THE ACCIDENTAL HERO

HERO IN PARADISE SERIES

BONZAI MOON

BonzaiMoon Books LLC
Houston, Texas
www.bonzaimoonbooks.com

This is a work of fiction. Names, characters, places and incidents either are the product of the authors' imaginations or are used fictitiously, and any resemblance to actual persons, living or dead, business establishments, events, or locales is entirely coincidental.

Angel Vane has been entertaining readers with her brand of crime thrillers for women. Now you can get one of her novellas for FREE, you just need to go to the link and tell her where to send it:

GET MY FREE SHORT STORY NOW
https://BookHip.com/SFTKRK

Prologue

Was it over?

The thought crept into her mind. Her lungs burned, pushing air in and out, fueling her frenzied race through the tangled branches of the dense forest.

Slowing down, she crouched low stepping under a thick branch and leaned against a plantain tree to catch her breath. Pain ripped through her lower abdomen. Gasping from the intensity of the cramps, her body involuntarily seized. Humidity clung to her, forming a thin film of sweat over her skin. Her eyes struggled to adjust to the dark maze of branches of the mountain jungle. Heart thundering, she struggled to hear any sound over her own ragged breathing as the tightness within her abdomen subsided.

A smile crept over her face.

The silence was deafening.

A welcomed delight. Proof that she'd actually gotten away this time.

She was finally free, but not without a high cost.

Taking a tentative step, she moved toward a canopy of flat elephant leaves, pushing them to peek through the opening. A few feet ahead, dark gravel met the edge of the jungle.

Muscles relaxing, she exhaled. This road led south toward the marina. At this time of night, she could slip onto one of the cargo ships and sail away from this awful island. She wished she'd never come here. The biggest mistake of her life. But it was almost over. Slipping her hand into the pocket of her pink windbreaker, she froze. Where was that damn cell phone? Had it fallen out of her pocket when she ran into the jungle? She grasped at both pockets, hoping to feel the small device, but it was gone.

She wouldn't be deterred. Clawing her way to freedom had been hard, and the loss of the cell phone wasn't going to stop her now. Walking toward the clearing, she stepped on the grainy hot gravel. The road stretched ahead, dark and deserted.

Turning back toward the overgrown copse of trees, she thought of him. She'd left him without a second thought, but now an unease had infected her, paralyzing her.

Was she doing the right thing? Leaving him behind?

After what she'd been through, he'd been the only bright spot. Truth was, she knew that there was no future for them. Going back for him would condemn her. She couldn't continue to suffer, not even for him. She hoped she wouldn't regret the decision.

A bright white light blinded her. Raising a hand to her face, she shielded her eyes as the car came into focus, driving slowly up the winding road of the St. Basil Mountains.

Stepping into the road, she waved her arms.

As the car slowed to a stop, she rushed toward the driver's door. The window rolled down.

Soulless dark eyes glared at her.

No. This could not be happening.

The car door swung open.

How had he found her?

"Bitch!" The growled word hung in the air.

Struggling to stay on her feet, she stumbled on weak legs.

"Don't know how you got away but you won't be escaping no more." The deep voice sent a chill down her spine. He stalked toward her with long strides. The moonlight shone bright, casting a bluish glow against his tanned skin.

"Stay away from me." She took small, tentative steps backward. "I'm not going anywhere with you!"

A scowl furrowed between his eyebrows. "You going back where you belong."

That wasn't true.

She didn't belong there.

She couldn't go back to that awful place where he'd taken her months ago.

The bastard had tricked her.

Pretending he was interested in what she had to offer, he'd told her she could make a lot of money. She'd agreed to go with him back to the hotel. Leading him to the bed, she'd crawled on top of him, smiling and giving him what she hoped was a sexy look as she thought of nothing but the cash she would score once it was all over.

Moments later, he'd maneuvered her onto her hands and knees. Grateful she wouldn't have to stare at another nameless face, she'd clutched the cheap sheets, bracing herself for his entry.

Instead, there was a painful sting as something thin and sharp pierced the side of her neck.

When her eyes fluttered open sometime later, she was …

Tears welled in her eyes as she pushed the past away.

He reached for her arm, but she jerked away from him. A strange look passed across his face as his gaze drifted down her body. "What happened to—"

His hand brushed against her abdomen. Instinctively, she shoved him and turned to run. His hands grabbed her shirt from behind, yanking her back against his body as he clamped his tattooed arms around her chest. Swinging wildly, she beat and scratched against his arms until his grip loosened.

Twisting from his grasp, she stumbled forward and sprinted across the road to the field on the other side. She ignored the fire burning through her muscles as she pushed her body faster, fueled by the chance, perhaps her last, to get free.

A loud blast pierced the silence.

A sharp pain slammed against her back.

Gasping in shock, she slowed to a staggering walk.

She stared down at the front of her white cotton t-shirt, stained red.

Another blast pushed her body to the ground.

Her vision blurred, and she began to cry.

The freedom she'd been desperate for would finally be hers in death.

Chapter One

Waves slapped the side of the yacht. Julian Montgomery reached over the edge of the chair and grabbed a Felipe beer from the ice chest. His eyes drifted toward two shadowy objects hanging from the railing, instruments of infamous dirtboarding down dozens of mountains. Wheels caked with mud and wood tattered from the pounding of saltwater, the abandoned boards now stood still.

Julian reached toward one of the cracked rubber wheels but pulled back. The mountain boards were a painful reminder of a life he no longer lived.

His eyes watered from the weight of the memories of his last run. His best friend Broman Garrison had convinced him to drive eight hours from Coronado to San Francisco and board down Hyde Street at three in the morning. Dressed in Navy camouflage combat gear, Julian had plummeted down the steep road in tandem with his best friend as the chilled wind pricked his skin. Avoiding the occasional car daring to interrupt their descent, they'd adopted the normal cadence of an urban ride—preferring synchronization of movements over competitive racing.

Julian would never have guessed that would be his last ride.

Taking a swig of the beer, he stared at a catamaran maneuvering into Crescent Moon Marina on the island of St. Basil. The smallest of the five inhabited Palmchat Islands, St. Basil had become his refuge, a self-inflicted exile.

Everyone thought he'd walked away from his life because of his last mission, an operation in Central Sulawesi. A ruthless terrorist cell on the small Southeast Asian island had attacked and killed several Navy SEALs. His survival of the brutal attack haunted him. Grief and guilt compelled him to abandon the life he'd known.

No one had been surprised that he'd left the military after he'd finally made it back stateside. Rumors of PTSD had swirled around him, giving him the perfect excuse to step away from the work he'd loved. But the rumors were far from the truth, which was too devastating, and had eroded his soul.

As the catamaran eased into its designated slip, Julian took another long pull on the beer. His cell phone vibrated. Snatching the phone from his pocket, Julian frowned at the screen.

Jacksonville area code.

Who could be calling him from back home? Muscles rigid, Julian turned his head, trying to relieve the tension clawing up his neck. He'd ignore them. If it was important, whoever it was would leave a message.

The phone buzzed in his hand for several minutes.

Or not.

Julian tapped the speaker button. "Hello."

"Julian ..." a female voice said, one he recognized—Dawn Garrison.

Julian sucked in air sharply, his heart banging against his ribcage. Was it really Dawn? How long had it been since they'd last spoken? Two years? Three? Remembering the last time he'd seen her, his stomach twisted. Hurling obscenities, clutching the letter he'd delivered, Dawn had crumpled to the ground. Tears streamed down her face as she pounded her fists against the scorched dirt.

"You're the last person I thought I'd ever call for help." Dawn cleared her throat. "But right now, you're my only option."

Julian gazed into the onyx waters rippling from the night breeze. "What do you need?"

"What I need is," Dawn said, then paused.

Her words hung in the air, indicting Julian for the mistakes he'd made three years ago. He should never have asked that question.

"You know if I could go back and change what happened, how it all went down, I would," Julian said.

"But you can't, can you?"

"I never meant for things to turn out the way they did," said Julian.

"You can't change the past."

Julian said, "I need you to understand how much I regret—"

"I don't give a shit about your regrets. I don't care how sorry you are. It doesn't change a damn thing!" Dawn screamed.

Julian knew he'd gone too far. Dawn had never given him a chance to apologize. But why should she? She didn't deserve the burden of relieving him of his guilt.

Julian closed his eyes and took a deep breath. "Tell me why you called."

Dawn sighed heavily into the silence of the phone, then said, "Broman always told me that no one on the planet could hide from Julian Montgomery. Ella is missing. I need you to find my sister."

Chapter Two

Tapping the messaging app on his phone, Julian accessed the audio file Dawn had texted him. A voice message from her sister. Julian dropped onto the oversized ivory sofa in his living room and placed the cell phone on the center of the glass coffee table. A shaky female voice, terrorized, spoke: "Help me! Help me, Dawn, please … I'm at a place called Genesis Gallery. He won't let me leave. I can't get out. You have to save me!"

Julian frowned. Ella's message seemed authentic, but her claim didn't make sense. The Genesis Gallery was one of the top tourist attractions in St. Basil, hosting hundreds of visitors daily. A cultural centerpiece of the island, the gallery showcased artistic works by renowned masters as well as up and coming talent. High profile social events were frequently held there. How could she be trapped at the gallery?

Julian drummed his fingers against the glass coffee table. Some kind of connection to the gallery wasn't out of the realm of possibility. Ella Sapphire was a hell of an artist.

The audio file continued to play. Near hysteria, Ella's words became jumbled and chaotic, indiscernible, as she wept through her pleas.

From what Julian could remember, Ella had been a hustler, bouncing from one get-rich-quick scheme to the next, not caring if her scams were legal or not. He'd heard that Ella's abrupt withdrawal from the University of Florida about five or six years ago had been related to a sex scandal with one of her teachers. According to Broman, she'd blackmailed a tenured professor into supporting her move to pursue art in St. Basil. For years, Dawn had made excuses for her little sister, running to the rescue—checkbook in hand—to bail Ella out of trouble. As the message continued, Julian wondered, was Ella in danger or was she trying to get Dawn to send her more money?

The message neared the end. Julian focused on the last whispered words Ella uttered, laced with terror and desperation: "Dawn, I really need you this time. I don't want to die here. Please ... I know he's going to kill me."

Leaning back on the plush sofa, Julian closed his eyes and tried to sort through Ella's crazy message. It didn't matter if he believed Ella was in danger or running a scam. The fact was Dawn believed Ella was telling the truth.

After everything he'd done, he had to help Dawn find her missing sister. Even if that meant revisiting his old life. Cutting open the old wounds that hadn't healed, he'd be forced to become the man he once was. The last time Julian had been on the hunt for someone, he'd left a trail of bodies in the wake of his horrible mistakes. Would this time be any different?

Bringing a shaky hand to his forehead, Julian glanced over at the steel safe tucked in the corner of the room. He pressed his palms against the glass table, willing himself to move, but his legs refused to obey. He didn't want to open that safe. He didn't want the memories to attack him.

Wiping his slick hands against the fabric of his jeans, Julian forced himself to stand. Grabbing the cell phone, he shoved it into his pocket and stared at the safe. Hesitant, he took tentative steps toward the dark gray cube. Entering the eleven-digit code, the safe beeped twice. The audible click of the lock opening reverberated within the room. All the remnants of his past he'd kept locked away for years were behind that metal door. If he opened it, all the demons would be released, haunting him for days to come. But if he didn't, he would never have a chance to make up for all the pain he'd caused Dawn.

Opening the door, Julian reached for the laptop. Rows of medals lay in a disheveled heap near the back of the safe. One caught his eye — the Silver Star awarded for gallantry in action against an enemy of the United States. Julian's gut twisted as he stared at the only medal in the safe that he hadn't deserved.

Snatching the laptop from the top shelf, he slammed the safe closed. Taking the narrow hallway to the dining room, Julian sat at the cherry wood table and booted up the computer. The familiar hum of the electronic whirring soothed him.

Julian opened a program on the screen and began uploading the audio file of Ella's voice message. His eyes followed the progress meter as an idea crossed his mind, a way to get information on Ella's whereabouts.

Pulling his cell phone from his pocket, Julian called his good friend Detective Kendrick Caillouet of the St. Basil Police Department. The first time he'd met the detective, Julian had been three sheets to the wind and doing a piss-ass job maneuvering his boat into the slip at the marina. His yacht had crashed into the outer boardwalk, causing damage to the pier and frantic calls to the local island police. He'd passed out momentarily, his drunken body slumped over the helm of the boat when the cop had found him.

Shaken awake, Julian had laughed through all the standard checks for inebriation, which he passed easily despite his dangerously high blood-alcohol level. Kendrick had taken it all in stride, amused instead of annoyed by Julian's antics.

Instead of taking Julian down to the police station, Kendrick, the kind of guy who never met a stranger, had listened as Julian recounted his fourteen-hundred-mile sail from Key West to St. Basil with nothing but the clothes on his back, a bottle of vodka and two boxes of Saltines. Taking over the controls, Kendrick steered the yacht into the slip and agreed to let Julian off with a warning.

When Kendrick left his boat, Julian hadn't planned on talking to the detective again.

The universe had other plans.

Over the next few weeks, he kept running into the detective as he explored his new island home. He often wondered if Kendrick was keeping an eye on him, the loner with nothing to live for. Maybe he was, maybe he wasn't. It didn't matter now. He was thankful that they'd become fast friends.

Kendrick was the nicest guy he'd ever met, a man always willing to lend a helping hand or give a stranger his last dollar. Selfless and sincere and honest—qualities that Julian had never had. He knew Kendrick would come through for him tonight.

"What's up, my friend?" Kendrick asked.

"I need a job," Julian responded, his fingers flying across the keyboard. He entered the phone number Ella had called from, then initiated the program to determine the last known location of the phone.

"You finally going to take me up on the offer to join the force?" Kendrick asked, excitement creeping in his words.

"I'm not the type of guy you want to serve and protect," Julian said, slumping back in the chair. "I need a job at the Genesis Gallery. Isn't your father on the board or something?"

"You're turning down police work, which you are qualified for, and instead want to work at an art gallery?" Kendrick asked.

"I'm looking for someone, and I think she hangs around the gallery," Julian responded. Lines of text scrolled across the laptop screen in a blur before stopping abruptly.

Device last known location: Genesis Gallery, St. Basil, Palmchat Islands 98% accuracy.

"So this is about a woman?" Kendrick asked.

"Don't start with me," Julian said, chuckling.

"Hey, one of us needs to hit the jackpot in love. My track record is abysmal," Kendrick said.

"You're too nice," Julian reminded him.

"And nice guys always finish last. Ladies these days want the bad boy, not the good guys like us," Kendrick said.

Julian frowned, rubbing the bridge of his nose. He wasn't one of the good guys, but Kendrick had no clue about his past.

"Hate to burst your bubble, but it's not like that. I'm trying to find her for a friend. Can you get me on at the gallery?" Julian asked.

"Any job in particular?"

"Doesn't matter."

Kendrick said, "Janitor role okay?"

"Hell no," Julian said. "Something somewhat related to my skills."

"Your skills are rusty from lack of use," Kendrick responded. "But I'll try to get you on as a security guard. Give me a day or two—"

The sound of shattering glass jolted Julian.

"What the hell was that?" Kendrick asked.

"Not sure, but I'm about to find out."

Chapter Three

A harrowing scream pierced the night air.

Julian sprinted to the side of his boat and peered over the edge. Stumbling off the back of the sleek black yacht docked next to Julian's, Wanda Campbell, wife of renowned island crooner Louis Campbell, landed with a loud thud onto the wooden planks of the pier.

Well-known throughout the island, Louis was the booming baritone who sung covers of hits by Teddy Pendergrass and Barry White on cruise ships for eight months out of the year. The remaining four months, he delighted locals and tourists in St. Basil with weekend shows at the famous King Street Lounge. The marriage between Wanda and Louis had been the scandal of last year since she'd been only eighteen while he was fifty when they tied the knot.

The young woman staggered across the wooden plank, her straight black hair whipping in the wind. The dark red satin negligee covering her thin waif-like body was torn at the shoulder, revealing a small, taut brown breast. Julian's eyes drifted toward her arms, clutching the left side of her abdomen. The satin fabric was stained darker. She was bleeding.

"Please help me! He's going to kill me!"

Julian strode along the side of his boat to the aft deck where the steps descended to the pier and jumped down. He landed in front of the wild-eyed, frightened woman as she collapsed. Dropping to his knees, Julian turned her body over slowly. A jagged cut gushed blood from her forearm. Julian could see torn muscles and the soft white of bone.

Pulling his t-shirt off, Julian ripped the cotton and fastened the cloth around the gaping wound, constructing a make-shift tourniquet to stop the bleeding.

"Are you stabbed anywhere else? Wanda, look at me. Did he stab you anywhere else?"

Wanda's response was a deafening cry as her eyes locked on something behind Julian.

Julian didn't need to turn around to know Louis Campbell had emerged from his boat.

Adrenaline pumped through Julian's veins, but his heartbeat remained calm. Julian focused on the familiar cadence, the metronomic pacing, slow and methodical thudding inside his chest. The wind caressed his skin as he honed in on the ragged breathing of Louis Campbell, ringing loudly in his ears. Julian was going to take down the coward who'd decided to use his wife as a human pin cushion.

Julian glanced over his shoulder. Campbell staggered down the pier, swinging a nine-millimeter Glock in his right hand. Only twenty feet separated them. The stench of alcohol and urine bridged the gap between the two men. Louis stalked forward, eyes bloodshot as he pointed the gun at Julian's head. Mistake number one. The head was too small a target. Maximum damage was done with two quick shots to the chest, the largest mass on a person's body, followed by a headshot to confirm the kill.

Standing, Julian walked toward Louis. An attack had to be carefully orchestrated, unhindered by any distractions or impairments. Weapons could be the biggest weakness, giving the holder a false sense of security and power. Louis Campbell had picked the wrong night to attack his wife.

The gun pointed at his face didn't slow Julian. The drunk husband yelled at him and then pulled the trigger. Dipping his head to the right, Julian felt the slice like fire above his right ear. Louis pulled the trigger again. A hollow click.

Two more strides and Julian was six inches away from Louis. Staring in the man's eyes, he saw the same look he'd seen in Wanda's—pure fear. Dropping the gun, Louis turned to run. Yanking Louis by the neck, Julian squeezed hard, his fingers digging into the crooner's soft, ample flesh, stopping his movement.

Julian pushed the stocky man from behind. Louis stumbled, landing on the wooden planks of the deck with a loud crash.

Julian's fist flew through the air, fast as lightning. Three jabs to the face broke Louis' nose. Two kicks to the ribcage and Julian heard the crunch of bone as Louis howled. Julian landed one last kick to the old man's nuts for good measure. Louis Campbell needed to learn that attacking a woman was never a good idea.

Sirens pierced the air. The red and blue flashing lights of the water ambulance danced off the surface of the bay as the hum of the boats grew closer. Julian stepped away from Louis' huddled form and turned toward the boat, watching as it docked next to the pier. Detective Kendrick Calliouet sat behind the boat captain, flanked by a team of EMTs and police officers. Two EMTs exited the boat and headed toward Wanda. Kendrick followed them, then jogged over toward Julian.

Julian said, "You got here fast."

"I was in the neighborhood," Kendrick said, a wry smile playing at the corners of his mouth as he stopped in front of Louis Campbell. "So much for not being the serve and protect type of guy."

The old crooner sat motionlessly, his head dipped low against his chest, blood oozing from his broken nose as a young police deputy handcuffed him.

Ignoring Kendrick's comment, Julian said, "You need my statement tonight?"

"I can get the official version in the morning but give me a quick rundown on what happened after you got off the phone with me," Kendrick said.

Julian recapped the events. Satisfied with the information, Kendrick allowed him to leave the scene of the incident.

Grabbing onto the side of his boat, Julian hoisted himself to the lower level and collapsed on the deck, trying to ignore the endorphins invading his body. The thrill of protecting the innocent. The gratified release from taking down another threat. Actions and feelings he'd banished surged back with a vengeance.

And nothing good would come of it.

Chapter Four

Mena Nix peered at the bulging eyes and flared nose of the statue showcased on a carved mahogany pedestal. A miniature bocio figure from West Africa stared back at her. She'd studied these figures while getting her Masters degree, but had never seen one in person until now.

Mena's eyes trailed down the statue, wrapped in fiber rope. Reaching toward the wooden face, she resisted the urge to run her finger along the wide lips and feel the grooves in the wood. As the conservator for art and sculpture at the Genesis Gallery, Mena knew first-hand how the oils and dirt from human hands could ruin art.

The artist's technique was brilliant. Preserved in its original condition, the piece showed no signs of restoration.

Coarse and abrasive, the tightly bound cords that formed the statue's body were believed to be symbolic of the violence and trauma suffered by West Africans for centuries through the slave trade. If she remembered correctly, the bocio figures were important to West African tribes practicing the Vodun religion. They believed the miniature statues would empower them with strategies to face difficult and threatening social conditions. Mena took a long swallow of champagne and then placed the flute onto the empty tray of a passing waiter.

She could use her very own bocio right now.

If not for tonight's gala celebration, Mena would have been locked in her apartment, soothing away the painful memories with culinary pleasures. The anniversary of the biggest mistake of her life still stung, reminding her of how she'd been duped. Mr. Wrong had been disguised as Mr. Right, luring her toward devastating heartbreak. How could she have missed the signs? How could she have been so wrong about the debonair Dr. Michael Marsh? He'd obliterated her trust in him and the sanctity of their relationship. She wasn't sure if she'd ever be able to trust anyone again. The risks were too high.

Mena would have given anything to be back at her condo but that wasn't an option. There was no way she could be anywhere but right here, standing in a luxurious banquet hall as a hundred guests milled around the spectacular mansion on the island's glamorous north shore, known as The Bluffs. St. Basil's well-to-do elite had gathered to celebrate the fifth anniversary of the Genesis Gallery for Indian, African and Caribbean Art, owned by Priscilla Dumay, Mena's boss.

Jovial conversation, laughter, and island music swirled through the atmosphere as moneyed art patrons mixed, mingled, and enjoyed the chance to view a priceless collection of the best ethnographic art from all over the world, courtesy of Priscilla's private collection.

Priscilla was much more than Mena's employer. She'd been her savior. Inexperienced conservators, only a couple of years out of grad school, didn't get the opportunity to head up the conservation department at renowned galleries. But Priscilla had given Mena the chance of a lifetime. The gallery owner had also provided Mena an escape from the wreck that had become her life when she'd needed it most.

"Foie gras?"

Mena stared blankly at the waiter, overwhelmed by the clusters of couples congregating in herds around the room. Engaged in intriguing conversations, they clutched the hands of their significant others, sneaking adoring glances at each other. Mena declined the hors-d'oeuvre and stepped closer toward the wall where a small Polynesian painting hung. She needed distance from the disgustingly happy couples converging upon her.

"Girl, you look like you need this." Omar Johnson, the curator at the gallery, shoved a short tumbler filled with amber liquid into Mena's hand.

Mena rolled her eyes as she took the glass, sniffing it. The strong alcohol shot up her nose, and she almost coughed.

"What is this?" Mena asked.

"Hennessy straight with a splash of water," Omar said, taking a sip of the liquid from his glass. "I see you found the Gauguin. Looks like a half-finished page from a ghetto coloring book if you ask me. But Prissy insisted on having it. Four hundred thirty-five thousand dollars later, here it is hanging on the wall in her uber mansion in all its glory."

Mena took a sip of the potent liquor. Omar was right. She was going to need some help to make it through the rest of this evening.

"Why are you so quiet? And why did you have the nerve to step up in an event like this without a date?" Omar asked, slapping at Mena's shoulder. "You are too beautiful to be here alone. This dress is stunning on your perfect body. If I wasn't gay, I'd definitely be your boo."

Mena glanced down at the sleeveless, sapphire to pink ombre sequined dress that fit her body like a glove. She had been happy to find something that fit at the Marina Boutique before rushing to the gala. She hadn't given the dress a second thought. She gave Omar a small smile and shrugged. "It's not like I haven't been trying."

Her love life had been on self-imposed life support since she moved to St. Basil—for a good reason. Six months ago, Mena had finally been ready to date again, and maybe even to trust herself to fall in love, but dating was so hard now. Her options were limited to tourists looking for local hookups or local Island guys seeking American sugar mamas—none of which gave her any desire to find a love connection anytime soon.

"Do you know who you're talking to? I've seen the men you've been dating. They are not boyfriend material and far from husband material. If I didn't know any better, I'd think you were playing it safe with no intentions of trying to find your Mr. Right," Omar said.

Mena winced as Omar steered her toward the center of the room. Finding Mr. Right was overrated.

Soft calypso music played from a live band while a few gallery patrons took a moment to snap selfies of themselves with the exquisite pieces of art.

"No, it's nothing like that," Mena lied. "Dating just isn't that easy."

"Girl, please. Nothing is harder than a gay man trying to find a date on a tiny Caribbean island, and I've managed never to have a drought," Omar said, taking a sip of his Hennessy, pinky extended as he gave her a wink. "Now, I have Charlie, and I'm not looking anymore, but it's not as hard as you think.

You could find a good man if you wanted to. Question is, why don't you want to?"

Mena took another swig of the liquor. Omar was her best friend, but he didn't know what she'd gone through three years ago. Now was not the time to come clean. She didn't want his sympathy or his pity.

"As my mom says, love is a crap shoot," Mena explained, chugging the rest of her Hennessy. "Sometimes you roll sevens, and sometimes you roll snake eyes."

"Well, get ready to roll some sevens," said a bubbly voice behind Mena.

Chapter Five

Regina Patel, the third member of Mena's friend trifecta, thrust her cell phone toward Mena's face. "Have you seen this article in the *Palmchat Gazette?*"

Mena scanned the headline on the small cell phone screen and frowned: CRUISE SHIP CROONER CHARGED WITH ATTEMPTED MURDER by Sophie Carter. She'd skimmed the same article in the newspaper over breakfast. Louis Campbell, the famous St. Basil crooner, had been arrested after an ex-pat Good Samaritan stopped him from terrorizing his wife on their boat at the marina about a month ago.

"Such a tragedy," Mena said, confused as she glanced at Regina, bubbling with excitement, her false eyelashes fluttering with every rapid blink. Why was she so giddy over this sad article?

"Let me guess," Regina said. "You didn't scroll down to see this at the bottom." Using her thumb, Regina rubbed the side of the cell phone until a picture emerged.

Mena stared into the brooding, velvety chocolate brown eyes of the hero. Left brow raised, Mena looked closer. The man was sexy incarnate with sun-kissed golden tan skin, a strong square jaw with the barest shadow of a well-groomed beard, and smoldering lips made for kissing. He looked vaguely familiar, but Mena struggled to place where she might have seen him before.

"Don't you recognize him?" Regina shrieked.

"Let me see that," Omar said, snatching the cell phone and staring at the screen. "One word. Damn!"

"He's very handsome, no doubt," Mena said. "He looks familiar ..."

"He should. I'm a bit disappointed that he isn't here tonight," Regina said with a sly smirk. "I personally delivered his invitation to the security room."

"The security room?" Mena asked. Realization struck as she put the pieces together. She'd only seen him once, maybe twice, and admittedly hadn't paid much attention to him.

"He's our new security guard, Julian Montgomery," Regina said. "He was hired about a month ago."

"Why have I never seen this delectable piece of Italian crème cake before?" Omar's voice hit a higher octave.

"Because you, my dear, tend to ignore people you believe are beneath you," Regina said, giving Omar a playful punch in the arm. "I only met him because I do the orientation for all new employees. I thought I was going to faint taking him around. He looks so much better in person. He is the icing and the cake, trust me."

"Work of art. I'm not surprised Prissy hired him. The fact that he's a bonafide hero is the cherry on top," said Omar as he finished the Hennessy.

Regina gave Mena a wink. "I happened to notice yesterday that he was quite smitten with you, Mena."

"What are you talking about?" Mena asked. Heat marched up her cheeks. Was she blushing right now? Just because some hot guy might have admired her when she wasn't paying attention? Thank God for her deep brown skin.

"I was telling him about this party and how it was the social event of the year and how anyone who was anyone was dying to get an invitation. Then I noticed he wasn't paying attention to what I was saying," Regina said, pausing for dramatic effect.

"Spit it out, girl. We don't have time for your theatrics," Omar said, pursing his lips.

"Julian was enraptured with Mena. The moment she strutted through the lobby and waved bye to me, his eyes locked on her," Regina explained, her eyes wide. Looking at Mena, she continued, "He watched your every move until you sashayed out of the gallery to your car. It was only then that he turned to me and thanked me for the invitation."

"I'm sure you're reading too much into things," Mena said, folding her arms across her chest. The new security guard might have been attracted to her, but so what? The road from attraction to relationship was long and tumultuous. Mena had no intention of entertaining some workplace romance, especially not one based on hearsay from Regina.

"I'm on Mena's side this time," Omar said, handing the cell phone back to Regina. "Mena Nix is a highly educated black woman. She deserves more than a quick fuck with a sexy ass security guard. We need to focus our energy on trying to fix our girl up with one of these millionaires floating around this room."

"But, he's a hero," Regina whined. "Money isn't everything."

"Right, it's the only thing," said Omar. "How do you think Charlie snagged me?"

"Thanks for the ego boost," Mena said, not wanting to hurt her friend's feelings. Regina's attempt to create a love connection based on a glance the security guard may have passed in her direction was sweet but unnecessary.

"I know what I saw. Mark my words," Regina said. "The two of you would make an awfully cute couple. I read an article the other day that over half of relationships start in the workplace—"

"Priscilla is waving for me to come over," Mena interrupted, placing her empty glass of Hennessy on the silver tray of a passing waiter. The raven-haired benefactress of the Genesis Gallery beckoned for Mena to join her. "Will the two of you excuse me?"

Chapter Six

"Here's my favorite conservator!" Priscilla said, stretching her arms wide as she enveloped Mena in a tight embrace. "You look amazing, my dear."

Mena shrugged, then said, "Thank you. So do you!"

Stunning as usual, the gallery owner was impeccably dressed in a white pantsuit and sparkling ruby red Louboutin's. Her dark brown mane was upswept into a messy bun, with her long bangs perfectly framing her face and accentuating her deep green eyes.

"Congratulations on five years. I'm so thrilled to have been a part of your team for three of them," Mena said, smiling warmly at her mentor.

"You and me both. The conservator I had before you was a disaster—Norman Gale," Priscilla said, spitting the name as if it was something disgusting in her mouth.

"Norman Gale?" Mena asked, frowning. "I had a chance to go to a seminar of his when I was in grad school. He was always on the cutting edge—"

"He was a pain in the ass who was too busy trying to further his own self-interests at the expense of my gallery. I was not going to let him use me to boost his career. So, we parted ways," Priscilla said, then laughed. "It was not amicable."

Mena smiled stiffly. It had been years since she'd heard the name Norman Gale in the art circles. Once a shining star of conservation, traveling the world restoring priceless works of art, he had recently faded into obscurity.

"I wonder what he's up to now," Mena said, making a note to discuss it with Omar and Regina later.

"Probably lamenting the day he met me," Priscilla said and gave her a wink. "But that failed partnership led me to you, and it was the best thing that happened to us, don't you agree?"

"You know I do," Mena said, giving Priscilla a quick hug.

Priscilla pulled away, then waved a hand toward a regal and elegant woman entering the ballroom. The woman appeared to be Mena's age, yet she commanded respect as she glided toward them. Turning to Mena, Priscilla whispered, "Here's someone you need to meet."

"Ms. Dumay! Congratulations on your anniversary and thank you so much for inviting me to your celebration," the woman said, greeting Priscilla with a warm smile and a familiar embrace. Priscilla graciously accepted her congratulations and engaged in small talk before turning back toward Mena.

"I'd like to introduce you to the woman we spoke about on the phone. This is Mena Nix, the head of my conservation department," Priscilla said, guiding Mena toward the woman. "Mena, this is Wangari Irungu. She is the heiress of Africa's largest horticultural empire and the current director at the Tribal Museum in Kenya. She and her team administer and select the recipient of the Nairobi African Art Fellowship."

Mena's mouth went dry as she shook Ms. Irungu's hand. Each year since she'd graduated, Mena had applied for the fellowship fully expecting to add another rejection letter to the pile. She couldn't believe the woman responsible for selecting the recipients was standing in front of her.

"I've been singing your praises to Wangari. This fellowship would be perfect for you," Priscilla said.

"Based on what Ms. Dumay has told me about the advances you are making in laser conservation techniques, I believe you have a great shot at getting the Fellowship this year," Ms. Irungu said, smiling warmly at Mena.

"I should think so," Priscilla said, giving Wangari's hand a gentle squeeze. "I only hire the best at my gallery. You'd be lucky to get Mena."

Mena listened in awe as Ms. Irungu discussed the review of Mena's application and how impressed she was with Mena's accomplishments while at the Genesis Gallery.

"Wangari, do you remember the Cote d'Ivoire face mask on display on the second floor at the gallery? That was restored by Mena," Priscilla said and gave Mena a quick wink.

"Absolutely exquisite work. Your skills are amazing," Wangari responded.

Mena beamed, thinking of how her life would change if she got the fellowship. She'd be moving again, putting more distance between herself and the past she'd left behind. She wouldn't be running away this time, though. She'd be moving forward. A subtle change, but one that gave Mena hope.

Mena felt a buzz coming from her purse. Excusing herself from Priscilla and Ms. Irungu, she removed the cell phone. Staring at the screen, she recognized the number—her workshop at the gallery. Who was still there at this time of night?

She answered the phone.

A chill ran down her spine as she listened to the panicked words. Forcing her voice to remain calm, Mena said, "I'm on my way."

Chapter Seven

"Bear with me for a moment." The tall, lanky man leaned against the edge of the metal desk lining the side wall of the security room of the Genesis Gallery. "We must remember that silence is the friend of grief, and meditation is its lover. A moment of meditation is always wise when approaching subjects of this matter."

Julian leaned back in his chair, glaring at the man with long dreadlocks, thicker than sausages, stretching down his back. He wore a red cotton skirt that skimmed his knees and a faded black Bob Marley t-shirt with the arms cut out. Impressive artistic tattoos covered the length of both arms. Quark was his name. Julian couldn't believe this was the guy all the artists at the Co-Op insisted he should talk to.

"I loved her so much. She was the apple of my eye, the ying to my yang, the wind beneath my wings, my reason for being. She was my muse set on high, a delectable treat for my mind, bringing a smile to the art that I produced daily," Quark prattled on.

Julian was growing impatient. His boss could pop into the security room at any minute. The last thing he wanted to do was explain why this hippie artist was in a classified area. He couldn't risk exposing the real reason he'd been working at the Genesis Gallery for the past month.

"I'm sorry," the artist paused. "I just miss her so much. What was your question again?"

"When was the last time you saw Ella? I need a time or place. Her sister is worried, and I'm trying to find her," Julian explained for the third time, rubbing his index finger against his temple. As the days passed and he was unable to provide any leads on Ella, Dawn became more demanding. She'd hurled insults at him this morning, questioning why she'd ever been misguided enough to ask him for help and why it was taking him so long to find her sister.

Julian wondered the same thing.

His initial inquiries at the Co-Op had been promising. Many of the artists knew Ella. She'd been part of their community for the past two years. Known as a gifted sculptor, she focused on furniture carvings although she dabbled in the occasional human figure from time to time. Julian had gotten numerous leads on the places where she'd been seen. Over the past few weeks, he'd painstakingly investigated each location, coming to a dead end each time. His last viable lead was a man Ella was rumored to be infatuated with ... the elusive artist, Quark.

"I know the exact month she vanished from my life. My art has never been the same without her aura gracing my presence—"

"When was that?" Julian leaned forward, muscles tensing.

Quark recoiled, taking a step backward, then responded, "Seven months ago. She came by my studio at the Co-Op and agreed to pose for me, naked of course, for my birthday which was the next week. She gave me her word, but she didn't show up. I texted and called a few times, but never got a response. I haven't seen her since. A few weeks later, I couldn't bear to come to the Co-Op any longer. That's how much I miss her."

"Was anything unusual about the last time you saw her? Anything different that you remember?" Julian prodded. He was well trained at reading people, especially criminals, and this kid didn't have the balls to be involved in Ella's disappearance or alleged kidnapping. Still, there was a chance Quark had more information that could help him find Ella.

"No. The effervescence of her personality gave me a natural high, and we were in sync as usual—"

The door to the security room opened.

Adam Russell, the head of security, and Zak Webber, the regular night security guard, stormed into the small space, looking uncomfortable in their tuxedos and shiny shoes.

"Looking good, fellas," Julian said, glancing at Quark.

"Who the fuck is this?" Zak demanded, pointing a thumb at Quark. "No unauthorized personnel are allowed in this room!"

Visibly shaken, Quark retreated closer toward the door.

"Calm down," Julian said, squaring off in front of Zak, unmoved by his outburst. "This gentleman misplaced his cell phone and came to see if it was in lost and found. If you don't want unauthorized personnel in the room, you shouldn't keep lost articles in here."

A small smile passed across Adam's face, but he didn't respond. Adam walked toward the sixteen screens arranged in four rows mounted on the wall above the curved metal desk. Julian followed his movements and glanced at the screens. Each focused on a different area of the property—the gallery rooms, the upscale Genesis Restaurant, closed for the night due to the gala, the six workshops lining the outdoor courtyard behind the main building, the Artist Co-Op building, and the front and rear parking lots. All was quiet on the grounds.

"Get the fuck out of here," Zak spat at Quark. Terror in his eyes, the artist stumbled out of the room.

"Was that necessary?" Julian asked, crossing his arms.

Zak grinned, then pushed past Julian, shoulder checking him as he walked toward the center of the room, near Adam.

"I still don't understand why I have to go to some stupid bullshit party," Zak complained, yanking at the knot of his bow tie. Reaching for the only other chair in the room, Zak scraped the metal legs across the floor before slumping down onto the seat. "Julian is too green to cover my shift alone. What if something goes wrong?"

"Ms. Dumay wants you there, simple as that. Not many of her employees have been with her since day one like you and I have," Adam said, moving toward the back wall where the master control panel and security logs were mounted. "It's important to her that we're there to celebrate this milestone."

The Genesis Gallery's five-year anniversary celebration was being held at Priscilla Dumay's sprawling mansion on the north shore of the island. Julian had been invited but agreed to skip the gala after Adam asked him to cover the night shift while the rest of the employees were at the party.

Julian glanced at his watch. Almost eight o'clock.

"Party started a couple of hours ago. Shouldn't you get going?" Julian asked, hoping to prod them along.

"Just wanted to make sure you have everything you need," Adam said, checking the settings on the control panel. The man was younger than he looked, with dimples, green eyes, and a plain face many women would consider forgettable. "Looks like you set all the perimeter alarms and the infrared motion detectors. Good."

As the newest member of the security management team, Julian was still subjected to micro-managing by Adam. The job was simple. Julian had memorized the layout of the gallery grounds. He knew every possible entrance and exit onto the property. He knew the weaknesses where someone could enter undetected by the intricate security systems.

A web of overlapping devices protected the art in the gallery: Closed-circuit TV cameras, a video analytics system, real-time suspicious behavior scanning, high-def megapixel security cameras, thermal heat and infrared motion detectors, perimeter pressure triggers, and silent alarms. The artwork had been appraised in the millions of dollars, but Julian thought the measures seemed like overkill for the size of the collection. This was no Met.

"I think I'll stay here," Zak said, giving up on the tie and wriggling out of his coat.

"No, you won't. Our ex-pat hero can handle one night on his own," Adam said, flipping the pages in the security log.

"That's right. U.S. military vet saves the young wife of Louis Campbell from bleeding to death, taking out the old singer in the process. Have the panties showed up in your mail yet? Bitches love heroes," Zak said, rubbing a tattooed hand over his dark mohawk.

"No lingerie yet," Julian responded, wary of Zak's probing gaze. A month later and that damn *Palmchat Gazette* article was still hounding him. Julian had ignored the reporter's calls, but she'd managed to get details from Kendrick for her story. Julian wasn't upset with the detective. Kendrick was too nice a guy to turn down a newbie reporter desperate for an interesting slant to impress her editors.

Julian walked toward Adam. "Everything in order?"

Julian had meticulously documented each security check on the log. He wasn't going to let a technicality get him booted from the job, at least not until he'd found Ella.

Adam gave a slight nod.

"No panties at all?" Zak asked, then laughed. "That's a damn shame. Groupies usually lose their minds over a dude who'll jump off the top of a damn yacht, get the girl to safety, then beat the shit out of her abusive husband. Sounds like some special ops type of shit if you ask me. You're a Navy vet, right? What part?" Zak asked.

"Intelligence," Julian said. Not exactly a lie, but not the whole truth either.

"Hmm, makes sense. You seem like a smart dude," Zak replied, but there was a challenge in his gaze. A hint of unbelief fusing the air with tension.

"Eight o'clock fellas. The party's going to be over by the time the two of you get there." Julian walked over to the security monitors, plopping down on the metal chair in the center of the curved desk. He glanced at the front parking lot camera. The area was empty except for Adam's car and Julian's motorcycle.

Zak stood, grabbed his jacket from the back of the chair, and walked to the door.

"You have my number," Adam said. "Don't hesitate to use it."

Julian nodded as the door closed. Reaching into his backpack hidden under the desk, he finished connecting his laptop to the security system and verified the blocking software was in place. Necessary measures to ensure that he could hack into the security footage files without alerting the cyber defenses of the gallery's IT systems. More importantly, he had to make sure his illegal use of classified U. S. Navy software wasn't detected. He was close to building a timeline of activity for Ella at the Genesis Gallery. The military's facial recognition software would search the footage for any patterns of people Ella had been seen with at the gallery over the past two years.

He was taking a monumental risk, one that could land him in jail for a long time.

But, he owed it to Dawn and Broman to do whatever it took to find Ella.

He couldn't let them down.

Not again.

Chapter Eight

Damn it! Mena heard the heavy footsteps of a man approaching her from behind. Shouldn't Zak be at the gala celebration right now? A confrontation with an overzealous security guard was the last thing she needed. Her sweet, but professionally inept assistant, Uma Fischer, was suffering inside the studio, trying to manage a barrage of questions about the authenticity of a sculpture that had cost the gallery a fortune. Mena wasn't ready for the truth to come out yet. She couldn't trust Uma to keep her mouth shut until she had time to do more analysis.

"What are you doing here at this late hour?" A deep baritone voice, commanding and arresting, called to Mena from behind. Turning around, Mena's lips parted, but no words came out. It wasn't Zak after all. Staring back at her were the dark, soulful brown eyes of the hero from the newspaper. The picture didn't come close to doing him justice. Confused thoughts jumbled in her mind as she struggled to remember what he'd asked her.

"Ms. Nix, what are you doing here so late?" he asked again.

"You know my name?" Mena licked her lips, which had gone as dry as the Kalahari Desert.

"Security manager," he said, giving her a slow, sly smile as he pointed to the title underneath the gallery logo on his navy polo shirt. "It's my job to know your name. Now it's your turn to answer my question."

Mena reached a hand toward her face, brushing a wayward strand of her wavy jet-black hair behind her ear. Her heart thudded against her chest. With a forced, even tone, she replied, "Irving Bond needs me to answer some questions about a very expensive piece of art. I need to get into my workshop and address his concerns."

The door to the workshop opened, and Uma stepped outside, relief flooding her tear-stained, flushed face.

Wiping away her tears, Uma said in between sniffs, "I'm so glad you're here. I tried not to tell him, but he kept pushing me, asking a ton of questions after I called you. I didn't know what else to say, so I told him the truth. He's so angry. I don't know what else to do."

Mena took a deep breath and exhaled slowly. She hadn't gotten here in time, and now she had to deal with the issue of the Master of Sinasso sculpture before she was ready. What was Uma still doing at the workshop? And why had Irving Bond, the director of the gallery, chosen tonight to examine the sculpture? They both should have been at Priscilla's mansion for the celebration.

Mena wrapped an arm around Uma and steered her toward the sidewalk that led to the employee parking lot.

"This is not your fault, Uma. I'm not upset. Go home. I'll take care of everything from here," Mena said, trying to soothe her whimpering assistant as she struggled to suppress her anger. She should fire the woman for caving to Irving Bond's inquiries. Uma was only average at her job, and now she'd done the one thing Mena had told her not to do. How hard could it be to tell Irving that he should wait until the procedures were finished? Why had Uma cracked under pressure?

"Are you sure you're not mad at me?" Uma asked, stepping back to look up at Mena.

"I'm not mad," Mena lied. "Go home. We'll talk tomorrow."

Uma shuffled along the sidewalk, her whimpers intruding on the otherwise serene, quiet night.

Now, Mena had to deal with Irving. One more deep breath, then she turned, headed down the sidewalk, and rounded the corner to the front of the workshop.

The hero was still there. Waiting. He was taller than she'd realized, at least six foot five. He stared at her, expressionless.

Mena took a deep breath. So much for Regina's declaration about the security guard's interest in her. He was all business tonight, dutifully performing his role in protecting the gallery grounds.

"Excuse me," Mena said, sidestepping past his large muscular frame, careful not to accidentally touch him. She turned and pressed her thumb on the knob—two short beeps. Access granted. Opening the door, she walked into the entryway.

"Ms. Nix," he said from behind her.

She turned and looked at him once more. Her breath caught at the full sight of him.

"Dial zero when you're ready to leave. I'll walk you to your car."

The offer was unnecessary. Fighting the urge to decline, Mena gave in.

"Thank you … " Mena hesitated, unable to remember the security guard's name from the article.

"Julian," he responded, extending his hand.

Mena reached her hand toward his. As their hands touched, a shiver spread through her body, awakening a smoldering craving within her. His eyes locked with hers, expressionless no more. She recognized that look. The last time a man had given her that look, a chain of events had been set into motion that almost destroyed her. After moving to St. Basil, she'd vowed never to get caught up again. She would engage with men on her terms or not at all.

Right now, Mena couldn't afford to be distracted by tall, hot, and handsome. She had to deal with Irving Bond. Pulling away from his grasp, Mena turned and walked into the workshop, then glanced out the side window. Julian jogged down the sidewalk. He caught up with Uma and placed a reassuring hand on her shoulder as they disappeared behind the Artist Co-Op building to the employee parking lot.

"Am I to understand that you believe the sculpture is a fake?" Irving Bond held the small sculpture to the light, peering at it closely.

Mena fought the urge to let out a primal scream. Stifling the rage boiling within her, Mena took a few deep breaths, allowing her heart rate to return to normal. She would get through this disaster. She needed to remain calm and composed.

"Irving, you know the process of authenticating artwork is complex and especially difficult for pieces from Africa. I can't provide a premature conclusion before all the tests have been completed," Mena said, stalking toward the director. As she got closer, Irving turned toward her, the sculpture still extended in the air. Mena grabbed it from his hand and placed it on the table.

"Cut the bullshit," Irving demanded, adding an exaggerated pause between each word. His eyes were focused, challenging her.

"There are contusions in the wood that are more typical of carving techniques utilized in the last thirty to forty years. If the sculpture was created by the Master of Sinasso, the techniques used would be different. My hunch is that when I do some further analysis to validate the age of the piece, it will prove that it is a fake," Mena said. She'd detected the anomalies quickly, which made her question the sculpture's authenticity almost immediately. How Irving hadn't done the same was a mystery to her. But, Omar always said that Irving wasn't as qualified as he wanted people to believe. Many of Irving's acquisitions in the past had been suspect, and Omar was disappointed that Priscilla didn't do more to scrutinize the purchases.

"You need to run the tests again," Irving insisted.

"That is exactly what I planned to do before I talked to you and Priscilla," Mena said.

"But you still believe it's a fake. You believe others would come to the same conclusion?" Irving asked, his voice hollow.

Mena hesitated, reluctant to convey how convinced she was that the sculpture had been a waste of gallery funds. She gazed at the diminutive female statue with delicate features and a rotund body symbolic of fertility. Priscilla was going to be disappointed that the statue couldn't be featured in the upcoming African Art auction at Christie's. The last Sinasso sculpture had sold for over ten million dollars, and the piece hadn't had the luxury of being restored by techniques that Mena specialized in.

Taking a deep breath, she said, "I'm sure of it."

"I will let Priscilla know." Irving stormed out the room, slamming the door behind him.

Chapter Nine

A slow smile spreading across his lips, Julian hung up the phone and leaned back in his chair. She'd called. It would take Mena seven minutes to walk from her workshop across the central courtyard to the main lobby, where she'd asked him to meet her.

He hadn't expected Mena Nix to take him up on his offer to walk her to her car. He wasn't sure why he'd tried.

The last time Julian had put in an effort to be near a woman was over a decade ago. He wasn't arrogant by any means, but he knew how he looked. Women made his life easy, pursuing and seducing him. He never had to work for what he wanted from a woman, which wasn't much. The women in his life had offered themselves freely even though Julian gave them nothing more than fun days and steamy nights in return. Intentional heartbreak was never in his plans. Frank, upfront conversations had made him the king of casual relationships. His honesty was usually rewarded with friendly companionship, hot sex, and none of the emotional baggage of a deeper connection. Any chance of being boyfriend material wilted the day he'd enlisted in the Navy and died the day he boarded the chopper, leaving Central Sulawesi and the carnage he'd caused there.

Julian checked the progress meter on the computer program—32%. It would take several more hours for the program to complete its analysis, providing him with a report of people to investigate further. The results would accurately discover leads, but without a connection to the Navy servers, it was taking a lot longer than Julian liked.

Memories of Mena flooded his mind. Her deep brown skin, smooth and flawless, was the perfect canvas to high cheekbones and deep-set mahogany eyes crowned with long eyelashes. Her lips were perfect, full, and begging to be kissed.

Warmth flooded his body, and Julian checked his thoughts before they led to an embarrassing situation. What the hell was he doing anyway? His life in St. Basil was different from the one he'd lived before, but commitment was still an issue. What could he offer someone as sexy, stunning, and intelligent as Mena Nix? Why would he get a chance with her or anyone after what he'd done? Since coming to the island, Julian had satisfied his sexual needs with occasional one-night stands with lusty tourists—fleeting and temporary dalliances with no chance of a real connection. No chance to get hooked on someone he couldn't have. Most of the time, he was celibate, locked away on his boat, watching the days go by.

Mena didn't strike him as the type to indulge in casual hook-ups.

He wasn't sure that's all he wanted anyway.

Julian had noticed her his first week on the job, during a tour of the grounds, guided by Pricilla Dumay's spunky, purple-haired assistant. Mena had been in the courtyard instructing a small group of students from the local college. Her back was to him, but he caught the salacious looks the young male students gave her as she spoke. Julian glanced at her as he passed by, curious to see why the guys were gawking.

One look was all it took to understand.

Was he more impressed that she was breathtaking or that she seemed utterly oblivious to the attention she was getting? Julian wasn't sure, but he watched the alluring woman maintain her professional demeanor while seemingly ignoring the infatuation.

Shaking his head, Julian pushed the thoughts away. He was working at Genesis Gallery for one reason, and it wasn't to pick up a beautiful woman. Grabbing a flashlight, Julian stood and left the security room. Mena should be in the lobby now.

Walking along the hall, Julian passed a smaller gallery containing native Mayan and Aztec art. The door was ajar, which was unusual. Glancing inside, nothing looked disturbed. He pulled the door shut and tapped the enter button on the keypad twice. The security code scrolled across the screen, confirming that the overnight motion detectors had been activated. Satisfied that everything was in order, Julian proceeded down the hallway.

A single light shone ahead as he got closer, illuminating the center console of the lobby where the receptionist greeted gallery patrons and visitors during normal business hours. Julian quickened his pace as he heard muffled voices.

"Please, I'll give you whatever you want." The voice was distant but recognizable. It was Mena Nix.

"Don't move. I mean it, don't take another step," a woman's voice barked back.

"Just take my keys," Mena said, a tremor in her voice.

"Shut up! I can't leave you here. You'll have to come with me," the woman screamed, near hysteria.

The woman's voice seemed familiar, nagging at Julian's memories. Where had he heard it before? Julian eased along the side of the wall, still out of view of Mena and the unidentified woman. Sliding his right hand along his waistband, he reached for his gun. The holster was empty. Damn it. He'd left it on the desk in the security room, right next to his cell phone. There was no time to go back for either of them now. He knew he could diffuse the situation without a weapon. He had a knife in his ankle holster if things took a turn for the worst.

Reaching the end of the hallway, Julian peered across the lobby. From his position near the Colonial grid windows on the right wall of the gallery, he saw Mena standing eerily still with her hands raised. Her eyes were wide and panicked, locked on the woman standing in front of her.

Julian's gaze shifted from Mena to the woman. She was average height, with honey blond mid-back length hair that rested against the bright pink of the windbreaker jacket she wore. Her body twitched with nervous energy as she pointed something at Mena.

"Turn around and take me to your car. Now!" The woman yelled, turning slightly.

Julian saw the gun.

Mena took a hesitant step back before turning toward the front doors of the gallery.

Julian glanced toward the center console. The silent alarm was below the receptionist's desk, but the console was about twenty-five feet from where he stood. The St. Basil police station was an hour away, and it was unlikely a patrol car would be in this area at this time of night. Mena and the woman were only a few feet from the entrance doors.

Certain he would reach the woman in the pink jacket before she hustled Mena out of the gallery, Julian decided to forgo the silent alarm.

"You're not going anywhere." Julian's voice echoed off the walls of the gallery as he stepped into the lobby. Relief flooded Mena's face as she lowered her arms and stared at him.

The woman turned quickly and pointed the gun at him.

Restraining the woman would be no problem. But he couldn't be impulsive. He didn't want Mena to get hurt or shot because of his reckless reaction. The first minute of a conflict was the most critical. Battles were won and lost from the choices made in those initial sixty seconds.

"Stay back!" The woman screamed.

A bulge protruded beneath her pink jacket.

She was pregnant.

And not just a little. From the size of her round abdomen, he guessed she was at least seven or eight months along. What the hell was a pregnant woman doing at the gallery after hours? How had she gotten onto the property without triggering one of the many alarms?

"Calm down, I'm not going to hurt you," Julian said, extending his hands to show he was without a weapon. He could get his knife and disarm the woman, but he didn't want to take the chance now that he saw she was pregnant. The last thing he needed was to hurt an innocent unborn child with a wayward throw.

Taking another slow step, Julian stopped. Moonlight pierced through one of the windows, illuminating the woman's face.

He recognized her.

"Ella?" Julian gaped at the woman. Was it really Ella Sapphire?

Julian couldn't believe it, didn't know what to think.

The gun in Ella's hand shook as she took a few steps back.

"How do you know who I am? You're one of them, aren't you? Stay back!" Ella's voice shook as she wiped sweat from her forehead. "I swear I will shoot you."

Ella turned and pointed the gun at Mena, then back at Julian. Tears flooded her eyes as she tugged at her jacket.

"You're not going to stop me from leaving here. I'm getting out of this place," Ella screamed. "Stay back!"

Julian took a slow step toward the women and then another. "Ella, I'm not going to hurt you. I'm trying to—"

A loud pop permeated the air as Ella pulled the trigger.

Mena screamed.

A sharp sting pierced Julian's left leg. Pain like fire burned his thigh. Julian crumpled to the floor. His eyes trained on Ella and her gun as another series of shots burst like flames from the pistol and headed directly for his head.

Chapter Ten

Mena jerked the car to the left as piercing, guttural screams shook her to her core. Easing the sedan into Park, she was afraid to turn around. She didn't want confirmation of what was happening to the woman who held her at gunpoint. She'd been driving the mad woman for almost an hour, weaving through the curvy scenic route from the Northwestern area of the island to downtown Marluna. The road took twice as long to get to town but was deserted at this time of night. Mena suspected that was why she'd been commanded to take this road. Arms tense, Mena's hands throbbed as she gripped the steering wheel. Sneaking a glance in the rearview mirror at the woman, she watched her captor panting as beads of sweat emerged on her face.

Julian, the security guard, knew the woman. He'd called her Ella, which had been the one mistake he'd made. The pregnant woman had shot him multiple times.

Had she killed him? Was Julian dead?

Mena choked back a sob.

Had she witnessed a man being murdered before her eyes?

She had to make sure she didn't end up a victim of the same fate.

Staring straight ahead, Mena slowed the car to a stop. Ella's screams grew more intense. After the tragedy that had already transpired, she didn't think the night could get any worse. But it had.

Ella was in labor.

The crazed, pregnant gun-toting lunatic was about to give birth in the backseat of Mena's Lexus.

Mena's heart raced. She knew nothing about delivering a baby. She wasn't CPR certified. How was she going to deal with helping the woman who had tormented her for the last hour? Did the crazy woman deserve her help?

The person who needed her, who Mena was most worried about, was Julian. The local hero had been gunned down, trying to protect her. Mena couldn't bear to think of him riddled with bullets, bleeding to death on the gallery floor. If the woman had taken her keys, Mena could have helped Julian. She could have called an ambulance and stayed with him, holding his hand and promising not to leave him until the paramedics came—

Another piercing scream jolted Mena.

The stakes were higher than she could have ever imagined. She couldn't focus on Ella and the terror she'd inflicted that evening. There was an innocent life to consider. A child that had no part in what its mother had done. Mena had to push away the rabid anger she felt toward Ella and do what she could to help the baby have a chance at life.

Ella let out another round of horrific screams. The contractions were coming closer together.

"You better fucking help me now!" Ella screamed.

Releasing her seatbelt, Mena turned her head slowly to look into the backseat.

The barrel of the gun was pointed directly between Mena's eyes.

A dull ached radiated through Mena's cheeks as her jaw clenched tightly. She glared at Ella. With everything this woman was going through, Mena couldn't believe she was still holding the gun, trying to threaten her.

There was no way Mena would allow the pregnant woman to shoot her, too. While Ella was in labor, Mena would get away, somehow, and call the police.

Mena had to be careful. She didn't want to provoke an extreme reaction from Ella.

"I don't know what you expect me to do. I've never helped anyone deliver a baby before," Mena said, choosing her words carefully. She had to remain calm.

Ella responded with another deep, husky groan. The gun dropped lower as a contraction racked Ella's body. Eyes dazed, Ella's breaths were short and shallow as sweat dripped from her face.

Mena was torn.

She could take this moment to overpower Ella, snatch the gun from her limp grasp and turn the tables on her tormentor. And yet, she had to think of the baby. How could she help the child and save herself at the same time? Would Ella have the strength to fight back after delivering her baby? Or, would Mena have a chance to take advantage of Ella's weakened state?

"You have to help me!" Ella screamed.

"I have blankets and water in the trunk. I'm going to get them and then help you deliver this baby," Mena said. Her words sounded foreign to her own ears as she smothered her emotions, focusing only on the task at hand.

Ella nodded slowly, wiping sweat from her brow. Her blond hair was plastered to the sides of her head. For the first time, Mena saw something other than anger in the woman's pallid and ashen face. Her lips trembled as her eyes darted about, blinking rapidly. Ella was afraid.

Mena exited the Lexus and opened the trunk. She pulled out a blanket and a towel from her impromptu trip with Regina to the beach this past weekend. She spotted her cooler tucked toward the back of the cavity. Opening the cooler, Mena slumped as she stared at the empty container. Remnants of ice had melted and formed a thin layer of water at the bottom. Would it be enough to clean the baby once it was born?

Mena grabbed the cooler from the trunk and walked around to the back door. Placing the cooler on the ground, Mena dropped the blanket and the beach towel on top, then reached for the door handle. Through the window, she could see Ella crying, her body trembling as she grimaced from another contraction.

For a moment, Ella's heinous crimes faded, and Mena felt sorry for her. What could Ella have been going through that led her down this path in life? Mena couldn't imagine this was how Ella thought she'd be giving birth to her child.

Driving away the thoughts, Mena opened the car door. A dark wetness covered the crotch of Ella's gray sweatpants and soaked part of the right pant leg.

"My water broke," Ella whimpered. "Please help my baby. Don't let my baby die because of me. Please!"

Terror clouded Ella's face as another round of sobs erupted from the woman. Groaning under the pain of another contraction, Ella clenched the sides of her swollen belly.

Mena focused on Ella's hands, trembling, muscles contracted.

The gun was missing.

Her gaze darting across the back of the car, Mena tried to locate the weapon. Where was it?

Another scream from Ella arrested Mena.

The gun would have to wait. A baby was demanding to be born, and Mena had to help the child, despite her feelings for the mother.

"Can you raise up?" Mena asked after the last contraction ended.

Ella nodded.

As quickly as she could, Mena grabbed the edges of the sweatpants and pulled them down Ella's legs.

"Oh Lord," Mena whispered and took a step back.

Ella wasn't wearing underwear.

Mena could see the crown of the baby's head between the woman's legs. This was really happening. Mena was about to deliver a woman's baby in the back of her Lexus. She couldn't fall apart. The baby needed her.

Grabbing the blanket from the top of the cooler, Mena placed it between Ella's legs. She wasn't sure what to do but figured the baby would appreciate coming out onto something soft.

"You're going to have to push," Mena said, remembering the clichéd line from countless medical dramas.

"I can't do this!" Ella shook her head, pushed herself back in the seat, and closed her legs slightly.

"You don't have a choice." Mena grabbed Ella's hands and gave them a gentle squeeze. "The baby is already coming out. I can see the head. You need to push."

Heartbreaking sobs poured from Ella, her eyes squeezed shut. "I can't. I can't."

"You can do this. When the next contraction happens, go ahead and push as hard as you can," Mena encouraged. "Can you do that?"

"Why are you doing this? Why are you helping me after everything I did to you?" Ella asked.

Mena ignored the comment. "Let's focus on your baby. Can you push?"

Ella nodded her head as another contraction rocked her body. With a primal moan, the woman bared down. Her face crumpled into a tight grimace of wrinkled, reddened skin, glistening with perspiration.

Mena watched the opening and braced herself. Some labors took hours, but this baby had other plans. Sliding out in one fluid motion, the baby laid listless on the blanket in Mena's hands.

Mena held her breath as she looked down at the small, fragile body. It was a boy. His skin was pale and tinged purple. He was eerily silent, his eyes closed and mouth slack.

The baby wasn't breathing.

Chapter Eleven

Mena's hands shook. Was the baby boy stillborn? Had the trauma of his mother's actions tonight caused him to stop breathing?

The rumble of a motorcycle jolted her. Turning toward the sound, Mena squinted as a single high beam light flashed across her face. Blinded, the light disappeared as quickly as it had appeared. Seconds later, a tall, muscular man jumped off the motorcycle and ran toward her.

"Julian," Mena whispered, unable to believe what she was seeing. Her heart flipped, and a fluttering filled her stomach.

In a blink, he was next to her, ruggedly handsome with his silky brown hair windblown from the ride. The heady scent of his cologne made her punch drunk as she stared into his eyes.

Julian was alive. Her eyes drifted down to his blood-soaked pant leg. He limped as he approached her.

Mena blinked back tears, thankful that Ella's spray of bullets hadn't killed him.

Julian squatted down next to Mena. "What do you have here?"

"The baby," Mena said, voice quivering. "He's not breathing."

"It's okay. You did good," Julian said, wrapping his arms around her.

The warmth of his skin was comforting, and Mena leaned into his embrace. Closing her eyes, she thanked God for Julian's arrival.

"Listen to me," Julian said. Reaching in the bottom of his pant leg, he pulled out an object and held it at his side. Moonlight glinted off the sharp blade of the skeleton frame knife.

"Hold the baby tight while I cut the umbilical cord," Julian commanded.

Mena gently squeezed the baby. His skin was cold to the touch, draining her of the last sliver of hope. The baby couldn't die. Not after everything that happened tonight. Mena needed him to be the one good thing to come out of this whole disaster.

With a swift move, Julian cut the umbilical cord and then lifted the baby from Mena's hands. He walked toward the light shining from the single beam of his motorcycle, several feet away from the Lexus.

Grabbing the towel and the cooler, Mena followed him.

"There's water in the cooler, not much, but you might need it," Mena said. If anyone could save the baby, Julian could. With Ella nearly passed out in the backseat of the car, Mena knew the nightmare was almost over.

Julian nodded. "I'll need it as soon as I get this little guy breathing."

Rubbing his large hands in smooth circular motions over the baby's chest and back, Julian whispered into the baby's ear. Mena took a step closer. Julian's bulging muscles were taut, yet his touch was gentle on the baby's small body. He paced slowly, alternating between massaging the body and pressing the baby's face close to his, perhaps feeling for any sign of breathing.

Minutes felt like hours as Mena clasped her hands in prayer. She wanted nothing more than for the baby to have a chance at life. Maybe his birth could be a turning point for Ella. Maybe the little boy could change her life.

Julian dropped to one knee and placed the baby face down on his extended leg. Sweeping a finger in the baby's mouth, Julian cleared remnants of the birth from the passageway, then continued to massage the baby's back.

Mena blinked away tears as she watched the scene. The baby's skin appeared to be changing subtly. It was no longer a faint purple, but she wasn't sure if her eyes were deceiving her in the dark night.

Breathe little guy, come on and breathe.

Turning the baby over, Julian placed two fingers near the center of the baby's chest and pressed down in quick succession. His movements were light but forceful. After a moment, he placed his mouth over the baby's face and blew slowly. Leaning back, Julian raised the baby from his leg and cradled him in his massive muscular forearm.

And then Mena heard the most beautiful sound.

A strong wail erupted from the little boy. His face scrunched and red, he continued to wail and cry as Julian let out a soft laugh.

Mena knelt next to Julian. Opening the cooler, she dipped the towel into the container, wrung the water out, and handed it to him. Julian cleaned the afterbirth from the baby's body and wrapped him securely in the towel.

"You saved his life," Mena said. The smile Julian gave her in return almost took her breath away.

"We did it together," Julian said. "How are you? Did she hurt you?"

"I'm fine," Mena said, but she wasn't sure if that was true. Her body and mind were numb.

Julian handed the baby to Mena.

Cradling the tiny baby in her arms, she hummed a lullaby she remembered from her childhood. The sound must have soothed the baby because he slowly stopped crying.

"You're a natural," Julian said, winking at Mena. "Stay here. I'm going to go check on Ella."

Mena nodded. Both Ella and the baby would need to go to the hospital immediately. Mena hoped Julian would leave his motorcycle and drive them there. She didn't trust herself behind the wheel right now.

"What the hell?" Julian muttered.

"What is it?" Mena asked and walked over toward the Lexus. Mena looked at the baby, rosy-tinted and breathing steadily.

Julian said, "Ella's gone."

Chapter Twelve

Julian yanked open the curtain of the cubicle in the hospital emergency room, walked inside, and sat on the edge of the bed. He'd refused the wheelchair with disdain, barking at the nurse to focus on evaluating Ella's baby. The blood soaking the fabric of his cargo pants could wait. He knew his injuries looked worse than what they were. What he didn't know was whether Ella's son had suffered any adverse effects from oxygen deprivation during birth. He needed the staff to focus on the baby, not on him.

A woman wearing yellow hospital scrubs pushed the edge of the curtain back and entered the space. Warm and welcoming, her smile revealed a set of deep dimples on each cheek.

"Mr. Montgomery," the woman began, a soft melodic lilt in her voice. "I'm Robyn Bean, the PA working with Dr. Gillis tonight. Looks like a lot of blood on that leg. Let's get your vitals and then I'll give your leg a look."

Grimacing, Julian pushed back onto the bed, giving his leg more support. The adrenaline still pulsing through his body dulled the burning ache—for now anyway. Robyn placed the blood pressure cuff on his arm and stuck a thermometer under his tongue, then focused her eyes on the gash in the fabric. She reached behind her and grabbed a pair of scissors. The cotton blend fabric fell to the floor as she cut the cargo pants off his left leg above the gunshot wound.

Julian closed his eyes as she peppered him with the normal medical history questions, dutifully answering each one.

Her hands, donned in latex gloves, touched his thigh gingerly as she examined the wound.

"Appears you were very lucky, no major damage to muscle or bone, but it will be painful to walk on this leg over the next few weeks. Your temperature is higher than I'd like, so Dr. Gillis may want to keep you overnight to watch for any further signs of infection. But she'll let you know that for sure after she finishes checking on the baby," Robyn said.

"I'm not staying here overnight," Julian responded, shifting in the bed, sending a sharp pain through his leg.

"Dr. Gillis will need to determine if it's appropriate to release you—"

"I don't care what the doctor thinks. It won't change the fact that I'm not staying here," Julian said. A hospital stay for a flesh wound was beyond ridiculous. Looking for Ella was out of the question tonight, but he planned to get started in the morning after sleeping in his own bed.

"You'll have to sign a waiver acknowledging your refusal of recommended treatment," Robyn said, looking perplexed.

"No problem." Julian leaned back on the bed and peered through the gap in the curtain. Across the hallway, Mena Nix sat still on the edge of a chair against the wall. Kendrick stood in front of her, partially blocking Julian's view. Kendrick must have been assigned to investigate the crime. A bit of unexpected good fortune, Julian thought. Not only would he have an inside track on what the cops uncovered about Ella's disappearance, but Kendrick could arrange to have his laptop removed from the Genesis Gallery security room before Adam Russell discovered it. Julian didn't want the head of security to know that he'd been secretly canvassing old surveillance footage to search for Ella. He didn't need anyone knowing he had any connection to the missing woman, at least not until he could figure out why she'd been on the property tonight.

Robyn droned on about the significant amount of dirt and debris embedded in the wound and the need to perform deep sterilization and trimming before she sutured it closed. Julian nodded in response, not caring about his leg at the moment as he strained to hear the conversation between Mena and Kendrick.

Mena's voice wafted from the opposite side of the emergency room. "She was angry and agitated. Once she went into labor, that's all I focused on. Everything else is like ... a blur. I'm sorry."

"How long had you been driving before you stopped the car on the side of the road?" Kendrick asked.

"I ..." Mena started, then stopped. "I don't know."

"It's okay. Do you remember if the woman gave you a location to drive to? Do you know where you were headed?" Kendrick asked.

"I can't remember."

Mena had seemed strong and unshaken earlier, but Julian could hear the toll that the night must have taken on her.

"Ms. Nix, how about you go home and come to the police station in the morning. Maybe after a good night's sleep, you'll be able to remember more details of what happened tonight," Kendrick suggested. He folded his notepad and stuffed it into the back pocket of his jeans.

"I can't go home yet. I need to check on Julian. I want to see that he's okay," Mena said.

Julian smiled.

"Let me go over and get his statement first and then you can see him. How about that?" Kendrick asked.

Mena nodded as she rested her head in her hands.

Kendrick turned and strode across the hallway to Julian's cordoned off space. Pulling the curtain back, he poked his head inside.

"You up for a visitor?" Kendrick asked.

"Get in here," Julian said, grateful to see his friend.

"Hey Robyn, can you give us a minute?" Kendrick asked the PA.

Robyn sighed heavily. "Kendrick, this wound needs to get cleaned now, or Mr. Montgomery could get a nasty infection—"

Kendrick flashed her a big smile and rested his arm around her shoulder, then said, "C'mon, I'll only be a few minutes."

"Fine," Robyn said as Kendrick gave her a quick peck on the cheek. "I'll be back in ten minutes."

"Surprised to see me," Kendrick said, dropping down on the stool.

"Hell yeah," Julian replied. "I thought the renowned Detective Desmond François would have been assigned to investigate. How'd you manage to get the gig?"

"He passed it up. The prince of Palmchat Islands police royalty believes a missing person case is beneath his talents," Kendrick said with a laugh.

As nice as Kendrick was, Julian knew his friend resented the meager opportunities given to any detective without the last name François. Despite making detective three years ago, Kendrick had been relegated to petty gang crimes, domestic disputes, and robberies, while all the high-profile cases went to one man—Detective Desmond François.

Kendrick asked, "What happened at the gallery?"

Julian recapped how he'd found a pregnant woman holding a gun on Mena in the lobby. Taking his time, he talked Kendrick through every detail up to the point where they'd arrived at the hospital.

Kendrick looked up from his notepad, where he'd been taking notes as Julian spoke. "Any ideas on who the pregnant woman is?"

"You won't believe who she is—Ella Sapphire," Julian said.

"Is that name supposed to mean something to me?" Kendrick asked, raising an eyebrow.

"Ella Sapphire is the reason I asked you to get me a job at the gallery," Julian said. "She's the sister of my best friend's wife, Dawn Sapphire Garrison. A month ago, Ella left a disturbing message for Dawn," Julian explained. He gave Kendrick a play-by-play of Ella's terrifying voice mail, his investigation into her disappearance, and how Ella had appeared out of the blue tonight at the gallery wielding a gun.

"You believe her hostage story?" Kendrick asked, his expression doubtful.

"Can't say I believe she was being held hostage, but I do think she has some kind of link to the gallery or the Co-Op. All the artists there knew her," Julian said.

"Typically hostages aren't the ones with the guns. I know the gala was going on this evening. Was there anyone else at the gallery other than you and Mena Nix?" Kendrick asked.

"My boss and another security guard were there until around 8 p.m.," Julian said.

"What are their names?" Kendrick asked.

Julian told him, then continued, "And there were two other employees in the conservation workshop. I'm not sure how long they'd been on the grounds," Julian said, explaining the incident between Irving Bond and Uma Fischer. "I walked Ms. Fischer to her car and watched her leave. Not sure when Bond left. Neither of them was in the main building when Ella shot me and took off with Ms. Nix."

"Still, they might know something to help us locate Ella," Kendrick said, jotting down the names.

"I know something else that might help," Julian said, thinking about his laptop.

"What's that?"

"I was doing a little scraping on the security videos to see if Ella showed up on any of the footage over the past two years. My laptop is still plugged into the gallery security system, running the analysis. It's in the Security Office, underneath the desk near the hard drives. If you grab it before anyone notices, I'll share the results with you," Julian said.

"Deal. I'm headed over to the gallery with my team now," Kendrick said and stood.

"Keep me posted," Julian said.

"You got it." Kendrick pulled the curtain open.

Standing on the other side in a sparkly dress that faded from blue to pink, hugging the curves of her ample assets, was Mena Nix. Julian held his breath, mesmerized as she swept a strand of hair behind her ear and bit her lower lip.

Kendrick gave Julian a thumbs up, then turned and walked through the curtain into the hallway, giving Mena a slight nod as he passed by.

"How are you doing?" Mena asked. She tilted her head, causing her dark hair to brush against the smooth skin of her collar bone.

Julian stifled a smile and responded, "Better now."

Chapter Thirteen

Appreciatively, Mena's eyes traveled the length of Julian Montgomery. Framed by the inky blackness of the sky, he stood in front of the ceiling-to-floor windows of her condo overlooking Crescent Moon Bay. She had no doubt he'd broken hearts in the past, and she didn't want to add herself to that list. But, a girl could enjoy the view.

Especially after what she'd gone through.

"The bay is beautiful at this time of night." Julian lifted his arm and pressed a palm against the glass, leaning forward. "You probably have the best view of the bay. I bet on a clear day, you can see clear across to St. Felipe."

Indeed Mena could, which was one of the reasons she'd selected this condo. Located at the edge of the sprawling property, it boasted an angular view of both the bay and the Caribbean.

"That's my boat over there," Julian continued, pointing down toward the boats docked between slips at the marina.

Mena walked over and stood next to him. Her eyes drifted to the massive super-yacht in the slip near the boardwalk and the Cartier store. She'd noticed that yacht several times during treks to the luxury stores in the marina. She and Julian were separated by a ten-minute walk along a meandering palm tree-lined pathway. Amazing that she'd never met him before.

"Nice boat," Mena said, then placed a hand on his arm. "The doctor's orders were clear. You're supposed to stay off that leg for the next twenty-four hours. Did you take the pain medicine?"

Julian grimaced, then shook his head as he limped over to her ivory curved sofa, centered in the middle of her living room, and sat.

"You didn't need to offer up your guest bedroom." Lifting her navy and white striped throw pillow, Julian plumped it in his hands before placing it behind his head.

"And you didn't need to risk your life to save mine, but you did," Mena said, reflecting on Julian's astonishing bravery. Despite suffering a gunshot wound, he'd managed to save both her and Ella's baby boy. "The doctor seemed concerned about you being alone. So I figured it was the least I could do to pay you back for everything you did to help me."

"You don't owe me anything," Julian said, looking over his shoulder at her. "Actually, in a strange way, I owe you."

"For what?" Mena asked, intrigued. She walked over toward the couch, hesitated and then decided to sit in one of the wicker pod chairs adjacent to the sofa.

"For being kidnapped at gunpoint by Ella."

"Excuse me?"

"That didn't come out right," said Julian, dragging a hand down his face. "What I meant was, if Ella hadn't kidnapped you tonight, I might never have found her."

Mena said, "I don't understand."

"I've been looking for Ella for the past month," said Julian.

"Why?" Mena asked, picking at a string on the cushion of her chair.

"She's important to someone very important to me, so I had to do whatever it took to find her," Julian responded.

"She didn't seem to know you," Mena said.

"More like she didn't remember me. It's been a while since we've seen each other," Julian said, shifting on the couch. He grabbed the other navy and white striped pillow and propped it underneath his arm.

"Was Ella in some kind of trouble?" Mena asked, wondering why she was pressing him for answers. Maybe it was better that she didn't know the details. But, a part of her couldn't resist trying to understand why a pregnant woman would take her hostage and then abandon her baby after he was born.

"Dawn seemed to think so," Julian yawned. "I'm not so sure."

Dawn.

A woman very important to Julian.

Mena swallowed past the lump in her throat. She stood and took a step toward Julian, reaching a hand to help him up from the couch. "It's getting late, and my guest bedroom is a lot more comfortable than my sofa."

"How are you doing? Really?" Julian asked, holding her hand in his. The intensity of his gaze arrested Mena, as she realized a generic response was not going to suffice.

Hesitating, she focused on the contrast of her dark brown skin against his. "One minute I'm trying to explain to the director of the gallery that an expensive piece of art he purchased is a fake and the next I'm being held at gunpoint, driving like a lunatic down a dark road before having to deliver a baby in the middle of the night. Not exactly how I thought this evening would end. Knowing that you're alive and the baby is okay, and the police are searching for Ella helps, though."

Julian stood from the sofa. The distance between them diminished as he looked down at their intertwined hands, still clasped tightly. Julian swept a wayward strand of her black hair from her face and tucked it behind her ear. "I'm worried about you."

"You have no reason to be worried," Mena insisted. "Don't I seem fine? I'm not freaking out or having a panic attack or drowning in tears. Tonight was tough, but I got through it."

She'd summoned every ounce of her willpower to not crumble in the middle of her floor and wail from the senselessness of it all. The last time she'd felt this way was three years ago when a woman had rung her doorbell and shattered her life as she'd known it. Tonight, that lost, helpless feeling had returned, rocking her to her core. But she'd stayed strong and survived, like she had back then.

Julian stared at her, a gentleness in his eyes.

"Yeah, that's what worries me," Julian said, leaning closer to her.

"I don't understand," Mena whispered, feeling like the room was suddenly too small for the presence of Julian. Heat flooded her face, and a sly tingling awakened within her.

Julian licked his lips slowly, sending a lustful jolt through Mena. He said, "It's the lack of reaction. Just because you aren't showing emotion doesn't mean you aren't feeling a whole hell of a lot of it."

Mena flinched.

Julian leaned forward and softly caressed the side of her face, sending a wave of heat through her body. His fingers lingered before pulling back.

Mena stared ahead, afraid of how her body would respond if she looked at Julian, disturbed by the magnetic attraction pulling her toward him.

"Which way is the guest bedroom?" Julian asked.

"Down the hallway, second door on the left."

As Julian left the room, Mena sank down into the chair, disturbed by the feelings brewing inside her.

Chapter Fourteen

The knocking grew louder, more insistent, pressing through the haze of sleep. Pushing his face deeper into the pillow, Julian groaned and opened one eye to check the time.

Squinting against the sun, glaring in through the single window in the corner, he stared at his watch.

The blurred numbers came into focus.

Half past noon.

The knocking grew louder.

Where was Mena? Why wasn't she answering her door? Was she hurt?

Pushing off the bed, Julian rushed out of the room into the hallway, ignoring the throbbing of his thigh. The living room was quiet and serene.

The knocking resumed. Julian walked to the door, yanking it open.

Kendrick stood in the doorway. "Anything you want to tell me about you and the lovely Ms. Nix?"

Julian hesitated, not ready to articulate what he felt about Mena. Not yet. Not when he needed to focus on finding Ella.

Kendrick smirked, then walked past Julian into the condo, passing the foyer where two large paintings of bright colored island flowers hung one on top of the other against the backdrop of the blue and white striped wallpaper. Julian followed the detective into the living room.

"Look, she felt sorry for me. I didn't want to stay overnight at the hospital, and the doctor made a fuss about me being alone on my boat in case something happened with this damn gunshot wound. So, she volunteered to look after me for the night."

"Guess that's the trick. Get shot and get the attention of a beautiful woman," Kendrick responded, with a sly smile. Reaching into the messenger bag slung across his shoulder, he pulled out Julian's laptop and placed it on the table next to a wooden platter filled with lemons, limes, and oranges.

"Thanks for getting this," Julian said.

"I also had your bike towed back to the marina parking lot this morning," said Kendrick. "Took the guy a while to find it, but it wasn't damaged."

"Any sign of Ella?" Julian asked.

"Nothing yet," Kendrick replied. "But I got the gallery staff interviews done this morning."

"What did you find out?"

"No one knew her. Some thought she looked familiar. A few said they might have seen her at the Co-Op, but they weren't sure."

"What about the security cameras?"

Kendrick shook his head. "There was no security footage recorded by the cameras last night."

"That's impossible." Julian limped over toward the bar and rested his elbows against the counter, relieving pressure from his injured leg. "The gallery archives the daily security videos and backs them up. Nothing gets deleted."

"I watched as a—" Kendrick reached into his pocket and pulled out his notepad. Flipping through pages, he stopped and said, "Zakariah Webber accessed the folder with the videos from yesterday. Nothing but white noise on each file. Webber claimed he found a loose connection that was the cause of the lost footage."

"A loose connection would have caused the same effect on the monitors in the security room," Julian said, confused. "They were crystal clear."

"But, you weren't in the room the whole night, right?" Kendrick asked.

"No, but after I dealt with the issue in the conservation workshop, I went right back to the security room. The monitors were fine," Julian insisted.

"You think your laptop may have the footage from last night?" Kendrick asked.

Julian jerked one of the white mesh, rounded-back chairs from the table and sat. Disgusted, he opened the laptop and booted it up. It didn't hurt to check, although he suspected his little project may have been the reason the security recordings for yesterday were damaged.

All of his efforts to find Ella, and maybe somehow make up for all the pain he'd caused, had failed miserably. Pinching the bridge of his nose, he thought about the conversation he needed to have with Dawn. After he told her about Ella, she'd probably hate him more than she already did. Julian couldn't blame her. Not only had he destroyed her marriage, but he'd blown a chance to reunite her with her sister. Julian never should have made promises he couldn't keep. Even if he had found Ella, he knew in his heart, it wouldn't have changed things between him and Dawn. Nothing could make up for the mistakes he made three years ago.

The computer flickered, and Julian accessed the folder with the saved files. Inside were over six hundred date-labeled files—the security videos for the last two years compressed and saved on his computer. He scrolled through the dates. The video file for yesterday was missing. Julian turned the laptop to show Kendrick the disappointing results.

"A bust for last night but looks like you have copies of security footage going back almost two years," Kendrick said, scrolling through the files in the folder. "I can use these files to figure out where Ella could be right now."

Julian closed the classified laptop he wasn't supposed to still have in his possession and pulled it away from his friend. "If I give you this footage, I'd be making you an accessory to a crime."

"Say no more." Kendrick rubbed a hand down his face and shook his head. "But if you happen to find something interesting, you need to give me a heads up."

"You'll be my first call. Do you have any other leads?" Julian asked.

"We recovered the gun and a cell phone from the back of Mena's car. Forensics is working on getting fingerprints from the weapon to run through the criminal databases, and the tech team is trying to crack the password on the phone," Kendrick said.

"That could be Mena's cell phone," Julian guessed.

"I asked her about it already. She said she'd never seen it before and that it wasn't her phone," Kendrick said.

"When did you talk to her?" Julian asked.

"I got her statement this morning when I was interviewing the rest of the employees at the gallery," Kendrick said.

"Mena is at the gallery?"

"You didn't know that?"

"She didn't tell me." Julian stood. His date with the security footage would have to wait. Mena Nix had some explaining to do.

Chapter Fifteen

"What the hell are you doing here?"

Mena locked the door to her workshop, then turned. Staring back at her were the soulful brown eyes of Julian Montgomery. He looked so different from last night, dressed in jogging pants and a t-shirt that couldn't hide his well-toned physique. Nothing like she thought a man suffering from lack of sleep and a gunshot wound to the leg would look. He was refreshed and ... scowling at her.

"You shouldn't be here." Mena grabbed his hand, steering him toward the narrow pathway lining the back of the workshop buildings. The stone walkway connected the perimeter of the gallery grounds.

Walking through the shadows of the workshop buildings, below the outstretched branches of the mahogany trees clustered along the walkway, Julian matched her strides as she hurried toward the employee parking lot.

"Look, I don't want anyone at the gallery to know that I was Ella's hostage. I don't need that kind of attention. So, it's probably not a good idea for the two of us to be seen talking to each other," Mena said, as she looked back for signs that anyone was watching them.

After two hours of police interrogation in the conference room of the gallery, rehashing last night's events, Mena had found a moment to speak to Priscilla privately. Her boss had assured her that no one other than Adam

Russell, the head of security, would know about her involvement in the break-in last night.

Mena hadn't told Omar and Regina about being held hostage. She didn't want to worry them now that everything was over. And honestly, the last thing she needed was a barrage of questions from her best friends about how it felt to be held at gunpoint and forced to deliver the baby of her captor.

Detective Caillouet had confided that her name was being withheld from the news as a common protocol of an ongoing investigation. Mena had been relieved. The last thing she needed was her father, Caleb Olivier, a seasoned reporter for the *Palmchat Gazette*, finding out about Ella taking her hostage. She hoped he didn't find out at all.

"You went through hell last night, and you thought it was a good idea to come to work this morning?" Julian stepped in front of her, blocking her.

"I could say the same thing to you," she responded. "You shouldn't be walking on that leg."

"I've lost count of how many times I've been shot," Julian said. "I know how to get through this. How many times have you had a gun pointed at your head?"

Mena shrunk back, stung by his words. She knew he'd been in the U.S. military but hadn't figured his life had been on the line so many times. Her life had been in danger only once before last night. That one summer afternoon when a woman, a stranger to her, rang her doorbell and changed her life as she'd known it. She'd never imagined that the simple act of answering her front door would destroy the foundation of the life she'd built with her then-husband, Michael. She couldn't imagine going through that type of trauma again.

Julian said, "Look, I didn't mean to—"

"I'm fine. Really, I am," Mena said. She folded her arms across her chest and looked toward a group of hibiscus bushes clustered around a stone fountain in the park. The weight of a thousand burdens settled within her, causing her body to slouch.

The breeze picked up, blowing a strand of her dark hair across her face. Julian caught the strand between his fingers and smoothed it back behind her ear. The slight brush of his fingers along the side of her face was hypnotic.

"You gave your statement to the cops this morning?" Julian asked. His eyes searched hers, and she detected a hint of concern and worry in his face.

"How'd you know?" Mena asked, growing irritated. She didn't need or want Julian to care or worry about her. She didn't need that type of complication in her life right now.

"The detective on the case, Kendrick Caillouet, is probably the only friend I have on the island. He told me he questioned you," Julian said.

"Your only friend?" Mena asked, a hint of a smile playing at the corners of her mouth.

"I keep to myself for the most part," Julian admitted.

"I thought police investigations were supposed to be confidential," Mena said.

"He didn't give me details, but I heard you talking to him last night at the hospital. I know it was hard for you to remember what happened. Was it easier this morning?"

Mena took a deep breath. "Yes and no. Some parts are crystal clear, but not the parts that the cops want to know about. I can't remember much of what Ella said to me in the car before she went into labor," Mena said. "I'm not sure I want to remember."

Julian slipped an arm around her waist and guided her toward a stone bench underneath a large mahogany tree. Sitting down, Mena rested her purse on the bench, then turned toward Julian. He didn't look back at her, his attention focused on a chipmunk scurrying across the manicured lawn of the courtyard beyond the workshop buildings. She figured he was willing to listen to her or to sit with her in silence as she tried to process the chaos in her mind.

She knew she needed to talk to someone. What she hadn't anticipated was that she'd actually *want* to talk. But not just to anyone. To Julian. She knew she could trust him.

Mena said, "Ella was pregnant. Why would she risk breaking into the gallery and taking me hostage? She has a son that she's never met. And now because of the crimes she committed, she won't get a chance to raise her child. They could be separated for years. I don't know what I'm saying. The crazy woman tortured me last night. I'm lucky to be alive today. Why should I care?"

Julian smiled at her and said, "Because you're a good person. You're different from the Ella's of the world. She was selfish, always in trouble, hanging out with the wrong crowds, always looking to make a quick buck no matter who got hurt. Can't say I'm surprised that she pulled a stunt like this."

"But ... Dawn ... she still wanted your help to find Ella?" Mena asked, remembering the woman who was important to Julian. The reason Julian had been looking for Ella in the first place.

"Dawn always saw the best in her sister, even when the rest of us couldn't," Julian said.

"Does your only friend have any leads on where Ella could be?" Mena asked.

"Not yet," Julian said.

"Do you know why Ella was at the gallery?"

Julian hesitated. "I have suspicions ..."

"Like what?" Mena felt compelled to know.

"Ella was always scheming, but she had a real talent for art. She was a sculptor and studied art history before she dropped out of college. I don't think it's a coincidence that she showed up at the gallery two years ago and started hanging out at the Co-Op. I think she was transitioning her petty schemes to more criminal activities," Julian said.

"Art theft," Mena said, thinking of several high-value pieces Ella could have easily smuggled out of the gallery in the pockets of her pink windbreaker.

"It's possible," Julian said. "You would think if she was casing the joint, she wouldn't have disappeared from the Co-Op seven months ago. But that could have been part of her plan to not raise suspicion when she came back to steal from the gallery."

"And I stumbled right into the middle of her getaway and ruined everything," Mena said.

"That's the theory at least," said Julian. "But enough about Ella. How about I take you somewhere that will help you relax."

"Where?" Mena asked, frowning.

"It's a surprise. Have you ridden a motorcycle before?" Julian asked.

"You're not the only one that owns a Harley."

Chapter Sixteen

Pressing her thighs against the sides of the steel gray, sleek Harley Davidson Road King, Mena leaned forward and opened up the throttle. The bike accelerated faster, roaring along the long stretch of mountain road. She and Julian had been riding for almost twenty miles heading east, away from the Genesis Gallery. With each passing mile, the strong island winds had blown away all thoughts of last night. A blur of mahogany and almond trees whizzed by as she guided the motorcycle down the gentle slope toward the uninhabited east side of St. Basil.

Julian had read her mind. Somehow, he'd known instinctively what she needed. The open road and wind in her face freed her mind from the onslaught of memories.

How could he know her so well, yet not really know her at all?

She didn't believe in coincidences, but Julian was doing everything right. The feel of his arms wrapped gently around her abdomen, holding her close, had her whole body on high alert.

Julian seemed perfectly at ease with her at the helm of the Harley. Not once in the past hour had he given her any pointers on how to drive the bike. He settled in behind her and let her take control, only occasionally giving her a nudge to turn onto a different road.

Mena wondered how Julian remained so calm. She knew Ella's disappearance bothered him. After all, he'd been trying to find her. For Dawn.

Dropping everything at Dawn's request had to be based on more than a casual friendship. But, from what she could tell, Dawn was no longer in Julian's life. Had they been lovers in the past? Was Julian harboring residual feelings for her?

Stop it.

Why was she thinking about Julian and Dawn? Whatever their relationship was, it had nothing to do with her.

Mena pushed the motorcycle faster. The mosaic of passing trees created a beautiful canvas as the bike glided along the road. Ella's attack had terrified her, but Mena was proud of how she'd handle the unsettling situation. Avoiding the peaks and valleys of emotional outbursts, she'd stayed relatively even-keeled, unlike the last time a crazed woman had tried to kill her.

After the trauma she'd experienced three years ago, Mena had worked closely with a therapist, learning how to process the unexpected attack, and how to stop herself from unraveling or having a meltdown. She'd taken Krav Maga for over a year to build up her physical strength as well as her emotional strength. Never again would she let the actions and behaviors of others ruin her life. Her last relationship hadn't left her with much, but it had taught her that one valuable lesson.

Easing on the throttle, Mena took the last curve of the road and saw two large rocks blocking the pavement ahead. Squeezing the brake, she brought the motorcycle to a stop.

Julian jumped off the back and grabbed her hand, helping her off the bike.

"What is this place?" Mena asked, allowing herself to be pulled forward. Julian's strong grip on her hand comforted her as she easily matched the pace of his light jog toward the boulders.

"Just a little hidden gem we discovered about a decade ago," Julian said and winked at her before heading toward a narrow opening between two massive boulders.

"We?" asked Mena.

Julian stopped and faced her. The look on his face was contemplative and a bit wistful.

"My best friend Broman and I found this place after dirtboarding down the

Cashew Hiking Trail near Warber's Peak in the St. Basil Mountains," Julian said, his smile tinged with a hint of sadness.

"What the hell is dirtboarding?" Mena asked, intrigued.

"Skateboarding down a mountain. Broman and I dirtboarded some of the best mountains in the world, but the mountains on the Palmchat Islands became our favorites. Can't tell you how many times we skidded to the bottom of that mountain," Julian said, pointing to the small opening in the jungle at the foot of a steep mountainside across from the boulders. "Then we would head here to swim before trekking back to our campsite. Some of the best days of my life were spent here with Broman."

"Sounds like fun," Mena said.

"We thought so," Julian said with a low laugh. "Dawn didn't agree. She's Broman's wife. She gave him hell every time I lured him away on one of our dirtboarding weekends. She and I have never seen eye to eye, but we had Broman in common and tolerated each other."

Mena resisted asking more questions about Dawn, distracted by the relief that flooded through her body. She shouldn't have been interested in Julian's relationship with his best friend's wife anyway.

"Broman is the reason why I agreed to look for Ella," said Julian. "Despite my beef with Dawn, because of Broman, I couldn't say no. I owe it to Broman to help his wife."

Finding out that Julian was helping Dawn find Ella because of his best friend changed something within Mena. Something that she wasn't ready to acknowledge.

"Come on." Julian's broad shoulders brushed against the small opening between the rough rocks as he twisted his body through the gap. He slowly disappeared until all she could see was his arm, extended toward her, beckoning her to follow him.

Stepping cautiously, Mena turned and eased through the crevice. On the other side of the boulders was an enchanting beach enclave. Mena took a deep breath, awed by the natural beauty before her. A maze of massive boulders dotted along the pristine sugary white sand. Light turquoise waters stretched into the distance leading to the Caribbean Sea. She would never have imagined a place like this existed on the other side of the Basil Mountains.

"Stunning," Mena whispered as she followed Julian around two smaller stones and out to a small clearing of sand. The water, as smooth as glass, pooled along the edge, the sky and sun reflecting on the surface.

Julian walked to the edge of the water. Reaching down, he unlaced his boots and stepped out of the shoes, throwing them back toward a large boulder.

Mena stepped out of her loafers. She ached to feel the soft white sand beneath her feet. Surveying the rocks, Mena walked to an oval-shaped boulder, placed her shoes on top of it, and then headed to the edge of the water to stand next to Julian.

"Are those coral reefs out there?" asked Mena.

"That's what stops the waves from destroying this place," Julian said as he lifted the t-shirt from his body, revealing a well-toned chest and sculpted abs. His body was chiseled, but not in the overt, gym rat way. The muscles were more natural, built from heavy lifting in the course of everyday life.

"I can't tell you how many times I've come out here and floated for hours. The best feeling ever. You wanna go in?" Julian asked.

"I'm not dressed to go swimming."

Julian winked at her, then unbuttoned his jeans and let them fall to his ankles, revealing navy blue boxer briefs that accentuated all of his assets. "You undress to go swimming. You gotta feel this water. Take off your clothes."

Chapter Seventeen

Mena glanced down at her clothes—a pale pink Brooks Brothers jacket and matching pants, perfect for a professional look in a humid climate but not for swimming. Underneath, her underwear was respectable—not sexy but not granny panties either. She didn't want to miss the chance to go into the water. A quick swim might keep her mind off the jumbled memories of last night. Maybe help her get some clarity to remember details of Ella's rantings before the gun-wielding woman went into labor.

Mena walked over to the oval-shaped boulder where she'd placed her loafers and took off her suit. She decided to keep her white-laced tank top on, giving her body a bit more coverage. She wasn't ready for Julian Montgomery to see her in lingerie, not yet, or maybe, not ever.

Mena laid her clothes on top of the five-foot rock. She turned and noticed Julian staring at her, a smoldering passion in his eyes.

He was stunningly handsome. A sly tingling crept through Mena's body, heading for a distinct place. She forced the feeling to subside. A distraction was what she needed, but not that kind.

Regina's words filtered into her mind, *Julian was enraptured ... he watched your every move until you sashayed out of the gallery.*

So what if Regina had been right. She couldn't act on it. Mena had had flings since she moved to the island. Short romances. Sometimes the sex had been good. Other times, average. But she'd only been mildly interested in the men. There was never a threat that things could get out of control like they had three years ago when she'd been played for a fool.

Just because Julian and Dawn didn't share a romantic past didn't mean she was going to let her defenses down with the sexy security guard. She didn't trust herself to engage in a sexual dalliance. She'd worked hard to keep those kind of complications out of her life. Keeping Julian at a distance was for the best, no matter how many seductive looks he threw her way. She took a few tentative steps toward Julian, water skimming the top of his knees.

"Should you get that wet?" Mena motioned toward the bandage on his left thigh where he'd been shot.

"Like I told you before, it's not my first rodeo. Come on into the water." Julian walked backward, further out into the sea.

Mena stepped into the water. "It's so warm. This water has got to be near ninety degrees."

"And it's not from the sun," Julian said, stopping to dip his body into the water. "I've been out here in the middle of the night, and the temperature has felt the same."

"What do you think is causing this?" Mena eased forward, allowing her body to get acclimated to the warmth.

"Gotta be some underground geothermal activity, but none of the research I've done on this island has indicated that's possible. It's the only thing that makes sense to me, though," Julian responded, then disappeared behind another rock formation.

Following him, Mena stood in waist-deep waters surrounded by a circle of rocks that stretched toward the sky. Leaning against one of the boulders, she felt the tension leave her body. The soft howl of the wind and the waves crashing against the coral reef lulled her into a serene state.

Water splashed against her face. Mena shrieked as her eyes fluttered open.

"I can't believe after all this time you've lived on the island, you haven't learned not to splash water on a black woman's hair by now," Mena said, slapping at Julian's arm.

Julian let out a loud, deep laugh. The brilliant smile spreading across his face tugged at Mena's heart, sending a burst of warmth cascading through her body. Mena leaned back against the rock, thankful for the support as her legs threatened to melt.

"I've been told, but I'm not too good at sticking to the rules," Julian said, rushing toward her. Mena knew she was trapped. Julian bent down toward the water. Rising, he splashed a cascade of water onto her face and body.

Mena howled with laughter and trudged through the water toward three towering rocks on the opposite side of the enclosure, trying to get away from Julian, who continued to douse her with the warm water.

Her hair was already ruined, but she didn't care.

Mena couldn't remember the last time she allowed herself to frolic and play, unconcerned about letting go. When was the last time she'd truly let herself feel anything?

Mena knew the answer, and it was a time in her life she didn't want to revisit. She'd followed her heart right to heartbreak and danger. She wouldn't make that mistake again.

But maybe she was overthinking things.

Julian was an attractive man, but there was no danger with him. They weren't involved. They'd shared a traumatic experience and needed an escape. Cavorting on the beach with Julian was a far cry from sentencing herself to another heartbreak. She knew better than to let that happen again. This was innocent fun with a sexy man.

Pushing the thoughts away, Mena turned on the offensive. She dipped underneath the water, then rose and pushed toward Julian, drenching him.

"I guess the gloves are off now," Julian said, his sexy laughter piercing through the wind as he waded toward her and tousled her hair before he dipped underneath the surface.

Mena giggled as she felt his hands playfully tickling her abdomen.

"No! I'm ticklish! Stop it!" Mena squealed as she bounded through the water, trying to find her way through the maze of rocks back to the shore. Julian was close on her heels, peppering her back with more water.

Mena stopped and turned. Scooping water in her hands, she flung it against Julian's face. The droplets of water cascaded down his skin slowly, sending her body into a sizzling sensual frenzy. Thoughts of touching his bare chest consumed her mind, and she got lost in the fantasy as another deluge of water sprayed against her body.

Jerking forward, Mena broke from the porno running through her head and put some distance between herself and the object of her desire.

Stepping between two smaller rocks, she felt something slithering around her legs.

Terror shot through Mena's veins as her body grew stiff.

A howl erupted from her throat.

"You okay?" Julian asked, swimming toward her.

Mena thrashed in the water, panic overwhelming her.

"I don't know!" Mena screamed, clawing through the water back toward the shore. "I think it's a jellyfish or something!"

They were too far away from the hospital to deal with a jellyfish or Portuguese Man-O-War sting. She could die before she got medical treatment. Mena felt herself growing hysterical. The shoreline seemed too far away.

She fought back tears as her body was lifted from the water. The sea breeze floated across her skin, giving her goose bumps as Julian's muscular arms wrapped around her. Grasping his neck, she was acutely aware of the strength of his body brushing against hers as he ran through the water, navigating the maze of rocks back to the beach.

Easing down onto the sand, Mena stared into his worried brown eyes before he looked away and focused his attention on her legs. Mena propped her body on her elbows and peered at her lower body, embarrassment threatening to overwhelm her.

She'd gotten tangled in some type of pink shirt. Julian took his time freeing her legs from the fabric, but instead of laughing at her, he was frowning.

An icy chill shot down Mena's spine as she focused on the article of clothing.

Julian held up the pink material.

Mena instantly recognized the jacket.

Ella Sapphire had worn it last night when she'd taken Mena hostage.

"How did that get down here?" Mena asked.

"We're almost twenty-five miles from the Genesis Gallery. Ella couldn't have made it this far by foot," Julian said. "I need to call Kendrick and tell him what we found."

Julian walked past Mena to his jeans, laying on the sand and reached into the pocket.

Mena stood and walked toward the rock where she'd left her clothes. Reaching for her jacket, Mena put it on as the wind blew her pants off the rocks into a crevice a few yards away. Rushing toward the pants, Mena caught them before they fell into the water. Grabbing them with one hand, she turned and stopped.

Long strands of blond hair floated in the crystal-clear water.

"Julian," Mena said, her voice hoarse.

Stepping closer, Mena peered around the rock. A young woman's pale, bluish-tinted face bobbed above the water, her neck twisted at an unnatural angle. Lifeless eyes stared at Mena.

"Julian!" Mena screamed, louder this time, her cries echoing off the sides of the cliff.

Taking another step forward, her breath caught.

"What is it?" Julian's voice boomed from behind her.

Mena stared into the woman's dull green eyes. "It's Ella. She's dead."

Chapter Eighteen

Julian squatted next to the pale, lifeless body.

How was he going to tell Dawn that her sister was dead?

Once again, Julian found himself in the unenviable position of giving Dawn Garrison news that could destroy her life.

Three years ago, Julian had been the one to tell Dawn about Broman. Flashes of that horrible day assaulted his mind. The porch of the Garrison home had needed repair and a coat of paint. The wooden boards creaked loudly under the weight of his body as he ascended the steps.

Tears had stung his eyes as Dawn stood in the doorway, glaring at him.

He'd forced the words from his dry mouth, then stood stiff as she beat against his face and chest with her fists until she collapsed to the ground. Trying to comfort her had been a mistake. She'd lashed out, pushing him away before she said, "It should have been you!"

Leaving her with her grief, Julian couldn't deny the truth of her words.

Now, he'd be the messenger of devastating news to Dawn once again.

Julian slapped his hand against the rock, the rough surface scraping his skin. Gritting his teeth from the stinging pain, Julian swallowed the bitter taste in his mouth. He couldn't help but think that he hadn't done enough to prevent Ella's senseless death. Last night, his primary focus had been Ella's newborn son. Ensuring that the baby was safe and secure at the hospital was most important.

But, after he'd known the baby boy was okay, why hadn't he resumed his search for Ella? The gunshot to his leg was a flesh wound. He should have spent all night looking for her. If he had, would Ella still be alive now?

Julian stared toward the mountainous landscape. In the distance, Mena climbed the gradual slope toward the massive boulders that hid the entrance to the secluded beach. Julian had asked Mena to go back to the motorcycle. He'd wanted her to wait for the police to arrive so she could guide them to Ella's dead body.

He didn't want her lingering around the gruesome scene. She seemed to be handling the shock, but Julian wasn't fooled. The haunted, vacant look in her eyes told a different story.

A shaft of sunlight shot through the rocks, casting a harsh glow onto Ella's distorted form. Her skin was almost translucent. Her face registered no pain, almost as though she had been resigned to her fate. Vacant green eyes stared toward the sky. Julian wanted to close the lids but resisted. He knew better than to tamper with a crime scene.

Examining the length of Ella's body, his eyes were drawn to a tattoo in the hinge of her elbow: PC-5.

Julian frowned.

The PC-5 was more than a petty, local street gang. A ruthless organized crime syndicate, the gang controlled the flow of illegal activities throughout the Palmchat Islands and the Caribbean.

Why would Ella have the gang logo tattooed on her arm?

Julian's eyes trailed down to the white cotton t-shirt, stained red with blood. Reaching toward the hem of the shirt, Julian lifted the fabric from Ella's wet skin and pulled it up toward her breasts. Two bullet wounds, both jagged and torn, with pieces of muscle and bone protruding from the skin. Telltale signs of exit wounds.

Please ... I know he's going to kill me.

Ella's message to Dawn roared in his ears.

Julian laid the fabric back against Ella's body and stood. Whoever shot Ella hadn't wanted her body found, but obviously had no clue about the patterns of the tides in the area. Julian had spent many sleepless nights in this enclave over the past few years. At night, the tide covered the cove, but only by a few feet. The waters generally receded quickly upon daylight. The murderer must not have known that Ella's body wouldn't be carried out to the Caribbean Sea never to be seen again. Otherwise, the killer would have dumped Ella somewhere else.

Julian stood as the pounding steps of boots against wet sand filled the air. Turning, he looked into the concerned eyes of Detective Kendrick Caillouet and said, "Someone murdered Ella."

"What did you say?" Kendrick asked, his face frozen in shock.

Julian pointed down at the lifeless body laying listless in the water. "This is Ella Sapphire."

"Are you sure it's her?" Kendrick asked.

Julian wished he wasn't. He nodded grimly, then took a step away from the body to allow Kendrick a closer look.

"I'm sorry, man. I can't imagine how hard this must be for you to find her ... like this." Kendrick kneeled next to Ella's body. Lifting the fabric of Ella's shirt, Kendrick sighed. "Two shots from behind. I'll get the techs to scour the cove, drag the sand bed, and see what evidence we can find."

Julian looked away. He'd promised Dawn he would find her sister and he'd failed. He hadn't been able to prevent Ella's death, but perhaps he could make amends to Dawn by helping to find Ella's killer. Having his friend as the lead detective on the case would make that prospect a lot easier.

"Check out that tattoo on Ella's arm," Julian said, pointing to the dark black ink etched into Ella's pale skin.

Kendrick nodded. "That's the brand of a prostitute for the PC-5."

"You think they could have killed her?" Julian asked.

"I doubt it. Typically, the PC-5 wouldn't worry about killing a hooker, even if she stole money from them. They might beat her up to teach her a lesson, but murder would be extreme, even for them," Kendrick replied. He beckoned for the crime scene technicians, then walked with Julian to allow the team to collect evidence.

"What if she wasn't just a hooker? What if she did more?" Julian asked.

"More like what?" Kendrick asked.

"I don't know. Maybe the murder was personal," Julian wondered out loud. "Crime of passion. Ella's message to Dawn mentioned a man she thought was going to hurt her."

"I think it's about time you shared that voice message with me," Kendrick said. "If we can figure out who this guy is, we can bring him in for questioning."

"I'll send it over as soon as I get back to my boat," Julian said.

Julian looked back toward the rocks where crime scene investigators scurried like ants around Ella's dead body. A heaviness infected his muscles as he turned away and headed toward the entrance of the secluded beach. Julian squeezed through the two boulders leading to the road. Paramedics ambled along the shoulder, while a group of officers stood nearby discussing the murder. His eyes locked onto Mena. Her dark wet hair laid slick against her head, twisted into a bun at the nape of her neck. She looked regal, sitting on the flat rock almost motionless with her knees pulled tightly to her chest. Her pink suit clung to her wet body.

Julian sat behind Mena and placed his hand next to hers but didn't touch her. He wasn't sure what she needed right now, but he wasn't going to let her be alone.

Mena turned to Julian, her troubled eyes clouded with sorrow. "Can you take me home?"

Supporting her as she rose from the rock, Julian led her back to the Harley as the flashing lights from the police cars, ambulance and fire trucks danced across their skin.

Chapter Nineteen

Julian stumbled down the hallway, following the smoky flavor of goat bacon lingering in the air. Around the corner Mena stood at the stove, hovering over what must have been professional grade cookware. With a pan on each fire, she moved between them, tossing different ingredients into each—a pinch of salt, a dash of cilantro, an egg.

Entranced, Julian resisted the urge to envelop her in his arms. Watching her sleep through a crack in her bedroom door last night, he'd worried as she tossed and turned. Standing in command of her kitchen, she showed no signs of trauma from finding Ella's dead body yesterday.

"I can feel you watching me," Mena said, without turning. "Have a seat at the bar. Breakfast is almost ready."

"All this for me? Not that I'm complaining. Let's see, some goat bacon, my favorite. Caribbean scrambled eggs with vegetables, home fries, and ..." Julian strained to see around Mena's curves to the last pan on the stove. "Is that French toast?"

"Made with brioche and vanilla cream, one of my specialties," Mena said, turning and flashing him an alluring smile.

"Who are you? Superwoman?" Julian teased, settling into the bar stool.

"No, that would be my mother. She passed on her love for culinary creations to me, but not all of her amazing skills. The remarkable Chef Dee Nix, owner of one of the top restaurants—"

"In Jacksonville. Kaleidoscope. Beyond Southern influence, downright country food like your grandma would make. Some of the best damn food on the planet," Julian said, memories of the restaurant flooding his mind. He and Broman had never missed a chance to eat at the restaurant when they were back home in between breaks from training for SEAL Team missions.

"You're from Jacksonville?" Mena leaned on the bar.

"Just like you," Julian said, marveling that he and Mena were from the same city in Florida. How many times had their paths crossed before they'd finally met on a tiny island in the Caribbean?

"When did you move to St. Basil?" Mena heaped food onto two plates.

Julian's stomach growled loudly as he shifted in his chair. "About three years ago. You?"

"Three years ago, this month," Mena said, handing him one of the plates.

Julian grabbed his fork and dug into the French toast. The flavor explosion in his mouth sent him to the stratosphere. He had to disagree with Mena. She'd inherited a lot of her mother's skills in the kitchen.

Placing her plate on the bar, Mena walked past Julian, pulled the stool from the opposite side, and sat.

A series of beeps emitted from Julian's laptop. He looked behind him and saw it next to the wooden platter of fruit where he'd left it last night. Reluctantly stepping away from his breakfast, Julian grabbed the laptop and returned to the bar, sitting the laptop next to his plate.

"Your laptop has been beeping like that all morning," Mena said.

Julian let out a deep breath, then stuffed his mouth with goat bacon. "I had a program running to analyze videos from the gallery grounds for any signs of Ella. She was a frequent visitor before she disappeared. I'm hoping the program found her on some of the footage and maybe there's some pattern of who she interacted with that could help me figure out why she was at the gallery with a gun."

"The cops asked the gallery security team to help with the investigation?" Mena asked.

"Something like that," Julian said, not sure why he'd divulged the information to Mena. Julian glanced at the clock, ten past seven. "Looks like I have enough time to get back to my boat, shower and change before heading in to work."

"You're leaving?" Mena asked, then quickly continued, "I'm sure you'll be grateful to sleep in your own bed. Thanks for staying with me last night. I felt safer knowing that you were hovering in my doorway."

Julian laughed. "You caught that, huh?"

"It was sweet," Mena said, then slipped a forkful of scrambled eggs in her mouth. Julian didn't understand how she could make eating breakfast a sensual experience.

Polishing off the last of his scrambled eggs and home fries, Julian wiped his mouth and leaned back. Mena slipped into a comfortable silence, pushing food around on her plate and pausing to take a small bite every few minutes. She avoided his gaze, staring intently at the movement of her fork. He knew he needed to leave but walking away from Mena was proving harder than he'd realized it was going to be. Staying a little while longer wouldn't hurt.

Flipping the lid of the laptop, Julian entered his password and opened the program. Clicking on the report, he scanned the results. The program had detected two statistically significant patterns in videos where Ella was a match —two men showed up on the footage with her. Sometimes all three of them were together. Other times, Ella was with one or the other. Clicking the next page, he saw still shots taken from the video footage of a face he expected. The artist, Quark. The next set of shots captured from the video was a complete surprise.

"Why do you have photos of Quark and Irving on your laptop?" Mena asked.

Julian wondered the same thing. He knew Quark and Ella were involved in a weird artistically-driven romantic relationship, but what type of interactions could Ella have had with the director of the Genesis Gallery?

"These are the results of the video analysis. Based on the algorithms, there's a statistically significant number of instances where Ella was with Quark and Irving Bond on the gallery grounds over the past two years," Julian said.

"Quark makes sense. He was known to have muses, multiple girlfriends at a time, many of which he picked up at the Co-Op. But I think the program got it wrong with Irving. I've never known him to spend much time hanging around the Co-Op artists," Mena said, wagging a piece of goat bacon between her fingers before taking a bite.

"If Irving Bond didn't care about the artists, why was he caught on camera with Ella so many times?" Julian wondered out loud. He clicked through the video still shots of Ella with Bond.

Mena leaned forward, peering at the cascading images on the laptop. The heady scent of her sandalwood and orange perfume arrested Julian, distracting him from the task at hand.

"Strange. These shots seem very casual and almost ... intimate. I've never known Bond to take such interest in any of the starving artists at the Co-Op. He cares about important artists. Take Quark, for instance. He'll bend over backward to make sure he's happy. The rest of the artists mean nothing to him since they haven't made a splash in the art world yet," said Mena.

Julian's phone buzzed in the pocket of his jeans. Holding up a finger to Mena, he pressed the green button.

"Good morning. I see you had another sleepover with the beautiful Mena Nix." Kendrick's voice invaded his ear.

"What makes you think that?" Julian asked, savoring the view of the dark beauty.

"I'm on your empty boat right now," Kendrick said. "How long will it take you to get over here?"

"Ten minutes. I have some interesting results to share with you from the video analysis," Julian responded.

Swiveling around on the bar stool, he stood and placed the laptop underneath his arm. Everything he'd brought to Mena's condo was on his body. Nothing to stop him from leaving, yet he felt drawn to stay. Disappointment settled within him at having to leave her so soon.

"The program got some good hits?" Kendrick asked.

"I'll give you the details when I get there," Julian said.

"Sounds good," Kendrick said, then paused. The next words he uttered were slow and measured. "I spoke to Dawn this morning. She's on the way to the island to give us a positive ID on Ella."

A sharp pain shot through his thigh as Julian walked to Mena's floor-to-ceiling windows and peered at his boat in the distance. He could barely make out Kendrick's figure on the top deck.

"How'd she take it?" Julian asked, his voice a low whisper.

"She didn't react at all. I told her the whole story—from Ella giving birth and how you saved that little boy to Ella being missing until you and Ms. Nix found her body. She didn't say much, just that she'd be on the next flight to the island," Kendrick said.

Julian swallowed past the hard lump in his throat. "I'll see you in ten."

Ending the call, he turned.

Mena stood in front of him. "I guess I'll see you later at work."

"You should probably take the day off. No need to push yourself after everything you've been through the past couple of days."

"Don't worry about me. I need the distraction," Mena said.

Julian stared at Mena. "Call me if you need ... anything."

Mena nodded as he forced himself past her and out the door.

Chapter Twenty

Mena approached Regina's desk at the end of the hallway in front of the double doors that led into Priscilla Dumay's office suite on the second floor of the main gallery building. She'd debated staying home like Julian had suggested, but everything in her condo was starting to remind her of him. The pillow he slept on smelled like his cologne. The cushions in a pile near the center of the couch had supported his aching leg. The breakfast plate lay empty, with only remnants of the food he'd inhaled from the massive breakfast she wasn't even sure why she'd made. Deep down, she suspected she knew the reason. She just wasn't ready to admit it to herself. Staying home would be a different kind of torture, and she knew her first mind was right. She needed to work, to lose herself in restoring art.

Sitting in one of the black contemporary armless chairs facing the desk, Omar turned and beckoned for her to come quicker.

"You have some explaining to do," Regina said in a rushed whisper as Mena slumped down into the chair next to Omar.

"Inquiring minds want to know what you and Julian were doing on a secluded, romantic beach before some damn dead body interrupted what could have been." Omar sat with his legs crossed and a perturbed look on his face.

"Are you and Julian hooking up? Are the two of you really a couple like the newspaper said?" Regina asked, a gleeful hopefulness in her tone.

The newspaper? Oh, God no! If her name was in the newspaper about finding the body, then she was in trouble. Fumbling with her cell phone, Mena accessed the *Palmchat Gazette* online and tried to find the article.

"Wait a minute." Mena shook her head, looking up from the phone. "Neither one of you want to talk about the dead body I found yesterday. You just want to know what, if anything, is going on with me and Julian? Unbelievable."

"Look, this ain't the first island that some tourist has accidentally drowned on and it won't be the last," said Omar, pointing a finger in her face. "What is up with you sneaking off with Julian without giving us even a little hint?"

"Omar is right. Mena, you tell us everything—"

"All the boring ass details," Omar said.

"—About all the guys you've dated so far on the island," Regina continued.

"The fact that you kept this little nugget a secret means there's something real going on with you and that sexy ass security guard, and we deserve to know!" Omar said.

"I thought you didn't think Julian was suitable for me," Mena said, stalling. She wasn't sure how to explain the closeness she shared with Julian without telling her friends about being held hostage by Ella two nights ago.

"He's not. But that doesn't mean you can't dip your chocolate in a little bit of milk until a man worthy of your stature and intelligence comes along," Omar said.

"You're not being fair. Julian is not some dumb jock. He was in the Intelligence Department of the U.S. Navy before he came to the island," Regina said. "Says it right here in the latest article on the *Palmchat Gazette* website. Maybe he's a better match for Mena than you think."

"Trust me, he ain't," Omar said, pursing his lips before looking away.

"You two have the wildest imaginations," Mena said, crossing her arms. "You know me. The truth is a lot less interesting than what you're conjuring up in your heads."

"I'll be the judge of that," Omar said. "Spill it."

"My car is still ... in the shop. Julian lives ten minutes away from me—much closer than the two of you. So when he offered me a ride home, I accepted,"

Mena said. Not a lie but not the full truth either. The police still had her car as evidence from the night Ella took her hostage.

Regina's eyes grew wide, as her face dawned a brand-new realization. "Omar, Julian rides a Harley to work."

"Oh damn, I bet you took over that Harley and went joy riding," Omar said, shaking his head.

"Basically," Mena said, deciding to go with Omar's story. "I took a wrong turn, and we ended up at a dead end and decided to explore the beach behind the rocks."

"That sounds so romantic!" Regina squealed. "I can't believe nothing happened between you two."

"Something did happen. We stumbled across a dead woman and had to call 9-1-1," Mena said. "We were questioned by the cops, and then Julian offered to stay with me after he drove me home. I guess he realized the whole finding a dead body thing had me a bit shaken."

"So ... Julian stayed with you last night? In your condo? Just the two of you?" Omar asked, leaning toward her, his eyes dancing with mischief.

Damn it. She couldn't believe she let that little tidbit of information slip out. "Get your mind out of the gutter. Nothing happened between us. He was a gentleman."

"Whatever, girl. What's the real story?" Omar demanded.

"Stop it, Omar," Regina jumped to Mena's defense, then added, "That was really nice of Julian."

Regina didn't bother to hide her smirk. Mena knew her two best friends were skeptical, but she didn't care. She wasn't going to tell them about the playful, sensual tension that had transpired between her and Julian before they found Ella's body. He'd been amazing through it all, taking the time to comfort her when she knew that he had a bigger concern looming before him— comforting his best friend's wife as she dealt with learning her sister had been killed.

"Can we focus on work now? Regina, I checked all my records, and I didn't see the Kuypers on any of my work orders," Mena said, avoiding Omar's penetrating stare as he pursed his lips at her diversionary tactic.

"Thanks for checking. I got another call this morning, from Yorick Kuyper this time, not his wife, Nora. They are still insisting on a refund, but he wouldn't give me any details about the purchase either. Just insists that Prissy knows exactly what they bought. But I don't want to bother her with this. If I can find the invoice, I can initiate a refund without wasting her time on this mundane stuff," Regina said.

"I'll check my records. I have copies of all manual invoices," Omar said. "Now to change the subject again. Mena, I need you to take a look at the Gabonese mask ASAP. Your girl, Uma, cleared it for the exhibit, but something doesn't seem right. I'm not going to put it on display until you tell me it's okay. Can you squeeze that in?"

"Of course, where is it?" Mena asked.

"In my office, on the bookshelf to the left," Omar said. "You can grab it on your way back to your workshop."

As Mena headed toward Omar's office to get the Gabonese mask, her cell phone buzzed in her hand. Glancing at the screen, Mena let out a low moan. This was the last person she wanted to talk to right now.

Chapter Twenty-One

Mena stared at the screen of her phone, dumbfounded. Her name written in black and white was in the first paragraph of the article on Ella's murder published by a reporter from the *Palmchat Gazette*.

A local couple, Mena Nix and Julian Montgomery—the hero who rescued Wanda Campbell months ago from a brutal attack by her husband, crooner Louis Campbell— discovered a dead body of a woman while on a relaxing getaway from work.

Mena put the phone back to her ear as she ducked into the conference room on the opposite side of the executive offices. "Yes, I'm still here, Daddy."

"I have worked for this newspaper for over twenty-five years. Not once have I ever asked for any special treatment," Mena's father, Caleb Olivier lamented over the phone.

"It's a big news story. This happens all the time in St. Killian, but things like this don't normally happen in St. Basil," Mena said, still dazed from skimming the article. Mena and Julian had only given statements to the cops and had left the crime scene before any reporters had arrived. How had the *Palmchat Gazette* found out about them?

"You listen to me. Those rich people do favors for their friends all the time. I watched first hand as Burt Bronson kept important news about his family out of the paper," Caleb yelled into the phone. "The one time I ask for a favor, that boy of his shuts me down like I don't have journalistic integrity."

"No one is questioning your integrity, Daddy. Maybe the new editor is trying to impress Burt," Mena said, leaning against the rectangular mahogany wood conference table.

"He should have found another way to do it! Putting your name in the paper was irresponsible and unnecessary," Caleb continued his rant. "You could have all kinds of kooks and crazies on your doorstep, trying to ask you about what you saw."

"Daddy, it's alright. The only thing anybody is going to hear from me is 'no comment,'" Mena assured him.

"Well, it's not alright with me. I have a good mind to quit! Leo Bronson is going to ruin the good name of the *Palmchat Gazette*," Caleb said.

Mena knew arguing with her father was an exercise in futility. She appreciated his attempts to protect her, but she couldn't let him quit his job just because he hadn't been successful. He was the most tenured reporter at the paper. Even though he didn't cover high profile stories anymore, he was still revered across the island as the reporter who'd covered the murders and eventual arrest of the serial killer, The Fury. It had made him a local legend.

"You can't quit, Daddy. The paper wouldn't be the same without you," Mena said, rubbing a finger against her temple.

After grudgingly agreeing not to leave the paper, Caleb asked one last time if he should come to St. Basil for a few weeks to protect her. She'd declined, and he'd dropped the matter, for now.

Ending the call, Mena stepped out of the conference room and headed toward Omar's office. After she grabbed the Gabonese mask from Omar's bookshelf, she was going to take the stairs. And not because she needed the exercise. The stairwell at the end of the hall led down to the first floor and opened directly across from the security room. She was curious to see if Julian had made it into work by now.

"What the hell are you doing in here? I thought I told you not to come to my office." A tense male voice wafted into the hallway.

Mena looked toward the half-opened door of the office of Irving Bond, Director of the Genesis Gallery. She recognized his voice.

"I know. I'm sorry. I just can't do this anymore," a female voice responded, weak and timid. "I need to give this back to you."

It was Uma Fischer, Mena's assistant conservator. Why was Uma in Irving's office?

"You can't walk away from me so easily—"

"I've always done what you asked me, but I can't keep this up. When the detective came by yesterday to talk to me, I was so nervous. I knew I couldn't keep doing this," Uma said.

"What the fuck did you tell the cops?" Irving whispered angrily.

"Nothing! I promise I didn't say anything. But I can't keep doing this," Uma said, then paused. Mena strained to see inside the office.

Uma's arm extended, dropping a small Louis Vuitton backpack on top of Irving's desk.

"What is this?" Irving asked.

"It's all of the money. You can count it, it's all there," Uma said, her voice quivering with emotion.

"You think giving back the money ends things between us?" Irving grabbed the backpack and threw it against the wall with a loud bang.

Mena took a few steps back and ducked into the conference room. Peering out, she tried to hear the rest of the conversation.

"I'm done with this and with you, Irving," Uma said, her voice rising in defiance.

"Don't be stupid. I decide when we're done. And don't even think about trying to cross me," Irving said.

"I'm not afraid of you. I'm getting out of this mess one way or another," Uma said.

A chilling edge to his tone, Irving responded, "You better watch out. You know what happened to Ella. You don't want to end up with two bullets in your back."

Chapter Twenty-Two

Mena exited through the doors of the conference room in time to see Uma rushing toward the stairwell.

"Uma! Uma!" Mena called out as she followed the assistant conservator through the stairwell door.

Uma stopped and turned back to look at Mena. Her caramel-hued skin was splotchy and red. Her eyes swollen from fresh tears.

"What's wrong? Why are you crying?" Mena asked. "Did Irving do something—"

"I'm sorry, Mena, I need to go home and deal with a personal matter. I'll give you a call in the morning," Uma said, then turned to walk down the stairs.

Mena followed her. "Is there anything I can do?"

"I can't talk about this with you," Uma said, wiping a hand under her runny nose. "It's private."

Mena raised her hands in surrender. "I'm sorry for prying. I hope things get better."

"Thanks," Uma whispered, then exited the stairwell to the first floor.

Mena took a deep breath. What the hell was going on between Uma and Irving? Normally she would stay out of Uma's life, but Irving's chilling last words to Uma changed everything. She needed to talk to Julian.

Pushing through the large metal door, Mena headed down the hallway to the security room. The door opened as she was lifting her hand to knock.

"What happened?" Julian asked, concern in his velvety brown eyes. He reached for her hand and pulled her into the security room, shutting the door behind him.

Mena's mind went blank as Julian's presence filled the small room, blocking her from thinking clearly.

"Did you remember something about the night Ella took you hostage?" Julian implored. He grabbed the chair from behind the curved desk and pushed it toward her, beckoning for her to sit down.

Mena felt her knees grow weak. Collecting her thoughts, she shook her head as she eased into the chair.

Julian squatted in front of her, placing his hands gently on her thighs. "Tell me why you're upset."

"I overheard Irving and Uma talking," Mena said her heart pounding. "Irving told her that she shouldn't think about crossing him or she'd end up like Ella with two bullets in her back."

Julian leaned closer, his gaze intense. "Did he use those exact words? Two bullets in the back?"

Mena nodded. "He did, but that didn't make any sense because Ella drowned, right?"

Julian looked away.

"Right, Julian?" A sinking feeling settled in Mena's gut.

"She was shot twice in the back," Julian confirmed.

Mena felt as if she'd been sucker-punched. When she found Ella, she'd focused on the pale, lifeless face as she'd stumbled away from the body. The *Palmchat Gazette* hadn't listed a cause of death. She'd assumed Ella had drowned.

"The cops are investigating Ella's case as a homicide, but they don't want details of how she died released to the public yet," Julian continued.

"Her death wasn't an accident." Mena leaned back in the chair, feeling dizzy. "Someone killed her."

"Irving Bond may know something about that," said Julian. "Why did Irving threaten Uma? What else were they talking about?"

After a deep breath, Mena recounted the details of the conversation between her assistant and the gallery director.

"Uma gave Irving a backpack filled with money?" Julian asked.

"That's what she claimed was in the bag. She was giving it back, so she wouldn't have to keep doing what Irving was asking her to do. Something about talking to the cops yesterday made her nervous, and she wanted out," Mena said.

"Did she say what she was doing for him?" Julian asked, his expression growing more serious.

"No, she didn't."

"I need to talk to Bond." Julian squinted, his face a mask of deep thought.

"How are we going to do that? I doubt he's going to come clean if we ask him. But we have to find out what he knows." Mena said, her thoughts racing.

"We?"

"Irving has my assistant involved in something, and he used Ella's murder to threaten her. I have to find out why," Mena said.

"Why do you have to find out why?" Julian asked.

Mena looked away, pain and sadness welling within her. "I don't understand why Ella took me hostage. Was I in the wrong place at the wrong time, or did she pick me on purpose? And is any of that related to Irving threatening my assistant. I wouldn't be able to live with myself if Uma was killed and I did nothing to stop it."

Julian leaned close to Mena. "You've been through hell, and you want answers. You want closure. That's natural, but there's a limit to how much you can do ... how much you *should* do."

"I have to do something," Mena insisted.

Placing his hands on her shoulders, he stared at Mena, fully understanding her desire to help. "How about I take you to see Kendrick? You can tell him what you overheard."

Chapter Twenty-Three

"I don't understand how Bond could have known that Ella was shot twice in the back," Detective Caillouet said.

A cool mountain breeze blew through the towering trees of Dumay Park, a two-hundred-acre park located on the southern end of the Genesis Gallery complex behind the Artist Co-Op building. A flurry of napkins floated off the stone table where Mena sat with the detective and Julian.

Mena focused on the plate of spaghetti Bolognese she no longer desired. She glanced over at Julian, sitting next to her. He crumpled the empty wrapper from the meatball sandwich he'd eaten and threw it into the trash can adjacent to their table.

His dark eyes intense, Julian said, "Neither do I. You haven't released those details to the media."

Kendrick shoved a large forkful of Caesar salad into his mouth, chewed slowly, and then said, "Maybe Bond knew about the bullets in Ella's back because he put them there."

Worry crept through Mena's body. "You think Irving killed Ella?"

"Most victims know their killers, and Bond knew Ella. On the video footage Julian showed me, there were numerous instances of Ella and Bond interacting with each other at the Co-Op," Kendrick said. "But, when I questioned Bond, he said he didn't know her, didn't recognize her and had never seen her before."

"Bond lied to you," said Julian.

Kendrick nodded in agreement, then glanced at Mena. "And I wonder if your assistant, Uma Fischer, lied, too. Maybe she helped Bond murder Ella."

Mena shook her head. "There's no way Uma could be involved in a murder. She's too sweet and kind."

"You said Uma was returning money to Irving and declaring that she wasn't going to help him anymore. Sounds like she's not as sweet and kind as you think."

Stunned, Mena said nothing.

Julian looked at Kendrick. "What's your next move?"

Kendrick said, "I'm going to talk to Bond. He needs to explain why he never mentioned knowing Ella when we talked to him after she broke into the gallery. I'm also going to ask him about his connection to Uma. If Bond and Uma murdered Ella, I'm going to find out."

"I really don't think Uma could be involved with what happened to Ella. I'm sure she's innocent in all of this," Mena said, worried that she'd inadvertently put a target on her assistant's back with the cops.

"Maybe you're right. At this point, I'm following up on every lead and tip I get. The info coming in is getting wilder by the hour," Kendrick said.

"Anything you can share?" Julian asked.

"The bullets found in Ella's body—"

"Wait," Julian shook his head and held up his hands. "How could you have bullets from Ella's body? There were two *exit* wounds."

"Can't believe I forgot to tell you. There were also gunshots to Ella's butt and thigh and those bullets were extracted by forensics," Kendrick said, rubbing a hand down the side of his face.

"And the ballistics results?" Julian asked.

"The bullets matched a gun used in a shootout at an art museum in St. Mateo a year ago," Kendrick said.

"I remember that. Didn't they draw anti-establishment slogans on the walls of the Palmchat Islands Museum?" Mena asked.

"Yes, and similar attacks happened in the months following that initial attack at other museums across the Caribbean, Central, and South America. The perps would vandalize, and graffiti tag the museum buildings. When security showed up, they'd shoot their way out to waiting getaway cars. They never damaged or stole any of the artwork, though," Kendrick said.

"Any ideas on who was behind it?" Julian asked.

"Initially, the attacks seemed politically motivated. Likely activists protesting the use of funds for art when poverty is still so rampant in the areas that the museums were located," said Kendrick.

"What changed?" Mena asked, wondering what could have incited the attacks.

"Fingerprints on one of the guns left behind at the museum in St. Mateo matched a gang member in the PC-5. After that, evidence suggesting PC-5 involvement was identified at other vandalized museums. We believe the museums were targeted by the PC-5, but none of the cops across the jurisdictions could figure out why," Kendrick explained.

"How could the gun found at the museum have been used to kill Ella? Wasn't it in police custody?" Julian asked.

Mena pondered the same thing.

"PC-5 has moles in all the police stations across the Palmchat Islands. Detective Richland François of the St. Mateo police department confirmed that the firearm had been lost during a move and was no longer in their evidence room," Kendrick said.

"So, a PC-5 gun was used to kill Ella. Ella has a PC-5 tattoo on her arm, tagging her as one of their prostitutes. Does that mean she could have been on the PC-5 Death List?" Julian asked.

A cold chill ran down Mena's spine at the mention of the Death List. Everyone living on the islands knew that the PC-5 had a running list of people who had angered or crossed them and were marked for death. Sometimes they killed quickly. Other times, years passed before they exacted their revenge. The one thing everyone knew for sure was that no one survived once their names were added to the list.

Kendrick said, "Our informants claim Ella was never a PC-5 hooker, but I'm not convinced. They don't give those tattoos out randomly."

"Let's assume she was turning tricks for the gang. If Ella got pregnant and decided to stop being a prostitute, would that be enough to put her on the Death List?" Julian asked.

"You never know with the PC-5. I need to follow up on every possibility," said Kendrick.

Mena took a deep breath. She'd hoped the conversation she'd overheard would unlock critical evidence in Ella's murder, but she'd never thought that two of her co-workers might be killers. And if the PC-5 was involved, unraveling the reason behind Ella's death could be more complicated than she fathomed.

Chapter Twenty-Four

Julian leaned over the railing of the yacht, his arm brushing against the rusted dirtboard hanging on the rail. Reaching a finger toward one of the wheels, he pushed softly, watching as the wheel spun around and around. Raising the bottle of vodka to his lips, he took another swig, enjoying the slow burn of the bad liquor down his throat. Broman never graduated to sophisticated brands, preferring the cheap ones they'd gotten drunk on in high school. Julian had followed suit, holding on to the same practice for old times' sake.

The call from Kendrick this morning had been expected, but still shook him up. Dawn had arrived on the island and was escorted by police caravan to the station where she caused a ruckus in the squad room. After verbally assaulting the officers, she made her way to the morgue, where she'd become unhinged.

Julian heard Dawn's wails reverberating through the phone as he talked to Kendrick. He'd heard those pained cries before when he stood on her porch three years ago. He hadn't wanted to hear them again.

"She's been in there for three hours, won't budge. You think maybe if you come down to the station, you can get her to go back to her hotel?" Kendrick had asked him.

Julian had been a coward. His presence at the morgue would be no help to

Dawn, no comfort for the grief she was enduring. He was the last person she needed to see right now.

Instead, he'd left his friend to deal with the grieving sister and retreated into a bottle of vodka.

His eyes, blurred from the alcohol, drifted toward the marina. Happy families and tourists milled in and out of the restaurants and luxury stores that bordered the bay. He wanted to be like them again, carefree, and enjoying life.

The crowds moved along the boardwalk at a glacial pace, but Julian's eyes were drawn to one woman. A petite blonde dressed in a floral jumpsuit and jean jacket. Her shoulder length, side-swept hair blew in the breeze as she pounded down the boardwalk, zagging in between the laconic tourists.

The bottle of vodka slipped from Julian's hand and plunged into the bay waters below as his body tensed. Turning, he took the stairs two at a time down to the first deck of the boat, then jumped off the side to the pier and walked briskly along the boardwalk until he was standing face to face with the woman.

She shot him a venomous look as her hands tightened into fists. Quicker than he could deflect, her arm swung in a sharp arc, and her fist slammed into the side of his face.

He deserved her wrath.

Stunned from the surge of splitting pain detonating within his head, Julian managed not to move from the fury of the blow.

He looked into the splotchy, tear-stained face of Dawn Garrison, his best friend's wife, and Ella Sapphire's sister. Words eluded him. What could he say to Dawn that would make her feel anything but pain at this moment? All he could do was tell her the truth of how he felt and how he was determined to bring Ella's killer to justice.

Julian said, "I'm so sorry about Ella—"

"No," Dawn snapped at him. "You don't get to be sorry."

"I never meant for things to happen this way. I thought I would be able to find her, to help her." Dizzy from the vodka coursing through his veins and the mid-afternoon Caribbean sun baking his skin, Julian struggled to stay on his feet. He'd heard his own words before, three years ago, the first time he'd fumbled through an apology to Dawn.

He thought this time would be different.

It wasn't.

"I'm starting to understand that help from you is a one-way ticket to tragedy. The papers talk about you like you're some kind of hero," said Dawn with a short, scornful laugh. "These people don't know the truth about you. They don't know what you've done."

No one knew the truth about him. Three years ago, he'd stood in the tent of his commanding officer surrounded by a small group of naval leaders as the Silver Star for gallantry in action against an enemy of the United States burned in his hands. The simple ceremony had lauded him for courage and bravery in his attempts to rescue his fellow SEAL Team from a brutal, unexpected attack. Julian was rigid as the record of everything he'd done that fateful day was announced. Everything except the one critical mistake he'd made.

The night Ella had disappeared was different, but the outcome had been the same. Nothing had changed for him, no matter how much he'd wanted things to be different.

Julian said, "I had to make a choice that night. Ella had run off, but her son's life was on the line."

Dawn looked away from him, her eyes downcast as he continued. "He wasn't breathing. I did CPR, but I didn't know if he would survive. He became the priority. I thought I'd have time to find Ella after I got her son safely to the hospital."

"But there wasn't time, was there?" asked Dawn.

Julian avoided her blazing stare, looking to the sky. A seagull swooped down toward a piece of bread discarded on the boardwalk, angling its beak to pluck the morsel. Missing the mark, the chunk of food tumbled into the water and disappeared beneath the waves as the bird circled in vain to find it again.

"Dawn, there's no way I could have known that Ella was in trouble—"

"Really? No way? How about the voice message she left on my phone about some man who was going to kill her! How about the fact she was desperately trying to flee the place where she told me she was being held against her will!" Dawn screamed.

"I did everything I could to find her, but it was too late," Julian tried to explain. His words sounded hollow even to his own ears.

Dawn jabbed her fingers into his chest. "You made me doubt her. You made me think that she was being dramatic. Like you'd find her lounging in some hammock, smoking weed and laughing about driving her big sister crazy with worry. But she wasn't crying wolf this time. My sister would still be alive if it weren't for you."

Her words were like daggers, piercing his skin, and deflating his soul. She was right. He hadn't taken the threat seriously enough. He should have given Kendrick a copy of the voice message earlier. He should have asked for help from the police to find Ella, instead of thinking he could ride in and save the day. He'd been selfish and consumed with his own motives.

Finding Ella and saving her for Dawn would have given him a chance to make amends for some of the pain he'd caused her in the past. Nothing had gone as he planned. Ella had been impossible to locate on the island for weeks until she'd showed up unexpectedly at the Genesis Gallery with a gun pointed to Mena's head.

He should have let Mena take the baby to the hospital and tried to find Ella that night. He should have canvassed the area immediately after saving her son. If he had, would he have found Ella before the killer had? Would she be happily reunited with her sister at this moment? The fact that he would never know tormented him.

"Listen to me. I can still help," Julian said, thinking about the strange conversation Mena had overheard between Irving Bond and Uma Fischer. Kendrick might not be able to get them to come clean about what was going on between them and how it related to Ella, but Julian wasn't bound by the same rules of law enforcement. He could get them to tell the truth with other methods. "I'm already tracking leads on people who might know something about Ella's killer. I'll do whatever it takes to find out who murdered her and why. I won't rest until you get answers."

Julian placed his hand on Dawn's shoulders. She'd begun to weep silently, a hopeless pain etched across her face that tore Julian's heart apart.

Dawn said, "Stay out of it. You'll only make things worse. Broman was wrong about you. You aren't the man he thought you were. And as far as I'm concerned, you are the one who is dead ... to me and to my family."

Chapter Twenty-Five

The tall lamp lights dotted along the marina walkway twinkled against the deep blue sky as night settled on the island. Julian slowed his pace to a light jog as he passed the Louis Vuitton and Harry Winston stores.

Hours had passed since he'd talked to Dawn and he knew she was right. He should stay out of the investigation, despite having to suppress his desire to uncover clues that could help identify Ella's killer. He didn't want to do anything else to hurt her. For once in his miserable life, he was going to put the needs of Dawn before his own. She'd made it clear that she wanted him to stay away from her family and he would honor her wishes.

Snaking through tourists ambling in and out of the shops, Julian reached the end of the dock between his yacht and Louis Campbell's.

Mena walked toward him gingerly in orange stilettos, careful to avoid the gaps in the wooden planks of the pier. Her body was amazing in an orange knit halter top and crisp white pants.

"You weren't at work today," Mena said, stopping a few feet in front of him. A warm breeze blew across the bay, billowing her wavy dark hair around her face. His body had a distinct reaction to this sexier version of her, one he didn't want her to notice.

Julian shrugged, "My day off."

"Well, I have some bad news. Not sure if you've heard from Kendrick already," Mena said.

"I haven't been home most of the day. What happened?" Julian asked.

"Kendrick came to the gallery and talked to Uma and Irving again. They both denied the conversation happened. Then Uma came back to the workshop and screamed at me for telling the cops about what I overheard. She told me that I should have stayed out of her business with Irving," Mena said.

"Might not be bad news after all," Julian said as he considered this new twist in the information surrounding Ella's murder. "She lied to Kendrick, which means she's hiding something. She, and possibly Bond, might know about Ella's murder."

"You might be right." Mena's eyes traveled the length of him, a baffled expression clouding her face. "Where've you been?"

Julian glanced down at his green tank top, long cargo pants and military-grade combat boots, all remnants of the life he used to live. "Running on the beach. Down to Marluna and back."

"That's over twenty miles … one way," said Mena. She reached a hand along the side of his sweat-soaked tank top and twisted the end of his backpack strap between her fingers, then added "wearing all of this."

"Nothing compared to what I had to do in BUD/S," Julian said as his body tensed. It had been years since he'd admitted his role in the U.S. Navy to anyone, yet with Mena, the words had tumbled out.

"Were you a Navy SEAL?"

"I used to be." Julian walked past Mena toward his boat. Ascending the stairs, Mena followed him on board. He wasn't disappointed. "Have you had dinner?"

"Nope. You cooking?" Mena asked.

"Hell no, not for you. I don't want to embarrass myself," Julian said, chuckling. He glanced at his watch. Almost nine o'clock. Still time to call for takeout. "I'll order some food from the marina restaurant. The busboys deliver it out here to the boats pretty fast."

An hour later, after eating their fill of grilled goat, conch fritters and mango kale salad, they sat at the table. Mena sipped a freshly made Palmito from a wine glass while Julian had water.

"So," Mena said, then hesitated. "Kendrick mentioned that Dawn arrived on the island this morning. Have you seen her? How's she dealing with all of this?"

"Identifying her sister's dead body was hard for her, and that's putting it lightly." Julian rested his head against the back cushions of the bench.

"I can't imagine the pain she's going through right now. Losing her sister must feel like losing part of herself. It's so sad," Mena sympathized.

"That's exactly what it's like." Julian thought of Broman. Not his brother by blood, but by every other way that truly mattered. "A piece of you dies at the same time. Memories become bittersweet, and you know you'll never be the same."

"Hopefully seeing you made things a bit better for her." Mena scooted closer to him, the smell of her sandalwood and orange perfume lingering in the air between them.

"A day when Dawn has to see my face is never a good one for her. I've caused that woman enough pain for several lifetimes," Julian said.

"But she asked you to help her find her sister. Why would she do that if she didn't consider you a friend?" Mena asked, a puzzled expression passing across her face.

"She was desperate. Trust me, if she could have gotten help from anyone other than me, she would have," Julian said. The sweat soaked clothes had begun to irritate his skin, and he wanted to get away from everything that reminded him of his time in the Navy with Broman. Peeling the tank top from his body, he kicked off the combat boots.

Mena pressed her hands over his, giving them a gentle squeeze. The feel of her light touch tantalized and comforted him. "From what you've told me, you put your life on hold to look for Ella. Finding her was your sole priority. I don't know what happened in the past, but I think your actions over the past month are worth a lot more than you're giving them credit for."

Experiencing this tragedy with Mena had forged a connection between them, a closeness he'd never felt before in his life. It felt natural to open up to her. But what if that was a mistake? What if he said too much? Could he come clean about the damage he'd done and not scare her away?

"She ... umm ..." Julian paused, surprised by the quiver in his voice. "She thinks it's my fault Ella was murdered. She doesn't believe I did enough to save Ella."

Mena waved her hand dismissively. "There's no way you could have known

Ella would be shot to death after you found us on the road that night. That's ridiculous."

"It's not as ridiculous as you'd think, but I don't want to get into all that," Julian said, a weight settling within him as the memories threatened to cave him in. Dawn had every right to blame him for Ella's death and so much more.

"I'm sure it was her grief talking. Once she has time to reflect, she'll realize that you did everything you could to find Ella. You can't be blamed for someone else killing her," Mena said.

"Why can't I? When she disappeared from your car that night, I didn't try to go after her—"

"Because you were helping her son! And me. We needed you. None of us could have ever imagined that would be Ella's last night alive. I wouldn't have made it through that night without you," Mena said.

"You don't know the things I've done to Dawn in the past, mistakes I've made. I'd give anything to make it up to her. I thought finding Ella would help me do that," Julian admitted. "But I made it worse."

"There's still a chance you can help Dawn. Uma and Irving lied to the cops, but that doesn't mean we can't get one of them to tell you the truth. What if Uma has some information that could help with the investigation, but she doesn't realize it?" Mena asked. "She's my employee. I know where she lives and how to find her. You can talk to Uma and see what she knows."

Julian stood and walked toward the railing of the boat, away from the dirtboards that hung on the opposite side. Turning back toward Mena, he crossed his arms and watched her watching him from the bench. "Why would you do that for me?"

"Honestly, it's more for me than it is for you. Being traumatized, like I was by Ella, changes you. Wondering if you'll live to see the next day is sobering and frightening." Mena lifted her head and stared at the stars in the sky. "Trust me, I know firsthand what that does to you because it wasn't the first time something like that has happened to me. You learn a lot about yourself going through life or death situations. It reveals the real you, every action, every thought magnifies who you are deep inside. After it's all over, it's a struggle to get back to some semblance of normalcy. But I did before, and I will again."

"What happened to you?" Julian took a step toward Mena. She held up her hand, stopping him.

"That doesn't matter. What matters is how I got back to normal. The only thing that got me there was knowing why it had happened and why to *me*," she emphasized the last word, then continued. "Once I had those answers, I could move on."

"You don't have those answers with Ella," Julian acknowledged.

"I hide it well, but it's driving me crazy. Why did Ella take me hostage?" Mena stood and paced across the deck of the boat. "Was it a random act of violence? Was I in the wrong place at the wrong time? Or did she need it to be me? Why didn't she stay with her newborn son? Why did she get killed?"

"There's no guarantee that you'll get answers to those questions," Julian said, reflecting on the fact that Dawn hadn't gotten the answers she needed three years ago, even though Julian could have given them to her.

"And there's no guarantee that you can find something that will help solve Ella's murder and ease Dawn's pain," said Mena. "But we won't have a chance if we don't try."

Julian approached Mena slowly, staring at her. Dawn had warned him not to get involved in Ella's murder investigation because he would make things worse. But didn't he have to help Mena get closure? And Kendrick was being lied to by a potential suspect. If Julian could get Uma to talk, he could help his friend with the investigation.

Grabbing Mena's hands in his, he leaned closer, then said softly, "This could be dangerous if we're right and Uma knows something about Ella's death."

"I'm not saying that we go rogue and try to take over the case. I'm not that foolish. But I did overhear a disturbing conversation between Irving and Uma. The cops couldn't get them to tell the truth. I know we can get Uma to come clean and explain why she and Irving were arguing. It could be the break the cops need to find Ella's murderer." Mena squeezed his hands, her touch searing into his skin, changing him by the second. "Whether you want to admit it or not, you know you need to do this. The question is, are you going to?"

Chapter Twenty-Six

Julian twisted the end of the binoculars, bringing the small pink home with a red tile roof into view. The sun was beginning to set behind the house, making it harder to see if there was any activity inside. All the pent-up energy and anticipation that had built up during the day as Julian worked security at the gallery, counting the hours until it was time to stakeout Uma's house, had dissipated. Where the hell was Uma? Three hours had passed, and she still hadn't come home.

Mena had been sitting patiently next to him in the nondescript rental car he'd gotten for the occasion. Uma lived in the heart of Melhor Province, a middle-class neighborhood on the outskirts of Downtown Marluna. The car was partially hidden by overgrown bushes and trees at the dead end of the narrow, gray stone street facing her house.

"You think she saw us and turned around?" Mena asked.

Julian shook his head. "No way she could see us before she drove into her driveway. Something must have delayed her. We need to be patient."

"This is the not so sexy side of investigating," Mena exhaled, donning her sunglasses as she adjusted the seat to incline. "The waiting is annoying, but I'm determined to talk to Uma tonight."

Julian stole a glance at Mena. The fading sunlight glowed against her deep brown skin, and he was struck once again by how beautiful she was. The waiting hadn't been so horrible for him. One because he was used to it and two, it had given him a chance to get to know her better. She'd talked about her job at the gallery and her adventures hanging out with her best friends, Omar and Regina, to pass the time. It had been a long time since he'd gotten to know a woman and he found himself enjoying the experience ... probably more than he should.

"Let me see the binoculars," Mena said, grabbing for them.

"No, you won't know what to look for, and I could miss something," Julian said, shaking his head.

"C'mon! I'm about to die from boredom over here. I've talked your ear off, and now I need something else to stop me from going crazy," Mena said, pushing the sunglasses on top of her head. She reached over and placed her hand on his abdomen, her hands caressing his six pack. Julian froze, unsure of what to do next. The binoculars hung in the air between them.

A burst of laughter erupted from his mouth before he could stop it as Mena tickled him. The binoculars fell from his hand and bounced onto the center console before coming to a rest in her lap.

"Got it!" Mena said, with a giggle.

"You're not playing fair," Julian said, leaning toward her, decreasing the space between them in the small sedan. His leg brushed against the volume knob of the car radio, and the sensual bass of "Sweetie Badness" by Coco filled the air. Julian rested his hands on Mena's as she gripped the binoculars. Their eyes locked on to each other as the world melted away. He was consumed by the taut sexiness of her body. Her breasts, pressing against the orange tank top, threatened to break free. His body responded in the only way it could, growing harder as his hands caressed her arms and rested against her neck. She smelled of sandalwood and oranges as he leaned closer to her face. His gaze dropped to her full, luscious lips. He wanted nothing more than to kiss her ... right now.

The binoculars fell from Mena's hand and landed with a loud thud on the floorboard of the car. She reached her hands to his face and pulled him closer. Slowly, he pressed his lips against her neck and breathed deeply. Mena let out a soft moan as he trailed kisses down the side of her jawline. Reaching her chin, he pulled back and looked into her eyes. The passion burning in her gaze matched the blaze erupting within him. In an instant, his mouth was on hers, as he hungrily sucked on her lips before exploring her mouth with his tongue.

She didn't resist and matched his fervor with her own as they indulged in the decadence of the kiss.

Seconds faded away as he allowed his hands to roam over her body, enjoying her willingness to be touched and caressed. Her hands moved sensually under his shirt, stroking his back in a rhythmic massage.

The music stopped and segued into a commercial for cell phones.

Mena pulled back. "Julian ... look!"

Julian held her close, not wanting to break the trance of her hypnotic kisses. He ached to feel her lips against his once more.

"Julian, it's Uma! She pulled into her driveway," Mena said, pushing him away.

Julian turned his head toward the front window of the car. Uma exited her Toyota and walked to the edge of the white stone fence bordering her pink home. She waved to someone out of his view.

Grabbing the binoculars, Julian saw Uma holding an empty box in each hand.

A minute later, a large truck pulled in front of the house. Two men left the cab of the truck and followed her inside. Julian shifted the binoculars to read the name on the side of the truck: Marks & Sons Inter-Island Movers.

"Looks like Uma may be leaving the island," Julian said, lowering the binoculars.

"What? She can't leave now. Not until she explains what she and Irving are up to," Mena said, opening the driver's door.

Julian said, "Mena wait—"

Mena was out of the car, slamming the door behind her and running toward Uma's house before he could get his door open.

Julian cursed under his breath as he exited the car and followed Mena. As they reached the front door of Uma's small home, Julian said, "Let me do the talking."

Mena ignored him and knocked on the door.

"Let me handle this okay," Julian reiterated.

"I'm the one who knows her, not you. If anybody can get her to come clean, I think it's me," Mena said, turning to the door. Using her fist this time, she banged louder.

"We only have one shot at this, so I need you to stand back and let me get the information out of her—"

The door swung open.

Eyes puffy and skin pale and sallow, Uma looked haunted, scared, and sad. Her shoulders slumped, she stared at Mena.

"What are you doing here?" Uma asked.

"What is going on with you and Irving? Is he making you leave town?" Mena demanded.

"Irving is not making me do anything. I'm leaving because it's what's best for me," Uma said. "I was going to turn in my resignation tomorrow, but I might as well give it to you now."

"Why are you resigning? What is going on?" Mena asked. "I know you gave money back to Irving for something and that he threatened you. I can help you with the cops and with Priscilla. You don't have to give up your life because of him."

"Don't you get it!" Uma screamed. "Irving was my life."

Julian took a step forward and asked, "What was the nature of your relationship with Irving?"

"Oh God! Mena, I can't believe you got the security team involved in this. I told you it was a private matter, nothing related to work," Uma said, then broke into sobs.

"I'm sorry, Uma. Can we come inside, please? I promise we won't stay long," Mena said.

"Fine. Just stay out of the way of the movers." Uma stepped back, allowing Mena to enter. Julian followed.

Inside, boxes were piled in the center of the room. The place had been emptied, with no sign that anyone had ever lived there.

"Did you and Irving have a ... personal relationship?" Julian asked.

Uma nodded. "I was his girlfriend, but I knew I needed to keep it a secret from everyone at work. I just didn't know that keeping our relationship a secret also meant keeping it a secret from his other girlfriends. I was one of many. He never loved me, not like I loved him."

Mena said, "So, what I overheard between you and Irving was—"

"I was ending our relationship. He lied to me. I was such a fool," Uma said.

"What about the money?" Julian asked.

"It was money he'd given me to help pay my bills, get my hair done, typical stuff that a guy would give to his girlfriend. After I found out about the other women in his life, I didn't want any of it. That's why I gave it back to him,"

Uma said, then waved her hand around the room. "That's also why I'm moving out of this place. It seems that Irving sets up all his girlfriends in rental properties. I was no different. I'm sure he'll move some other bitch in here after me."

Julian and Mena exchanged a glance as Uma erupted into another round of tears. Mena embraced Uma, comforting her as she continued to cry.

Mena pulled back from the embrace. "Uma, tell me the truth. Why are you really leaving? Is it because Irving threatened you? He told you not to cross him, or—"

"He never said that to me." Uma frowned, shaking her head. "You heard wrong. I'm leaving because it's the only way I can make sure I won't go back to him."

"What about Ella Sapphire? Do you know her? Was she one of Irving's other girlfriends?" Julian asked, detecting a strange look in Uma's gaze, one he couldn't read.

"I never heard of her," Uma said.

Chapter Twenty-Seven

Mena kept her hand steady on the controls of the laser robotic arm as another layer of dirt disappeared before her eyes. The painstaking process of removing decades of grime from the Mayan Fresco that would be on display in the Genesis Gallery's new exhibit had been her only focus for the past five hours.

"Hey, you got a minute?" Julian's voice sent a tremor through her body.

Mena's head jerked up as she dropped the controls. She hadn't expected him to be at the gallery today. After the visit to Uma's had been a bust, Julian told her he'd be spending his day off giving Kendrick an update on what they'd learned.

"Can you wait for me out front? I just need five minutes."

Turning toward the laser, she powered down the machine and placed the fresco in an archival case. Her heart thumped in her chest as she thought about seeing Julian for the first time since last night. They hadn't had a chance to discuss what happened between them—the blistering kisses that had left her dazed and dizzy with lust. She'd thrown herself into the most tedious aspect of her work to stop obsessing over their make-out session.

It had taken every ounce of her willpower to not spill the tea to Regina and Omar over lunch. Omar had thrown a tantrum because she'd forgotten about the Gabonese mask he'd wanted her to analyze. As Omar fussed, Mena had been consumed by her own thoughts about last night's rendezvous with Julian.

Mena didn't understand why she'd let the sensual connection occur in the first place. She and Julian had gone through not one, but two, traumatic events. Of course, they felt drawn to each other. But she'd known him less than a week, a total of five days. Five days! Not long enough to jump his bones, no matter how sexy those bones were.

But the pesky thoughts lingered around the edges of her mind.

What did the kiss mean to Julian?

Was she ready to try to start a new relationship?

Or was she misreading the whole situation?

Would the passion flame out as quickly as it had sparked?

Mena wanted to bang her head against the wall. She didn't have time to deal with these raging emotions. Checking her reflection in the mirror on the opposite wall, Mena smoothed the wrinkles of her pencil skirt down over her hips and ran her fingers through her hair to give it a tad more body. Times like these, she wished she'd opted for a kitten heel over her ballerina flats, but there was nothing she could do about that now.

Stepping out of the back room into the wide-open space of the workshop, she saw Julian standing near the front windows. His broad shoulders and chiseled back evident through the classic dark brown polo he wore with khaki pants.

"Hey there," Mena said, her voice wispier than she'd planned.

Julian turned and looked at her. She could see the same smoldering fire in his eyes she'd seen last night before they'd interrogated Uma about her argument with Irving Bond.

In seconds, he was next to her, his shoulder touching her shoulder, igniting a flurry of sensations through her body. "Gave Kendrick the update about Uma. He doesn't think there's anything more to explore. But, he did get some new information on Ella."

"What kind of information?" Mena asked.

"They were able to track down a student loan Ella applied for about nine months ago. She'd been trying to enroll in the Art Institute in St. Killian. The application had Ella's address listed as a high-rise condominium downtown called Harmony Towers," Julian explained.

"Aren't those the new luxury condos that opened a year ago? Omar thought about moving there. A studio costs a half million dollars. How could Ella afford a place like that?" Mena asked.

"That's exactly what Kendrick and I wondered. The cops went over there this morning and talked to the manager, a woman named Lucy Hargrove. Apparently, the condo Ella listed as her address is owned by a company called Zygatica Investments and is up for sale now. Kendrick believes Zygatica could be a PC-5 shell company, which would explain why the manager refused to give him any information on who the tenants were," Julian said.

"I don't understand," Mena said.

"If the PC-5 owns Ella's condo in Harmony Towers, the manager wouldn't want the cartel to find out that she gave information about their property to the cops. It wouldn't be good for her career—or her livelihood."

Mena could tell there was something else he wasn't saying. "But ... you think we may be able to get more information out of the manager."

"Only if ... we ... were a couple looking to buy a new condo," Julian said. "You up for it?"

Glancing at her watch, Mena grabbed her purse from her desk. She'd only be skipping her last hour of work. "Let's go."

Thirty minutes later, Mena walked hand-in-hand with Julian into the cool air conditioning of the luxurious tower.

"We have an appointment to see Lucy," Julian said to the concierge, seated behind the ornate white desk carved with golden harps.

"Mr. Montgomery," a voice called from behind them.

Mena turned to see a pretty woman, her red hair shaved in a low fade with the "I Love Lucy" logo from the iconic television show tattooed on the side of her head. She was impeccably dressed in a teal pantsuit and silver stilettos.

"This must be your beautiful wife," Lucy said.

Mena shot Julian a look. He gave her a sheepish smile in return, a plea in his eyes to go along with the ruse.

Mena nodded as Lucy ushered them into an elevator to see the available condo. For the next hour, Mena and Julian dutifully played the role of a newlywed couple as Lucy showed them around the condo, which still had the furnishings of the previous owner. The condo was immaculate and expensive, selling for one million dollars.

"What do you think?" Lucy asked after completing the hard sell for the property.

"It's just as beautiful as Ella said it was," Julian replied.

Mena noticed the immediate recognition on the woman's face.

"You knew Ella?" Lucy asked, sadness marring her features.

"We're old family friends," Mena added.

"Such a tragedy what happened to her," Lucy said, dabbing a finger at the corner of her eyes, which welled with tears.

"Did you know her well?" Mena asked, trying to keep the woman talking, hoping to get information about Ella that she and Julian could pass on to the detective. Something that could help Detective Calliouet get a warrant to search the condo.

"We were friends, not besties, but we had some good times. I used to hang out with Ella and her friend Uma at the rooftop pool after work, but the boyfriend put a stop to that once he found out. So, instead, we'd go and get drinks at the bar across the street on nights he wasn't at the condo. I miss her," Lucy said.

"Uma Fischer?" Mena asked, wondering if her assistant had lied again. This time about not knowing Ella.

"You know, I don't know what Uma's last name is. Could've been Fischer. She only hung out a few times with us. Mostly it was just me and Ella," Lucy said.

"Her sister never liked the guy," Julian said, then tapped a finger against his head. "Can't remember his name."

"Bugs," Lucy replied. "Well, at least that's all I ever heard Ella call him."

"When was the last time you hung out with Ella?" Mena asked, wondering if Lucy had seen Ella during the time when Ella had disappeared from the Co-Op.

"Gosh, has to be about six months ago. Right around the time I got my promotion. I was too busy to hang out, and I didn't have time to see her as much. How's her sister doing with all this?" Lucy asked.

"She's pretty torn up, as expected," Julian said.

"You know, I have something I think you should give to Ella's sister." Lucy led them out of the condo, then locked the door. "Wait here."

Lucy walked briskly down the hallway and disappeared into one of the condos at the end of the hall.

"So, husband, seems like Uma knew Ella after all. When Irving threatened her, she knew exactly who he was talking about," said Mena.

Julian cleared his throat, his jaw clenched. "I'll bet Uma knows exactly why Ella was killed."

"I'm guessing you have some stealthy SEAL tricks you could use to find out, right?" Mena asked, stopping short as she noticed Julian flinch. Had she gone too far? His guarded look made her wonder if his past in the SEALs was a subject he didn't want to discuss.

Lucy returned a few seconds later and handed Mena a mahogany box the size of a briefcase. Holding the case, Mena's eyes roamed over the surface. The wood was carved with an intricate island scene filled with swaying palm trees, hibiscus bushes, and seashells along a trail leading to the sea.

Mena said, "This is stunning."

"Ella carved that herself. She was incredibly talented," Lucy said.

Mena tried to open the lid, but it wouldn't budge.

Lucy continued, "When I heard the news about Ella, the first thing I did was get her box from the condo. Her sister deserves to have it."

"I'll make sure she gets it," Julian said.

Mena and Julian followed Lucy back to the elevator down to the first floor.

As they walked through the lobby, Lucy turned to them.

"I hope you decide to buy the condo. I think the two of you would love it here. Please let me know what you decide and give Ella's sister my condolences," Lucy said, then shook both of their hands.

As they walked out of Harmony Towers, Mena handed the box to Julian.

Julian took a closer look at the box. "Looks like some kind of intricate locking system. Doesn't matter. At least we have a lead about Ella's past to give to Kendrick."

"Don't you want to see what's in the box before we give it to the cops? Maybe try to figure out who Bugs is," Mena suggested. Her curiosity was raging out of control. Before they handed over the box, she needed to know what was inside.

"I'm not sure that's a good idea." Julian hesitated.

"How about you think about it," Mena said, looping an arm through Julian's as they walked over to his motorcycle, parked in the circular driveway of Harmony Towers. "Over dinner."

Chapter Twenty-Eight

Julian glanced down at the bag of groceries filled with food and a bottle of Sauvignon Blanc as Mena fumbled with the key. She finally unlocked the door and pushed it open. As she walked away from him and into her kitchen, Julian took a moment to watch the sensual sway of her hips. He followed at a slow pace, grateful for the distraction of memories from their sizzling make-out session last night. No doubt they would have ended up making love in the rental car if Uma hadn't decided to come home at that very moment. He could no longer deny that being around Mena made him happy. Happier than he'd been in years, but it was a happiness he knew he didn't deserve.

"Let me help you with that," Mena said, reaching for the paper bags he'd placed on her kitchen counter.

"No way. I lost the bet. I'm cooking tonight," Julian reminded her, ushering her out of the kitchen. He'd made the mistake of underestimating Mena's knowledge of the Harley. She'd suckered him into a bet he had no chance of winning. Google had proven her right and him wrong on the first year Harley released their signature Road King design, an embarrassment to him as the owner of that particular version.

"Just because you're cooking doesn't mean I'm okay with you being unsupervised in my kitchen," Mena smirked.

Julian opened the bottle of wine and grabbed one of the empty wine glasses hanging underneath Mena's wine bar. Pouring her glass full of the white wine, he placed it on the bar. "Sit. You can watch everything I do from there. I promise I won't set anything on fire."

"You better not or I'll own that boat you live on right now," Mena said, a challenge in her gaze. "What's on the menu? You were so secretive in the store."

After leaving Harmony Towers, they'd driven the rental car to an open-air farmer's market to grab food for dinner.

Julian said, "I got some mahi-mahi and thought I'd grill it with a jerk marinade and pair it with sautéed vegetables and rice in coconut milk. Then for dessert, I picked up a key lime pie. I grabbed a bag of Oreos in case you need a snack while I cook."

Mena's eyes lit up, "Gimme!"

He handed her the bag, then turned to start prepping the fish.

"Have you decided what to do about Ella's box?" Mena asked, running her fingers over the carved surface.

Julian tossed the mahi-mahi steaks in the jerk marinade. "Part of me thinks I should give it to Kendrick and let the cops deal with it. Dawn made it clear that she wants me to stay out of her life and stay out of the investigation into Ella's murder."

"But what if the cops miss something like they did with Uma? We found out more about her conversation with Irving than they did and that there's a good chance she was close friends with Ella," Mena said, as she licked the icing off one side of an Oreo cookie.

"None of that matters. You called Uma, and she denied knowing Ella and Lucy Hargrove. Doesn't matter what Lucy says if Uma is going to deny hanging out with her and Ella at Harmony Towers," Julian said, trying unsuccessfully to ignore Mena's perspective.

"I know that. Fact still remains that we found out more than the cops. The same thing could happen with the box," Mena countered.

Julian knew she had a point. He worried that Dawn would find out he was still investigating Ella's murder despite her insistence that he stay out of it. But if there were some evidence in the box, something that led to Ella's killer, maybe Dawn would be grateful that he'd kept looking into things. She just might forgive him for all the pain he'd caused her.

"I'm going to drop it off with a locksmith in the morning," Julian said, making up his mind in the moment. "They should be able to get the box open without damaging it or the contents. Once I see what's inside, I'll know what to do."

"I think you're making the right decision. If there's nothing in there but Ella's sketches or something like that, it could be a big waste of time for the police. You can arrange to have it sent to Dawn and be done with it. But if there's something more …"

"Something like Bugs' real identity or proof that he had a motive for killing Ella—"

"You think this Bugs person could be involved?" Mena asked, taking another sip of her wine.

"Dawn asked me to look for Ella because she got a disturbing voice message from her sister. In the recording, Ella said she was at the Genesis Gallery and that he," Julian raised his hands in air quotes, "was going to kill her. 'He' could be the man known as Bugs."

Mena tapped her fingers on the bar, her eyebrows crinkled into a cute frown. "Doesn't the name Bugs remind you of some gangster."

"Ella did have a PC-5 tattoo on her arm. Kendrick's informant said Ella wasn't a hooker, but it doesn't make sense why she'd have the tattoo if she wasn't turning tricks for the gang. The PC-5 could be lying, trying to distance themselves from Ella's death to keep the heat off the cartel," said Julian.

"And maybe Bugs was her PC-5 pimp. But we'd need to know his real name to find him," Mena said.

"If we find out who he is, we'll tell the cops and let them handle it," Julian said, growing weary of the decision he'd made. He wasn't convinced he was doing the right thing. What if his interference caused problems with the investigation and Dawn got hurt … again. How would he live with himself?

"You're right. The PC-5 is dangerous. I wouldn't want you getting hurt trying to help me get closure. I don't know if I could live with myself if something bad happened to you because of me. You've already risked your life to save me, a stranger to you."

"We're not strangers anymore," Julian said, looking over his shoulder at her.

Julian saw a hint of a smile emerge on her face.

"No, we're not," Mena said.

Chapter Twenty-Nine

Hours later, Mena was finishing off the last bite of her key lime pie after devouring the dinner Julian had prepared.

"That was delicious," Mena said, leaning back in her chair. "Where'd you learn how to cook?"

Laughing under his breath, Julian said, "It's all because of Broman. When he was dating Dawn, he wanted to do something to impress her. So in between training sessions at BUD/S, we'd sneak off and take these cooking classes. He was such a klutz in the kitchen. Couldn't follow a recipe to save his damn life!"

Mena laughed. "I'm guessing you fared much better?"

"Not too shabby, I suppose."

"Did Broman finally get a chance to cook for Dawn?"

"He did on the night he proposed. Dawn screamed at him for destroying the small kitchen in her apartment and told him it was the worst damn dinner she'd ever tasted in her life. Then she said that he'd be banned from the kitchen ... after they got married," Julian said.

"That's romantic, in a weird way," Mena said.

Julian picked up the bottle of Sauvignon Blanc and filled Mena's wine glass, before topping off his own and then sat back down in his chair.

"Their whole relationship was weird to me, and I tried to stay out of it as much as I could. She was jealous of the time that Broman spent with anyone other than her. So that put a target on my back as his best friend. Things got worse when we were assigned to the same SEAL team," Julian responded.

"Did you always want to be in the Navy? Growing up, I mean?" Mena asked.

Julian was relaxed and didn't mind answering the question. He had already opened up to Mena more than he had to any other person in his life, except for Broman. It felt good sharing parts of himself again. He liked not feeling like the fuck up who didn't deserve to have a life anymore. He wanted to take a risk with Mena. He just hoped she wouldn't run away if he decided to share more of his past with her. The things that haunted him. The things he was ashamed of and could never forget, or forgive himself for …

"For as long as I can remember. My dad didn't think I was Navy material, but I proved him wrong. Both my mom and dad have a long lineage of family in the Navy. Generations and generations of sailors and naval airmen," said Julian.

"And Navy SEALs?" Mena asked.

"No," Julian paused. "I was the only one."

"I bet your parents are very proud of you."

"Yeah, until I screwed it all up," Julian said, a cloak of sadness descending upon him. "Doesn't matter now. That part of my life is over. What about you? What brought you from Jacksonville to St. Basil?"

"A boring story," Mena said, hesitating.

"Well, whatever the reason, I'm glad … unless you came because something bad chased you here."

"Worse than bad. A disaster."

"What was a disaster?" Julian asked, concerned.

"My marriage."

Julian let the words settle in the air. The idea that Mena had loved some other man enough to marry him felt like a punch to the gut. He knew she had a life before he met her. He never imagined that there was a husband in her past.

"Difficult marriage and even more difficult," Mena paused, inhaling sharply as she pinched the bridge of her nose. "Divorce. After that was over, I needed a fresh start. So, I moved here."

"What caused your marriage to fall apart?" Julian had to know.

"Some relationships aren't meant to be," Mena said. "Wish I had seen the signs earlier, but I didn't."

"Hard to see the signs sometimes," Julian added, thinking back on the biggest mistake of his life. The signs had been there, subtle warnings that things wouldn't go as he'd thought, but foolishly he'd ignored them.

"Good thing is we both lived to see better days," Mena said, clinking her glass with his.

"And I'm thinking our days could get even better," Julian said.

"How so?" Mena took another sip of wine.

"We could pick up where we left off the other night," Julian said, sliding his chair closer to hers.

"That shouldn't have happened," Mena said, chugging the rest of her wine.

"Why not?" Julian asked.

Mena was silent, but her eyes were locked onto his.

"I've been fighting these feelings from the very first moment I laid eyes on you in the courtyard at the gallery." Julian paused, watching for her reaction. Mena looked intrigued and that was all the encouragement he needed to continue. "I want to know everything about you. The woman that restores priceless pieces of art and teaches university students and drives a Harley and stops worrying about getting her hair wet to splash in the water with me."

"I'm not going to pretend that I don't feel what you're feeling right now," Mena said, standing and walking toward the window. "But I know going through a traumatic experience like the one we went through with Ella can fool people into thinking they feel some deep connection. Desire and passion can be a coping mechanism to work through post-traumatic stress."

Julian stood and walked over to her. "Let me make this clear. This thing building between us has nothing to do with Ella. It has everything to do with the beautiful, magnificent, intelligent woman that you are—"

"So, why rush it?" Mena asked. "It's only been five days. Why can't we take more time to get to know each other before jumping into anything deeper?"

Julian inhaled sharply, disturbed by his actions. He'd let his feelings run rampant, trying for something he knew he didn't deserve. Mena was awakening feelings within him that he thought had died three years ago. What made him think he deserved a chance at a happy ending now? Why should he have the life he'd destroyed for Dawn and Broman?

Julian stepped closer to Mena, unable to resist the urging from his heart.

Diminishing the space between them to mere inches, he leaned forward and brushed his lips softly against hers. Her mouth parted slowly, a subtle invitation. Wrapping his arms around her waist, he pulled her closer, increasing the intensity of the kiss. As their mouths moved in perfect harmony with each other, an insatiable hunger built that could only be assuaged by more of each other. Mena's fervor matched his own, emboldening him to continue his pursuit of the delectable taste of her mouth.

Breaking the kiss, Julian pulled away. He knew in his heart he wouldn't be able to stop himself from pursuing Mena, even if that led him straight to heartbreak. But he could delay the pain for as long as possible. "You're right. We can take this slow. I have all the time in the world for you."

Chapter Thirty

Muscles burning, Julian pushed his legs faster as his feet sunk into the soft sand with each step. His body was efficient, refusing to succumb to physical exhaustion. Remnants of his prior training and mental focus kicked in right when Julian didn't need it. What he needed was a distraction from Mena. She was consuming his thoughts, altering his ability to think about anything without memories of her creeping into his mind. He knew that taking things slow between them was the right move, even if every cell in his body wanted to ravish her last night. He wanted a chance to build something lasting with her, and he was willing to wait as long as it took.

Running past the old lighthouse on Saffron Beach, Julian saw Kendrick ahead. The detective stood at the end of a rock jetty jutting into the Caribbean Sea, his face obscured by the bright rising sun.

Crossing over the rocks, Julian slowed to a stop. Something was wrong. Kendrick's clothes were disheveled. Julian took a few steps closer.

"Kendrick ..." Julian called out.

Kendrick turned, a look of relief cast across his face. "Julian, what are you doing out here this early?"

"I could ask you the same thing. What the hell happened to you? You look like shit," Julian said, moving closer to his friend.

Kendrick laughed. "Feel like it too. I hit a wall with the Ella Sapphire case, not sure what to do next. François is hovering, waiting for me to slip up and make a big mistake so he can snatch the case from me. I feel like I'm letting everyone down."

Julian maneuvered down onto the rock jetty and sat.

"What do you know so far?" Julian asked. He'd spent years analyzing evidence as a SEAL. If there was one thing he was good at, it was finding information to track down criminals. Maybe he could help Kendrick get out of his funk, help him see a connection that he might have missed.

"Remember I told you that the bullets found in Ella's body matched a gun used in the shootout at the museum in St. Mateo," Kendrick said, sitting on the rocks next to Julian.

"Yeah, some PC-5 gang member's prints were on the gun from the museum attack, but no one knows why the gang targeted the Palmchat Islands Museum or the other museums," said Julian.

"Well, I didn't mention this, but we found blood and skin underneath Ella's fingernails like maybe she tried to scratch her attacker. I thought the obvious next move would be to see if there was a match between the blood under Ella's nails and that gang member," Kendrick said.

Wasn't a bad first move on the detective's part. Julian asked, "Was it a match?"

"Not even close. We ran the DNA against every PC-5 gang member we had in our database and got no hits. I got Irving Bond to give a sample, but he wasn't a match either. Now, I'm trying to get the DNA run against a few international crime databases, but the paperwork for that is insane. Going to take a week or more before we can start the search." Kendrick rubbed his fingers over his eyes, then rested his head in his hands.

Julian knew how bureaucratic red tape could mire an investigation, especially when it involved countries sharing their intel. Because St. Basil was a small island, the process might be harder, but he was certain Kendrick would get access eventually.

"That's normal, man. Just know that those kinds of requests never get denied, but there are formalities that you have to follow," explained Julian.

"It's still frustrating. But, what's bothering me is what we found on the cell phone," Kendrick said.

"Cell phone?" Julian didn't remember a cell phone.

"The one we found in Mena's car," Kendrick said. "It's a burner. I'm calling it the Mystery Burner because I don't know who owns it."

Julian eased his hand into the water as a school of tiny fish darted by. "What did you find on the Mystery Burner?"

Kendrick hesitated, a look of concern in his eyes. "Whoever owned the Mystery Burner may have wanted Ella dead."

Julian's head jerked up. "What do you mean? How do you know that?"

"One of the last text messages sent from the Mystery Burner said something like 'I can't deal with it anymore. I need you to take care of her like we discussed.'"

"Who did the Mystery Burner send that text to?"

"The text was sent to the cell phone of a Lawrence Rubin," said Kendrick. "An eighty-year-old man who passed away last year. I think the Rubin phone was stolen because the texts were sent months after the man died. When I contacted the family, they told me they thought the old man lost the phone."

"Well, that's a dead end."

"So, the Mystery Burner sent the text about 'taking care of her' to the Rubin phone," Kendrick continued. "Then the Rubin phone replied back requesting a photo. The Mystery Burner sent a picture of Ella Sapphire."

Julian turned toward Kendrick. "When were those texts sent?"

"Seven months ago," Kendrick said. "That was the last time the Mystery Burner had been used."

Stunned, Julian said, "The last time most of the artists at the Co-Op said they saw Ella was seven months ago."

Kendrick continued, "Other than that last set of texts, all the other texts, hundreds of them, were between the Mystery Burner phone and one other number. The texts dated back to about a year and a half ago."

"What was in those texts?" Julian asked.

"Raunchy stuff about all the freaky things they planned to do to each other. I never understood why people do that," Kendrick said.

"You won't understand until you try it. Stop being a prude," Julian teased.

"Let's save the love life lecturing for another time," Kendrick said. "Now, there are a few dozen texts in between the sexting that alluded to art pieces. Stuff like 'got the mask, almost done with it' and 'this painting was hard, but I think I did a good job.' Ella was a talented artist, so I thought maybe the other number belonged to Ella, and she was texting the Mystery Burner phone. But, we couldn't track the owner of the other number either."

"Two burner phones texting each other. The one Ella had when she got into Mena's car, the Mystery Burner, is the same one you think Ella was sending texts to from another burner phone? Why would she have the phone of the person she'd been texting? That's strange, don't you think?" Julian said. The puzzle pieces were coming in fast, but they didn't seem to fit. There had to be something they were missing.

"I thought about that. Couldn't figure it out," Kendrick admitted, then continued, "A few weeks before the Mystery Burner found in Mena's car was last used, the texts from the other number, who could be Ella or some other artist, became more threatening. The person demanded a bigger cut of the money. A couple of the texts were threats about going to the cops if more money wasn't sent. Some of the responses from the Mystery Burner made it seem like extra payments were made, but a lot of the later texts were ignored," Kendrick said.

"Let's assume for a moment that Ella was the person texting the Mystery Burner," Julian started, his mind racing with this new information. "She was definitely talented enough to forge art and make it look believable from what the other artists at the Co-Op told me. She also was no stranger to blackmailing. She'd done that a few times in the past, but on a small scale. She was lucky the people paid up instead of telling the cops."

"What did she have on these people?" Kendrick asked.

"She'd sleep with married men and then get them to pay her a few thousand dollars to stop her from telling their wives," Julian said, remembering the stories he'd heard from Broman.

"Interesting ... so, Ella could have been forging art for someone—possibly a fence—to sell. She might have become unsatisfied with her cut of the profits and demanded more money. She got some money, but then that person decided the blackmail was getting old and tried to stop her. But whatever the person did seven months ago didn't involve killing Ella, since she was alive up until a week ago," Kendrick surmised.

"But we can't be sure the person sending texts to the Mystery Burner was Ella. What if she stole the Mystery Burner or found it somewhere while she was at the Genesis Gallery and had no clue about the texts on the phone. Did you check Ella's bank accounts? Any sign of these money transfers?" Julian asked.

"We didn't find any evidence that Ella had an account at any bank in the Palmchat Islands. I also talked to Dawn about it, and she wasn't aware of any bank accounts," Kendrick said. "Another dead end."

"Any idea from the text messages which art pieces were being copied?"

"No. Just vague references about a mask or statue or painting," Kendrick said, then leaned back. "But you can see for yourself when I drop the Mystery Burner off at your boat later today."

"Really?" Julian asked.

Kendrick nodded. "Our tech team hasn't gotten a lead on the owner of the Mystery Burner or who was sending texts to the phone. Technically, everything I'm telling you is bending the rules. Why not bend them a bit more if that means bringing a killer to justice."

Julian ran his hands through the warm water of the sea. The warmth of the rising sun stung his skin. The biggest regret of his life was a result of him bending the rules, doing something he thought was good that had disastrous consequences. Julian hoped his friend wouldn't suffer the same dire fate as he had three years ago.

Kendrick stood and walked back along the rock jetty toward Saffron Beach. Julian stood and followed behind his friend. Kendrick's shoulders slumped, carrying the weight of the burden of trying to solve the complicated case.

Kendrick stopped at the edge of the jetty, turning to face Julian. "One more thing. In the texts, the sender referred to the owner of the Mystery Burner by a peculiar name."

"What was the name?" Julian asked.

"Bugs."

Chapter Thirty-One

After he and Kendrick had discussed Julian's conversation with Lucy, the manager at Harmony Towers where Ella last stayed, they'd both been more convinced that Ella could have sent the texts to the Mystery burner. Ella's alleged boyfriend, Bugs, was likely the elusive owner of that phone and might have had something to do with Ella's death, especially if Ella had been blackmailing him for more money related to whatever art scam they'd been running.

Missing from the texts was any connection to the Genesis Gallery. Julian had read the text messages dozens of times over the weekend, pouring through the details for any clues that could have been missed. Not once was the gallery mentioned, nor anyone associated with the gallery. That didn't mean Ella and Bugs hadn't met at the Co-Op. Ella had mostly been seen with two men on the security footage of the gallery grounds—Irving Bond and the artist Quark. One of them could be Bugs, but he was beginning to think that neither of them had been Ella's boyfriend before she disappeared. If Ella was involved in criminal activities with Bugs, it would make more sense that the two of them would limit their interactions with each other in person and avoid being seen.

So, what did that leave him?

Julian reached for the coffee machine and pressed the open button. After he'd placed a coffee pod inside, the machine gurgled as the brew begin to drip into the mug below.

Trying to track the movements of Ella and Bugs through their cell phones was the only option. The Mystery burner was locked down, used only for text messages. No calls in the call log or apps were on the phone. Nothing to help Julian find the owner.

The number of the phone he suspected was Ella's was a different story. There were apps downloaded onto the device registered to the phone number, based on Julian's hack into the databases of Palmchat Wireless. He'd analyzed the listing of apps on the phone and found two that could get him location data: a weather app and one used for maps and online directions. Apps granted location tracking by cell phone owners typically gathered data on the phone's location every ten seconds and were accurate within several feet. After accessing the phone's location data, Julian would have extensive information on Ella's movements. Information that could help him figure out the identity of Bugs.

Grabbing the coffee mug from the machine, Julian took a sip of the bitter black brew. The warm liquid burned down his throat as he stepped out into the stifling humidity of the island morning. He took the curved staircase up to the upper deck of his boat, sat at the table, and faced his laptop.

A myriad of activity flashed across the computer screen. He'd hacked into the weather app, which had the weaker cybersecurity profile and was running twelve separate programs to attack the master data collected by the app. No results yet, but he was getting close.

The wind whipped through the canopy that blocked the blazing sun. Kendrick would stop by soon for a report on Julian's findings, and he had nothing to give him.

His eyes drifted across the bay. From his vantage point, he could see Mena's corner condo. His preoccupation with getting evidence from the phones hadn't stopped him from watching the condo after he returned home from his shift at the gallery each night. He was glued to his laptop, working on a break in Ella's case, trying not to notice when the lights were on and when they were off in Mena's condo. Trying not to wonder if Mena was thinking of him or missing him. She'd been more than understanding when he explained how he was working with Kendrick on Ella's case and couldn't afford to be distracted by her this weekend.

Not seeing her had been harder than Julian wanted to admit. In one short week, he'd grown to like her presence in his life, and the void created by her absence left him with a longing stronger than he'd ever felt before.

"Good morning," Kendrick's voice wafted from behind Julian. "Brought you breakfast."

A brown paper bag dropped onto the table. Opening it, Julian peered inside.

"Donut holes? This is your idea of a good breakfast?" Julian asked, closing the bag. Memories of the feast Mena had cooked for him days ago assaulted his mind. His stomach growled at the thought of savoring the goat bacon and French toast. His heart ached at the thought of feeling her lips against his again.

"Better than vodka and coffee," Kendrick said, tapping the side of Julian's mug. Kendrick sat in the chair next to Julian's, then reached for the bag of donut holes.

"No vodka, just black coffee. But I was tempted," Julian admitted.

"Any breakthroughs?" Kendrick popped a couple of donut holes in his mouth.

"Nothing yet. I'm attacking the files from twelve different angles—"

"I think this is the part where I don't need to know the details," Kendrick interrupted.

Julian shrugged, knowing his friend was right. Admitting to a member of law enforcement that he was hacking into confidential corporate files was not the best move. At least Kendrick didn't know he was violating U.S. laws with his unauthorized use of classified Naval programs and hardware to assist with his hacking.

"Good point. What about you? What's in the folders?" Julian asked, noticing the files tucked underneath Kendrick's arm.

"While you were doing your top-secret thing, I thought I should go back through some of my cold case files that seemed similar to Ella's case," Kendrick said.

"Did you find anything?"

"One of them could be connected," Kendrick handed a file folder to Julian. "That one is the case of a missing woman named Samantha Fox. She was a PC-5 hooker and had the same tattoo on her arm that Ella had. She was rumored to be pregnant when she disappeared. Her family has been adamant that the

PC-5 kidnapped her and are holding her somewhere against her will, but we haven't been able to find evidence of any crime. She'd been staying at the Guava Sunset apartments and disappeared around the time her lease was up. Landlord claimed she didn't want to renew and her apartment was cleaned out like she moved on purpose. Nothing to suggest she was in any trouble or that any foul play was involved. My PC-5 informants claim they have no idea where Samantha could be."

"How long ago did Samantha go missing?"

"Three years. But the pregnancies and the PC-5 tattoos are the main links between the two women," Kendrick said.

"Did you find out if Ella was on the PC-5 death list?" Julian asked.

"She wasn't and my informant was right about her never being a prostitute for the gang. Shortly after she arrived in St. Basil, she hooked up with Beaujean Ali, a director in the PC-5 and was his girlfriend. Not sure why she ended up with the hooker tattoo, though."

"Did you talk to this Ali guy? Get any info out of him?" Julian asked.

"He's not talking. He's been in a coma at the Rakestraw Blake Center on the Aerie Islands for the past few years," Kendrick explained. "I also checked to see if anyone in the PC-5 goes by the name Bugs. Didn't find anything on that."

"I scraped through social media accounts of a lot of the suspected PC-5 gang members over the weekend, too. Not an exhaustive search, but pretty extensive. I didn't see any mention of the name Bugs. Guess we'll have to wait to see what your informant finds out. What's the other cold case?" Julian asked.

"A missing teacher named Tamara Gardner. She was estranged from her family due to childhood molestation claims, but close to her co-workers at the elementary school in Cashew Groves, my neighborhood," Kendrick said, handing Julian the file.

Julian opened the manila folder and skimmed the contents.

"Says here, the principal at the school reported her missing after she didn't show up for work on the first day of school and she hasn't been seen since," Julian said.

"The principal insisted she would never have abandoned her job, and all of her co-workers' statements were consistent. Tamara loved her job, loved teaching children, and was dedicated to her career. Yet, she disappeared. This part is similar to Samantha. Tamara's house was cleaned out like she'd moved on purpose too, but no indication that she'd put it up for sale. The house was fully paid for, and there were no signs of foul play," Kendrick said.

"Any suspected pregnancies?" Julian asked, wondering if that could link Tamara's case to Samantha's and Ella's.

"Not that we were told about," Kendrick said. "But one of the teachers claimed she owed money to a PC-5 gang member before she disappeared. The teacher didn't know the gang member's name, and I couldn't find anyone else to corroborate that claim."

Julian turned the pages of the report, reading the transcripts of the interviews with each of the teacher's co-workers. Tamara Gardner seemed like a lovely woman, well-respected, and making a difference in the lives of her students. She could have decided to move for some reason that she didn't want to share with her co-workers, except—

Julian paused, his eyes locked on a name on the page.

"Did you see this?" Julian asked, handing the page to Kendrick.

Kendrick stared at the page. "I don't get it. Transcript from one of the other teachers, but no smoking gun that I can tell. What caught your eye?"

"The co-worker said she'd broken up with her boyfriend at the beginning of that summer," Julian said. "Do you see the name of the boyfriend?"

Kendrick scanned the page, then said, "Quark. Damn, I completely missed that."

"Quark was also seen with Ella on the security footage of the Genesis Gallery dozens of times. He could have been one of the last people to see Ella before she disappeared seven months ago. I talked to him about a week ago. He admitted that Ella was his muse, but claimed he had no clue where she was," Julian said.

"And this file links him to another woman who has mysteriously disappeared," Kendrick said. "Looks like I may need to talk to Quark and it looks like your computer has discovered something."

Julian glanced over at the computer screen. A flashing cursor awaited further action.

"I'm in," Julian said, pulling the laptop closer. He typed in the unique identifier for the app from the phone suspected to be Ella's and waited as the program filtered for all the location data points tagged to the identifier in the master data file. Thousands of data points filled the screen from dates over the past year. Julian copied the latitude and longitude coordinates into his mapping program and waited for the results.

Kendrick leaned over his shoulder. "This is the breakthrough we've been waiting for."

"Damn right," Julian said. The dots appeared on the map, all within the island of St. Basil. "Look here. There's a cluster around Harmony Towers, the Artist Co-Op at Genesis Gallery, a couple of grocery stores ..."

Kendrick pointed to a cluster of dots in the middle of the Basil Mountains. "And this spot in the middle of the forest. What the hell could that be?"

Julian knew exactly what was at the location, the place that he and Kendrick needed to go next.

"That's Quark's Treehouse."

Chapter Thirty-Two

The air had a distinctly different feel at the high altitude of the second highest peak of the Basil Mountains. A damp coolness permeated Julian's bones. He shivered in the shadows of the towering trees as he hiked up the slope, Kendrick at his side.

"I can't believe this is where the guy lives. There's nothing around for miles," Kendrick said as they reached the top of the ridge. Ducking underneath the low hanging branches of a cluster of trees, they trudged higher up the mountain. No trails marked the location of the treehouse from the road, and without the GPS, the house would be impossible to find.

Climbing over a rock formation, Julian headed left, glancing at the satellite GPS on his phone to ensure they were still heading in the right direction.

"A little more to the left, and it should be straight ahead," Julian said, as Kendrick walked past him.

"How'd you find out this was where he lived?" Kendrick called back to Julian.

"One of the cleaning ladies for the gallery. She also cleans for Quark weekly and told me about his treehouse in the skies. The only way I got him to come to the gallery and speak to me was by threatening to put his mountain hideaway location on social media for his fans to see," Julian explained.

"I'll be damned," Kendrick muttered as he stopped in his tracks.

Julian looked up from the GPS and walked ahead to where Kendrick stood.

A mystical treehouse modeled after a traditional French chateau loomed before them, nestled amongst the mahogany and almond trees. The main building was flanked by four towering turrets and sat on a large wooden deck. Extending from each side of the deck were bridges to the adjacent trees. The deck surrounding the tree to the left housed a pool, Jacuzzi and lounge chairs. The tree to the right was surrounded by an even larger deck covered with a sheer fabric canopy. Underneath were a series of paintings on easels, some finished, others in progress, and a large rectangular table covered with brushes and littered with small paint cans in hundreds of colors. A single, spiral wooden staircase descended from the main building down to the forest floor.

"Shall we go up?" Julian asked, walking past Kendrick. Time for Quark to come clean about what he knew about Tamara Gardner and Ella. After seeing the location data from the cell phone he suspected was Ella's, Julian was convinced Quark knew more than what he'd originally said about both women's disappearance.

Reaching the top deck, Julian followed Kendrick around to the front entrance of the home. From this side, a sweeping panoramic view of Crescent Moon Bay stretched before Julian's eyes. He could see why Quark chose this location. The views were stunning.

Kendrick knocked on the ornately carved, glass double doors of the home. Several minutes passed. "Maybe no one is home."

Julian stepped around Kendrick and knocked harder. Listening for any movement inside, Julian heard nothing but the rustling of the trees from the wind blowing. "Where the hell could Quark be at nine o'clock in the morning?"

"Let's hang out and wait for him to come back," Kendrick said, walking toward an intricately carved wooden bench tucked in an alcove of the home.

Julian pulled out his cell phone and sent a text to Adam Russell to let him know he wouldn't be coming to work today. Quark could be back in five minutes or five hours for all he knew, and he wasn't going to let Kendrick wait alone. Pressing send on the text message, Julian walked over and sat on the bench next to Kendrick.

Several hours passed, the air had warmed under the noonday sun.

Running his finger along the carvings, Julian traced the pattern down to the curve of the handle and stopped. He stared at the carving underneath his finger.

ESapphire

"My precious bench was carved by the beautiful spirit of Ella Sapphire. May her spiritual presence rest peacefully in the clouds of the afterlife," Quark's voice rang through the air.

Julian and Kendrick looked to the right as the artist ascended the staircase.

"Do rise. I don't allow anyone to sit on the priceless art I have on my property," Quark said, as he passed them. Dreadlocks swaying in the wind, the artist was dressed in what looked like a burlap bag with red paint splattered on the front and back, and his feet were bare.

"Detective Caillouet and Mr. Montgomery, to what do I owe this displeasure?" Quark asked, ushering them into the open doors of his treehouse. Inside, the decor was meticulously appointed with oversized French furniture. Quark led them to an expensive looking couch and waved a hand for them to sit down.

"Do you know a woman named Tamara Gardner?" Kendrick asked, easing down onto the couch. Julian decided to remain standing, his eyes scanning the home.

Quark gasped. "Did you find her? Where is my beloved? Where is she?"

The desperation in Quark's voice surprised Julian. He turned to look at the artist, shocked to see tears welling in the man's eyes. What the hell was going on with him?

"So, you do know Ms. Gardner?" Kendrick asked.

"Of course, I know Tamara. Her soul merged with mine while we dated. She was and will always be my number one muse. I still sketch her beautiful face weekly. Wait here," Quark said, then sprinted into one of the side rooms. He returned minutes later with a sketch pad, flipping the pages. Each one featured the face of the same woman with varying expressions. "She is beauty incarnate, is she not? I wanted nothing more than to exist within her, but she tore my heart to shreds when our relationship ended."

Kendrick said, "You know that she hasn't been seen—"

"Since the summer two years ago, yes!" Quark exclaimed. "Has she come back to the island? Have you seen her?"

"No, we haven't found her yet," Kendrick confirmed. "If you tell us why your relationship with her ended, we may have a better chance of locating her."

Quark swiped at the tears flowing down his cheeks. "She believed I was unfaithful to her, but in my heart, no one could hold a candle to her. Her light shone brighter than the sun, burning away all the others."

"Did you cheat on her?" Julian asked, annoyed by the artist's responses.

"By earthly terms, I suppose the answer is yes. I'm an artist. I'm not of this Earth, and I do not need to adhere to the arbitrary rules of love imposed here," Quark said.

"So that's why the two of you broke up?" Kendrick asked.

"No. We broke up because I didn't want to be a father. Tamara was ready to settle down and procreate. I don't believe that any child should be born into this cruel world and refused to be the father of her child. When she learned of my feelings, that was the final straw. She dumped me," Quark said.

Julian stared at the artist. The hurt expression on his face was genuine.

Quark continued, "I spent the whole summer in Belize trying to repair my shattered heart. When I got back, I found out she'd left her job and her home, and no one knew where she'd gone. She'd disappeared."

Kendrick exchanged a glance with Julian. Quark's account of the events lined up with the information obtained by the cops when Tamara went missing. She had been active on the island throughout the summer that Quark was away, based on the notes in the cold case file. Quark had given them enough information to validate his alibi for the time when Tamara went missing.

"You said the bench outside was carved by Ella Sapphire, right?" Kendrick asked, changing the focus of the conversation.

"It was. I bought the plain bench, and she turned it into a wonderful work of art," Quark said.

"Where were you last Sunday night? The night when Ella was murdered?" Kendrick asked.

Quark's mouth dropped open. "I ... I ... I didn't kill her. I would never harm another living creature, let alone a woman that I loved deeply. She was my number two muse. Without her, I've struggled to produce my work. The source of my inspiration gone."

"Sounds like you lost your top two muses. Strange coincidence, wouldn't you say?" Julian asked, taking a step toward Quark.

The artist shrank back under Julian's gaze. "I didn't do anything to Tamara or Ella. I want nothing more than to have them both back in my life. Last Sunday night, I met with Mr. Montgomery at the Genesis Gallery and answered questions he had about Ella. Then I headed to the park in downtown Marluna for my monthly painting in the park party. There were a hundred tourists and locals hanging out with me until the early hours of the morning, painting and drinking. You can ask anyone on the island. Everyone knows that's where I was."

"I think that's all we need for now," Kendrick said, standing.

"One last thing," Julian stopped, glancing at his cell phone. "Can you give me the last phone number you had for Ella?"

Quark looked confused, then nodded, pulling his cell phone from his pocket. Swiping his finger across the screen, the artist tapped on the phone a couple of times and then read out the numbers.

Julian listened, matching each one to the number that had texted the Mystery burner found in Mena's car.

Chapter Thirty-Three

Mena stood in front of the security room on the first floor of the Genesis Gallery. She'd been halfway to her car in the employee parking lot, ready to go home, when she'd spotted Julian's Harley in a secluded space near the back entrance. Regina had found out after lunch that he'd called out today. But there his bike was on the gallery grounds this evening. She couldn't deny how much she'd missed him over the weekend, but he'd been busy working with Kendrick trying to track down evidence to identify Ella's murderer. How could she demand some of his time when he had more important things to focus on?

Walking briskly across the manicured lawn, she'd entered the side door of the main gallery building and headed toward the security room. She raised her hand, then lowered it and raised it again. Poised to knock, she hesitated once more.

She could do this another time. Julian needed to concentrate on Ella's killer. And hadn't she said they needed to take things slowly? She was in no hurry to jump into another relationship, not after everything she'd gone through with her ex-husband, Dr. Michael Marsh. Mena took a step back. She could talk to Julian tomorrow, or—

The door jerked open.

Julian stood in the doorway. He seemed larger than she remembered, more imposing, dressed in a black t-shirt and black jeans. He'd gotten a hair cut, his dark brown locks smoothed into small peaks on his head.

Seconds that felt like hours passed as they stared at each other.

Mena's heart pounded in her chest loud enough for the whole gallery to hear. She needed to say something, anything—

"I missed you," Julian said.

"Don't say that," Mena responded, a flurry of sensations shooting through her body.

"Why not?" Julian asked, his voice low. The softness in his eyes, the longing, and veiled hurt tugged at Mena's heart. "It's true. Didn't you miss me too?"

Mena took a deep breath. "Maybe just a little."

Julian smiled and took a step back inside the security room, motioning for her to follow.

Mena's legs felt like jelly as she forced herself to move into the room. Julian pulled a chair from the corner of the room, and she sat slowly. Grabbing the chair near the security monitors, Julian sat directly in front of her, their legs touching. His dark eyes sparkled as he reached for her hand. "I'm taking things slow, like you wanted."

"I know. I'm not sure I'm ready for some kind of relationship, and after what I went through with my marriage, I don't know that I'm ready to commit to anyone," Mena said.

"That's not what I'm asking for," Julian said, his fingers drawing small circles on the back of her hand, sending her body into a frenzy. "All I want is to spend time with you. And if you enjoy the time we spend together as much as I do, then we can spend a little bit more time together. That's it."

"You make it sound so simple," Mena said.

"For me, it is. I want you to live in the moment. One moment at a time and share a few of those moments with me. You think you can do that?"

"I want to give you a lot of moments of my time," Mena said, then giggled.

"Is that right?" Julian said, smiling. He leaned in and brushed his lips against hers.

Heat roared through Mena's body from his touch, and she wanted nothing more than to taste his mouth on hers. Placing her hands around his neck, she delved into the kiss, caressing his lips. His hands stroked through her hair as their kisses deepened. Mena's body ached for Julian, but it was too soon. She had to slow down.

Breaking the kiss, Mena pulled back and let out a shaky laugh. "Wow."

"Wow indeed," Julian said, his voice barely above a whisper. "How about we start with dinner at Stars Beach Bar tonight? We can meet there, no pressure."

"Stars Beach Bar?" Mena asked, thinking of the high-end, exclusive restaurant near The Bluffs. Charlie had proposed to Omar there last year. "Fancy. How about we take your Harley instead."

"Alright, but you're driving," Julian said and pulled her into a passionate kiss.

Chapter Thirty-Four

"What a way for the night to end," Julian said, scratching his left temple.

"This was probably the best first date I've ever had," Mena said, laughing as they strode along the boardwalk toward Julian's yacht. "Even if I had to pay for dinner and taxi you home."

"Not exactly how I wanted to impress you. I'll pay you back tomorrow after I get my bike from the pound. You must think I'm some worthless bum."

"A sexy, worthless bum," Mena said, teasing him.

"You sure you had fun?" Julian asked. The night had been embarrassing for him at every turn. He'd left his wallet in the back compartment of his motorcycle, and when he'd gone out to get it, a tow truck was carting his bike away along with two other cars that were illegally parked along the cliffs. Julian had missed the "No Parking" sign, telling Mena to squeeze in between the two cars already parked there, despite her hesitation.

Even with the missteps, he had to agree with Mena. The date had been perfect. She looked amazing in a flowered sleeveless top and low-rise denim skinny jeans that gave him a nice view of her luscious ass. Just the distraction he needed to take his mind off of Ella's case for the night.

Mena nodded as she turned and wrapped her arms around his neck, squeezing him tight. She whispered in his ear, "Are you going to invite me in for a Felipe beer?"

The warmth of her breath against his skin stirred his cock, and it took every ounce of his will power not to succumb to the feeling.

Linking arms, they walked along the planks toward his boat. Julian led her to the back steps and watched as she ascended to the deck. Her jeans shifted lower onto her hips, giving him a nice view of her pink thong. He was officially aroused.

Taking the steps slowly, he reached the deck and looked around, but Mena wasn't there. What was she up to?

Julian walked toward the front of the boat in time to see Mena turn the corner and head into his living room.

"Have I told you how amazing this yacht is?" Mena asked, plopping down on the leather couch.

Julian couldn't take his eyes off of her. She was meant to be here on this boat with him. She was meant to be in his life.

Walking past Mena into the kitchen, Julian pulled two bottles of Felipe beer from the refrigerator and kicked the door closed.

"Would you like an official tour?" Julian asked, handing her one of the bottles.

"I'd love one. How many bedrooms do you have?" Mena asked.

"Just one straight ahead. I converted the other cabins downstairs into a workout room and a game room," Julian said.

Mena rose from the couch and walked toward his bedroom door. He could definitely get used to that view. She turned back slowly, her dark hair falling over the smooth brown skin of her back.

"You going to join me?"

There was something about the look in her eyes that told Julian this would be a night he'd never forget.

In two steps, Julian's body was pressed against Mena's. The tautness of her nipples through the thin fabric of her top delighted his senses. He cradled her head in his hands, loving the soft feel of her thick tresses intertwined between his fingers. His tongue trailed across her lips, then plunged in her mouth, swirling in concert with hers as their kiss deepened.

Julian released his hands from Mena's hair as she pushed his sport coat from his body and then deftly unbuttoned his cotton shirt, pushing it to the floor. Her soft lips ravished his chest with kisses, starting near his collar bone and blazing a trail down below his belly button before she broke away to crawl back onto his bed.

Breathless, Julian watched as Mena unzipped her strapless top and let it fall. Slipping her fingers along the band, she ran a finger lazily around the button before unzipping the jeans and pushing them down. Stepping around her crumpled clothes on the floor, Mena stood before him like a centerfold in a sexy lacy bra and matching thong. Curling a finger toward him, Mena beckoned for him to come closer.

Julian relieved himself of clothes in record speed, revealing the full extent of how much he wanted to make love to Mena. A small moan escaped her mouth as he approached the bed and lowered his body onto hers.

A sizzle of electric desire pulsated between them as their skin rubbed against each other. Caressing her body, Julian relieved Mena of the constraints of her lacy underwear before delighting himself in the taste of her skin. A perfect symphony long meant to be played, their bodies fell into a perfect rhythm, rocking in sync with the motion of the boat on the water as they brought each other to climax. Blissfully exhausted, Julian wrapped Mena in his arms as they drifted off to sleep.

Chapter Thirty-Five

Pain shot through Julian's left thigh as he walked gingerly toward the entrance to the local hospital. Last night had been more than he'd thought was possible. Several rounds of sweaty, unadulterated passionate lovemaking had left him listless and spent. Waking up to Mena in his bed felt better than every orgasm he'd experienced last night.

After she'd rushed back to her condo to get ready for work, Julian had noticed the blood on his bed sheets. The stitched-up gunshot wound had begun to bleed, no doubt aggravated by the intense movements of his sexual encounters with Mena during the night.

If he was going to keep up with the dark beauty, he needed to be one hundred percent, and that meant going back to the hospital to have his wound taken care of.

"What are you doing here?" a woman's voice called from behind him.

Julian stopped, recognizing Dawn's voice. "Getting my leg checked."

Julian didn't bother turning to look at her. He knew Dawn would prefer to never see him again.

"I'm here to see my nephew," Dawn said, catching up with him and falling in step with his strides. "I've been coming every day since I got to the island. He calms me. I call him Elliot. That's what I'm going to name him when I finally get custody of him."

Julian stopped in front of the entrance to the hospital and looked at Dawn. He couldn't believe that she didn't have legal custody of Ella's son yet. "What's causing the delay?"

"Palmchat Islands Child Protective Services has strict rules on trying to locate both parents before awarding custody to a family member," Dawn explained, running a hand through her blond hair. "The department has to make a good faith effort to find the father of the baby through news releases and social media postings."

"How long is that going to take?"

"Two weeks. Well one more week now," Dawn said.

"And then you'll get custody?"

"No, then they do a DNA test to prove that I'm related to little Elliott and once it comes back a match, I can have custody of Ella's son," Dawn explained.

"That's bullshit," Julian said, frustrated by the process.

"Tell me about it. I want to go back to Florida. It's hard being away, you know. I need to get back there, but I'm not leaving without my nephew," Dawn said.

Julian knew exactly why Dawn needed to get back home and how difficult it must be for her to be away for so long.

"Anyway, I wanted to thank you for saving his life," Dawn said.

Reaching for the glass door, he held it open for Dawn to enter and followed her inside. The hospital was a flurry of activity. Nurses and doctors running around, armed police officers rushing back and forth.

"What the hell?" Dawn muttered.

An officer passed by, and Julian grabbed his arm. "What's going on?"

"A baby has been kidnapped. We're locking down the hospital until we can locate him," the officer said.

"What did you say?" Dawn screamed. "Which baby was taken?"

"I'm not sure ma'am. Is your child here?" the officer asked.

Dawn pushed past the officer and ran to the physician on duty. It was the same doctor who'd been at the hospital when Julian brought the newborn in over a week ago.

"Dr. Gillis, what baby was taken? Tell me now!" Dawn yelled.

"I'm sorry, Mrs. Garrison, it was Ella's baby," Dr. Gillis responded. "We are searching for him now—"

Dawn's fist slammed into the woman's face.

"How could you lose my nephew?" Dawn screamed. The two women sank to the ground. Dawn's fists pummeled the doctor's body as she demanded answers. "Where is he? How could you let this happen?"

An officer ran from the opposite side of the room and grabbed Dawn before Julian could get to her. Dawn squirmed within the officer's grasp, tears streaming down her face as she screamed for the baby to be found.

Julian felt numb as the chaos surrounded him.

Someone had kidnapped Ella's son.

Kendrick entered the room from one of the enclosed administrator offices and barked orders at two deputies before he made eye contact with Julian. As he passed the officer trying to comfort Dawn, Kendrick said, "Get her out of here, now."

"What the hell happened?" Julian asked Kendrick.

"Ella's baby was stolen this morning," Kendrick said, his face laced with concern.

"Any leads on who took him?" Julian asked.

"Surveillance videos in the hospital and the parking lot were conveniently offline. But we got a clear view of the kidnappers from the CCTV camera at the stop light on Bishop Boulevard," Kendrick said.

"You got a good view of the kidnapper?" Julian asked.

"Crystal clear. You'll never guess who we saw holding the baby in the front seat of the getaway van."

Chapter Thirty-Six

Mena tapped her fingers on the rectangular mahogany wood conference table. The faces of her co-workers sitting across from her blurred as her eyes teared with another yawn. Regina, sitting next to an empty chair usually occupied by the gallery owner, dutifully took meeting minutes. Omar sat next to Regina, not bothering to hide his boredom as he focused on his cell phone, oblivious to what was being discussed. Odd that Priscilla Dumay was late for this meeting. Mena couldn't remember a time in the past three years when the gallery owner had missed the Tuesday morning status update meeting.

The Director of Accounting, a short round-faced man with tightly coiled hair forming a cap on his large head, rose from his seat and waddled to the front of the room. Stopping next to the oversized monitor built into the mahogany wood paneled wall, he began the overview of the gallery's financials for the past week in his typical monotone fashion. Mena usually enjoyed the weekly meetings but focusing on today's agenda was proving to be impossible.

As the projector displayed a large graph of the gallery's assets, Mena zoned out, her mind flooded with memories of a magnificent night with Julian capped off by some of the best sex she had ever had. She was not one prone to exaggeration, and her assessment of last night's sexcapade was not hyperbole. When she'd agreed to live in the moment, as Julian suggested, she hadn't expected to become the aggressor. Julian had been the one exercising restraint, patiently willing to forgo intimacy to focus on getting to know each other. But her attraction to him had proven to be insatiable, spurred on by his charismatic personality, humor, and stunning body. In the end, he'd allowed her to seduce him on their first official date, and she'd enjoyed every salacious moment.

When morning came, waking up next to him had been perfectly natural and comfortable. Inevitably thoughts of starting a new relationship worried her. Where was this going? Would they always live in the moment? Or could this intangible thing between them blossom into something more committed and everlasting? Mena halted the thoughts as soon as they started.

She wasn't ready to think about a serious relationship with Julian and what that could mean, especially after the disaster of her failed marriage. The Julian she'd gotten to know was caring, open and honest. But Mena had fallen for a caring, open and honest man before and knew better than anyone how easily you could be fooled, especially when matters of the heart were involved.

Taking things slow was her only option. No premature attachments or thinking ahead of what could be. For now, she was going to follow Julian's mantra. If one night of hot, rugged, passionate love was all she would get from Julian Montgomery, then she'd savor the memories of that delectable treat with no regrets.

Damn it!

Mena pressed a hand against her temple and let out a heavy sigh, eliciting a raised eyebrow from Regina. Mena smiled to reassure her friend she was fine and tried to regain her composure as the Director of Accounting droned on through his tenth slide. Mena wanted Julian to be more than a one and done. More than just mind-blowing sex. Julian made her realize how much she craved true companionship and a relationship again.

Mena rested her head in her hand and stole a glance toward Omar. He rolled his eyes as another slide filled with tiny numbers and accounting charts filled the screen. Mena stifled a smile as her stomach growled.

She'd had to pass on breakfast with Julian. Giving him a rushed kiss, she'd dashed off the boat and hurried back to her condo to get ready for work.

The doors to the conference room slammed open as Priscilla Dumay, dressed in a tailored couture pinstriped pantsuit, stomped into the room. Following her was the head of security, Adam Russell, and the night security guard, Zak Webber. The Director of Accounting ceased speaking mid-sentence as all attention in the room turned toward Priscilla and her security team.

A sheen of sweat glistened on Priscilla's face. She bumped into the edge of the table, cursing under her breath, before noisily pushing her chair away from the table and dropping down onto the seat. Pointing toward the projector screen, she looked over her shoulder at Adam and Zak, mouthing the word "go."

The Director of Accounting scurried back to his seat as the two security guards marched to the front of the room.

"We have an emergency security announcement," Priscilla said, through gritted teeth. "Adam Russell will give the details and instructions going forward. Adam."

The room went eerily quiet as heads turned toward Adam Russell. What could have happened? Priscilla and her security guards were pensive and angry. Mena couldn't help but notice that Julian was missing. Had he done something to spark the ire of Priscilla Dumay? Mena gripped her hands in her lap, hoping that Julian hadn't been fired.

Zak pushed a jump drive into the laptop.

A picture of Irving Bond filled the screen.

The staff all looked around as if for the first time noticing that Bond was missing at the meeting. What was going on? Mena glanced at Omar, who looked attentive, his eyes focused on the two security guards.

"A detective with the St. Basil Police Department met with Ms. Dumay and me this morning to inform us that they have issued a warrant for the arrest of Irving Bond for kidnapping an infant from the St. Basil Hospital in Marluna this morning," Adam Russell announced.

Audible gasps erupted within the room. Priscilla tapped against the table with her perfectly manicured nails, asking everyone to please remain quiet while Adam finished his update.

Mena's thoughts went to Ella's baby. Was he the baby who'd been kidnapped? Was that why Julian wasn't here? Did he know Irving had kidnapped Ella's baby? Did Dawn?

"Effective immediately, Irving Bond's employment at the Genesis Gallery has been terminated. His access privileges have been revoked," Adam continued. "The police have video surveillance showing Irving leaving the hospital with the child, which he removed from the premises without consulting any medical staff. He is considered unstable and dangerous at this point, and every effort is being extended to locate him and the child."

"Why would Irving steal a baby?" Regina blurted out.

"He always seemed shady to me," Omar said, huffing under his breath.

The room fell quiet, awaiting Adam's response.

"I don't have any information on Irving's motives or what would drive him to commit such a horrible crime against a defenseless child. Needless to say, it is very important for all of you to alert me or someone on my security team if you see Irving on the premises or at the Artists' Co-Op," Adam said.

Mena sat motionless as Priscilla fielded a barrage of questions from the shocked staff. Her thoughts raged with concern for Julian. She couldn't let him go through this alone. She reached in her pocket. It was empty. She'd left her cell phone back at her workshop. She couldn't text Julian to find out if he knew about the kidnapping.

As Priscilla brought the meeting to a close, Mena was the first to stand. Turning to exit the conference room, she stopped short. Zak stood in her way. His black eyes were menacing, sending a chill down her spine.

"We need you to stay in the conference room until we've had a chance to search the outer workshops and the Co-Op for Irving Bond," Zak said, giving her a smile that looked more like a sneer. He crossed his tattooed arms across his chest.

"I need to go grab my cell phone," Mena said.

"That will have to wait," Zak said, his tone firm. "Please go back inside and have a seat. We should be done in a few hours."

Chapter Thirty-Seven

"Find him … promise me … you'll find Ella's baby … bring him back to me." Dawn's words slurred as her eyelids drooped from the sedative.

Julian grabbed Dawn's hand, squeezing it tight between his own. "I'll find him. I promise."

The stress eased from Dawn's face as tears streamed down her cheeks. She closed her eyes and drifted to sleep in the hospital bed. The shock of Irving Bond kidnapping Ella's son had everyone reeling, even Julian. He didn't understand why Bond had taken Ella's baby. Video surveillance from the gallery had shown Bond and Ella together dozens of times. Julian was certain there was some sort of connection between the two of them, but what was it? And did that connection have something to do with Ella's baby boy?

Checking the cell phone vibrating in his hand, Julian saw a text message from Kendrick. The detective was waiting outside the hospital for him. Satisfied that Dawn would be okay, Julian left the small room. He hoped Kendrick and the cops had made some progress on tracking Bond down. Pushing through the glass door leading out to the hospital parking lot, Julian saw Kendrick huddled with a few other police officers near a cluster of hibiscus bushes.

Kendrick waved for him to come over as the other officers headed toward a parked police car.

"How's Dawn doing?" Kendrick asked.

"The doctor gave her a sedative. I think we were all afraid she'd give herself a stroke from the stress of the situation. I'm glad she allowed them to give her something to calm down. Any news on Bond's location?" Julian asked. He'd promised Dawn he would find the little boy and this time he wouldn't let her down. He would find the baby and bring him back alive.

"We located the getaway van abandoned near a barbershop in Marluna. No one in the area saw Bond or the baby. So, I decided to see if there were any clues on the security footage from the gallery, focusing on Bond this time," Kendrick said.

"What did you find?" Julian asked.

"Bond seemed to be a ladies man. We found just as many videos with him and other females, some employees and some artists from the Co-Op, as we found of him and Ella. Nothing to indicate that Ella was getting any special attention from him," Kendrick said.

Julian asked, "What about the night Ella took Mena hostage? Bond was there that night. Any ideas where he went after he left the gallery?"

"Irving has a rock-solid alibi for that night. Around the time you and Mena ran into Ella in the lobby of the Genesis Gallery, Bond was checking into the Seafoam Motel with Alexandra Vincent," Kendrick responded.

"Isn't that the wife of Bimbo Vincent, the owner of King Street Lounge?" Julian asked.

"The same Bimbo Vincent who filed for divorce citing infidelity by his spouse. His private investigator has extensive videos and photos of Alexandra meeting up with several men, one of which was Irving Bond on the night that Ella was killed. We cross-referenced the surveillance from the P.I. to the security cameras at the motel and confirmed that Bond was with Alexandra Vincent."

Julian said, "So that just leaves Bugs, the guy Ella was likely dating based on my conversation with her friend Lucy Hargrove, the manager at Harmony Towers."

"I have a lead on who Bugs could be," Kendrick said.

"Who is he?" Julian asked.

"DNA analysis of the skin and blood under Ella's nails matched a perp named Teo Juarez. There's nothing in the databases for Teo Juarez past his juvenile criminal record, so I don't know much about him. I think he could be Bugs and I should find out if Ella knew a guy named Teo Juarez."

"Lucy might know," suggested Julian. "You could try asking Quark."

Kendrick nodded, scribbling on a notepad.

"We also need to find out if Irving Bond has a connection with Bugs. From the texts Ella sent to the burner phone, we know that she had a sexual relationship with Bugs and they could have been involved in some kind of art forgery scam. Bugs could be the father of Ella's baby. And if, let's say, Irving was their fence, Bugs could have blackmailed Bond into stealing the baby from the hospital," Julian said, thinking out loud.

"That's a damn good theory," Kendrick said, then looked down at his cell phone. "It's the Chief. I have to get back to the station. I'll let you know if we get any other leads on the baby's location."

Kendrick jogged across the parking lot to his car.

Julian couldn't wait on the St. Basil Police Department.

Finding Ella's baby was his number one priority, and he didn't need the cops slowing him down.

Chapter Thirty-Eight

Gripping the railing, Julian paused at the two dirtboards dangling on the edge. The lights from the marina walkway reflected off the boards, giving them an eerie glow against the darkness of the night. Running his hands along the surface of both boards, he closed his eyes and took a deep breath. A strong breeze whipped across the bay, ruffling his t-shirt. The feeling reminiscent of the rush of wind blowing past his body as he pressed his feet against the dirtboard, dodging tree limbs and bouncing off rocks, trying to catch up with Broman on the dirt trail in front of him. Julian had bested Broman in every task they'd ever tackled, but he'd never beaten him down a mountain on the boards.

Stepping backward, he turned and entered his living room. Crouching in front of the safe, he entered the code and jerked the door open. Pushing his hands along the medals and ribbons on the base, he felt for the one thing he needed right now. His fingers brushed against metal. Pulling it forward, he glanced down at the small bronze key in the palm of his hand.

Minutes later, he descended into the bowels of his boat, walking through the engine room to a locked door in the corner. Inserting the key, he unlocked the door and stepped inside. Running his hands along the side wall, Julian felt the small round knob and pushed it inward, flooding light into the cabin. Julian looked around, his heart pounding in his chest.

A metal desk stretched before him with six computer monitors mounted to the wall above it. Three keyboards rested against the flat surface in front of three square hard drives. Two tall computer servers stretched from the floor to the ceiling, one to the left and the other to the right of the table. In the middle of the desk was a red switch.

There was no time to waste.

Flipping the switch, the computers roared to life, blinking green and red. The monitors illuminated with white text filling each screen. The hum of the servers filled the air, growing louder with each passing second. Julian adjusted the height of the stool and sat. His fingers flew across the keyboard. Time was critical. He had to find Ella's baby. He would worry about solving the mystery of the connection between Bond, Bugs, and Ella later.

Tapping into the hundreds of CCTV cameras across the island, Julian downloaded Irving Bond's picture from the Genesis Gallery website and started the facial recognition software. Within ten minutes, he was watching footage from five minutes ago of Irving Bond exiting a black Mercedes at a warehouse along the waterfront. Two keystrokes and the address flashed in front of him on the second monitor. The warehouse was only ten minutes away from the marina.

Adrenaline blasted through his body as he stood, knocking the stool over. Reaching below the desk, he yanked the drawer open and stared down at the rows of Beretta M9 pistols lined in foam padding next to dozens of magazines. Snatching one of the guns, Julian slammed a fifteen-round magazine into the base and kicked the drawer closed. Racing off the boat, he ran toward his Harley in the Marina parking lot.

The wind roared past his ears as he pushed the Harley faster through the backroads between the marina and the waterfront. This part of town between the airport and downtown Marluna was the heart of PC-5 territory. He wasn't afraid of the island gang. He'd stared down more deadly criminals on his SEAL missions. He could handle anything the gang punks threw at him.

As he reached the edge of the waterfront, Julian cut the engine and glided his bike toward one of the outer warehouses. The moon was a sliver in the night sky, providing little light to combat the cloak of darkness shrouding the buildings of the waterfront.

Three buildings down, the black Mercedes sat empty in front of a large warehouse door. Julian took a breath as his heartbeat steadied, then slowed, and his senses heightened. Crouching low, Julian sprinted toward the Mercedes, then ducked in between the two buildings. He detected no other movement outside. The waterfront was deserted at this time of night. The rumbling of airplanes taking off from Jasper Bishop Inter-Island airport a mile away was the only sound penetrating the silence.

Most likely, Bond was in PC-5 territory to pass off Ella's baby to Bugs. If that happened, the baby might never be seen again, especially if Bugs was the father as he and Kendrick suspected.

Hunching forward, Julian darted across the sidewalk to the car. The smell of exhaust filled his nose, threatening to choke him. Placing one hand over his mouth and the other on the Beretta, Julian opened the car door and leaned inside, gun raised.

Empty.

Checking the passenger side, he reached for a small plastic medical tag, cut in half. Turning it over, he stared at the name he'd expected: Baby Boy Sapphire.

Julian knew he was close to rescuing the little boy. Folding the bracelet in half, he stuffed it into the pocket of his jeans, then slid out of the car, closing the door behind him. Partially obscured by the car, he could see inside the open corrugated door of the warehouse, illuminated by a series of overhead LED high bay lights. A maze of wooden crates the size of coffins were scattered across the massive space, some stacked as high as the ceiling in a haphazard pattern.

The back wall of the warehouse was another wide corrugated pneumatic door, partially lifted just enough for a man to walk under. A boat was loosely moored to a cleat on the dock that extended into the Caribbean Sea. From his spot to the boat was about a hundred yards. If Bond emerged, Julian knew he could stop him before he made it to the boat. But the warehouse seemed empty. Where could Bond have disappeared to? Was he too late?

He couldn't afford to wait any longer.

Julian crossed in front of the car and took a step into the warehouse. The room was quiet except for the sound of the wind rushing through the room from the bay. Picking up his pace, Julian walked toward the center of the room.

The distinctive sound of guns cocking stopped him.

Four, maybe five gunmen surrounded him, hidden behind the crates. He knew the position of three of them, but the other one or two were further away. He couldn't get a read on their position.

"You should not be here. This is private property," a man called out from behind a crate. "You can leave alive, or you can leave dead. It's your choice."

Julian tightened his hold on the Beretta.

No way was he leaving without Ella's baby.

He listened for movement behind the crates, but all was quiet.

Dropping low, Julian spun his body in a one hundred eighty degree arc and pressed the trigger of the semi-automatic pistol. Two, four, six shots in quick succession before he hit the ground and rolled behind a stack of three crates.

Surprised howls of pain filled the warehouse as bodies crashed to the ground.

He'd taken out three of the targets, but not the man who'd spoken to him.

Julian peered around the crate.

"Go! Go! Go!" The man emerged, tall and thin, dressed in all black with a brown bandana tied around his head. Another man darted across the warehouse behind him as they both rushed toward the boat waiting at the back of the warehouse.

Irving Bond emerged from behind one of the crates, rushing toward the two men.

Julian stood and ran toward Bond.

A blaze of gunfire erupted, bullets whizzing through the air around him.

Julian dove toward a series of crates, taking cover. Thrusting an arm out from behind the crate, he pulled the trigger. Three shots and another body crash to the floor.

He'd shot four. But there was one gunman left.

Julian knew it was now or never.

Darting from his hiding place, he pressed his body against the gritty, cold concrete floor, as a bullet zipped past him almost taking off his ear. Julian didn't slow down, crawling closer to the back entrance.

Bond looked back at him. Their eyes locked. He could see fear in the man's eyes as he stepped onto the boat, clutching the baby close to his chest.

Julian scrambled to his feet, running as a flurry of gunshots erupted from the remaining lone gunman. Dropping to the ground, he rolled onto his back and shot in the direction of the bullets. A howl pierced the air as a body landed on the ground in a loud thump.

Flipping over, he heard the boat roar to life as the tall, thin man untied the spring lines securing the boat to the dock from the cleat.

Julian lunged through the rear door of the warehouse.

A sharp blow knocked the wind out of him as a man in an Adidas jogging suit slammed his leg into Julian's chest, sending his gun flying into the choppy waters of the sea. Stunned from the blow, Julian stumbled back as the boat sped away from the waterfront with Irving Bond and Ella's son on board.

The man crashed his fist into Julian's stomach, detonating like a bomb within his body. A sharp pain exploded in his head as the man slammed his elbow into the back of Julian's skull.

Dazed, Julian reached for the knife in his ankle holster as his body collapsed to the ground.

"Freeze! St. Basil P.D. Put your hands in the air," A voice rang through the warehouse.

Julian rolled over on his side, gripping his abdomen, as a dozen deputies raced into the building with their weapons raised.

Chapter Thirty-Nine

Headed toward the Marina Restaurant, Mena gripped the carved wooden box under her arm and forced herself to put one foot in front of the other. The island had been abuzz since Irving Bond stole Ella's baby from the hospital yesterday morning. After hearing the news, she'd waited in the conference room of the gallery for hours until she'd gotten the clearance to leave the grounds. Racing to Julian's boat, she'd found it empty.

She'd made a trip to his yacht this morning before work and this evening after he was absent from work ... again. She needed to show him what she'd found in Ella's box, but he wasn't around. He hadn't responded to any of her phone calls or texts either.

He was probably consumed with finding Irving. But worry seeped into Mena's mind.

The fear threatening to grip her heart was strange for Mena. She couldn't imagine that her feelings for Julian had grown so strong in such a short time, but they had. The passion between them was intense. She felt it every time she was near him, burning bright within and threatening to consume her. She had to admit that he was right about their connection. Whatever was building between them scared the crap out of her.

She needed to slow down, corral her raging feelings, and put things in perspective. Over the past three years, she'd reconstructed the way she handled relationships, careful to keep her emotions in check and avoid making hasty decisions. Julian had unraveled every strategy she'd put in place to avoid another failed relationship. She couldn't risk jumping into a situation with a man she barely knew. She wouldn't set herself up to be duped again.

Opening the door to the Marina Restaurant, Mena walked inside and asked the hostess for a table for one, something near the bay but inside. The place was sparse for a Wednesday night. She was grateful to avoid the typical noisy, rowdy crowds.

Following the hostess to a small table on the edge of the outdoor deck, Mena sat and ordered a diet soda before perusing the menu. She should know it by heart, as much as she ate there. Normally, she had goat stew, but she was in the mood for something different. Leaning back, Mena could barely make out Julian's boat docked in the last slip of the pier.

Where the hell was he?

The waiter came to her table and placed the diet soda in front of her. After ordering goat fritters and a Caesar salad, Mena felt her phone vibrate in her purse. Fumbling with the zipper, she thrust her hand inside and pulled out the device, glancing at the screen.

A wave of disappointment shot through her.

It wasn't Julian.

"Hello," Mena answered.

"Hi Mena, its Priscilla."

"Hi, what's going on?" Mena asked, surprised her boss was calling her after work.

"I wanted to let you know I had a very exciting conversation with Wangari Irungu about you. You've made it to the final round of candidates for the Nairobi African Art Fellowship. Congratulations!"

"Are you serious?" Mena asked. The conversation she'd had with Ms. Dumay and Ms. Irungu felt like a lifetime ago.

"With everything that happened to you last week, I asked Wangari if I could give you the good news myself. Your final interview with the Board is scheduled for this Friday at 2 p.m. I told Regina to clear your schedule so you won't be interrupted," Priscilla said.

"I don't know how to thank you." Mena absently checked her calendar and saw Regina had indeed cleared her day and placed the interview on the schedule. Mena waited for excitement to flood her body at the chance of getting the Fellowship she'd coveted since college, but it didn't come.

"No thanks necessary. You deserve this chance, and it's the least I could do, considering how you were attacked at my gallery. Don't get me wrong, I'd be sad to see you go. You are such an amazing conservator, one of the best I've ever worked with. But this is an amazing opportunity for your career. I could never stand in your way."

"Thank you, Priscilla," Mena said, trying to inject more enthusiasm into her tone.

"When you get this fellowship, don't forget about my little gallery and your humble beginnings. I'll be rooting for you," Priscilla said and ended the call.

Mena dropped the cell phone back into her purse and stared at the food as the waiter placed it on her table.

The phone call was unexpected.

She had forgotten about applying for the fellowship.

No doubt the opportunity was amazing. So, why didn't she feel more excited about making it to the final round? She knew she had a great chance of getting it, especially with Priscilla Dumay's connections and endorsement. She just couldn't muster up any enthusiasm—

"This seat taken?" The deep, baritone voice interrupted her thoughts.

Chapter Forty

Mena looked up and stared at Julian.

His face was weary. Dark circles under his eyes stole the sparkle from his irises. A beat up "CoCo Live in Concert" t-shirt covered his broad, muscular chest, and he wore dingy cargo pants.

"Where have you been?" Mena demanded. "I've been calling and texting you since yesterday. Did you hear about Irving Bond kidnapping Ella's baby?"

Julian slumped down into the wrought iron chair, dragging his hands down his face. "I know. Bond was at a warehouse last night with some PC-5 gangbangers. I tried to stop him from taking off with the baby in the boat, but I got attacked. Had to spend the night in the hospital. They released me an hour ago. I'm sorry for not calling you back."

Mena reached for his hand, lacing her fingers between his. She was shocked by what Julian had gone through over the past twenty-four hours, but she was relieved to see him alive and safe.

"Don't worry about that. Have you eaten?" Mena asked, noticing Julian eyeing her goat fritters.

"Hospital food is disgusting. I didn't touch that shit today," Julian said, as he plucked one of her goat fritters from the plate and popped it in his mouth.

Mena motioned for the waiter to come back to the table. She ordered a bowl of goat stew and two Felipe beers, then watched as Julian continued to ravage the food on her plate. She let him eat in silence for several minutes as she picked at her salad.

As Julian finished off the last fritter, Mena cleared her throat, then asked, "So, is Irving a suspect in Ella's murder?"

"Bond has an air-tight alibi, and so does that weirdo Quark," Julian said, then explained how the cops had turned their focus to the mysterious Bugs, whose real name they believed was Teo Juarez. He was the new prime suspect in the murder of Ella Sapphire.

Mena fought to keep up as Julian relayed information about text messages on the cell phone Ella had dropped in Mena's car. The texts varied from sexual flirtations to confirmation of forging art pieces to a series of blackmail threats for more money for forging the art. Bugs, the suspected owner of the cell phone, had sent a text to a mysterious third number requesting for Ella to be 'taken care of.' The cops weren't sure how Ella had gotten possession of Bugs' phone, but Julian suspected that Ella could have been trying to get the phone to the police to save her own life.

Amazed, Mena listened as Julian explained how he'd confirmed that the sender of the texts to Bugs' burner phone was Ella through an infiltration of the location data collected by apps on the sending number's phone. A visit to Quark had given them Ella's last known phone number, which matched the number that sent the hundreds of texts to the burner phone, confirming that they were indeed from Ella.

"So, Ella was forging art, and Bugs was selling the forged pieces. She kept demanding a bigger piece of the pie, and you think Bugs got fed up and decided to kill her?" Mena asked, trying to grasp the motive for Bugs killing Ella.

"That's the current theory. We also think Bugs is the father of Ella's baby, and he wants custody of his child without having to go through the proper channels. CPS has been issuing alerts to identify the father, but if Bugs killed Ella, he's not going to come forward and risk being connected to that crime," Julian said. "He has to know the cops have his DNA from the blood and skin they found under Ella's fingernails."

"How did Irving get entangled in all this? It doesn't make any sense," Mena said, rubbing her temples.

"It does if Bond found buyers for the fake art Bugs and Ella peddled and took a cut of the profits. Bugs could've blackmailed Bond to get the baby for him by threatening to reveal Bond's role in the scam to Dumay and the cops." Julian leaned back in his chair and took a long swallow of Felipe beer from the bottle. "This is all speculation, though. We won't be able to complete the puzzle until we can confirm that Bugs is Teo Juarez and locate where he is."

Mena's mind was reeling. She'd had no clue what she was getting into when she first asked Julian to help her get closure on the tragedy with Ella. The truth was more complicated than she could've imagined. She was hit hard by the irony of being in the wrong place at the wrong time. One minute earlier or later, and she could have avoided being entangled in Ella's mess. But then she wouldn't have connected with Julian, either.

Mena took a sip of her Felipe beer, craving something stronger at the moment. "I'm not surprised you risked your life to rescue Ella's baby. I almost forgot—"

Mena reached down to grab the carved wooden box from the floor and placed it on the table. "I figured out how to get Ella's box open. A series of small wooden pegs were used to lock it. Maybe there's something in here that could help?"

Julian's face lit up. "I'd forgotten all about Ella's box."

"It's been at my condo since the day Lucy gave it to us," Mena said.

"Did you look inside?" Julian asked. He wiped his fingers, then reached for the box.

Mena nodded. "There's a laptop. The battery was dead, so I charged it. But it's password protected. I couldn't see what was on it. There was also a small remote control with tiny numbered buttons on the front. Could be some type of garage door opener or a remote for a home security system. There's no logo or anything on it."

Julian held the remote to the light, peering at it curiously, before placing it on the table. He grabbed the laptop and sat it next to the plates of food.

"Let's see if I can get past Ella's password," Julian said. He turned the computer on and waited for the login screen to appear. As Julian typed onto the keyboard, Mena saw a black screen appear and a series of lines of text emerging, then disappearing on the screen.

In a matter of minutes, the desktop appeared.

"Haven't met a civilian laptop I can't get into yet," Julian said, giving Mena a wink.

"Impressive," Mena said. Julian turned the screen toward Mena to give her a better view.

Dozens of file folders cluttered the desktop. Julian clicked and opened a few. They scoured through various Photoshop files of Ella's art, some excel files with crude budgets and Word files with poetry, resumes, and query letters to galleries.

An hour passed, and they hadn't come across anything out of the ordinary.

"Should we keep checking all the files?" Mena asked. She was starting to believe this search of the haystack wasn't going to uncover any needles.

"This folder is unusual. Ella has named each folder except this one, which is still called Untitled. Let's see what's inside," Julian said, then double-clicked the folder.

The folder contained over a hundred MPEG files, each named with a single date and some with "part 1" or "part 2" at the end.

"Those are video files," Mena said.

"The last file was dated about eight months ago." Julian double-clicked on the file, and the video filled the screen. Naked, Ella walked across the view of the camera. Seductively leaning over the mattress, she eased onto the bed, rubbing her breasts as she purred and said, "Get over here, Bugs."

A fully clothed man entered the room from the right side of the camera. Ella demanded that he strip for her, repeating "Dance for me, Bugs" as she continued to caress and finger her body in intimate places. Bugs hastily discarded his clothes, moving his body in awkward gyrating dance moves. As his clothes fell to the floor, he reached over to pick them up, filling the screen with his wide, pale ass. He turned and threw the clothes toward the camera.

Mena gasped.

"Well, I'll be damned," Julian said as he paused the video on the man's face filling the screen.

Chapter Forty-One

"Irving Bond is Bugs," Kendrick repeated into the phone. "I'm in possession of sex tapes that clearly show him being called by that name."

Julian sat on top of the two-drawer file cabinet in Kendrick's office at the St. Basil Police Station as the detective continued to talk on the phone. The call with the judge was going well. In a matter of minutes, Julian expected Kendrick to announce that the warrant had been approved to search Irving Bond's possessions at his home and at the Genesis Gallery.

He'd reluctantly abandoned Mena at the restaurant last night after discovering that Irving Bond was Bugs. She'd been understanding, recognizing the importance of getting the evidence in the hands of the police.

"Got it," Kendrick said, placing the phone in its cradle, a smile spreading across his face. "Now, I need to send a copy of the warrant to the officers I dispatched to Bond's home and to the gallery an hour ago."

Kendrick leaned over his keyboard, typing frantically.

Julian ran a hand through his hair, a heaviness settling in his stomach. He wasn't as certain as Kendrick that the case had been solved. Something about Irving Bond orchestrating Ella's death didn't quite fit.

With one final tap on the keyboard, Kendrick cleared his throat. "Why don't you look happier? If it wasn't for you, we wouldn't have uncovered Ella's laptop or the video files that prove she and Bond were involved in a multi-country art scam."

Julian had pulled an all-nighter helping Kendrick pour through the files on Ella's laptop. They'd uncovered concrete evidence that the PC-5 helped Irving Bond steal pieces from museums and replace them with fakes created by Ella. She had meticulous records of how they sold the real art on the black market to private collectors. There was enough evidence on Ella's laptop to put Bond in jail for years. But it still didn't explain why the skin and blood under Ella's nails belonged to Teo Juarez. Who was he and how was he connected to the scam Irving and Ella had going with the PC-5?

Kendrick stepped from behind his desk and walked closer to Julian. "Calls are already coming in from the museums targeted by the gang in other countries. They're searching for any fakes in their gallery, and a couple have already identified them. All ethnographic art pieces. We got what we've been looking for."

"No, we don't. Bond has an alibi for the night Ella was killed. We don't have anything to connect him to Ella's death. You can lock him up for the art scam, but at this point, Ella's murder is still unsolved," Julian said.

"I have the text he sent from the burner phone with the picture of Ella. That's enough for probable cause. It clearly identified her as the woman he wanted the receiver to 'take care of' and we have tons of proof on the cell phone that Ella was blackmailing him," Kendrick said.

"Yeah, but where's the definitive proof that the burner phone belonged to Bond? The fact that texts on the phone refer to Bugs, like Ella called him on the video may not be enough to make that stick. Plus, that text was sent months ago. Why was Ella kept alive all that time?" Julian asked, bothered by the timeline of events.

"Maybe Bond found out Ella was pregnant with his baby. He wanted the child but not her because she was blackmailing him. As soon as the baby was born, he gave the word to take Ella out," Kendrick said.

"So, Bond's a family man now?" Julian scoffed. "How could Bond have known Ella was going to give birth that night and send a hitman after her if he was fucking Alexandra Vincent at the Seafoam Motel at the time it all went down?"

Kendrick leaned back against his desk, scratching his head absently. "I don't have an answer for that ... yet. That's what the warrant is going to help with. We'll go through every aspect of Irving Bond's life until we find the connection to Ella's murder. I promise you that."

"If it's one thing I've learned, you do keep your promises," Julian said, reflecting on the news reports of the PC-5 shoot out at the waterfront. "Thanks for keeping my name out of the press this time."

"We didn't want outrage spreading across the island if the public found out the missing baby everybody is praying for was at the scene of a shootout. Plus, it helped that the five gang members you mowed down all survived their injuries," Kendrick said.

After Julian's first year as a SEAL, he'd stopped keeping track of the number of his confirmed kills. The Navy had other ideas, delivering commendations when he reached new milestones. In his head, he justified his actions by focusing on the fact that he was ridding the world of terrorists and criminals. Two nights ago, he hadn't thought twice about adding five PC-5 gang members to the list. But when he'd had to tell Mena about what went down, everything had changed for him. His heart was reminded that every life he took was a human being with parents or siblings or spouses or children who mourned their loss. He was relieved that the gang members hadn't been taken out by his actions. He'd only wanted to save the baby, not play judge and executioner to the ones involved in the kidnapping.

Kendrick continued, "None of us on the force could have survived the mayhem at the warehouse. What you did was miraculous, and you almost saved Ella's baby, too."

"Almost doesn't count," Julian said, then glanced at his cell phone vibrating in his hand. A text from Dawn. She wanted to see him. Now.

Chapter Forty-Two

"Where's your boyfriend been hiding lately?" Omar asked, walking next to Mena as they approached Priscilla Dumay's office.

"That's what you want to know right now? Not why the cops were swarming around Irving's office this morning or why we've been summoned by Priscilla?" Mena asked. She regretted spilling the details about her growing closeness to Julian over lunch with her two dear friends. Both Omar and Regina had instantly announced that she and Julian were a couple, fast-tracking their budding attraction into a full-blown committed relationship. "Like I told you, we are exploring things and living in the moment. No strings and no attachments."

"Whatever, boo. I can tell you're falling hard for that man," Omar said, placing an arm around Mena's shoulders. "As for the Dragon Lady, I have no clue why she wants to see us."

"Don't call her that. You think it has something to do with the Kuypers refund?" Mena asked. Regina wasn't at her desk as they entered the first set of doors leading to the seating area outside of Dumay's office.

"Could be. I couldn't find anything in my manual invoices. I had that nerd in accounting go through the sales files, and the Kuypers weren't in the system as a buyer of anything from the gallery in the past," Omar said.

"So strange," Mena said.

"And don't think I didn't notice you avoiding my question about Julian. Where the hell has he been?"

"Dealing with some medical issues from his gunshot wound," Mena said, adopting the lie that Julian had been giving to Adam Russell when he'd bailed on work each day this week. The gallery employees had been relieved that Julian survived Ella's break-in with just a flesh wound. None of them knew Mena had been held hostage that night. Priscilla had kept her word, keeping that part private.

Omar held open the second set of double doors for Mena. As she walked inside the office, the frigid air caused goosebumps to stand on her skin.

Priscilla sat still, her mouth twisted into an ugly grimace, unlike the normal, benign smile she usually wore. Adam Russell stood next to her, arms crossed over his chest. Priscilla motioned for them to come forward and take a seat.

Speaking slowly, she began, "Irving Bond committed the ultimate betrayal by daring to use my gallery as a haven for his side hustle art scam."

Priscilla's hands were clenched, revealing white knuckles. "After everything I did for that bastard, he dares to do this to me. Putting my reputation on the line for his greed."

Mena and Omar exchanged confused stares. What was Priscilla talking about? "I'm sorry, Priscilla. What art scam was Irving involved in?"

"And does it have anything to do with why he stole that innocent little baby from the hospital?" Omar asked.

"The police were here this morning with a warrant to search Irving's office because they have uncovered a mountain of evidence that he was involved in stealing art from museums and replacing the pieces with fakes. Then he'd sell the real art on the black market," Adam interjected.

Priscilla took a deep breath. "The detective provided me with a list of items owned by the gallery that they believe are forged. Apparently, whoever Bond was working with kept meticulous records on each piece they stole, forged, and resold on the black market. I will need both of you to work quickly and confidentially to reassess every piece in our inventory to confirm the listing from the police and identify if there are any other fakes. Tell no one about what you are doing, not even Regina. That sonofabitch used his merry band of forgers to steal from me and trust me, he will regret it."

Mena's eyes grew wide as she thought back on the Sinasso sculpture that

Irving had pressured her into evaluating the night of the gallery gala. The same night Irving had been in the conservator workshop with Uma Fischer. Had the Sinasso been one of the fakes he was trying to pass off as real? Had he used Mena to determine if the forgery could fool others?

Omar asked, "Who was working with him to forge the art?"

Mena knew exactly who Irving used—Ella Sapphire.

"We won't get into that information as it's part of an open police investigation." Adam's dismissal was stern. "As Ms. Dumay has said, the main priority is to ensure that Irving didn't scam the Genesis Gallery."

Omar took the listing from Priscilla, scanning the contents. "Damn. The Sinasso is on the list. So is the Gabonese mask I'd asked you to take another look at, Mena."

"That reminds me. Mena, I need you to check anything your former assistant, Uma Fischer, cleared for display in the gallery. I have reason to believe that little bitch was signing off on Irving's fakes," Priscilla said.

Mena nodded, her head spinning. Had Uma lied to her? Had she really been giving Irving back money that he paid her to authenticate fakes for display at the gallery?

"What about the Kuypers? You think they figured out their purchase was a fake and that's why they wanted a refund?" Omar asked.

Priscilla waived a hand dismissively. "No, that has nothing to do with Bond. I was brokering a sell for the Kuypers with another gallery, but the shipment has been delayed. I'm taking care of fixing that issue. I need the two of you to work quickly so we can inform the police about any additional forgeries you find."

"We can do that. Mena and I will get right on it," Omar said.

"Thank you, I knew I could count on you both," Priscilla said.

As they exited Dumay's office, Omar erupted into laughter. "Can you believe this shit?"

"I'm stunned. How can you laugh at a time like this?" Mena said.

"Because I warned Prissy over and over that Irving wasn't the golden boy he pretended to be. She dismissed me every time, thinking I was jealous of him. Which I was. She was always overlooking his mediocre efforts at running the gallery, even though I tried to warn her. Look who she needs now!" Omar said.

Mena frowned. "Where should we start?"

"Irving's secret closet," Omar said, heading through the open seating area adorned with various sculptures.

Mena followed closely behind him. "Secret closet?"

Omar pushed the door open, walked around Irving's desk and headed toward a row of bookshelves along the back wall.

Omar pulled a small remote out of his pocket that looked strangely familiar to Mena. Where had she seen that before?

"The door is hidden in the bookshelf. It's a fire-resistant room where art can be stored to protect against any element — fire, rain, wind. Prissy wanted it this way in case we ever needed to protect the most important art pieces from a sudden threat. I use mine to keep expensive pieces that I've recently sold or purchased. When the cops were here, I didn't remember to tell them about the space. I'm guessing Irving didn't either, or they would have asked to search mine. He could have hidden evidence of his crimes in here," Omar said.

"So that remote will open the door?" Mena asked.

"With the right code. I happen to know that Irving's is 4-8-6-6," Omar said as he punched the tiny buttons on the remote. A panel of the wall popped open.

Mena pulled the door open wider and reached her hand in to flip the light switch. Inside the closet was a utility stairwell with concrete stairs descending down.

"Does your storage closet look like this?" Mena asked.

"I feel like the Wizard of Oz," Omar said, laughing. "You're getting a glimpse behind the curtain. We have a basement where excess inventory is stored. You've only seen the tip of the iceberg of the amount of art Dumay owns. There's hundreds of pieces down there, but nothing that she wants going in rotation in the gallery exhibits. Those pieces we keep in the storage buildings surrounding the courtyard."

"So, we need to look down there?" Mena asked.

"Hell no. Nobody goes down there. I have a storage chest on the landing in my closet. I figured Irving had the same but looks like he doesn't. I was sure we'd find something incriminating in here," Omar said.

Mena's heart pounded in her chest. Julian and the police still didn't know where Bond had disappeared to with the baby. Could he be hiding in the basement of the gallery? Bond would know that no one went down there anymore. It could be an easy hiding place for him, especially since the entrance to the stairwell was undetectable from inside his office.

"Start pulling the pieces from the police listing off the gallery floor," Mena instructed Omar. "I'm going to head to the workshop to prep my equipment for the analysis."

But before she did, there was one person she needed to call.

Chapter Forty-Three

Julian reached into his pocket, pulled out the remote, and handed it to Mena.

"You remember the code, right?" He'd been stunned to hear about a hidden basement under the main gallery building. None of the original floorplans he'd reviewed with Kendrick that afternoon had indicated that the basement existed, yet Mena had seen the stairwell to the lower level used for storage when she and Omar were searching the secret closet for art forged by Bond.

Kendrick was annoyed that Dumay hadn't been more forthcoming with the information when he and his officers had come to search the gallery after Ella's break-in, Ella's murder and Bond's kidnapping of Ella's baby. The detective had made arrangements for a fourth visit to the gallery in the morning to search the basement, but Julian was worried. Would it be too late?

Julian had to see if Bond was in the gallery basement tonight. After talking to Dawn this afternoon, he was more determined to find Ella's baby. Dawn was sinking further into depression, mired by the compounding grief of her sister's death and the missing baby. He had to find a way to ease her pain. Returning Ella's baby to Dawn was the only way to do that.

The only issue was Mena. He'd made a mistake allowing her to tag along with him to break into the gallery in the middle of the night. He should have forced her to give him the code to the remote and then wait for him at her condo where she would have been safer. But he liked the fact that she was with him, supporting his efforts to find Ella's son.

"4-8-6-6," Mena said, entering the code into the remote. Julian pulled the bookshelf forward and stepped into the stairwell with Mena close behind him. They took the steps down to the basement level, where an oversized steel door led to the storage rooms. Slowly pulling the door open, Julian peered down the dark, narrow hallway that stretched ahead. A single light cast a faint glow on the dreary gray walls covered with dust and cobwebs. About ten feet away, there was another hallway perpendicular to the one they stood in, but Julian couldn't see around the corner to where it led. Judging from their location and the narrow width of the corridor, he guessed that the passage formed a U-shaped perimeter around a massive room in the center. But he saw no door, no way to enter whatever was in the middle of the building on this level.

Holding Mena's hand tight, they walked along the edge of the wall, careful not to make any sound. Darkness shrouded them. A light shone at the end of the passageway. After seconds that felt like hours, Julian neared the corner. Unease crawled along his skin as he looked back at Mena. The dim yellow light tucked in the corner shone down on the top of her hoodie, casting a shadow that obscured her face from view.

Releasing Mena's hand, he took the last few steps to the edge, then stopped as words floated through the air. Was that Bond? Had Mena been right? Had Bond been down in the basement hiding out all this time?

"Yes, things are fine," said the male voice, strong and confident. "No complications at all."

There was a pause, then the footsteps drew nearer to the hallway where Julian stood still. Julian thought about grabbing his gun but decided to wait. If the baby was nearby, he couldn't take a chance of the child getting caught in the crossfire if there was any gunplay. He could subdue Bond without using a weapon and reduce the chance of the baby getting hurt.

"Please don't remind me," the man said and sighed heavily.

Julian hadn't spoken to Irving Bond much, but he knew the voice wasn't that of the missing director. Who was the man and why was he down in the basement at this hour?

"Ella Sapphire could have caused a lot of problems for us, but thankfully she's been eliminated. I will let you know when I'm leaving," the male voice said.

Heat rushed up the back of Julian's neck as his muscles tensed. Whoever the man was, he knew Ella and was happy she'd been killed. What was going on down here? Julian placed a hand over his gun and waited.

Quiet settled in the hallway as the man ended his call. Julian paused, trying to gauge which direction the man might head. As the footsteps grew distant, Julian heard Mena take a deep, shaky breath.

Julian glanced around the corner.

The hallway was empty.

Along the wall to the right was a counter where a single computer rested. There was an opening next to the counter, some type of room without a door, then the wall continued until the next corner, leading to what Julian could only guess was another hallway.

"Go back to the stairwell and wait for me," Julian said to Mena, then sprinted to the computer. A generic screensaver of moving boxes flashed across the monitor. Next to the computer were dozens of folders stacked in slanted wire file holders on the desk. Julian took out his cell phone and snapped a picture. He picked up a few of the files and read the labels: 0112FOX, 0325GARDNER and 1026SAPPHIRE. Julian stared at the last file, dropping the others on the table. The name couldn't be a coincidence.

Opening the 1026SAPPHIRE folder, Julian thumbed through the contents —a purchase order for "Asset" with a value of $250,000 was stamped as PAID in large red letters. Behind the purchase order was a letter with wire transfer information signed by Irving Bond and addressed to Y. Kuypers. Stapled to the top corner of the wire transfer letter was a magenta colored mail receipt confirmation label from Palmchat Postal indicating a letter sent had been successfully received.

What the hell could this be?

A rush of wind moved through the air as he felt a hand touch his back.

Turning he dropped the file and ripped the Beretta from his waistband, pointing the gun, his finger inching toward the trigger.

A squeal pierced the air, as Julian recognized Mena.

Lowering the gun, he pressed his free hand against her mouth, stifling the sound. Her eyes stared back at him, wide with terror.

Shit!

What was she doing back here? Releasing his hand from her mouth, he could see her body shaking as she mouthed the words, "Somebody is coming down the hallway."

Grabbing her, he tucked the gun back into his waistband and held her close as he looked for a place to hide. A few feet up the hall from the counter was the dark, door-less room.

Darting inside, Julian pressed his body against Mena's and waited. The hum of a printer filled his ears as he stared at the only lights in the room, the small LED square on the front of the machine.

"Quentin, get the fuck out here," a rough voice demanded.

Julian recognized Zak Webber's voice.

A dark-skinned man, tall and bald, dressed in black scrubs passed by the opening, oblivious to Julian and Mena hiding inside.

"Keep your voice down," Quentin demanded. The voice was the same Julian had heard earlier.

"Whatever," Zak said, his tone laced with the familiar defiant bravado Julian had grown used to hearing from the brash security guard.

"Why are you here?" Quentin asked.

"Did you use Bond's remote tonight to get down here?" Zak asked.

Julian fingered the remote in his hand. The device must have been on a certain frequency that alerted Zak Webber. But why? What was down here and why did Zak sound concerned?

"Of course not," Quentin responded. "Did Bond show up? Is he here?"

Julian detected the panic in Quentin's voice. Both men were worried about Bond being on the premises, which meant neither one of them had seen Bond yet. Bond and the baby were not down in the basement.

Zak said, "It appears so. Initiate Operation X. Get the rest of the assets prepped. I'll have trucks ready for transport in an hour."

"Operation X will take hours to complete. We can't get it done before the gallery opens," Quentin complained.

"You have one hour, Quentin," Zak said. "Make it happen."

Zak's heavy footsteps became fainter as Quentin passed the opening, heading around the corner as a flash of light nearly blinded Julian.

Grabbing at the light, Julian ripped the cell phone from Mena's hand, hoping that Quentin hadn't noticed.

Julian frowned at Mena then looked down at her cell phone screen.

A crystal clear picture of Quentin stared back at him.

Chapter Forty-Four

"Why did you do that?" Julian growled, his voice low as he pushed Mena further back into the room and pinned her body against the wall. The last thing he needed was for Quentin to have noticed the flash from the cell phone and decide to investigate. Julian wasn't in the mood to hurt anyone tonight, especially not in front of Mena.

"I don't know," Mena started, then stopped. "I was trying to help—"

"Don't," Julian said, softening his tone. Mena's body quivered against his, and he knew instinctively that she was afraid. Ignoring the danger he'd led her into was a mistake he never should have made. At that moment, he knew he'd sacrifice anything and everything to protect her.

Taking a step back, Julian glanced over his shoulder, pausing to listen for any sound. The basement was quiet except for the low hum emanating from the printer.

"I'm getting you out of here," Julian said, pulling the hoodie down to cover more of her beautiful face. Operation X was scheduled for one hour from now, but he and Mena wouldn't be around to witness it. A door slam echoed along the hallway. Julian turned and took a step toward the opening, pushing Mena behind him.

The sound came from the right of the printer room.

Mena's hands clutched the back of his sweatshirt. Grabbing the Beretta,

Julian paused and hoped he wouldn't have to shoot his way out of the basement. The sound of wheels rolling on the cracked linoleum floor and cabinets opening and closing persisted for the next few minutes.

Julian focused on the beating of his heart, slow and calm. His breathing was steady and focused. He'd never been one to get an adrenaline spike right before the critical action of a mission. His body regressed and slowed, his senses heightened as his body instinctively shifted into the ideal state to fight or defend.

A door opened and then closed, and the hallway was eerily quiet again. Taking a chance, Julian peered around the corner. There was no sign of Quentin. A series of doors lined the right side of the wall. He counted four, but there could be more. What was behind those doors, hidden within the walls of the bowels of the gallery? Why were Zak and Quentin worried about Bond coming back? What about the file he'd found with Ella's last name on the label? And what was Operation X?

"Are we trapped down here?" Mena whispered from behind him.

Julian turned to Mena and gave her what he hoped was a reassuring smile.

"We're leaving ... now. I want you to run as fast as you can back to the stairwell," Julian said. "Don't worry about making sounds and don't worry about me. Just get to the stairwell. Wait for me there, do you understand?"

Mena nodded. She looked confident and brave, despite the wave of tremors that shuddered through her body.

"But what if the Quentin guy comes back or Zak Webber is waiting in the stairs or ..." Mena stammered.

"Look at me," Julian said, his hands cradling Mena's face. "This will not be a repeat of what happened the night Ella took you hostage. I'm going to get you out of here safe and sound. I promise."

Mena placed her hands over his, the smoothness of her touch drawing him closer. Julian kissed her lips softly, then whispered, "Go."

Mena sprinted out of the printer room and turned left, heading down the hallway. Julian released and reloaded the magazine in his gun, then took off behind her. Every few seconds, he peeked over his shoulder to make sure no one was following them. By his estimation, Quentin was too busy securing the assets to pay attention to any sounds in the hallway.

Rounding the corner, Mena increased her speed and Julian followed suit, overtaking her before they reached the door of the stairwell. Gun poised to shoot first and ask questions later, Julian pushed the door open.

Relief flooded through him at the empty stairwell.

Gripping Mena's hand, they took the stairs two at a time until they reached the top. Mena pressed against the paneled door.

The door didn't budge.

"You think we need to enter the code again?" Mena asked, her breathing heavy as she paced back and forth.

"That's not an option," Julian responded. Entering the code would alert Zak Webber, and they'd surely get caught this time. Shooting the door open would be too noisy. Julian glanced at his watch. About forty-five minutes until Zak would be back to transport Quentin and the assets for Operation X. He had to come up with a way to get out of the stairwell before that happened.

Running his fingers along the edge of the door, Julian felt for something, anything that would open it—a latch or emergency release. Nothing. Pressing his back against the door, it was heavy and strong. No way could he muscle it open.

"Now what?" Mena asked, her pacing continued.

"I made you a promise, didn't I?" Julian asked.

"You did," Mena responded. "But this isn't looking too good."

"I need you to trust me—"

"There's no one that I trust more than you, Julian," Mena responded.

Julian was struck by the conviction and confidence in her words, moved by the utter certainty of her faith in him.

"I'm distracting you. I'm going to sit here and let you think. I know you'll come up with something," Mena said, then sat on the top step.

If only it were that easy. A beautiful, intelligent woman putting her trust in a rusty ex-Navy SEAL who'd led her into a dangerous situation. What a mess. Julian took a step away from the door and felt a tug at his ankle.

His knife.

Ripping the blade from its holster, Julian inserted it into the thin gap to the left of the door. As the steel slid down, it hit an obstruction. Julian placed more pressure on the blade, forcing it downward.

The door released, revealing a small crack.

Mena turned, her face illuminated in the most stunning smile he'd ever seen.

Guess he wasn't too rusty after all.

Mena stood and wrapped her arms around Julian's neck, delighting him with a passionate kiss.

"I knew you could do it," Mena whispered into his neck as she hugged him.

"Let's get out of here," Julian said, pushing the door open.

"I think you may want this," Mena said. Reaching inside her sweatshirt, she pulled out a file folder. "I saw you staring at it before you held a gun to my face. Figured it was important."

Julian took the file out of Mena's hand and glanced at the label.

1026SAPPHIRE

Chapter Forty-Five

Stretching her arms across the soft bamboo sheets, Mena rolled over to her side and refused to open her eyes. Not yet. She wasn't ready to wake up. The gentle sway of the boat lulled her into a dream-like state. Last night had been surreal. Working with Julian to figure out if Irving was hiding in the basement of the Genesis Gallery was something she'd never expected she would do.

Her plan had been to pass along the information about the basement and leave it to him and the cops to find out what, if anything, was going on down there. But when she'd seen his soulful brown eyes staring back at her, she'd wanted nothing more than to help him. She forced him to take her along or forgo finding out the code that would give him access.

What the hell was going on with her? One minute she was disciplined and cautious in matters of the heart and the next, she was running side by side with Julian trying to hunt down a baby kidnapper. She'd been nervous and tense, but never afraid. And she knew why. Julian would never let anything bad happen to her. He'd told her as much, but she hadn't needed to hear the words. She knew it was true in her heart.

But was she ready for this? A relationship with a reclusive ex-Navy SEAL who'd done something to screw up his military career. Something that involved his best friend, Broman. She'd watched him work day and night trying to make amends to Dawn for the devastating mistake he'd made in the past. But what could he have done? And how much longer could she be with him without knowing?

She'd been fooled by a man with a past before. Her ex-husband, the debonair Dr. Michael Marsh, intruded into her mind. Michael had been sophisticated and sweet with romantic gestures that turned out to be lies. She'd been swept away by a man who'd been too good to be true. Could she be making the same mistake with Julian? Was the mistake he made in the past something that could change the way she saw him? Stop her from wanting to be with him?

The old-fashioned clock ring tone pierced the air.

Saved by the bell.

Mena opened her eyes and glanced at the small nightstand next to Julian's California king-sized bed. Rolling over twice, she pulled the phone toward her with the tips of her fingers.

A number she didn't recognize. International 254 and 020 area code.

Tucking her hair behind her ears, she answered the line.

Anxiety flooded her body as the board members for the Nairobi African Art Fellowship greeted her.

Mena shook involuntarily. She'd forgotten about the interview today. She glanced at the clock on the side wall. Two p.m. The exact time Priscilla had told her the interview had been scheduled. Mena was unprepared. She'd been too busy playing cops and robbers with Julian over the past two days. How could she have forgotten?

Mena bolted up from the bed and closed the bedroom door. Gathering her thoughts, she withstood an hour of intense questions and commentary from each board member until they seemed satisfied that they understood her motivation for seeking the fellowship, her background in restoring art and laser conservation techniques and how she and the art world would benefit from the exclusive study supported by the fellowship.

Ending the call, Mena collapsed on the bed and fought tears. She had to readjust her priorities. She couldn't let her career get derailed by Julian or the madness surrounding the murder of Ella or Irving kidnapping Ella's newborn son. Her calling wasn't law enforcement, it was the preservation of art to enhance the cultural enrichment of current and future generations.

A soft knock on the bedroom door startled Mena.

"Come in," Mena called out, wiping away a single tear.

"Sounded like you were on a business call," Julian said, peeking his head in the door. "Everything okay."

Mena rubbed her hands over her eyes, then took a deep breath. "I hope so."

In seconds, Julian was laying next to her, his hands lazily stroking her hair.

"Anything you want to talk about? Not sure I could help, but I'm a pretty good listener," Julian said, his eyes filled with concern.

She wondered why he was asking. Could he tell she was upset? She couldn't open up to him about the fellowship, not when she'd most likely blown any chance of getting the prestigious appointment. What would be the point in discussing it?

"Nope, I'm good. Just got caught off guard. But I handled everything fine," Mena lied. Turning toward him, her heart caught at the intense scrutiny in his eyes. The emotions playing underneath the surface couldn't be denied. His feelings for her were deeper than she'd acknowledged or was even ready for. She wasn't willing to think about her feelings for him, feelings unlike she'd experienced with anyone before.

"Okay, let's get some food in you," Julian said, standing. He grabbed her hands and pulled her up gently, then wrapped her in his arms.

Mena stood still, enjoying the strength and comfort of his embrace. His lips brushed the top of her head as he whispered, "You know, there's nothing I wouldn't do for you. But I can't guess what you need. You'd have to tell me."

Pulling away, she stared at him and pushed all of the distress of forgetting about the interview and confusion on whether she should or shouldn't pursue a relationship with him to the deep recesses of her mind.

Live in the moment.

Chapter Forty-Six

Walking next to Julian, Mena exited the interior cabin and was greeted by the glorious Caribbean sun shining brightly in a deep blue sky filled with popcorn clouds. She felt more carefree than the tourists milling about the island thankful for another perfect day in paradise.

Mena scooted onto the bench seat as Julian sat a plate of goat tenders and French fries in front of her. Taking a bite, Mena savored the smoky flavor of the meat, realizing she was ravenous.

"Any progress on figuring out who Quentin is? What his relationship is to the gallery?" Mena asked, squeezing ketchup onto her fries.

Julian was quiet.

"Julian ..." Mena looked up. She couldn't read his expression.

"I'm grateful for everything you've done to help me try to find Bond and Ella's baby, but you need to get back to your real life. You don't need to be involved in this anymore," Julian said.

Mena's heart pounded in her chest. Was he giving her what she wanted that easily without her having to ask? Was that what she truly wanted? Now that the offer was on the table, she wasn't sure she wanted to accept it.

"I guess I'm a pretty lousy partner. Nothing close to what you're used to from the SEAL teams," Mena said, trying to make light of him pushing her away. She was on the verge of tears, and she couldn't understand why. Being with Julian made her feel too much.

"Taking you with me to hunt down Bond was wrong. You could've gotten hurt. I won't put you in a situation like that again," Julian said.

"I'm probably more of a distraction than a help, anyway," Mena acknowledged, still conflicted about losing another chance to be around Julian. His commitment to finding Ella's baby and proving that Bond murdered her was all consuming. Would he make time for her?

"A little bit," Julian said. "I'd much prefer you to distract me in other ways."

Mena laughed and winked at Julian. "I could think of some naughty ways to distract you."

Julian's eyes danced with passion as he stood. Sweeping the plates to the side of the table, he leaned over and brushed his lips against hers. Mena delighted in the ticklish sensation of his stubble as his tongue entered her mouth, scorching her with the intensity of his passion. Without breaking the kiss, she maneuvered her body from the bench seat, stood and wrapped her arms around Julian's neck.

His hands stroked her thighs as he lifted her in the air. Wrapping her legs around his waist, she could feel his body respond to hers, throbbing with anticipation. Mena ran her fingers along his short cropped hair, pressing herself against him with gyrating slow motions. Julian stepped back toward the cabin.

"Ahem, ahem."

Mena heard a male voice from behind, shattering the intense moment. Damn it! Whoever was on Julian's boat had the worst timing.

Opening her eyes, she looked into Julian's playful brown eyes staring back at her. His hands were still cupping her butt as he held her upright.

Giving her a last quick peck on the lips, Julian said, "Raincheck?"

Mena nodded as he released her. She slid down Julian's body, noticing that his erection hadn't dissipated. Taking a glimpse over her shoulder, she saw Detective Caillouet standing near the railing looking out toward the bay to give them some privacy.

Mena grabbed her plate of food and stepped inside the cabin as Julian closed the sliding glass door and walked over to the detective. She should go home to her condo and take a shower, but her curiosity got the best of her.

What had Julian found out about the basement of the Gallery, and why was the detective here?

Sliding the door open, the voices of the detective and Julian were clearly audible.

"Sorry, my friend," The detective said.

Julian shrugged. "Couldn't be avoided. We can't waste any time with Bond still on the loose with Ella's baby."

The detective nodded, then punched Julian in the arm. "Looks like things are progressing nicely with you and the lovely Ms. Nix. I'm happy for you."

"She is the most," Julian paused, as if searching for the right word, then continued "phenomenal surprise in my life. You know, Broman told me a long time ago that he knew Dawn was the one because she made him feel alive. He said I'd know it when I felt it."

"And Mena makes you feel alive?" the detective asked.

"More alive than I ever felt before. She made me stop wanting to get back the life I used to have. I mean, I still wish I could erase the mistakes I made, but I wouldn't give up this time I've spent with her for anything," Julian said.

"I want some of that," the detective said, clapping a hand on Julian's shoulder.

Mena pressed her body against the side wall, her heart pounding. She couldn't agree with the detective more. She felt guilty for eavesdropping on Julian's private thoughts, but she couldn't help but feel giddy about his unabashed display of affection toward her to his close friend. Maybe she'd been freaking out for nothing. Maybe Julian was worth taking the risk again.

Chapter Forty-Seven

"Explain to me why you and Mena broke into the gallery last night," Kendrick said, his voice drowned out by the strong wind blowing across Crescent Moon Bay. Thick popcorn clouds covered the sun, giving the marina a brief respite from the strong heat of the Caribbean afternoon.

"I thought Bond could be hiding out there with the baby. Think about it. A secret basement most people didn't know existed. Perfect hiding place for that bastard," Julian said, rubbing his temples.

"But instead you found Zak Webber and a man Zak called 'Quentin,'" Kendrick said, pulling his phone from his pocket.

Julian glanced at the photo on Kendrick's phone from the text message Julian had sent him this morning.

"Quentin knew Ella. He was talking to someone on the phone, and he said Ella was a threat that could have caused a lot of problems for them. But he was happy she'd been eliminated," Julian said.

"Who do you think he was talking to?" Kendrick asked, scribbling on his small notepad.

"Hell, I don't know. Maybe Teo Juarez?"

"Really?" Kendrick looked up.

"It's a guess but, it's the only thing that makes sense to me," Julian said, walking toward the railing of his boat. He glanced over at the tourists scurrying into the luxury shops lining the marina. "Zak knew Bond's remote was used to access the floor—"

"How could Bond's remote access the floor if he wasn't there?"

Knowing he'd withheld too much, Julian decided it was time to come clean with Kendrick. "There was something else in Ella's box other than the laptop. A small remote that I believe belonged to Bond. That's how Mena and I were able to open the secret door that led to the basement. I think Zak was alerted when we activated the remote."

"Why didn't you tell me about the remote? Anything else in Ella's box that I should know about?" Kendrick threw his hands in the air.

"When I found all those files on Ella's laptop, I didn't think the remote was important. It wasn't until Mena told me about an identical remote that Omar had, which opened the door in Bond's office, that we pieced it together," Julian said.

"Ok, so you used the remote to go down into the basement. Zak comes down and talks to Quentin and then what?" Kendrick asked.

Julian explained how Zak and Quentin freaked out about Bond's remote being used and then Zak demanded that Quentin initiate something called Operation X. "My guess is that it's an emergency protocol to protect the artwork in the gallery from some disaster. This wasn't mentioned in any of my training, but that's not necessarily unusual. Could be on a need to know basis. The main thing is that I saw no sign of Bond or Ella's son down there."

"Maybe not, but you've given me another lead to follow. I'm going to track down Quentin and bring him in for questioning," Kendrick said.

"One more thing from the basement." Julian picked up the file folder labeled 1026SAPPHIRE from the center of the table, then paused as Mena ducked out of the glass doors of the cabin. She pressed her hands to her lips and blew him a kiss, before waving goodbye. He hated to see her go, but there was no time for them to continue what they'd started.

"What's this?" Kendrick took the folder from Julian's hand and thumbed through it.

"Not that you need more evidence against Bond for his art scams with everything Ella had on her laptop, but we found this in the basement. Inside is a purchase order for an unnamed asset that he was selling to some guy for $250,000 and a letter signed by Bond with wire transfer instructions," Julian explained.

"Every little bit helps," Kendrick said. "Was this file just laying around down there?"

"It was on a desk with a bunch of other similar files. I guess he tracked the art based on the last name of the artist who forged the pieces that were used to replace the ones he stole. I tried taking a picture of the other files, but it's too blurry to see the labels on them." Julian reached into his pocket and accessed the photo. Zooming in, the text was a blurred black smudge, which he showed to Kendrick. "I remember a couple of the labels though. One was 0112FOX, and the other was 0325GARDNER—"

"Fox and Gardner?" Kendrick stuttered.

"Yeah, that mean anything to you?" Julian asked.

"You remember the cold cases of the two missing women I told you about?" Kendrick asked.

Julian nodded his head quickly. What could the files have to do with those women?

"The missing PC-5 hooker was Samantha Fox, and the missing teacher was Tamara Gardner," Kendrick said.

Chapter Forty-Eight

"Just the man I wanted to see," Kendrick said, taking a sip from a bottle of Felipe beer. The detective was sprawled on a park bench near the wading pool toward the eastern edge of Saffron Beach in Cashew Groves.

Julian sat next to him, then nodded his head toward the cooler, resting next to Kendrick's foot. Kendrick opened the Styrofoam top, pulled out a beer, and handed it to Julian.

Kendrick said, "The Chief is eating us alive because we haven't found Bond and the missing baby yet. We're getting hundreds of calls, but none of the leads are getting us any closer to finding that little boy. Please tell me you found something."

"I guess the search of the gallery basement came up empty?" Julian asked.

"Six rooms, all of them filled with various painting and sculptures. Nothing looked suspicious. We took some dust and hair samples, just in case," Kendrick said.

Surprised, Julian said, "Operation X wasn't related to moving art like I thought. I was sure the place would be empty."

"Adam Russell insisted that Zak Webber was the only employee on the grounds after hours."

"Either Adam is clueless about Quentin's presence in the basement, or he's hiding the real reason that Quentin was down there," Julian guessed.

"It might be the latter," Kendrick said. "When I got back to the station last night, the team had more details about Quentin."

Julian stretched his legs forward, trying to soothe the dull ache from his gunshot wound exacerbated by the uncomfortable bench. He wondered if Kendrick had the same information he'd uncovered. "I got some info on Quentin, too, but you go first."

"We found a match for him in the Caribbean Medical Association database. Dr. Quentin Tufa Ob/Gyn. Practiced for ten years at St. Killian General Hospital but spent most of his time in St. Basil at the hospital in downtown Marluna. I was at the hospital this morning, talking to the staff. Most of them remembered him fondly but said he abruptly resigned over a year ago. No one knew why he quit. I heard the gamut of rumors ranging from disagreements with hospital administrators to stealing medicine to an inappropriate relationship with a patient. No official reason was listed in his employment records, and no one seemed to know where he went, although one of the doctors heard he went to work in a rural hospital in his native Ethiopia. That could explain why he'd fallen off the radar," Kendrick said.

"But he didn't fall off the radar," Julian interrupted. "I saw him in the basement of the Genesis Gallery. He may have left town, but he's certainly back now."

"I have guys checking to see if we can trace his movements on the islands and we're still working on a connection between him and Bond."

"Let me tell you what you and your guys missed," Julian said.

Kendrick sighed, covering his face with his hands.

Julian chuckled. The small island police department couldn't match his skills, nor did they have the ability to tap into the systems he could to gather data quickly. "Tufa had a troubled childhood. His parents were killed by a rival tribe in Ethiopia, and he was left homeless. A humanitarian orphanage took him in, and five years later, when he was ten, a French family adopted him. He moved to Paris with his new family where he legally took their name. But when he graduated from high school, he legally petitioned for a name change back to Tufa."

Kendrick's eyes were wide as his hands dropped from his face. "How the hell did you find all this out? We tried to get access to Tufa's records from Ethiopia but were told they were sealed. We were denied access."

"If I tell you, I'd have to kill you," Julian joked.

"What was his name before he changed it back to Tufa?" the detective asked.

"Dumay."

"Dumay ... like Priscilla Dumay?" Kendrick asked, his mouth hanging open. "That has to be some kind of coincidence."

"It's not. I cross-checked his adoptive parents to the parents listed on Priscilla Dumay's birth certificate. They're the same," Julian confirmed.

"Priscilla Dumay's adopted brother was in the basement of her world-renowned gallery in the middle of the night. I suppose there could be a legitimate reason for him being there, but ..." Kendrick paused.

"What is it?" Julian asked.

"Dumay wasn't around yesterday. Adam said she had a family emergency, so I didn't get to talk to her. But, when she provided a list of the gallery employees after Ella's break-in, Quentin wasn't on the list," Kendrick said.

Julian wasn't surprised. He had a feeling that whatever Quentin was doing in the basement was not related to authorized gallery business. "I can help with that. It took me a while, but I tracked down his new employer. Siamood Storage in downtown Marluna."

"A storage company?" Kendrick asked. "Seems odd for a doctor to trade in his stethoscope to run some storage company."

"Not a stretch once you know that Siamood is a cryobank. The website says they transport embryos donated to research facilities and dispose of embryos marked for destruction. And guess who owns Siamood Storage," Julian said.

Hesitant, Kendrick responded, "Priscilla Dumay?"

Julian said, "The one and only. Her parents were doctors on the cutting edge of embryology at the beginning of the medical discipline and pioneered a lot of the techniques used for IVF today."

"So the adopted son goes into a similar field of medicine, leaves his job abruptly, and his sister lets him run the cryobank."

"I wonder what else Quentin Tufa might be involved in. Maybe he was stealing art with Irving Bond and selling it to private collectors," Julian said.

"But why would Quentin be freaked out about the idea of Bond coming back to the basement?" Kendrick asked. "How does that fit into the puzzle?"

Frustrated, Julian leaned back in his chair. "Haven't figured that out."

Kendrick said, "Looks like I need to pay a visit to Siamood Storage to see

Quentin Tufa. But this guy isn't going to talk to a cop, especially if he's connected to Bond's art scam. I need to go undercover."

"Undercover? Have you ever done that before?" Julian asked.

"Nope, but there's a first time for everything. Especially if I have a rusty ex-Navy SEAL by my side to help," Kendrick said.

Chapter Forty-Nine

"How do I look?" Julian scratched the top of his head as he fell into step next to Kendrick on the busy sidewalk. Nearing the Hurricane Memorial near City Hall, they passed a live band perched on the corner playing calypso music on steel drums. The grid of streets making up the small, modest business district of Marluna bustled with activity as the day neared lunchtime.

It had been two days since Julian agreed to go undercover with Kendrick at Siamood. He'd been consumed with the investigation, pushing aside everything else in his life. He'd had to be satisfied with a few texts and phone calls and sneaking off to Dumay Park for a secret lunch with Mena. He missed her more than he wanted to admit. Finding Ella's son was his priority now. After this was over, he'd have plenty of time to make it up to her.

"Nothing like the Palmchat Island Hero, that's for sure," Kendrick said, then burst into laughter.

"That was the point," Julian said, rolling his eyes. Kendrick's youngest sister worked at the St. Basil Theater and agreed to create a disguise for Julian so he wouldn't blow their cover. Earlier that morning, Julian had sat under the harsh lights of the small stage, resisting the urge to squirm like a petulant child while Sabrina Caillouet covered his short cropped brown hair with a longer floppy blond wig. She'd spent most of her time trimming the wig, so it would look natural against his face and then finished up the transformation by gluing a blond mustache and beard to his skin. Wearing the blue contacts had been his idea, a finishing touch to throw off anyone who might see through her work.

"She did a damn good job. If I didn't already know it was you, I wouldn't believe it," Kendrick said.

Satisfied that his transformation was enough to stop his cover from being blown, Julian said, "Let's go over the plan again."

"All cryobanks and storage facilities get randomly inspected annually by auditors from PIMA, the Palmchat Islands Medical Agency. We are two PIMA assistant auditors on loan from the St. Mateo branch to assist with audits this week. Jessica Dryden is the lead auditor based in St. Basil and will be expecting us. She's been briefed that we are new to the role and will need clear directions on what to do," Kendrick explained.

"Did they give you any details on what we'll be doing?" Julian asked. The set up of this undercover operation had come together quickly and lacked the rigor he was used to from SEALs missions. There were too many unknowns, too many ways things could go wrong without a clear plan of how to address them.

"Simple stuff. Checking inventory against the Cryobank records and taking temperature readings of the nitrogen tanks," Kendrick said as they crossed the street.

"And PIMA is fine with us high-jacking their audit?" Julian wondered why the organization had been so willing to allow them to go undercover as auditors.

"Things are different on the islands than what you're used to. It's very common for governmental agencies to work together this way. PIMA wouldn't have agreed to let us tag along if they thought we could do real damage," Kendrick explained.

"And you're sure this Jessica Dryden has no clue who we are?" Julian wanted to confirm. The last thing they needed was an inexperienced civilian trying to pretend she didn't know her assistants were undercover law enforcement.

"Clueless," Kendrick said. "Now stop worrying about that part. I need you focused on finding something that connects Quentin to Bond or some type of physical evidence that Bond and Ella's baby have been hiding out in the offices."

Crossing the street, they approached the arched entrance of the Pourciau

Market building. Standing near the oversized wooden doors carved with island motifs was a curvaceous, woman dressed in a khaki linen pantsuit and four-inch patent leather tan stilettos. A bright smile spread across her cherubic face as Julian and Kendrick approached her.

"You must be the assistant auditors," The woman said, stretching out her hand toward them. "I'm Jessica Dryden."

"Nice to meet you, Ms. Dryden," said Kendrick, shaking her hand. Julian followed suit.

"Today's going to be quick," Jessica said as she opened the door to the building. "This is the smallest Cryobank in the Palmchat Islands. They only have three nitrogen tanks to hold embryos scheduled for transfer to research facilities. We should be done in ten minutes. Sorry to have you come all the way down here for such a quick audit."

Julian and Kendrick exchanged a glance. Ten minutes was nowhere near long enough for them to search for a connection to Bond without being detected.

Stepping inside the cool air-conditioned building, Julian lagged behind Kendrick and Jessica as he surveyed the layout. He might have to break into the place later, after the audit, to get what they needed, which wasn't ideal.

Reaching the end of the hallway, they walked toward the last door on the right. Siamood Storage was written in small block letters on a plaque to the left of the door.

Jessica knocked on the door, then turned to Julian and Kendrick. "Let me do all the talking. I know the guys here pretty well. We'll be in and out in no time."

Kendrick nodded.

"What do you want us to do?" Julian asked.

Jessica said, "One of you can take temperature readings on the three nitrogen tanks, and the other can make copies of the receipt and transfer records, twenty-five each. They should already have the originals pulled for us."

Jessica knocked on the door again as it swung open.

Julian inhaled sharply, staring into the eyes of Adam Russell.

But Adam's gaze had locked on someone else entirely.

Glaring at Kendrick, Adam's eyes were cold and suspicious.

Stepping out of the room and closing the door behind him, Adam crossed his arms and said, "Detective Kendrick Caillouet, what are you doing here?"

"Detective?" Jessica asked, her voice rising an octave. "That can't be right."

Jessica glanced back and forth between Adam and Kendrick.

"I assure you it is," Adam said. "And I want to know why PIMA believes they need a police escort to perform their audit."

"What is going on here? Are you a detective?" Jessica asked Kendrick.

Kendrick lowered his head, pinching the bridge of his nose.

"Is there some reason why you're here, Detective?" Adam demanded.

"That's what I want to know," Jessica said, placing one hand on her ample hip. "No one told me you were a cop. I thought you were a new auditor. What is going on?"

"Yes, I am a detective with the St. Basil Police Department," Kendrick spoke slowly, stalling for time.

"Why are you here, Detective?" Adam asked again.

"I'm sorry Mr. Russell, I don't know what's going on," Jessica said, her eyes frantic. "Let me call headquarters and see if I can get some information."

Julian stepped behind Kendrick and placed a hand on Jessica's arm.

"Excuse me, Ms. Dryden," Julian said, changing his voice to avoid Adam Russell recognizing it. "Would you like me to run in and get those temperature readings real quick?"

"Would that be okay?" Jessica turned to ask Adam. "The rest of the sample support can be faxed over to my office later."

Adam barely looked at Julian as he gave a quick nod, his attention squarely focused on Kendrick.

Julian walked around Adam, entered the office and closed the door behind him, leaving Kendrick to fend for himself with Jessica and Adam.

The office was small and quiet with stark white walls and dark blue carpet. No place for a grown man and an infant to hide. A receptionist desk sat in the middle of the room with two fake palm plants on each side. There was no phone or computer on the desk. There were no chairs in the room. Julian checked behind the desk. No drawers, nothing on top of the desk, no sign of Bond or the baby.

Glancing to the left, Julian saw an open door leading into another room behind the receptionist's desk. The second room was no bigger than a closet. Three large nitrogen tanks about three feet tall sat along the back wall connected to a device that Julian had never seen before, likely something to keep the tanks at the correct internal temperature. Adjacent to the tanks was a single desktop computer sitting on what looked like a brown snack tray. A hard drive tower was underneath the tray next to a flatbed scanner.

Julian frowned. He'd searched for IT networks connected to this address and found nothing. Yet, there was a computer on the premises. Placing his hand on the mouse, he wiggled the device, bringing the screen to life. Checking the computer properties, he confirmed what he already suspected. The computer was not connected to the internet and probably never had been. There was no better way to ensure that information wouldn't be compromised or hacked than to never connect the computer to the internet in the first place.

Julian didn't have much time.

Grabbing the knife from his ankle holster, he worked fast unscrewing the side plate of the tower. With the container open, Julian removed the hard drive and stuffed it in the pocket of his blazer. Screwing the fasteners of the side plate back onto the tower, Julian slipped the knife back into the ankle holster.

As he exited the office, Jessica was huddled next to Adam.

Kendrick was gone.

Jessica said, "I assure you that I will find out why he was here and get you details as soon as I have them."

"Please do," Adam responded.

Jessica walked over and grabbed Julian's elbow, directing him toward the main entrance. She power-walked toward the exit, in a hurry to leave the building.

Julian fell into step with the lead auditor and followed her out into the bright sunshine.

"Where are the temperature readings?" Jessica asked, removing her portfolio folder from under her arm and unzipping it.

Julian turned toward her and adopted what he hoped was a sheepish grin. "Sorry, I couldn't figure out how to take the readings. I was going to ask for help ..."

"Forget it. Just go home. I'm going to go get a drink," Jessica said, stomping down the sidewalk away from Julian.

Tapping the hard drive tucked securely in his pocket, Julian walked away from the auditor.

Chapter Fifty

Sprinting up the concrete steps of the small orange and alabaster bungalow on a narrow rectangular lot in the Cashew Grove neighborhood, Julian knocked on the door. Wilted flowers in two ceramic pots sat near the edge of the porch next to a discarded, faded basketball. An old wooden rocking chair, missing one leg, was propped against the front of the home.

"Come on, open the door," Julian called out. After leaving Siamood, Julian had gone straight to the police station, expecting to find Kendrick there. Instead, in the squad room, he'd witnessed dozens of cops cackling with laughter at the expense of his good friend. Led by Detective Desmond François, officer after officer hurled insults about the naivety of Detective Kendrick Caillouet.

"That fool didn't even wear a disguise," one deputy said, between fits of laughter. "Everybody in St. Basil has seen his face plastered all over the news with the Ella Sapphire murder and the missing baby case."

"It's embarrassing. He didn't read the previous PIMA audit reports to realize the main contact for the audit visits had been the same man—Adam Russell—that he'd questioned, not once, not twice but three times already. He needs to have his detective badge revoked," Desmond had said, throwing fuel onto the fire.

"Come on, Kendrick's a nice guy, and he's never had to do anything like this before," a female officer tried to come to Kendrick's defense.

"Kacee, you've been on the force for less than three months, and I know you wouldn't have made a mistake like that," Desmond retorted.

"Damn right, I wouldn't have," Kacee said, erupting in laughter.

Julian's heart had ached for his friend.

Pounding on the door harder, Julian said, "I'm not leaving. I'll stay out here all damn night."

Seconds later, the door opened, and Kendrick stepped back allowing Julian to enter.

Julian closed the door and walked inside the spacious living room. An oversized black leather couch and chair filled one whole side across from a contemporary coffee table, and the seventy-inch television mounted on the wall. The indoor decor was sleek and modern, a stark contrast from the neglected exterior. The only confounding piece of furniture was a bright neon blue bean bag in the corner closest to the kitchen.

Kendrick plopped down on the bean bag and covered his face with his hands.

"It's not that bad," Julian said, slapping Kendrick's knee. He sat in the black leather recliner closest to the bean bag. Dark curtains blocked the sunlight from the afternoon sky, casting gloomy darkness over the room.

Kendrick gave him a depressed look. "Thanks for lying to me."

"Anytime," Julian said. "They're just being jerks. Tomorrow, they'll be on to the next thing."

"As brutal as having my whole department laugh in my face was, that's not the part that's bothering me," Kendrick said and sat up. "It was the first time I realized how sheltered I'd been here on the island. Most of my cases were investigating petty gang-related crimes, nothing of the caliber that you and Desmond François have seen. I don't have the experience to handle this case. I'm no good at this."

"And you never will be if you keep up that attitude. Trust me, we all make mistakes. This one you can definitely bounce back from," Julian said, a wave of regret washing over him. He'd give anything to have his mistakes limited to a professional slip up. The kind of mistakes he'd made ruined lives.

"I've lost all element of surprise. Adam Russell is probably giving Priscilla Dumay an earful about how the cops showed up at the cryobank. She'll ask her adopted brother about it, and Quentin will be tipped off that we're looking into him," Kendrick said, banging his fists against the bean bag. "I really blew it this time—"

A telephone ring pierced the air.

"What the hell? You still have a landline?" Julian quipped.

"I'm not the only one. Don't you?" Kendrick asked, rising from the bean bag and walking into the kitchen where the phone continued to ring.

"I live on a boat. So, the answer would be no," Julian said, pressing a button on the side of the chair, reclining back against the smooth leather.

"Caller ID says Siamood Storage. How the hell did they get my home number?" Kendrick asked.

Julian's body shot up from the chair. He sprinted into the kitchen and stood next to Kendrick, looking down at the caller ID on the phone. "Answer it, put it on speaker."

Kendrick nodded, then pressed the button. "Hello."

"Is this Detective Kendrick Caillouet?" a male voice asked.

Julian leaned an elbow onto the kitchen counter. Could it be Quentin Tufa? Maybe he'd found out about the detective's visit to Siamood Storage earlier.

"Who is this?" Kendrick asked.

"Irving Bond. I'm ready to turn myself in for kidnapping the baby. I just have one condition."

"And what would that be?" Kendrick asked.

"Protection. The same people who killed Ella Sapphire are trying to kill me."

Chapter Fifty-One

Mena squirmed in the plush, palm leaf motif designed chair tucked in the back corner of the upscale King Street Lounge and glanced at her watch again. Almost nine p.m. Julian had been ignoring her for days. Well, not ignoring her on purpose. She knew he was committed to finding Ella's missing baby. He was focused on more important things than her, but she couldn't help but feel frustrated from not seeing him. She missed him like crazy, and it was hard for her to process that he was too busy to miss her like she missed him.

When he'd finally texted her this afternoon asking her to meet him at King Street Lounge, she'd been ecstatic. Abandoning work early, she'd gone home to put on an outfit guaranteed to make his eyes pop out of his head.

As she twirled the remnants of her watered down Palmito, her excitement waned. Julian had yet to show up for their date. The decadent opulence of the restaurant with its lavish Swarovski crystal inverted dome chandeliers, crystal waterfall draperies and metallic purple palm fronds adorning the walls couldn't mask her disappointment.

Where the hell was he? She glanced at her cell phone again to make sure she hadn't missed a call or text from him.

Her vision went dark as strong hands covered her eyes.

She felt a gentle kiss on the top of her head, sending a jolt of excitement through her body.

"Sorry, I'm late," Julian whispered in her ear.

A war raged within Mena. She was thrilled they could spend time with each other after being apart for so long, but she was pissed that he was late and hadn't had the common courtesy to text or call her and explain why.

"Took you long enough," Mena said, avoiding his gaze. She snatched the knife from the table, tore into the cold roll of French bread, stabbing butter on the piece and then dropped the knife back on to the table with a loud clang.

Her anger was winning the battle. She stole a glance at Julian. The soft purple rays of the dim lighting within the restaurant accentuated the rugged handsomeness of his face, making him downright irresistible. Mena caught the glances of a few women in the restaurant, their eyes drawn to him as he sat across from her.

"I'm sorry for keeping you waiting so long. You look amazing," Julian said, looking genuinely contrite.

Mena turned away from him toward the stage where the band was setting up for the evening set.

Julian reached across the table and placed his hand on top of hers. Despite her commitment to resisting him, the tension in her hands eased at his touch. He caressed her hands in his until she turned to look at him. The look in his eyes made her heart skip. The pain and worry reflected touched her to her soul.

"Please forgive me," Julian said.

"That depends," Mena said, pulling her hand away.

"On what?"

"The reason why you were late," Mena said, crossing her arms over her chest. She wasn't going to let the thousand-watt smile stop her from getting a proper explanation.

"It's good news," Julian said.

"What happened?" Mena asked. If Julian looked this happy, there must have been a breakthrough in Ella's murder or with the case of her missing son.

Julian said, "Bond called and arranged with Kendrick to turn himself in tomorrow morning. He agreed to bring the baby."

Mena's eyes widened in surprise. "You've got to be kidding me!"

"No joke. Bond claims the person who killed Ella is also trying to kill him, and he needs police protection."

A sick feeling in her stomach, Mena said, "I can't believe Bond was involved in all these crimes that led to Ella's murder. You'd think I would have learned by now how people aren't what always what they seem ..."

"I probably shouldn't have said anything about this," Julian said, grabbing her hands in his.

Mena allowed his soft caresses to soothe her.

Julian continued, "We have to keep this a secret for the next twelve hours. Can't take a chance of Bond getting spooked and not showing up. I didn't want you to be in the dark about what's going on."

"I won't tell anyone, especially not Omar and Regina," Mena said. The gallery employees would be reeling once news broke. She had no desire to start the incessant conversations early. "Are you going to be there when Bond turns himself in?"

Julian clenched his jaw, then said, "No, Kendrick wouldn't tell me the details. He's afraid I'm going to get there before his team and mess things up like I did at the waterfront when Bond escaped with the baby."

Mena figured it was much more than that. Julian didn't want to help, he wanted to be the one to bring down the bad guys and save the baby. He didn't want to be on the sidelines while the cops accomplished the one thing Dawn had asked him to do. The one thing he probably believed would give him the forgiveness he wanted for his past mistakes. Mena wondered what Julian had done to destroy Dawn and Broman's family.

"If Irving claims Ella's killers are after him, who is he pointing the finger at? Who did he say killed her?" Mena asked.

"He's not giving up that information until the cops give him protection and immunity," Julian said, his voice laced with disgust. "But I think Bond will say Teo Juarez killed Ella."

"They found his DNA under Ella's fingernails, right?" Mena asked.

Julian nodded. "We haven't been able to figure out how Bond, Ella, and Juarez are all connected to each other. Kendrick is still working on pulling the evidence together, but he's close to solving this case," Julian said.

"Thanks to you," Mena added, leaning toward Julian. She felt a strong magnetic pull as his face came closer to hers. Her heart pounded as he reached forward and stroked her face, before kissing her gently on the lips. "I think all of this deserves a celebration. Don't you?"

"What do you have in mind?" Julian asked, his eyes dancing with excitement.

"Let me show you," Mena said, trailing a finger down the side of his face.

Chapter Fifty-Two

Mena stood on the deck of Julian's yacht, her hands wrapped tightly around him, caressing his back as they kissed with an abandon, oblivious to the fact that anyone walking along the boardwalk of the marina after midnight could see them. She didn't care if anyone stopped and stared. She'd had an amazing night with Julian and felt all her defenses against him had melted away.

For the first time tonight, she'd felt like she had Julian's attention. All of him was focused on all of her, with no distractions from Ella or Dawn. If this was what being in a relationship with Julian Montgomery would feel like, she knew she wouldn't be able to turn it down.

She felt him rub against her bare thighs, his hands making their way up under her strapless denim mini dress to squeeze her butt. The friction built between their pulsating bodies brushing against each other, delighting her senses. Licking his tongue along the edge of her lips, Julian sucked on the edge of her mouth before kissing her deeply. Mena moaned, eager to accept his kisses. There was no need for music as their bodies harmonized in a synchronized rhythm grinding against each other until Mena felt what she'd been waiting for—the unmistakable and formidable bulge expanding in Julian's pants.

Sliding her hands down the rock-hard muscles of Julian's back, she danced her fingers around his waist to the front of his pants. Julian let out a low chuckle.

"Stop. That tickles," Julian said, laughing more.

"Yes, but what I'm about to do next won't tickle at all," Mena said. Gripping the waistband, she loosened the buckle of his belt and unbuttoned the jeans, then lowered her body in front of him as she slowly pushed his pants down to his ankles. Enjoying the view from below, she gazed at his erect manhood, released through the gap in his boxer briefs.

"Come here," Julian's voice was husky and low, filled with intensity.

Mena stood and unbuttoned Julian's cotton dress shirt, pushing it off his shoulders as he stepped out of his boxer briefs and kicked them across the deck of the boat.

"Wait a minute. Let me look at you. Like really look at you," Mena said, teasing Julian. She took a step back and enjoyed the flash of red that engulfed Julian's face and disappeared as quickly as it had appeared. His taut muscles and rock-hard penis had her salivating for more of him. How had she become this addicted to him when she'd been trying to fight off falling for another man again? Julian was the full package, the right combination of honesty, caring, openness, integrity, and unbridled passion. He was everything she knew she wanted and all the things she'd had no clue she needed. This relationship they were creating felt different to her—more real, a little rough and rugged, rocky at times but oh so right other times. Her heart wouldn't be denied tonight. She belonged with him, and he belonged with her.

"You done?" Julian asked, taking a step toward her. He laced his fingers between hers and pulled her closer.

"We really going to do this out here?" Mena asked with a giggle, checking around the boardwalk for any passersby. The marina was empty of the early partygoers who'd already made their way down Bishop Boulevard to the club scene in downtown Marluna.

Julian's eyes were hooded and brimmed with desire. He yanked her toward him and whispered in her ear, "We can do this wherever you like."

Then he dipped his head and made a blazing trail of sensuous kisses from her ear down the side of her neck. Gasping, Mena grew more aroused. She couldn't hold out any longer. Pressing her hands on his biceps, she pushed him gently back onto the bench seat that bordered the railing of the yacht. Mena straddled him, panting from the frenzy of sensations flooding her as their bodies rocked in sync with the waves crashing against the yacht.

As the intensity grew, she rocked harder and faster against his thrusts, frenetically varying her pace and angle, squeezing her thighs to heighten his pleasure as he skyrocketed hers. She moaned his name as they climaxed simultaneously, sending a flurry of shudders from the violent pleasure rocking her body.

Julian whispered, "You're going to be the death of me."

His touch gentle and sweet, he lifted her in one smooth motion and carried her into the cabin for round two.

Hours later, Mena awoke, twisted within the sheets, her body draped over Julian's as he snored lightly. Lightheaded, she watched him sleep for a while, marveling at the man who'd come into her life and changed everything. She'd never thought she'd experience anything like this ever, yet here she was with Julian. Despite how they met, she couldn't imagine how life could get any better than this.

Slowly rising, she eased out of bed and grabbed Julian's robe from the chair in the corner. Burying her face in the soft terry cloth, she breathed in his scent trying to memorize it before putting the robe on. Another late night on the yacht. The clock read 2:34 a.m. as she slid the glass door open and walked out onto the deck.

Two dirtboards hung along the railing on the side closest to the boat in the next slip. Walking closer to them, she ran a finger along the cracked paint of the board.

Julian walked toward her, wearing dark jogging pants and a neon yellow Palmchat Islands t-shirt. He wrapped his arms around her. "Why'd you leave the bed? I missed you."

"Too wound up to sleep. Thought the sea air would be soothing," Mena said. "I didn't mean to wake you."

"My body knew the minute you left and sleepwalked to find you," Julian said. "I'm still asleep."

"You're silly," Mena laughed.

"You're beautiful and amazing and the best thing that I've ever had in my life. I don't deserve you," Julian said.

"Don't say that," Mena said. She didn't want him putting up any barriers for them, especially since she'd finally decided to tear down the ones she'd erected. "Are these the boards you used to dirtboard down mountains?"

"That one is," Julian said, pointing to the black dirtboard with the yellow trident in the middle. "The other one belonged to Broman ..."

Mena noticed a tinge of sadness in Julian's voice as he said his friend's name. Her eyes drifted to the white dirtboard with a sunrise in the middle. Underneath, the words read "Break of Dawn." She thought of Ella's sister and instantly made the connection. "Can't believe y'all did something so dangerous."

"We were SEALs. Nothing could compare to the danger we faced in our training or on a mission. But we tried to come close. Work hard, play hard," Julian said.

Compelled by Julian's openness, the vulnerability he'd shown her tonight, Mena did the one thing she hadn't intended to do. The one thing that could ruin the magical night they'd shared.

Her words were almost a whisper as she asked, "What happened to Broman?"

Chapter Fifty-Three

Julian squeezed the bridge of his nose. His shoulders slumped as he struggled with how to respond. The truth could change how Mena felt about him but lying would be no better. Didn't she deserve to know the truth before she got more involved with him?

Mena was quiet.

The roar of the water of the bay crashing against the boats intensified as Julian tried to steady himself. He wasn't prepared to answer the question. He'd avoided talking about Broman to anyone. He was the only one who could still tell the truth about what happened three years ago. The truth about what happened to Broman.

He could give her the official Naval response after the attack, and she'd probably be satisfied. But she'd also walk away from the conversation believing like everyone else ... that he was a hero when he was nothing of the kind. He'd never told anyone the secret he kept locked inside. The reason he'd exiled himself from the life he'd loved, a fitting punishment for the life that Broman would never have. Could he tell her the truth now? Would saying it out loud free him or crush him?

"We were like brothers, two peas in a pod my mom called us. We did everything together, so when I told him I was going into the Navy like my parents, he was right on board. Broman was the good one, born to serve and protect. Always willing to lend a helping hand, sacrificing himself to help someone else. He believed in doing the right thing and stopping the evil in the world. He was the real hero," Julian said.

"From what I've seen, you have a lot of that in you, too," Mena said, then leaned her head on his shoulder.

Julian cast his eyes to the floor. "My Dad never thought much of me. I was his weak son that could never live up to his expectations. But he was the weak one, pushing himself from one risky situation to another, trying to deal with the fact that his wife was more accomplished in the Navy than he was. But none of that mattered to me when I was young. I had to prove him wrong. I had to do everything that he did in the Navy and the one thing that he'd failed at ... becoming a Navy SEAL. I did it all, but now I wish I hadn't," Julian said.

"Despite what motivated you, there's no denying the good that you did in the world as a SEAL and after you left the SEALs. You are a true hero—"

"A true hero wouldn't have done what I did to my SEAL team, what I did to Broman," Julian said. He didn't look up. He didn't want to read the look in her eyes, to wonder what she thought about him now.

"What did you do? What happened to Broman?" Mena asked again.

"After years of trying, Broman and I finally got assigned to the same six-man SEAL team, and we were deployed to Southeast Asia for an intelligence mission on local terrorist cells. Missions in this area never see any action. They're strictly for reconnaissance," Julian started, the memories slamming into his mind like it was yesterday.

Julian rested his elbows on the table as he continued the security checks. He was pissed at the guys, bailing on the rest of their daily tasks to hit up the bar and meet up with some of the local girls. Even Broman had chided him, leaving his own checks unfinished and leaving him behind, knowing that Dawn would cut his dick off if he even thought about cheating on her with another woman.

Julian was done with the local girls. The sex had been good at first, but now he was bored with them. Scanning the computer screen, an anomaly emerged in the coding. Heart pounding, he began to type. The characters marched across the screen as his fingers moved faster.

His brain was in overdrive, deciphering the communication that had been snagged by his program. In minutes, his additional coding translated the language in real-time as Julian read the conversation. It didn't take him long to realize what he was reading.

Private communications between an independent terrorist cell and one of the most dangerous and elusive shadow facilitators in the world.

Enrique Rivera Ortiz. El Mago. The Magician.

The self-proclaimed magician had eluded international law enforcement for years, as he supplied stolen US and European military grade weapons to mafias, cartels, and terrorists.

Julian continued to read as the communications filled the computer screen. El Mago was on the island, less than five miles from their base. He was negotiating for a service. Julian waited as the terrorist cell finalized the payment amount and transfer directions. Reaching over, Julian wrote down the address and time of the drop on his notepad. What the hell did El Mago want them to do? And why was it worth twenty million U.S dollars?

Several minutes passed before Julian got his answer.

Damn it! This was worse than he thought.

El Mago knew the location of a confidential informant working with the U.S military. The informant was scheduled to testify, providing evidence that could destroy the shadow facilitator's entire empire. He wanted the terrorists to assassinate the informant.

Julian couldn't let that happen. He knew exactly how he could stop the transaction from going down, but it was risky. His actions would be criminal, and if his plan didn't work, he could be put in prison for treason. But what if it did work? He would have single-handedly brought down one of the most wanted criminals by the U.S. Military.

In a split second, Julian knew exactly what he was going to do.

Intercepting the transmission, he hijacked the communications of the terrorist cell and typed in new instructions. Five seconds later, El Mago confirmed his agreement. As Julian grabbed the sniper rifle from the corner of the room, he didn't bother to alert his team. The takedown would be quick and easy.

"I was only gone for a couple of hours." Julian hung his head low. "El Mago never showed up. On my way back, I heard the gunfire. Dozens of terrorist rebels had surrounded our house. The bullets penetrating the wood structure was deafening. I managed to sneak into the back of the house through the jungle."

"Julian ..." Mena started, then stopped.

He had to continue. No one knew the full truth of what he'd done. The shame he carried. The mistake he tried to erase from his life with every day he continued to live. Burning within him, he had to tell someone. No, he had to tell Mena.

Julian continued, "There was so much blood. Their bodies almost torn apart from all the bullets. They never had a chance. They never saw the ambush coming, and that's when I saw the communications had reconnected after I hijacked them. When I intercepted the transmission, the terrorists had identified what I'd done and traced the source back to our base. I led them right to where we were located and didn't realize it."

Mena was quiet, her face a mask of shock, sadness, and something Julian refused to acknowledge. He had to keep going. He had to tell his truth to someone he trusted even if that meant losing her.

"Do you know what I did? Before I checked to see if any of them were still breathing? I went back to that computer and corrupted any sign of what I'd done, the files I'd stolen on the informant's whereabouts and the communications I'd intercepted between El Mago and the terrorists. As I was covering my own ass, I heard a cough," Julian said.

"Broman?" Mena asked, her eyes full of hope. A hope he would soon dash.

Broman wasn't moving. Julian felt for a pulse. Thready, but it was there. He had to save Broman. He couldn't lose his best friend. Not like this. Lifting Broman onto his back, Julian trudged through the swamp to the safe point. The Blackhawk would be waiting.

Muscles burning like fire, Julian ran from the ambush. He could hear the helicopter in the distance. Tripping, he fell to the ground. Broman's mangled body was next to him, riddled from bullets and stab wounds. Julian looked at Broman's face, covered in blood and mud. The guilt and shame of what he'd caused threatened to suffocate Julian. How had things gone so wrong?

He'd been running for what felt like hours. His body was drenched in sweat. Broman clung to his neck like a dead weight, threatening to take him down. Julian ran faster.

Past the brush, a clearing appeared. The slow, methodical whips of the helicopter blades were deafening. Each step pounded the ground harder, his limbs becoming heavier as the end was in sight. Collapsing at the door of the helicopter, someone lifted Broman from his back. Falling to his knees, dizziness enveloped Julian as he descended into an abyss. His eyes focused on the soldier, leaning over him. The soldier's mouth moved, but Julian couldn't hear the words. He stopped trying to understand and allowed the darkness to envelop him.

Julian's voice cracked with emotion, "Broman was barely alive. I got him out of there. I got him to safety, to the hospital ..."

"But he still died," Mena said.

"Death would have been a blessing," Julian said. His body ached from the tension of the barrage of memories, the pain of the devastation he'd caused. "He's suffering a fate much worse than that. My best friend is in a long-term care facility, trapped in a coma and basically brain dead."

Mena's hands flew to her mouth, her eyes wide in shock.

The truth of what he'd done was out there. She knew the terrible things he'd done, the horrible person he was, a man who'd given terrorists a direct path to slaughter his SEAL team.

"I can't imagine what you must think of me now," Julian said. He was holding his breath, waiting for her to walk out of his life for good.

Mena turned away from him and took a deep breath.

A sound pierced the night sky, and Julian's head jerked toward the marina. The sound was faint but easily recognizable.

Floating across the pier from Louis Campbell's deserted yacht, docked next to his, the panicked wails of a baby rang in his ears.

Chapter Fifty-Four

Forcing open the swing door, Julian jumped over the four steps leading down to the bottom of the boat and crossed the plank connecting his yacht to the boardwalk pier behind the slips. In seconds he was climbing over the transom of Louis Campbell's sleek black, fifty-foot yacht, aptly named The Crooner.

Cries from the baby grew louder.

Was it Ella's son?

The sounds came from inside the boat cabin.

Julian peered through the glass floor to ceiling sliding doors. The room was pitch dark.

Louis Campbell had been remanded to police custody over a month ago for attacking his wife, Wanda. She hadn't returned to the scene of the gruesome attack, but instead had flown back to St. Mateo to stay with her family until the trial.

The yacht had been abandoned since.

The perfect hiding spot for Irving Bond and Ella's son?

Julian reached for his knife.

His hand brushed against the bare skin of his ankle.

Damn it!

He'd rushed off his boat without grabbing his knife or his gun.

The wails from the baby continued.

No time to go back.

Stepping toward the glass doors, Julian pulled the handle. The door swung open wide, resting flat against the wall.

Humid, hot air clawed at his skin as he stepped into the cabin.

Julian squinted.

His eyes adjusted to the darkness.

He was in a square-shaped galley with stainless steel appliances, pecan wood cabinets and light gray marble countertops.

The baby's cries lowered to a whimper.

He could barely hear the child anymore.

He couldn't tell which direction the sound had come from.

A half-level above the kitchen toward the bow of the boat was a living room area, with blond leather couches in a U-shape around a coffee table to the left and a smaller matching sofa lining the wall to the right.

The room was empty.

Everything was clean and undisturbed.

Walking through the living room, he glanced toward a set of stairs that descended to the staterooms below.

From the size of the yacht, Julian guessed the lower level held two maybe three berths.

The baby could be in one of them.

So could Irving Bond.

Descending the steps, Julian paused.

Footsteps pounded against wood behind him.

Turning, he saw a figure ascending from the curved stairs off the starboard side of the galley. The man was stumbling, breathing heavily. In his right hand was a syringe.

Julian charged back up the steps as the man turned and staggered out of the cabin.

Sprinting through the living area and the galley, Julian lunged through the open door.

Collapsing on the man's legs, Julian toppled the man down on the outer deck, pressing his knee into the man's back.

"Where's the baby?" Julian demanded.

He grabbed the man's arm and twisted it behind him.

The man howled and shook his head, struggling to breathe, his face smashed against the deck as Julian applied more weight to pin him down.

Legs flailing in a desperate attempt to be free, the man squirmed but seemed listless without the energy to fully fight back.

"Where's the baby? What was in the syringe? What did you do to the baby?" Julian screamed, disturbed that the baby's cries had stopped.

Raising his head and turning to the side, the man gulped air, then said, "I didn't ... do ... anything ... to ... that baby."

Julian recognized the man.

Dr. Quentin Tufa.

What was he doing on Louis Campbell's boat with the baby?

Julian leaned back, preparing to yank Quentin from the ground.

He looked up. The barrel of a Sig Sauer pistol was pointed directly at his head.

The gunman was dressed in a wet suit, his face covered with a swim mask.

Soulless dark eyes glared at Julian.

"Move away from him," the gunman demanded, his voice low and rough.

Julian stood slowly, raising his hands in mock surrender. But he wasn't the type to give up. He was biding his time.

"Get the fuck up," the gunman yelled at Quentin.

Quentin stumbled, using the bench along the aft of the boat to propel his body to a sitting position.

The gunman stepped down into the boat and glanced at Quentin. "What the fuck is wrong with you?"

The mistake Julian had been waiting for.

Raising his fist upward in a sharp swinging motion, Julian sent the Sig Sauer pistol flying over the starboard side of the boat.

The gunman tackled Julian. As their bodies flew backward, Julian crashed against the glass doors.

The gunman landed a punch to Julian's abdomen knocking the wind out of him. Gasping for breath, Julian pushed away from the gunman, then slammed an elbow down on the man's head, jerking his knee up sharply to connect with the gunman's chin.

"Go, go, go, go," the gunman screamed as he stumbled against the railing. Quentin scrambled across the bench seat and hurled his body over the boat, landing with a loud thud onto the pier below.

The revving engines of two jet skis roared from the bay, stopping along the back edge of the wooden pier behind the boat slips.

The driver of the first jet ski leaned over and dragged Quentin's body from the pier and onto the back of the jet ski, then made a sharp U-turn.

Water sprayed across the deck and the back of the boat as the jet ski zipped across the water back out to the sea.

The gunman swung at Julian's temple. Julian blocked the swing with a swift move of his forearm to protect his face. The gunman connected with a quick kick to Julian's left leg, sending pain detonating through his body as the blow landed near his gunshot wound. Julian crumpled to the deck.

Staring at the man's dark eyes, Julian saw malice and a trace of something he hadn't expected. Recognition. Did the gunman know him?

A sharp wail pierced the air.

The baby.

His eyes trained on Julian, the gunman jumped over the transom of the boat, falling onto the pier, then turned and scrambled toward the jet ski.

The baby's crying amplified.

Julian watched as the gunman leaped onto the back of the jet ski. The driver steered away from the pier and into the black night of the bay, leaving behind a wake of rippled water pounding against the yacht.

Julian turned and ran back inside the cabin into the galley. Next to the stainless-steel refrigerator, a set of spiral stairs led down to the lower cabin. As he reached the bottom of the stairs, the baby's cries grew much louder. The dark room was slightly illuminated by light from the marina shining through the round windows lining the opposite wall. A king size bed rested in the middle of the detached master suite, with a couch along the opposite wall.

Julian's eyes darted to one of the windows. A low whistle of wind could barely be heard under the baby's cries. He refocused. A single hole pierced the last window.

The baby boy was wrapped in a blue blanket resting in the center of the king-sized bed. Julian's eyes were drawn away, now focused entirely on something else.

The back wall was splattered red with blood and brain matter above a body slumped on the ground.

The dead man was Irving Bond.

Chapter Fifty-Five

The brassy clinking of the bell on the door of the Hullabaloo Coffee Shop jolted Julian from his thoughts. An elderly man with a large bag of donuts walked out of the building and into the bright morning sun.

Julian lifted the oversized coffee mug and took a long sip of the black Felipean brew as he stared at the article in the *Palmchat Gazette. ISLAND HERO SAVES KIDNAPPED BABY.* Below the heading was an oversized photo of him, cradling Ella's infant son, trying unsuccessfully to shield his face from the cameras.

As he'd emerged from the cabin in the early morning hours yesterday, police, EMTs, photographers, and journalists flooded the boardwalk. The flash of cameras lit the pre-dawn inky black sky as reporters tried to board the boat to get a statement from him. After some wrestling with aggressive photojournalists, Kendrick herded the baby to a roped off area near the Marina Restaurant that was guarded by police. By the time Child Protective Services arrived, the crowd had swelled to hundreds of onlookers praising the safe return of the little boy who'd been missing for over a week.

Julian witnessed the sunrise from the waiting area of the police station. The rest of his day had been spent giving his statement about what had transpired on the yacht. He'd barely seen Mena as she was swept away into another interrogation room to give her statement. She'd hung around for a while, the receptionist told him, until she realized Julian would be detained for a few more hours. She'd sent him a brief text. By the time he was finally allowed to leave, there was no time to meet with her to discuss the bombshell about his past. Dawn was distraught and needed him. He'd spent the rest of the day and night with her as she waited for CPS to give her information on when she could see Ella's son.

"Not your best side," Kendrick said, tapping a finger against the newspaper resting on the table. The detective pulled out the wooden bistro chair on the opposite side from Julian and sat.

Julian shrugged, then looked out the window at the waves rolling in from the Caribbean Sea and crashing onto the sand of Saffron Beach. He wasn't concerned about being plastered all over the news anymore. His only concern was how Irving Bond's death would affect Ella's murder case.

"Got some good news for you to pass on to Dawn," Kendrick said. Waving a hand toward the waitress, Kendrick ordered a goat bacon croissant with cheese and an espresso shot.

"She needs some good news. CPS hasn't let her see the baby yet," Julian said, recounting Dawn's rant on the phone with him this morning.

"There's been a big public outcry of support for her to get custody in the wake of the kidnapping, so CPS is bending the rules on searching for the biological father. They're going to do DNA tests on Dawn and Irving to see if they are a match to the baby," Kendrick said.

Julian sighed heavily. "So, if Bond is the father, then Dawn automatically gets custody once she's proven to be the baby's aunt."

"And if Bond isn't the father, they've agreed to provide an exemption for Dawn to get custody of her nephew," Kendrick said.

"Well, at least something is working out right." Julian finished off the rest of his coffee, then leaned forward, resting his elbows on the table. "Any leads on who murdered Bond?"

"The bullet that killed Bond matched the Sig Sauer pistol we found in the bay. Got a fingerprint from the barrel of the gun that matched our elusive Teo Juarez," Kendrick said.

"Teo Juarez. His blood and skin were found under Ella's fingernails, and now his fingerprint was on the gun that killed Bond," Julian said. The masked man he fought on the boat was Teo Juarez. The same masked man that seemed to have recognized him. Who was Teo Juarez? Why had he killed Ella and Bond?

"My guess is that Teo Juarez is a hired assassin. Dr. Tufa could have hired Juarez to kill both Ella and Bond, but I don't understand why? Why would Tufa want Ella and Bond dead? Was he trying to make sure they didn't rat on him about the art scam?" Kendrick asked. The question hung in the air between the two men.

"I don't think Tufa is calling the shots. If you'd hired a hitman to kill someone, would you tag-a-long while he committed the crime?"

"Not unless I wanted to be on one of those videos of the world's dumbest criminals," Kendrick said, laughing. "But here's the problem. I don't have any evidence to bring Tufa in for questioning."

"Why the hell not?" Julian asked.

"We couldn't find fingerprints or DNA from any of our samples that matched Dr. Quentin Tufa on Campbell's yacht," Kendrick explained, taking a sip of his coffee.

"How is that possible? I fought him on the boat. He fell. We struggled. And there's no DNA? No fingerprints?" Julian banged his hand on the table.

"I couldn't find any evidence that you were on the boat except in the bedroom where you found the baby and Irving Bond's dead body," Kendrick continued.

"A cleaner," Julian guessed. "A professional one too, to get it done with all the crowds and reporters around. Doesn't seem like a disgraced former Ob/Gyn would have the connections to pull that off."

"Brings us back to the question of why Tufa was on the boat," Kendrick said.

Julian could only think of one reason. "To get the baby. Think about it. We thought Bond was after the baby for his own selfish reasons, but what if he was the pawn? What if someone forced him to kidnap the child, but he was sloppy and got caught on video. So next they sent Tufa to get the baby and Juarez to shut Bond up."

"If you're right, then why is Ella's baby so important?" Kendrick asked.

Julian stood from the table, reached into his pocket, and grabbed a twenty-dollar bill. Dropping it on the table, he turned to Kendrick. "I don't know, but

I have something that can help me figure out that missing piece to this puzzle."

"Please enlighten me," Kendrick said.

"When we—" Julian paused as his cell phone vibrated on the table. He read the text message and felt his body grow weary. "It's Mena. Sorry man, I gotta go."

Chapter Fifty-Six

Mena pressed her fingers against the thorns of the cactus plant on the teak wood table on the upper level of Julian's boat. The intermittent stinging pain contrasted with the numbness that had taken over her body.

What was she going to do?

She had no clue how she was going to tell him. Everything had changed between them in one moment. She couldn't be with him anymore. She knew she'd be walking away from him today. Walking out of his life and closing this chapter in hers.

How was she going to tell him?

She'd cycled through all the possible ways he could process her decision to leave him. Resigned disappointment. Understanding that everything had changed for her. Anger and rage over the abruptness of her decision. Sadness for the loss of what could have been. But those were the flood of her emotions, the torrent attacking her, causing her to shut down.

She hadn't seen him since he'd jumped off the boat to save Ella's baby yesterday. After calling 9-1-1 and waiting on Julian's boat until the police arrived, she'd left when Julian emerged from the Campbell boat with Ella's son in his arms. A large crowd had amassed, and she'd escaped the madness by jogging along the pathway from the marina back to her condo where she'd watched the coverage on the local news.

An hour later, a police cruiser arrived with officers to escort her to the police station, where she'd given her statement to corroborate Julian's version of events.

She'd only seen Julian briefly, and he didn't look like a man who'd endured a dangerous fight to rescue a kidnapped baby. He was alert and fresh as he tended to Dawn in one of the interrogation rooms. Not wanting to interrupt, Mena had left the station and holed up in her condo, ignoring all the well-meaning phone calls of friends trying to check up on her. There was only one call she'd taken yesterday, and it changed everything.

She knew what she had to do, and she couldn't waste time. When she'd called Julian this morning and asked to meet, his tone was pleasant and … relieved. He had no clue what she was getting ready to do to him.

The slapping of bare feet on the small wooden stairs leading from the main deck to the upper deck sent a tremor through Mena's body. Julian was back. The moment she'd been dreading all morning was upon her, and she struggled to comprehend whether she could actually go through with it. But she knew she had to. She couldn't be with Julian anymore.

"Hey, you playing hooky from work to see me?" Julian asked, placing a tentative kiss on her forehead. He moved onto the cushioned banquette seating surrounding the teak wood table and leaned his head back.

Mena gave him a tight, forced smile as her mind raced. Julian looked pensive despite his casual tone. "Did you get an update from Kendrick?"

"The cops have determined that the prime suspect in Ella's murder is now the prime suspect in Bond's. Coast Guard found the gun and tests confirmed it was the murder weapon. A fingerprint on the barrel matched the same man whose blood and skin were found under Ella's fingernails," Julian said.

"Really?" Mena asked, chiding herself for not coming up with something more to say. She was so consumed with what she'd come to do that she was finding it hard to concentrate on the news about Ella's case.

Julian nodded. "Teo Juarez. The bastard is probably still on the island hiding in plain sight, but it's just a matter of time before he slips up and we're able to find him. Then he can lead us to who's really calling the shots."

"Us?" Mena asked.

Julian glanced at her. "You sound worried."

Mena looked away. She couldn't help the fierce protectiveness she'd developed for Julian, though she suspected she was about to break his heart.

Julian shielded his eyes with one hand. "I won't stop until I bring Ella's murderer to justice. Plus, if you haven't noticed by now, I do okay taking care of myself even when you're around distracting me."

Yesterday, Mena would have been giddy from Julian's subtle, playful flirting. Today, everything had changed. His teasing made her feel sick to her stomach about what she had to do. He was going to be blindsided by her decision and the reason.

Julian reached for her hand, intertwining his fingers with hers. "Okay, tell me what's on your mind. You look ... stressed. Beautiful but tense. Why did you want to meet this morning?"

Mena snatched her hand away, then looked down at the table. Her heart was pounding in her chest.

"Mena ..." Julian rubbed the back of his neck, his voice strained and low. He leaned forward, resting his hands against the table. "I think I know what this is about. We were in the middle of a pretty serious conversation when we got interrupted by Ella's son crying. I told you about my past. The horrible things that I did ..."

"Please stop," Mena whispered, jumping up from the seat. It was now or never for her. She took tentative steps toward the other side of the table, then turned to look at Julian. "I was awarded the Nairobi African Art Fellowship. It's an extremely prestigious position for conservators, highly sought after."

Confusion passed across his handsome face as he gazed at her.

Gripping the top of the chair in front of the table, Mena swallowed past the hot mass in her throat and continued, "The fellowship is a two-year program. I'll be moving to Kenya ... in two weeks."

"You're moving away?" Julian asked.

Mena nodded her head, biting her lower lip.

"What about us?" Julian asked, a frown creasing his brow. "You're just going to walk away from what we're building together—"

"Come on Julian!" Mena said, dizzy with angst as she gripped the chair tighter. "Think about it. There isn't an 'us' yet. We've only known each other for a few weeks. Most of our time has been spent chasing down clues about Ella's death. You don't really know me, and I don't really know you! This is too new to be serious."

"But you said we had time to get to know each other better," Julian insisted, reaching for her. "You said we didn't need to rush things. I thought we were—"

"Everything is different now. The fellowship is something I've been striving for since I graduated. It is the opportunity of a lifetime for me, and I can't let anything or anyone stand in my way now that I've finally gotten it." Mena tried to explain.

"You think I'd stand in your way?" Julian asked. His eyes grew dark and cold, but she saw the shadow of pain and hurt in his gaze.

"That's not what I'm saying. I just think that the timing works. This would be a lot harder if this thing between us had already developed into a real relationship—"

"It's a real fucking relationship to me! I opened up to you. You are the only person on the planet that I trusted with my darkest secret. You know things about me that could get me arrested. You're trying to tell me that isn't real? You feel nothing for me?" Julian bolted up from the seat, shifting the table several inches toward Mena.

Mena took a few steps backward as tears pricked her eyes. The silence stretched between them as his words hung in the air. Both of them were acutely aware that she wasn't just leaving for a career opportunity. She was ending any chance they would have of starting a relationship. She'd killed their future by accepting the fellowship.

Squeezing the bridge of her nose, Mena said, "Of course I feel something for you. These weeks have been amazing despite the tragic reason that brought us into each other's lives. But we don't know that we'd end up wanting to stay together after all of this blows over and we don't have Ella and her baby forcing us together."

Julian walked from behind the table. He stalked toward her until he was only a foot away, staring down at her. His eyes bored into her soul. She could see the pain he battled. Regret gripped her like a vice around the neck.

"So, you're only hanging around me because you want to know why Ella was killed? You need closure to make sense of everything, and once you get your answers, then what? I instantly stop being someone you want to spend time with? I don't understand what's fucking happening right now."

Mena took a deep breath. "What's happening is that I realize that I can't build a relationship with you or with anyone. The Fellowship is my top priority, and I'm leaving in two weeks. I hope you can understand why this is the best move for me."

Julian rubbed his hands down his face, letting out a heavy sigh. "Congratulations. I'm not surprised they picked you. You're brilliant. I'm proud of you," he said, his voice strained, though the words were sincere.

"Thank you," Mena said, her body shaking with disappointment. She knew she was doing the right thing, although her heart felt like it was cracking into a million pieces.

Everything between her and Julian was new and fragile. The feelings they shared were intense but hadn't existed long enough to establish strong roots. Better to end things now before it got any harder. A long-distance relationship would be torture for both of them. Why start something that could never be?

Julian stood rigid and motionless in front of her. A beautiful statue of a man who'd awoken her heart again. She would always be grateful to him for that.

Mena knew she should leave the yacht and go back home. But she couldn't force herself to move. She wanted to prolong this last moment she had with him even if it was to witness his pain.

"Goodbye, Julian," Mena said finally. The wind whipped through her hair as she turned away from him toward the aft of the boat. Jumping from the back stairs, she stepped off Julian's boat and right out of his life.

Chapter Fifty-Seven

Julian leaned over the granite counter in his galley, staring at the bottle of vodka.

On one side of the bottle was his cell phone, a picture of Mena he'd taken on their first date saved to the background, smiling back at him. A twinge of pain pierced his heart as the memory of her walking off his boat for the last time assaulted his mind.

On the other side of the bottle was a hard drive. The one he'd stolen from Siamood Storage days ago. Could the contents of that drive hold the missing pieces to why Ella and Bond were murdered? Did he have the strength to find out anymore, now that the one bright spot in his life had gone dark?

Julian grabbed the cell phone in one hand and the hard drive in the other and pushed through the door to the deck. As he jumped off the side of the boat, he dropped the cell phone into the bay, sending a spray of water up as the device disappeared into the blue abyss. He had to stop thinking about Mena and what could have been. The only way to do that was to lose himself in what he should've been doing all along. Doing what he knew Broman would want. Bringing peace to Dawn by getting justice for Ella.

An hour later, he parked his Harley in the narrow driveway in front of Kendrick's home. Jogging up the steps, the door swung open before he had a chance to knock.

Kendrick said, "I thought it would be better for us to meet here. Not sure who can be trusted at the station anymore after Louis Campbell's boat was wiped clean of all DNA. What mysterious evidence do you have?"

"Don't know yet," Julian said, crossing over the threshold and marching toward the kitchen. Reaching into his backpack, he pulled out his laptop and the hard drive and placed it on the modern glass dining table in the kitchen nook. "When we were at Siamood, I swiped a hard drive from a computer that was on the premises. The computer wasn't connected to any network or internet, so there's no way it could have been hacked externally."

"You never told me about that," Kendrick said.

"We got distracted when Bond called to turn himself in," Julian reminded him.

Kendrick nodded. "Now that we know Bond wasn't behind Ella's murder, maybe the computer at Quentin Tufa's new job will give us a clue as to what's going on and why both Ella and Bond were murdered."

"I'm going to need your computer to make this work," Julian said.

Kendrick disappeared into the bedroom, then returned with the computer. "Let me know if you need anything else."

Julian pushed the thoughts of Mena Nix out of his mind and focused on hacking into the hard drive. He couldn't be distracted by her anymore. She'd made it clear that her career was her top priority over everything else in her life. She hadn't given him the option to go with her. While his feelings had grown deeply for her, she obviously hadn't gotten to the point where she reciprocated the feelings like he thought she had. He'd misread the whole situation, and his heartbreak was his own fault.

Connecting cables between the laptop and Kendrick's computer, Julian replaced the hard drive with the one from Siamood and booted up the machines.

Three hours later, Julian had cracked the passwords and encryption software. Kendrick huddled next to him as they looked through the files.

"Embryo inventory records." Kendrick read the heading of the database on the computer screen. "They all have a barcode number, but some of them have a second identifier."

Julian focused on the text filling the screen of the monitor. The second identifier next to certain records was a series of four digits followed by a last name. He'd seen that pattern before. "Let's do a search for 1026SAPPHIRE."

Julian typed the text and pressed enter. No results.

"Let's try one of the women from my missing person cold case files. Try searching 0112FOX," Kendrick said.

Julian typed in the code and pressed enter. The identifier was next to four records, all with different barcodes. Julian clicked on one of the records.

"Some kind of form. Look here." Kendrick pointed to the screen. "Asset delivery date is four months from now. A check mark is in the column labeled 'Buyer confirmed' and in the column labeled 'Payment received,' but no check mark in the column labeled 'Delivered.'"

"There's an attachment," Julian said, clicking on the pdf file.

"Wait a minute. We've seen a purchase order like that before," Kendrick said, then grabbed a file from a stack near the edge of the glass dining table. "This is the 1026SAPPHIRE file folder you got from the basement of the gallery. See this purchase order for an asset valued at $250,000 and the wire transfer letter addressed to Y. Kuypers signed by Irving Bond. It's almost identical to the one in the pdf attachment."

"But the purchase order in the attachment was sent to J. Patterson," Julian said, then clicked on the remaining three records. Each had a check mark in all three columns: buyer confirmed, payment received, and delivered.

"Search for 0325GARDNER too," Kendrick said.

Julian typed in the code. "Same results. This one is next to three records, two delivered and one showing as canceled. You know what this means, don't you?"

"Bond's art scam was a side hustle," Kendrick said, nodding. "He and Tufa were stealing embryos."

"My guess is that they convinced these women to be surrogates and sold the babies on the black market for $250,000," Julian said.

"That's a hefty price tag for a child. Not to be crude, but I'm pretty sure you can get a baby illegally for much cheaper than that," Kendrick said. "Could they have been selling anything else?"

Julian shook his head. "Think about it. Bond and Ella were having an affair. If Ella agreed to be a surrogate but got pregnant by Bond instead, that costs Tufa $250,000. If he decided to sell the baby anyway, Ella could have reneged on the deal and got Bond to back her on it."

"And maybe because of that Tufa kidnapped her and held her hostage down in the basement so he could steal her baby. Ella's message to Dawn said she was being held at the Genesis Gallery and she thought someone was going to kill her," Kendrick said.

Julian added, "Ella gets free and threatens to blow the lid off the whole scam, so she was a liability. Bond wants his baby but was sloppy, and the cops knew he took the little boy. He arranges to turn himself in and hand over information—"

"Probably implicating Tufa in this whole scam," Kendrick said.

"And that put a target on his back," Julian said.

"Tufa could've hired Teo Juarez to get rid of Bond and Ella to maintain his baby-selling ring. I think we've nailed it. We just need proof. My two missing persons are probably laying low on purpose, collecting hefty fees for producing babies. Finding them isn't likely," Kendrick said.

Julian agreed. "That leaves the money or the buyers."

"I'll work on tracking down the buyers from the purchase orders in these files, starting with Y. Kuypers who bought Ella's baby. They've got to be freaked out for paying for a child that hasn't been delivered yet. Should make them more willing to talk," Kendrick said.

"I see you left the tough work to me," Julian said, laughing. "I'll trace the money trail. We're going to nail Dr. Quentin D. Tufa."

Chapter Fifty-Eight

"He in?" Julian asked the receptionist stationed at the front desk of the St. Basil police department as he walked through the metal detectors. Julian had spent the weekend at Kendrick's dining room table, racing through networks trying to follow the complex trail of money flowing through hundreds of accounts. Sleeping on Kendrick's leather recliner was preferable to staying on the yacht where Mena had dumped him. He couldn't deny anymore how hard he'd fallen for her. Maybe once she moved to Kenya, he could forget about her and get back to living like he did before she blew into his life.

In between researching the money trail, he managed to go to work at the Genesis Gallery. Luckily for him, or maybe not, running into Mena wasn't possible. She didn't work the weekends, and he didn't need to endure the pain of seeing her again, revisiting the heartbreak he'd suffered that was damn near crippling him. Losing himself in investigating the murders with Kendrick was the only thing keeping him going. He needed to find proof that Quentin D. Tufa was behind the murders of Ella and Bond. When Kendrick left for work this morning, Julian had been on fumes, having taken only a few quick naps over the past couple of days. He'd promised Kendrick he would come to the police station after his shift ended at the gallery.

The receptionist nodded her head as the phone rang. "Go on back."

Julian headed down the hallway, knocking on Kendrick's open door before entering. Kendrick sat behind the plain brown wooden desk, typing quickly on the keyboard.

Julian glanced over at the three rows of floating shelves on the adjacent wall filled with pictures of Kendrick with his friends and family, smiling and happy. There was one picture of him and Kendrick holding a thirty-five-pound barracuda they'd tag-teamed to catch off the coast of St. Felipe. Simpler times for both of them and moments Julian felt he didn't deserve to treasure and enjoy. Until Mena came into his life. She'd changed him. The guilt was still there, but he knew Broman would want him to move on, too. Reaching for the grey cushioned chair in the corner of the room, Julian pulled it closer to Kendrick's desk and sat.

"I called you like ten times today. What's up with not calling me back? Not to sound like your girl, Mena, but I know your work at the gallery couldn't have been that busy," Kendrick said, his eyes glued to the computer screen.

His girl. Mena. She wasn't anything to him anymore. She'd made that crystal clear. "Not my girl and I threw my phone in the bay. Haven't had a chance to get it replaced."

He regretted tossing his cell phone. At the time, it had seemed like the right thing to do, a way to stop himself from staring at the phone, hoping that Mena would call when he knew she wouldn't.

His time with Mena had expired.

He missed her like crazy.

But, he had to move on.

"Wait ... what did you say? You tossed your cell phone ... in the bay ... on purpose?" Kendrick asked, pausing from his typing. "What's going on with you two? Lover's spat?"

"I wish," Julian said. If they were dealing with a simple argument, he'd be in a much better mood right now. "She dumped me."

"You're joking," Kendrick said, his face clouding with concern.

"No joke. She got a prestigious art fellowship in Kenya, and she's moving there in two weeks," Julian said, sadness welling in his chest. He didn't want to feel these emotions all over again, but they were building like a wave threatening to crash over him and pull him under. They said it was better to have loved and lost than to never have loved at all. He'd tell all of them that they were dead fucking wrong.

"So what? You can handle a little distance. Hell, you could go with her," Kendrick said.

"She made it very clear that she didn't want that," Julian said.

Kendrick said, "I'm sorry to hear that. Some of my bad relationship luck must have rubbed off on you."

"Yeah, I got your cooties," Julian said, surprised by his ability to actually find humor in the situation. "Aren't we a pathetic bunch?"

"Only in love," Kendrick said. "The rest of our lives, we do okay. Speaking of which, let me fill you in. The results of the hair samples we collected from the basement of the Genesis Gallery came back today. We got positive matches for all three women."

"All three?" Julian asked, stunned. "Ella's hair was in the basement."

"And hair of my two missing women—Samantha Fox and Tamara Gardner," Kendrick said. "Priscilla Dumay is going to have to explain how hair strands from a dead woman and two missing women were found in the basement of her gallery. Maybe this will encourage her to give us the goods on her adopted brother. How's your search into the money trail going?"

"Better than I expected," Julian reached into his backpack and pulled out a file folder, handing it to Kendrick. "Zygatica Investments has a bank account at the St. Basil branch of the Porciau Bank. It's the same account that's on the wire transfer letters signed by Bond attached to each purchase order. These are copies of bank activity from last week."

Kendrick took the papers out of the folder and placed them on his desk.

"If you look at the activity for Friday, two hundred fifty thousand dollars was deposited into the Zygatica Investments account from a Swiss bank account. This morning, the same funds were withdrawn from the Zygatica account and sent to a bank in the Netherlands. The withdrawal from Zygatica Investments' account has an additional notation of 'refund 1026SAPPHIRE.' The receiving bank account at the Netherlands Bank is owned by a married couple: Yorick and Nora Kuypers. They originally sent the same amount to Zygatica Investments' account three months ago," Julian said.

Kendrick highlighted the names on the page. "You're fast. My guys are still working on getting information on Y. Kuypers and you've already beaten them to it."

"And I got travel documents for the Kuypers," Julian said, leaning over the desk to grab a page from the file. "Take a look at the date the Kuypers flew into St. Basil."

"That's the same day Irving Bond stole Ella's baby from the hospital," Kendrick said, a frown creasing his forehead.

"The same day I caught Bond at the docks with the baby in the warehouse," Julian remembered.

"Maybe that's why Bond kidnapped the baby ... to stop Tufa from giving his son to the Kuypers," Kendrick said, leaning back in his chair.

"The last page shows the trip the Kuypers booked last night to return to the Netherlands Friday morning. My guess is the Kuypers stuck around to force Tufa to refund their money since the baby wasn't delivered to them. Considering how the money moves through these international banks, they are probably waiting around to make sure the transfer clears before they head back home," Julian said.

"Does Tufa own the Zygatica bank account?" Kendrick asked.

"Still working on that. Even with the new laws in place in the Palmchat Islands to make it easier to determine who owns bank accounts, it's still nearly impossible to get that information. It may be faster for you to get those details from the Kuypers."

"Guess that means I have four days to track the Kuypers down and bring them in for questioning before they get on that plane Friday morning," Kendrick said.

Chapter Fifty-Nine

Mena grabbed the empty seat across the table from Omar at the open-air Genesis Grill and plopped into it, struggling to keep the tears from falling from her swollen eyes. The restaurant was bustling with activity as tourists and locals alike flocked to the popular hot spot for happy hour. While everyone around her was basking in yet another beautiful day in paradise, she was nursing a massive headache and hiding behind oversized sunglasses. She'd spent the weekend at Regina's house curled into a ball, crying. After ending things with Julian, she couldn't bear to go back to her condo where they'd shared so many memories, where she could see his yacht from her living room window, so close yet so far from her in too many ways.

Regina had begged her to talk about what happened, but she couldn't. After reassuring Regina that Julian hadn't done anything physically or emotionally abusive to her, she'd quietly explained that they'd had a "dealbreaker" argument and would no longer be seeing each other. Thankfully, Regina hadn't pressed for more information and instead had allowed her to grieve the lost relationship with Julian.

"Thank God Julian wasn't on the schedule today, or we probably couldn't have convinced you to come to happy hour," Regina said.

Mena didn't respond, although her friend was right. Mena had reluctantly gone home to her condo this week, keeping her curtains drawn to avoid looking out the window at Julian's yacht. She'd made it through half the week without seeing him by avoiding the main gallery building.

"Okay, somebody needs to fill me in on what the hell is going on," Omar demanded.

"She and Julian got into a big fight," Regina said, handing Mena a tissue. Taking off her sunglasses, Mena crumpled the tissue in her hand as she rubbed it over her face.

"Did that brute hurt you? Do I need to call my cousin in the PC-5?" Omar asked, reaching over to grab Mena's hand. "I'll have him in a body bag by the end of the day, you just say the word."

"No," Mena said, laughing softly at Omar's serious offer. She had no doubt that Omar and Regina would do anything she asked to make the pain go away. But there was nothing they could do. As her mom always said, time will heal those wounds. "Really, I'll be fine. I'm just disappointed that we never had a chance."

"I'm sorry Mena," Regina said. "The chemistry between you two was off the charts. I was rooting for you."

"I wasn't," Omar said, pursing his lips. Snatching the Kleenex from Mena's hand, Omar grabbed the monogrammed handkerchief from his coat pocket and delicately dabbed her tears away before handing it to Mena. "I never thought he was good enough for you. I hate to see you crying over that fool. He was for a fun time in the sack. You never should have caught feelings for him."

"Omar!" Regina screeched, frowning at him.

"It's okay. Maybe he's right," Mena said, blowing her nose into the handkerchief.

"Regina may be okay with letting you off the hook, but I'm not," Omar said, a sneaky look in his eyes. "What the hell was the fight about? And don't think of lying to me."

Exhausted, Mena didn't have the strength to resist her friend's well-meaning inquiries.

"I got the Fellowship. I'm moving ... in two weeks," Mena said, forcing a hesitant smile on her face. She should be exhilarated, planning her next life adventure, but instead, she was miserable bemoaning the loss of a man she had fallen for ... hard.

Regina let out a shriek and jumped from her chair. As her friend's arms wrapped around her, rocking her back and forth, Mena let out a shaky sigh.

"I'm so proud of you. Oh, my God. Omar, we get to go to Kenya. We're going to visit you all the time, at least twice a year if not more," Regina gushed.

Omar was quiet, his gaze shrewd.

Mena squirmed under his scrutiny.

"Regina dear, can you go check on what's taking our waiter so long?" Omar asked.

"Sure thing." Regina patted Mena on the arm, then sauntered toward the hostess stand.

"You fool," Omar said.

"What?" Mena asked.

"You dumb idiot," Omar said.

"Really?" Mena asked.

"You broke that man's heart because you have to move to Kenya? Are you crazy?" Omar asked.

"You don't even like Julian," Mena said, her heart thundering as regret seeped through her.

"It's not about what I like. For the past few weeks, I've watched you fall in love, and it looks good on you. I can't believe you of all people would let fear make you walk away from that man," Omar said.

Stunned silent, Mena looked toward the Caribbean Sea. Everything Omar said was true. Despite the heinous crimes that brought them together, she'd broken away from the emotional detachment that had kept her previous attempts at a relationship in St. Basil casual at best. All the walls she'd put up to make sure she wouldn't be a fool for love again had fallen, and it scared her. She couldn't face the idea of being rejected by Julian. So, she struck first.

"A long-distance relationship for two years would never work," Mena said.

"Who says?" Omar demanded. "And what makes you think the relationship would have to be long-distance? That man has no ties to St. Basil. He could pick up and float away on that expensive ass yacht of his at any time."

"I can't ask him to come to Kenya with me. That's a huge commitment," Mena said.

"What you are doing Mena is refusing to give him the opportunity to make that decision for himself. That's not fair. You made all the decisions and didn't give him a choice," Omar said.

"But, I thought I was doing the right thing … for both of us," Mena said.

"You don't get to decide what the right thing is for both of you. Both of you have to decide that," Omar said. "Stop being afraid and get your ass over to that yacht and fix this mistake you've made."

Mena looked down at her hands, resting in her lap. Was Omar right? Hell, she knew he was right. The question was: what was she going to do about it? Mena inhaled a shaky breath. "What if he turns me down?"

"Then at least you can go to Kenya with no regrets, knowing that you tried. Trust me, you need to do this," Omar said.

A memory blazed through Mena's mind. Julian had comforted her after the interview with the Fellowship Board that she'd been convinced was a disaster. He never demanded to know what had upset her. *You know, there's nothing I wouldn't do for you. But I can't guess what you need. You'd have to tell me.*

Regina returned to the table with a short, young man dressed in the all-white attire of the waiters.

"Sorry for the delay. What can I get you to drink?" the waiter asked.

"Nothing for me. I won't be staying," Mena said. Jumping up from her seat, she rounded the table and gave Omar a quick hug. "There's something important I need to do."

Chapter Sixty

The dreaded day off was finally close to an end.

Julian stared at the dark ceiling of his bedroom as the yacht rocked slowly.

He'd given Kendrick all the evidence he'd found to help with Ella's murder investigation. He'd hit a dead end trying to uncover the owner of the Swiss bank account, and it didn't matter anymore, anyway. Kendrick would find the Kuypers, and they would be able to finger Quentin Tufa as the man they'd purchased a baby from on the black market. Kendrick would put pressure on the ex-doctor and force him to admit that he'd put the hit out on Ella and Irving Bond. The case would finally be solved.

There was nothing left for him to do. Nothing for him to focus on, hide behind, or lose himself in.

An empty bottle of vodka laid next to him in the bed, nestled in the spot that should've been Mena's.

Pain seared through Julian's head as he stumbled out of bed and staggered to the galley. He opened another bottle of Burnett's. He'd been waiting for the liquor to numb the pain and dull his memories, but it had had the opposite effect. With each swig, memories of Mena became heightened, clear and vivid—splashing in the water with her at the secret beach, their first date, the feel of his arms around her as she drove his motorcycle around the island, the feel of her body as he made love to her, the sounds of her panting his name as she climaxed.

The memories always ended with the last time they'd seen each other. The day she'd ended things between them. The look on her face when she'd shattered his heart. She'd been so matter of fact as if the time they'd spent together had meant nothing. Just a passing distraction in her life.

Julian stepped out of the galley, a bottle of vodka dangling from his hand. She'd been hesitant to get involved with him. Maybe her divorce had eroded her trust in men, making her more reluctant to enter new relationships. But had they been in a relationship?

No.

Not yet.

He'd lured her with false promises. He'd led her to believe they could live in the moment with no strings, no labels, no pressure. He had no right to be upset with her because he hadn't been honest with her about what he really wanted. He hadn't been honest about what he really felt for her. He knew the moment he'd first seen her in the courtyard that she was special. He'd been drawn to her, propelled by some invisible force to create a connection with her, one that had grown deep and quick for him. He'd fallen in love, fast and hard. Now he was resigned to embrace the despair crushing him after losing his chance with her.

Stepping over an empty box of Saltine crackers, Julian stared at the choppy waters of Crescent Moon Bay. The bright orange sun shimmered in the cloudless blue sky signaling another beautiful day in paradise.

Fuck paradise.

Coming to St. Basil had been a mistake.

He never should have stayed on this stupid fucking island.

Walking to the coffee table, Julian lifted his leg and kicked the glass table across the room. The bottle dropped from his hand, spilling vodka all over the floor. He lunged at the couch and sent the pillows flying through the air. Swiping his hand across the bar, he sent plates and cups flying, the plastic clanking as it hit the wooden floor. Reaching for the curtains, he grabbed fabric in his hands and yanked them from the wall. Fighting through the folds of fabric, he kicked the curtains to the floor as he looked for something else to destroy. Sweat beaded along his brow as he threw cushions against the walls and kicked over another table. Collapsing from the futility of his destruction,

Julian laid on one of the bare couches and closed his eyes. Losing Mena was going to be a bitch to get over.

"Feel any better?" Her voice floated to his ears.

Julian blinked his eyes open, trying to focus. His heart thundered in his chest.

She came back.

"You didn't think I was going to leave without seeing you, did you?"

Julian shook his head and grabbed her hands.

"I'm so sorry," Julian started. "I never should have—"

"Shhh," She put her finger to his lips. "Don't tell me, show me."

She leaned forward and kissed him, her lips exploring his with a desperate passion. Straddling his waist, she fumbled with the buttons on his khaki shorts and tugged at the waistband of his boxer briefs as her kisses traveled down his face. She sucked on his ear as her hand found its target in his pants.

"Make this pain go away. Make me feel like a woman again." Her words floated to his ears as she licked and sucked on the side of his neck.

Julian squirmed under her touch.

Something was ... wrong.

Chapter Sixty-One

Speeding through the streets, Mena turned into the parking lot of the marina and pulled into an empty parking spot. Stepping out of the car, she paused to take in the exquisite sunset. She never got tired of watching the brilliant burst of light slipping below the horizon of the bay faster than her eyes could fathom.

Mena slammed the car door. She had to make things right, but she wasn't delusional. She had no misguided expectations of a fairy tale reunion where Julian decided to try out a long-distance relationship with her. She wanted forgiveness for the mistake she'd made. He, for one, should understand that.

Mena walked along the sidewalk leading to the boardwalk and boat slips. Julian's yacht was docked in the last slip of the row for oversized boats.

Picking up the pace, she wondered if he was home. There were no lights shining through any of his windows, and the boat looked deserted. He could be out with Kendrick trying to gather more evidence to solve Ella's murder. He could be living his life, having moved on. She could be a distant memory in his mind. A blip on the radar. He might have already gotten comfortable with her departure. He might not want a chance to resume their relationship. But, nothing was going to stop her from trying.

Reaching the back of the yacht, Mena ascended the four stairs to the bottom deck of the boat and walked around to the starboard side. Her heart was pounding out of her chest.

Rounding the corner toward the floor-to-ceiling glass doors to the inner cabin, Mena prepared to knock on the door. Raising her fist, she stopped. Frowning, she struggled to comprehend what she saw.

She couldn't breathe.

This couldn't be happening.

Fumbling backward, she couldn't stop looking at the scene playing out in front of her eyes.

Pillows were strewn across the floor.

The glass coffee table overturned.

Julian stretched out on the long sofa.

A petite blond straddled him, stroking his penis, as they kissed with reckless abandon.

Chapter Sixty-Two

Her touch was different.

His body wasn't responding as it had all the other times they'd made love. Pushing her back, Julian tried to get his bearings.

"Don't push me away. I need this. You owe me this. I've lost everything."

Julian grabbed her wrists and jerked her away from him.

He forced the fog from his head and looked at her face.

Dawn Garrison. His best friend's wife.

"What are you doing?" Julian demanded. He gently moved her leg from straddling him and stood from the couch. He needed to put distance between them. His mind was a confused mess of vodka, memories of Mena, and Dawn trying to make out with him.

"Help me get past this. I feel like my life is destroyed all over again. I need to feel something other than pain." Dawn stood and walked over to him, groping his body. "Please do this for me."

Placing his arm around her, he tried to comfort her in the only way he was willing. He could never be anything more to Dawn than a friend and not just because of how much Broman meant to him. He couldn't bring himself to think about being with another woman because of Mena.

"I can't. We can't do this. Broman—"

"Don't you say his name!" Dawn slapped him. Balling her fists, she beat against his chest and arms. "You took him away from me. He spent all his time with you instead of me."

Julian withstood her blows, which quickly lost steam as she collapsed in his arms. He led Dawn back to the couch.

Julian sank to his knees in front of Dawn and placed his hands on the sides of her face. Wiping the tears from her eyes, he said, "Broman loved you. He wanted nothing more than to make you happy. You made him feel alive."

"Is that what he told you? Broman was married to the SEALs, not to me," Dawn whispered.

"You know that's not true," Julian said, remembering all the times Broman snuck away from training missions to squeeze in time with his wife, risking the wrath of their commanding officers. "Every chance he got, he was trying to spend time with you."

"And what about the times you stole from me. Moments I should have had with my husband when he was off riding boards down another damn mountain with you! Why did he love you so much that he gave the time he should have been spending with me to you? Didn't the two of you spend enough time together?"

"We were best friends, but he never put me before you. Not once and you know it. You can be mad at me, but don't use your anger to destroy the truth of who Broman was. You were his life," Julian said.

"And he was mine. Now I have nothing. I have no life. How can I walk away from him? How can I move on when he's still here, living and breathing?"

"He would want you to move on. He would want you to love and be loved again," Julian said. He knew in his heart that was true. Broman would move heaven and earth to take away the pain Dawn was feeling right now.

"Finding another man to love me is impossible while he's still alive, while there's still a chance, even slim, that he could come back to me. The only bright spot I had was the chance to raise Ella's baby, but that got snatched away from me too."

"What?" Julian asked, his tone uncertain as his chest tightened.

"You didn't get my message?" Dawn asked, her words choked with tears.

Of course, he hadn't. His cell phone was somewhere resting on the sand at the bottom of Crescent Moon Bay. Not his smartest move, but he'd been too busy lamenting the loss of the woman he'd fallen for to care about keeping up with what was going on in the world.

"No. Tell me … what happened to the baby?" Julian asked.

"CPS ran the DNA test," Dawn started, then broke down into heavy sobs.

What could have gone wrong with the DNA test? If Bond was the father, then Dawn would have a clear shot of getting custody of Ella's son since Bond was dead. The test must have identified someone else as the father. Someone who was going to fight Dawn for custody of the child. Could it be Quentin Tufa?

"Bond wasn't a match for the baby," Dawn said, covering her face with her hands. "And neither was I."

Julian froze, his body rigid with disbelief. His mind raced as he struggled to make sense of the bomb she'd dropped. "How is that possible?"

"No one knows. All we know is that Ella was not the biological mother of the baby she was carrying."

Chapter Sixty-Three

"That was worse than I expected," Omar said, wrapping an arm around Mena. Walking past the huge windows across from the conference room on the second floor of the Genesis Gallery, they headed toward the elevators.

Driving aimlessly around the south side of the island, Mena had been on a downward spiral of self-reflection. The image of Julian making out with the petite blond was burned in her memories, threatening to consume her in regret. She didn't want to think about who the woman was or why he'd moved on so quickly after their quasi-breakup. None of that mattered anymore. She'd gotten the answers she was looking for—there was no chance of a reconciliation between them.

Priscilla had called, interrupting her woeful state, demanding an update on the work she and Omar had done on the gallery inventory. When she arrived, Omar was waiting for her. They'd tried to keep the truth from Priscilla as long as possible but had to come clean with their findings. With the assistance of Uma, Irving had stolen twenty pieces from the gallery and replaced them with fakes—more than double the amount the cops had told Priscilla about.

Omar said, "If Irving wasn't already dead, the look on Priscilla's face when you broke the news would have killed him in his tracks. I thought she was seriously going to pop a blood vessel right then and there."

"Can you blame her? I'm surprised she's not going to take the evidence we gathered to the police," Mena said.

"She can't let her reputation be tarnished any more than it already has been. Can you imagine the rumors that would swirl about all of us if it turns out Prissy had more than one employee who was a criminal? People would think we were all crooks duping unsuspecting art buyers and I'm not trying to be blacklisted. I think it's for the best. But little Uma Fischer better watch her back," Omar said.

The elevator dinged. As the doors opened, Mena stepped in and almost collided with Adam Russell, the head of security.

"Excuse me, Ms. Nix, Mr. Johnson." Adam paused, narrowly avoiding contact with Mena as he stepped out the elevator. "You two headed home?"

"I don't know about home, but we're about to get the hell up out of here. We deserve some drinks," Omar said, laughing.

Mena nodded.

Adam didn't seem to appreciate Omar's humor. Serious as usual, he said, "Well, drive safely and enjoy what's left of your evening."

"Thanks," Mena responded and pressed the button for the first floor of the Gallery.

"I know you don't want to talk about this, but I need to tell you how proud I am of you for what you did earlier with Julian. Doesn't matter that things didn't work out the way you wanted. You get huge credit for trying," Omar said.

Mena blinked back tears for the first time since she'd witnessed the compromising position of the petite blond and Julian. Stumbling away from the yacht, she'd been resigned. Doubts had clawed at her when she left happy hour with Omar and Regina as if she'd known that her attempts to reconcile with Julian would be futile. The fear and trust issues she thought she'd shed from her failed marriage had corrupted her relationship with Julian. When they hit a roadblock, she didn't trust him enough to talk through how to handle her move to Kenya. Maybe they would have ended up in the same spot, deciding to split up. Maybe they wouldn't have. Now she'd never know, and that was something she'd regret for quite some time.

"How could he have moved on so fast?" Mena asked.

"Because men are bastards," Omar said. "But, he could have thought there was no hope for the two of you. So, he tried to erase the memory of you from his mind the only way he knew how: banging some chick who's the exact opposite of you."

"Well, I think I'm going to leave for Kenya early," Mena said. The elevator doors opened, and they stepped out, heading toward the front lobby of the Gallery.

"Are you serious? Damn, I guess I understand. Why wait any longer, hanging around here where you have the chance to bump into that bastard again," Omar said.

"There's a lot I need to do, like find an apartment and get used to the area before I start the fellowship. So, I was hoping you could arrange to have my condo packed up and shipped to me," Mena said, placing an arm around Omar's shoulders.

"Of course, girl," Omar said. "I bet Prissy is sick that you're leaving early. She's always been your biggest cheerleader, and I'm sure she wanted to throw you a fabulous going away party—"

"I haven't said anything to her about it. I should go back upstairs and talk to her," Mena said.

"Want me to wait for you?" Omar asked.

Mena shook her head. "No, it's late. Go home to your man. But thanks for all your support. I love you so much!" Mena threw her arms around Omar and gave him a big hug.

Minutes later, she exited the elevator on the second floor. The sitting area was quiet and peaceful. Stepping toward the double doors leading into Dumay's office, Mena paused as she heard a male voice in the room, probably Adam Russell. She didn't want to interrupt their meeting. Priscilla was probably giving Adam an update on everything Mena and Omar had discovered about the fake art at the gallery.

She took a step forward, straining to hear if the conversation was wrapping up or if she should try talking to her tomorrow. She had a lot to do, starting with booking a flight to Nairobi, packing a bag for the trip and reaching out to Wangari Irungu's assistant for suggestions of apartment locators who could show her around. She didn't think Priscilla would care if she left a week early. She'd already completed the transfer of her work to her temporary replacement until a new conservator was hired.

Words flittered through the air from inside the office.

"Cops have hit a dead end," Adam said, serious and curt.

"Are you absolutely sure there are no more loose ends? Nothing that would lead back to us?" Priscilla asked, her voice cold and harsh.

"We've eliminated every threat to your operations. The assets have all been safely relocated without triggering any suspicion," Adam responded.

Mena felt a cold chill creep down her spine. Memories from the night she and Julian investigated the Gallery basement looking for Irving Bond and the kidnapped baby intruded into her thoughts. Zak Webber had told Quentin to initiate Operation X to move some *assets*. Were these the assets Adam was referencing? What were these assets, and why could moving them trigger suspicion?

"Good. I'm concerned about the high body count, but I couldn't afford to let Bond turn on me to save his sorry ass. He had to be taken care of," Priscilla said.

A sharp bang against wood reverberated in the air.

Mena jumped as her hands flew to her mouth. High body count? Was Priscilla responsible for Bond's death? How was that possible?

Priscilla Dumay was a pillar of the St. Basil community. She was the same woman who'd been an advocate for Mena's own career progression. In addition to giving her an amazing opportunity to lead the conservation department at a major gallery, Pricilla had influenced the Board to finally give her the coveted Fellowship.

A sob caught in Mena's throat. Could Priscilla have arranged for the murder of Bond? Mena pressed her body against the wall, straining to hear more of the conversation.

"How are things with my brother? I won't have him going down for that idiot," Priscilla said.

"Based on my sources within the police department, Quentin is the main suspect. I'm not sure we can protect him. We need to get him off the island and into our temporary facility tonight," Adam said.

"Damn that sonofabitch!" Priscilla thundered. "If Irving had thought with his brain and not his dick, my brother wouldn't be in this mess. You have papers ready for him?"

"Arrangements are being made as we speak. Don't worry. I've covered all the bases. The only two people who could cause problems for you have been silenced," Adam confirmed.

"Thank God we don't have to deal with that whore, anymore. If I'd known

Ella was blackmailing Irving over his art forgery scam, I never would have agreed to bring her into our operations," Priscilla said.

"That's behind us. Things will get back to normal soon," Adam said.

"Absolutely," Priscilla responded with confidence. "I also need you to ramp up the inventory of assets in our new location. Maybe send Zak down in advance to get them. I plan to increase production as soon as we get there, and our current assets can't bear the load."

Mena stumbled back from the door. She needed to get out of the Gallery without alerting Priscilla or Adam. She wasn't sure what to do with this information. She could barely comprehend what she'd heard. But she knew one person who'd know what to do.

Turning around, Mena slammed into a solid, muscular body. Staring up, her gaze met the flat black eyes of Zak Webber. Her body trembled as she stumbled to the side.

"Excuse me," Mena whispered.

Zak's response was brusque. "You're not going anywhere."

Chapter Sixty-Four

Dawn beamed as she crossed the hotel lobby toward Julian.

What could have her in such a good mood? Two days ago, she'd been a wreck, trying to seduce him, and now she looked like she'd won the lottery. Not at all what Julian had expected to see when he agreed to meet her before she boarded her flight back to the United States.

"I'm not leaving after all," Dawn said, her smile bright. "Why the hell don't you check your damn messages?"

Julian looked down at the new cell phone in his hand that he'd picked up late yesterday evening. He hadn't noticed the icon indicating three missed messages.

"I take it you got good news. Is this about the baby?" Julian asked.

"I applied to be a foster mother for him," Dawn said, steering Julian toward a set of wicker chairs tucked away behind the main check-in area of the hotel. She sat in one of the chairs and motioned for Julian to sit across from her.

"CPS said this type of scenario was unprecedented. They don't have protocols on how to track down the biological parents for the child or the financial resources to do so. While they work through their next steps, the caseworker said I had a good shot at becoming his foster mom. If they hit a dead end trying to find the parents, which the caseworker thought they would, it would put me at the top of the list to adopt him," Dawn explained.

Julian studied her face. He wasn't surprised Dawn wanted to be a mother to the baby. Raising the child would be a fresh start for her, the one bright spot in years of devastation and disappointment.

"That's great news … I'm happy for you," Julian said, looking out the window at the marble waterfall wall in the shape of a crescent moon that served as the entrance to the hotel. Sheets of water cascaded down the smooth black surface in harmony with the calypso music playing outside. He'd planned on giving Dawn a final update on Ella's murder case before she left the island, but now he wasn't sure she needed or wanted those details. Dawn didn't need him to help her get closure. She'd done that all on her own. Telling her about his role in tracking down evidence that brought them closer to bringing down Dr. Quentin Tufa for Ella's death now would be selfish.

"Don't look so worried. I know what I'm doing, and I know the risks. That little boy didn't ask to be born into this situation. He needs someone to take care of him. I can help him heal as he helps me heal from the pain of losing my sister. Doesn't matter if that's for the next eighteen hours or the next eighteen years."

"He's very lucky to have you."

"You don't mean that," Dawn said, with a deep laugh. She crossed her arms over her chest. "You and I will never be close. I don't like you, and you barely put up with me for Broman's sake. But, I feel like we've settled into an acceptable state of co-existence."

Julian raked his fingers through his hair. "I do mean it. No matter how strained things are between us and probably will continue to be, the best thing that could happen for that child is to grow up with you as his mother."

Months ago, he'd agreed to help Dawn track down her missing sister to get forgiveness for all the ways he'd hurt her in the past. Today, he no longer felt the need to convince her to forgive him. She had a right to blame him for Broman's condition. For Julian, sharing his deepest secret with Mena had broken the hold that mistake had over him. He still regretted what happened, but he no longer felt the need to punish himself continuously for the deaths that had resulted from his actions or for Broman's vegetative state. He couldn't say he had completely forgiven himself, but he had gotten to the point where he was willing to enjoy life again. Mena Nix had done that for him, and he'd forever be thankful for the short time that he was able to share his life with her. Because of Mena, Julian was satisfied knowing he'd done everything he could. Dawn didn't have to know about his role in getting justice for Ella.

Tucking a strand of her blond hair behind her ear, Dawn said, "I'm sorry about what happened between us a couple of days ago. I shouldn't have crossed that line."

Julian waved away her apology and leaned back in the oversized chair. "You've been through a lot."

"And you talked me off the ledge. If it wasn't for you, I don't know what I would have done after I found out the DNA test results, but it would have been something ... tragic. You kept my feet on solid ground and supported me through that shock, and I'm grateful for that. So, there's something I need to show you," Dawn said. She reached into her purse and pulled out a letter that Julian recognized immediately.

The same letter he'd promised Broman he would give to Dawn if anything ever happened to him. When Julian had stood on Dawn's porch that day, he'd been convinced that Broman would not make it through the emergency surgeries he was undergoing at that same moment.

Handing the letter to Julian, Dawn said, "Read it."

"Broman never meant for me to know what was in this letter," Julian said. The paper felt heavy in his hands, like it had that day. A single five by seven sheet of stationery from a small inn in Nepal where Julian and Broman had dirt boarded down a section of the Himalayan Mountains about a month before Broman's impromptu wedding to Dawn.

"Doesn't matter. I think you should read it," Dawn said, dabbing a finger against her eyes as tears began to fall. "I'd kept it with me since you gave it to me over three years ago, but I'd never read it. When I left your boat Saturday night, I finally read Broman's last words to me. Together, both of you helped me get past all the pain and the hurt. I think it will help you too."

Weighed down by the emotions of seeing his best friend's last words, Julian sucked in a deep breath. The message was what Broman wanted the woman he loved most in this world to know if he ever was killed on a mission.

Unfolding the paper, Julian saw the short block of writing and read the intimate note.

My beautiful Dawn, my body may have died, but my soul and my spirit will love you forever. You are the best thing that ever happened to me, and I wouldn't have become the man that I am without your unconditional love, your support, and your acceptance.

You took a broken boy and made him a whole man, and for that, I will always love you. In time, I hope you will find love again. But until then, lean on Julian to help you get through the pain. Our work is dangerous, and we sometimes make mistakes, but I know that Julian did everything in his power to bring me back to you alive. Sending love to you from heaven. Broman.

Folding the paper, he handed it back to Dawn.

Julian closed his eyes, overcome with emotion.

He and Broman had witnessed many of their friends, fellow soldiers, perish. They knew the risks they took each day to protect the world from the evils that existed. They knew they were human, fallible, and susceptible to mistakes, no matter how hard or how long they trained. Somewhere along the way, Julian had forgotten that simple truth. He'd convicted himself for a mistake he'd made when he now knew his best friend would never have blamed him for the state he was in.

Dawn had been right.

Reading Broman's letter was exactly what he needed.

"Thank you," Julian whispered.

Now it was Dawn's turn, waving away his gratitude. "Now that's behind us, there is something that I need from you. Your name carries a lot of weight on this island since you've saved a few lives and gotten a ridiculous amount of media coverage for your heroism. CPS needs a personal reference, and I gave them your name and number. So, can you check to see if you have a voice mail from them?"

Julian nodded, flipping his phone over in his hand. Accessing the app, he placed the phone to his ear and listened as the automated message conveyed that he had three messages. The first message began.

Kendrick's voice flooded through his ears. A surge of adrenaline flowed through his body as he listened to the message. Standing abruptly, the wicker chair tipped over, crashing to the floor.

"I have to go," Julian mumbled to Dawn as he rushed out of the hotel lobby.

Chapter Sixty-Five

"Julian," Kendrick said, leaning back in his chair. "We were just getting started, please come on in. This is Yorick and Nora Kuypers."

Julian entered the office and closed the door behind him. With long strides, he passed the couple, nodding at them, and took a position in the corner near Kendrick, leaning against a metal file cabinet.

Officers had been waiting at the airport to intercept the Kuypers before their flight after they'd been unable to locate them on the island over the past four days.

Kendrick raised a hand toward Julian, then turned his attention to the couple. "Mr. Montgomery has been consulting on the matter that I'd like to discuss with you today."

As Kendrick began the interrogation, Julian studied the couple. By his estimation, Yorick and Nora Kuypers were in their late forties, well-traveled and successful professionals. Having spent most of their lives building careers to be envied, they were now refocusing their priorities on having children. Julian guessed success eluded them in this area.

The Kuypers dutifully responded to Kendrick's line of softball questions for fifteen minutes—what brought them to the island, where were they staying, how long was their trip and how were they enjoying themselves so far. Yorick was cool and calm, weathering the questions with ease. He gave well-prepared answers, not too short, not too long. Enough detail to convey innocence, but not too much to accidentally spill information he wasn't prepared to divulge.

Nora was the enigma.

She kept her eyes downcast, unwilling to participate in the discussion, and deferring to her husband. Her hands, clasped tightly, rested in her lap and she hadn't uttered a single word.

The first kink in the couple's armor had come a minute ago after Kendrick had explained that the police were investigating abnormal transactions at the St. Basil branch of the Pourciau Bank. A rather large transaction between the couple and a local entity had been flagged, and Kendrick was tasked with investigating the origins and reasons for the transaction.

Nora glanced at her husband, fear, and worry in her eyes then returned her gaze to her lap. Yorick had rubbed a finger along the collar of his shirt, tugging on the material before responding.

"We had donated to the local art Co-Op here on the island, but in light of the incidents occurring over the last few weeks, we no longer believed that we should contribute to that organization," Yorick had finally responded.

"I assume you're referring to the Co-Op sponsored by the Genesis Gallery?" Kendrick asked, leaning forward in his chair, closing the space between himself and the Dutch couple.

"Yes, that is correct," Yorick responded.

Nora gripped her hands tighter, causing the knuckles to turn white.

"The deaths linked to the gallery were most unfortunate. But Mr. Kuypers, I'm sure you are well aware that the Co-Op is governed by a board of some of the most upstanding citizens of our islands and not by the Genesis Gallery. The deaths have had no impact on the good that the Co-Op is doing in this community. Do you often ask for money back from charitable organizations?" Kendrick asked.

Mr. Kuypers cleared his throat. "No, we do not, but again the Co-Op is also supported by the Genesis Gallery, and we were uncomfortable leaving our donation with an organization linked to two mysterious deaths. The Co-Op understood of course, and promptly refunded our money."

"That's interesting, Mr. Kuypers. The unusual transaction we are investigating was very large ... two hundred fifty thousand dollars, that's a lot of money," Kendrick said, whistling under his breath before continuing. "Now, my father is a member of the board that governs the Co-Op, and I happen to know that the organization has a dedicated account at the local branch of the St. Killian Bank, not the Pourciau Bank. Additionally, all of the Co-Op's funds are subject to extreme rigor since the Co-Op is a registered non-profit organization within our country."

Nora raised her head.

Julian could see her eyes grow wide, and she turned to look at her husband. Yorick patted her leg and let his hand rest there as Kendrick continued.

"I also know that any withdrawal or payment from the Co-Op's accounts over one hundred thousand dollars has to be approved by the Board. But that's irrelevant, isn't it? Because you and I both know that you didn't send a donation to the Co-Op or receive a refund from that organization," Kendrick said.

A tear welled in Nora's eye and rolled slowly down her face, then dropped onto the lap of her yellow sundress. A flurry of tears followed as she covered her face with her hands and began to sob.

Yorick wrapped his arms around his wife, rubbing her shoulders gently. Several minutes passed as Nora's loud sobs reduced to a faint whisper. Yorick kissed Nora lightly on the head before turning his attention back to the detective.

"Do you have children, Detective Caillouet?" Yorick asked, his voice soft and low.

Kendrick shook his head.

"And your colleague? Children?" Yorick looked at Julian.

Julian stared at the man and didn't respond. Keeping his arm's crossed, he had no desire to engage in banter with the couple. He needed the evidence he knew they could give. The critical link he needed to finally get justice for Ella.

"You men are young, still in your prime with plenty of years to procreate and raise children of your own. My wife and I are not so lucky. I was born with a genetic abnormality that results in azoospermia," Yorick explained.

"Azoospermia?" Kendrick asked.

"No sperm exists in my semen. I am unable to produce children. My wife and I took our time building our business and didn't try to have children until later in life. We didn't discover my issue until it was too late. We are in our late forties now, and it didn't make sense to continue to try to get pregnant with a sperm donor. Instead, we tried to adopt," Yorick explained.

"What stopped you?" Kendrick asked.

Julian wondered the same thing. A successful couple like the Kuypers should have no issues adopting a child in the Netherlands or anywhere for that matter.

"We were selfish!" Nora screamed as another round of sobs erupted from her body. "It wasn't enough for us to get a healthy baby. We wanted a perfect baby."

A perfect baby. Designer baby adoptions were well known on the black market. Couples that wanted to have a say in more than the sex of their baby. They wanted specific eye color and hair color while others wanted assurances of height and weight, intelligence, or predisposition to athletics or musical talent. Was that the reason for the high price on the babies? Were the genetic profiles of the embryos cataloged before implanting them into surrogates? Was that the service Dr. Quentin Tufa was providing?

"Judge us if you will, but we have gotten to the point in our lives where we are willing to do whatever it takes to get the baby of our dreams. Yes, we wanted a fair child, blond hair, blue eyes, one that would look like us," Yorick explained.

Julian thought of the baby Ella had given birth to—a boy with wispy blond hair and deep, cornflower blue eyes. Everything that the Dutch couple was looking for. But did the couple have any idea what people like Tufa were doing to get them the baby of their dreams? Did they have any idea how lives were impacted and destroyed in their quest for the perfect child?

Seething, Julian stalked toward Yorick, looking down at him and said, "So you set out to buy a baby like you buy a car? Picking the color and all the options you want? This is a child for God's sake!"

Cowering under his gaze, Nora hung her head low.

Yorick raised his hands and said, "Please, no. Our preferences weren't all superficial. Genetic testing and understanding genetic predispositions are critically important before adopting a child. These measures are frowned upon in typical adoptions, but we needed to know that the child we received had the best chance for living a long and happy life with us. This method of adopting a child included extensive genetic testing, beyond what is commonly available at most hospitals. Cutting edge genetic mapping that hasn't been approved for use in any country. You take a huge risk adopting a baby from strangers. We wanted certainty about the child we adopted," Yorick explained. "We understood the ... legal implications of our choice but felt that the reward outweighed the risks."

"So you paid two hundred fifty thousand dollars for what exactly?" Kendrick asked.

Yorick dropped his head, then said, "Certain adjustments were made to the embryonic DNA to ensure we received a child that was exactly what we wanted. This organization has had excellent results, despite the medical profession's disdain for this type of procedure. We did our research. The babies supplied to other couples were perfect, healthy, and resistant to most childhood diseases, with no negative side effects from the genetic modifications. Once we saw that, we knew that was the approach we wanted to take."

Genetically modified embryos? Julian couldn't believe what he was hearing. He couldn't understand why anyone would cross the moral and ethical boundaries to get a baby they thought was perfect. He felt sick, thinking of what the Kuypers, and who knew how many other couples, had wanted.

"And this organization confirmed that they could meet your specifications?" Kendrick asked.

"Yes, they assured us we would get the child we requested," Yorick whispered.

"But the broker lied!" Nora wailed through her tears. "Our baby is here, but he was given to someone else. Probably someone who paid a lot more than we were willing to pay."

"You dealt with a broker for this ... baby transaction?" Kendrick asked.

"The baby was born prematurely, and we were told to come to the island early. We've been waiting for weeks to take the baby home, and finally, we were told that the baby was no longer available with no further details or information. We could get another child, but it would take twelve months for them to secure what we wanted," Yorick explained, a tremor creeping into his voice. His body slumped in the chair, and he reached for his wife's hand.

"So, you asked for a refund," Julian stated.

"We could not wait twelve months for another suitable child to be available. We needed that money in case we were able to ..." Yorick hesitated before adding, "I don't think I should say anymore. I want to call my lawyer."

Nora continued to whimper, as she clung to her husband like a lifeline.

Julian took a step toward Yorick and bent down, leaning his head inches from Yorick's face. His tone slow and measured, Julian asked, "Who's your baby broker?"

"I'm not saying anything else until I have my lawyer present," Yorick said, shrinking back.

Julian stood, then glanced back at Kendrick and shrugged. Kendrick gave a slight nod.

With a swift kick of his foot to the back of the chair, Julian sent Yorick crashing to the floor. Nora screamed and jumped up from her chair. Julian held a hand out toward her, daring her not to move as he stood over Yorick, sprawled on the floor.

Nora stood frozen in place.

Dropping down to his knees, Julian pressed his elbow into Yorick's trachea. "I'm going to ask you one more time."

"Stop! Please don't hurt my husband," Nora screamed.

Julian looked up at Nora, without relieving any pressure on Yorick, whose face was turning bright red.

Nora wrung her hands, then uttered the words Julian had been waiting for.

"Priscilla Dumay," Nora whispered. "Our adoption broker's name is Priscilla Dumay."

Chapter Sixty-Six

"Can you believe Priscilla Dumay was behind this whole thing? The Kuypers are going to lawyer up and they should. Probably going to negotiate immunity from prosecution for their part, which I'm fine with as long as they give me enough evidence to nail Dumay," Kendrick said after the Kuypers were escorted down the hallway to an empty interrogation room being used as a holding cell until their lawyer arrived.

"The Kuypers didn't give us anything to connect Priscilla to Ella's murder," Julian said. He grew more irritated as he lifted the overturned chair from the floor and sat. Ella didn't have to die. She'd gotten caught up with immensely dangerous criminals and found herself sucked into their operations because of her own greed. She'd been taken most likely to protect Bond from her blackmailing attempts, then used by Dumay to be a surrogate for babies sold to couples like the Kuypers.

"The evidence is out there," Kendrick said, confidence in his tone. "We'll get what we need to prove that Dumay orchestrated Ella's murder."

There was a soft knock on the door, then a tall, thin woman poked her head through the partially open door. "Detective, I have the analysis on the hair strands found in the basement of the gallery."

Kendrick walked toward the door and took the folder from the woman, then closed it behind him. Opening the file, he was quiet for several minutes, reading the contents.

"The hair strand matching Ella Sapphire was old, decaying and fragile, but the strands matching Tamara Gardner and Samantha Fox were hydrated and healthy indicating that they had fallen from the heads of each woman within a couple of days of when we collected the sample," Kendrick said.

"Wait a minute. You're telling me that there's a good chance that both women were in the basement within days of when you searched the place?" Julian asked bewildered.

"Ella said she'd been kidnapped. You think it's possible that the surrogates aren't being paid for their services?" Kendrick asked.

"Like Dumay was kidnapping women and forcing them to have these genetically modified babies. It would explain why Ella was pregnant with a child that wasn't biologically hers and why Dumay had her killed after she escaped," Julian surmised.

"This is worse than we thought. If that's true, there's no telling how many women Dumay has forced to be baby-making slaves. We've got to find these women. Where could Dumay be hiding them now?" Kendrick asked.

"Operation X had to be moving the women to another location. We've got to start scouring other buildings and companies owned by Dumay to see where she may have taken them. But without knowing how many women, it's hard to know what size facility she needs," Julian said.

"But she will need access to medical equipment and medicines if she's caring for a bunch of pregnant women. That rules out remote locations, don't you think?" Kendrick asked.

Julian wasn't so sure. "Maybe. The Kuypers could be our key to finding them. They may know more than they realize—"

The lights flickered in the office, then shut off, bathing the room in darkness.

"What the hell?" Kendrick muttered.

A fractured round of gunshots sliced through the air.

Screams permeated through the walls from the near empty squad room as footsteps pounded against the floor. Most of the officers were on lunch break, beat duty, or out investigating crimes. A small contingent of administrative employees was manning the floor with a couple of first year officers in the squad room.

"Get down now!" A gruff, male voice screamed as another series of cries and whimpers filled the air.

"Grab the guns! On the floor! On the floor!" The male voice commanded.

Julian jumped from his seat, with Kendrick close behind him as they rushed toward the office door. Opening the door, a wave of smoke flooded into the office from the single hallway that traversed the squad room on both the east and west sides, lined with offices for detectives and interrogation rooms.

Poking his head into the hallway, Julian could make out three figures clad in black with ski masks covering their faces. Short shafts of sunlight filtered into the squad room from the windows at the front of the police station. The administrative staff huddled in chairs at the desks, handcuffed. Julian could see two officers in the middle of the squad room, their bodies pressed against the tile floor with their hands handcuffed behind their back.

"Let's go!" the gruff male instructed.

Julian got a better view of the man, wielding an assault rifle with a brown bandana covering the nose holes of the ski mask. Another man followed next to him, heading toward the hallway where Kendrick's office was near the middle. The third man remained behind, his gun trained on the heads of the two cops on the ground as the executive assistants muffled cries faded into the background.

Finger trained on the Beretta, Julian knew he might need to create a diversion to give Kendrick time to get to the Kuypers. His body was calm as he focused on the slow, steady cadence of his breathing. His throat burned from the smoke as the acrid smell tinged his nostrils.

Heavy footsteps charged closer, stomping the ground as each office door was kicked in. The smoke would provide limited cover for Kendrick to get to the interrogation room to protect the Kuypers, but Julian needed to time the move carefully. Sliding down against the wall, Julian opened the door wider. Kendrick squatted next to him, poised to run.

As the men stood near another closed office door, two up from Kendrick's, Julian waved a hand at Kendrick. He'd need to go now, and if the gunmen saw him, Julian was prepared for a shoot out to provide Kendrick cover to get to the Kuypers.

A heavy foot exploded against the door.

A fire blast lit up the hallway, and a loud pop detonated in the air as one of the gunmen fell to the floor.

"I'm hit!" the second gunman cried.

Kendrick brushed past Julian as he ran down the hallway. Julian followed, running backward, his eyes glued to the fight taking place in the hallway between the remaining gunman and one of the officers. In a matter of seconds, the gunman had subdued the officer, relieving him of his weapon and beating him unconscious on the ground.

Julian ducked into the interrogation room behind Kendrick and closed the door slowly. Pressing his back against the wall behind the door, Julian checked the magazine of the Beretta as Kendrick yanked his cell phone from his pocket and turned on the phone's flashlight.

The illuminated faces of the Kuypers were stiff with terror. Tears streamed down Nora's face.

"What's going on? What's happening out there?" Yorick demanded.

"Keep your voice down. We're going to get you out of here, just stay calm and don't make any noise," Kendrick whispered, then shut off the cell phone light. The room was coated in inky black darkness, the only sound the breathing of the four people inside.

"They've got to be here somewhere!" the lead gunman growled.

"Last two doors. Maybe they've already been moved," another man responded.

More steps pounded the ground of the tile floor outside the room. The steps fanned out, and then there was a loud bang as the door across the hallway was kicked in.

"Doesn't matter. We'll find them wherever they are. Yorick and Nora Kuypers will be dead by the end of the day," the gunman said.

Nora gasped.

The door to the room flung open, hitting Julian in the face.

Two men stormed inside, guns pointed at Kendrick and the Kuypers.

"Well, look what we have here," the gunman said, shining a flashlight on Kendrick and the Kuypers.

Julian stared at the back of the heads of the two men. He only had one chance to get this right.

Kendrick avoided looking in Julian's direction as he raised his hands in surrender. Yorick followed Kendrick's lead, raising his hands to show he had no weapons. Nora hesitated, her eyes downcast, then rising. Her gaze focused in Julian's direction. The lead gunman, stepped forward, then stopped, his head turning toward Julian.

Stepping out from behind the door, Julian dove across the room toward the Kuypers, unloading the Beretta at the men's arms. Crashing to the ground, Julian saw their weapons drop to the floor as they howled in pain from the bullets that had shredded their forearms.

Kendrick leaped from behind the table in the room, his gun raised, as he kicked the assault rifles toward the back wall. "Get on the floor! On the floor now!"

A uniformed officer burst into the room, jumping on one of the gunmen's back as the man made an ill-advised attempt to grab at the dropped weapon. The officer tackled him to the ground, securing his bloody arms in handcuffs.

Reaching into his pocket, Kendrick threw Julian the keys to his SUV and screamed, "Get them out of here now! Take the back exit!"

Julian caught the keys, then ushered the Kuypers out of the room and down the hall to an emergency exit. Breaking through the door, an alarm sounded as the bright sunshine of the afternoon nearly blinded him.

"Go!" Julian shouted as they ran across the parking lot. The heavy panting of the couple rang in his ears as they struggled to keep pace.

Opening the back door to the SUV, Julian pushed the Kuypers inside, then hurled his body into the driver side and started the vehicle. Putting the gear in reverse, the SUV skidded backward and then burned out of the parking lot as Julian pressed the gas pedal to the floor.

Chapter Sixty-Seven

Julian pushed through the gallery doors and walked past the lobby where patrons were taking their last glimpses of tribal art before the gallery closed in thirty minutes. He'd found the perfect spot to hide the Kuypers—Quark's secluded mountain treehouse. The *Palmchat Gazette* had run an article about Quark's visit to St. Mateo to unveil a building mural. Julian didn't have to worry about the artist being back for another week or more.

He knew exactly who wanted the Kuypers dead. But how the hell had Priscilla Dumay found out that the cops had the Kuypers in custody? And what would she do when she found out her kill team had been unsuccessful?

Working his evening shift at the Gallery had been the last thing on his mind until he realized it might be his one chance to figure out where Dumay had stashed the kidnapped surrogates. He was sure that both Adam Russell and Zak Webber were involved in Dumay's operations. One of them could give him information to help the cops save the lives of the surrogates being held against their will.

And then there was Mena.

He didn't want to frighten her, but she deserved to know that her mentor was not the woman she thought. He'd already left two messages for her and several texts, but she hadn't returned any of them.

Stopping at the elevator, Julian leaned his head back and watched Zak Webber sitting at the chair through the open door of the security room. Officially, he'd be relieving Zak and working the night shift at the gallery. But Julian had other plans. He was going to follow Zak and see if the security guard led him to Dumay or to the surrogates.

As the elevators opened, Julian entered and pressed the button for the second floor. If anyone knew where Mena was, it would be Omar Johnson. Julian stepped out of the elevator and headed toward Omar's office. He could hear the curator on the phone discussing the attack that had occurred at the police station earlier. Julian glanced toward Priscilla Dumay's office. The outer receptionist area and office suite were dark and quiet.

"I don't know what the hell is happening to our island. Two murders, a kidnapped baby and a guerrilla-style attack on our police department! I'm afraid to think of what's coming next ..."

Omar was quiet for a moment.

"Well, babe, the only thing I want is to be in your arms. I'm headed home now. Love you."

As Omar's call ended, Julian leaned his head in the door.

"What the hell do you want?" Omar asked, his lips pursed in a derisive sneer.

Taken aback, Julian stood in the doorway. He wasn't going to let the curator's attitude stop him from getting what he wanted. "Just wondering if you've heard from Mena ... maybe know where I can find her."

"Why the hell would I tell you where she is? You have some nerve coming around here asking about her," Omar said, slamming his laptop closed.

"Why would you say that?" Julian asked, growing concerned by Omar's rude reaction toward him.

"You know exactly why. You couldn't wait a week after you and Mena broke up before you'd fallen into bed with the next bitch. Jerk!" Omar stood and grabbed his Prada manbag from the coat hanger and placed it across his body.

"What are you talking about? I didn't fall into bed with anyone," Julian said, blocking Omar from leaving his office. "Is that what she told you? She thinks I had sex with someone else."

"She doesn't just think it, you asshole. She saw you in the act!" Omar poked him in the chest as he said each word.

How could Mena think that he'd ever turn to another woman? He wasn't ready to move on from her, and no other woman appealed to him right now. How had she got it in her head that he'd slept with someone else?

Fuck.

Dawn.

Had Mena come by when Dawn was on his boat, trying to seduce him to ease her own pain? Is that what Mena saw? Fuck!

"If you had managed to keep your dick in your pants for another few hours, you might have had a chance to get back with Mena. But you blew it," Omar said.

Confused, Julian stared at Omar. How could he have had a chance to get back with Mena? She had made it clear their relationship was over, hadn't she? "Tell me what the hell that means."

Omar sighed. "Mena realized she made a mistake, and she went back to your boat to try to make things right. She wanted to see if you'd be willing to have a long-distance relationship with her. But when she got there, you were getting it on with some other bitch, and it crushed her."

"That was Dawn, but we didn't have sex. I didn't do anything with her. She came on to me out of grief, but I pushed her away. It was all a mistake." Julian insisted.

Omar's eyes squinted, his head tilted as he asked, "Are you serious?"

"I didn't have sex with Dawn. I have not had sex with anyone since Mena told me she was leaving. I don't want to be with anyone but Mena," Julian said. He felt like his world had shifted on its axis and begun spinning backward at the same time. He never thought that he could have another chance with Mena. A chance to make things right between them, to be with her again. He hadn't allowed himself to dream of this possibility, but here it was, real and tangible for him to grab. "Mena changed her mind ... about us?"

"She did. I think she's in love with you."

"Where is she?" Julian asked.

"Far away from all this madness happening on the island. She flew to Kenya," Omar said.

"She already moved?" Julian asked, sadness pooling in his chest even though he was relieved she was far away from any danger from Priscilla Dumay.

"Yes. I'm taking care of having all of her stuff shipped to her."

Julian stepped aside, allowing Omar to pass by.

"You should still try to call her, maybe she'll believe you and the two of you can work things out." Omar turned and walked toward the elevator.

Julian was getting a second chance, and he wasn't going to blow it.

Mena Nix was going to find out exactly how he felt about her.

Chapter Sixty-Eight

"Damn, man, it's about time you showed up. I was about to call Adam and rat on your ass," Zak Webber said, clapping a hand down hard against Julian's back. "Did you hear about that attack on the police station today?"

Julian didn't flinch, resisting the urge to punch Zak and drag him down to the police station for his role in Priscilla Dumay's wretched operations. He knew he had to stay calm and not give anything away. Kendrick needed more time to ensure his case was solid. "I was watching it on the news like everybody else. I'm here now. You can leave."

"Not yet, man. I need help moving a ton of shit out of one of the workshops used for storage. Dumay wants to convert it to a studio to lure Quark back to the gallery. Hired some fancy interior designer to make it to his specifications," Zak said.

Julian followed Zak outside to the workshops that lined the far side of the courtyard.

"I'm hoping this shit don't take all night. I met this hot piece of ass over the weekend, and she texted me an hour ago. I need to get laid, bad," Zak said, with a lewd chuckle.

Julian would find out soon enough if Zak was going to get laid, or trying to throw Julian off his trail. If a late-night hook up was all Zak got into tonight, then Julian would return to the gallery and look for clues in Dumay's office.

Now that Dumay believed she was off the police's radar, she might have left behind compromising evidence.

Zak opened the door to the workshop and flipped the light switch. The room was filled with partially completed sculptures and carvings of various sizes, and art supplies—easels, paint brushes, various pencils and pens, large buckets of molding clay, and small pints of paints in hundreds of colors.

"What the hell?" Julian muttered, assessing all the pieces in the room. This could take all night.

"I know. This is some bullshit. Don't just stand there, help me carry this shit to the moving van," Zak said.

After four hours, Julian was drenched in sweat as he and Zak carried the last piece, a wooden totem pole from the Canadian indigenous people delicately wrapped in lambskin and loaded it into the moving van.

Julian checked his cell phone, accessing the security pods he'd placed around the treehouse to detect any movement. None had been activated for over ten hours, around the time he'd set them up after securing the Kuypers in one of Quark's guest bedrooms. No messages from Kendrick and nothing that indicated Dumay had discovered the Dutch couple's hideout.

Julian looked over at Zak, who appeared near collapse and was also drenched in sweat.

"I didn't think we'd ever get done," Julian said, as he leaned against the back deck of the truck.

"We ain't done yet. Got some stuff in the car that needs to be brought into the gallery. After that, I get to go, and your ass is stuck here until the morning," Zak said, laughing as he staggered toward the black town car parked several spaces over from the moving van in the otherwise deserted parking lot.

Dusk had receded into an inky black sky and stars dotted the horizon. The rustling of the trees grew louder as hot wind whipped through the buildings, brushing against Julian's skin like fire. The night was hotter than usual. Shifting the gun into the back pocket of his pants, Julian lifted his polo shirt over his head and let it fall to the ground. Freed from the shirt, he felt his body starting to cool.

"You got the right idea," Zak said, wiggling out of his soaked cream-colored polo and dropping it to the ground. Zak unlocked the car, illuminating the inside of the vehicle. A stack of easels rested in the back seat. "I'm gonna grab these easels. You get the mounting machine out of the trunk."

Julian pressed the button to release the trunk and looked inside.

"What the hell is this?" Julian asked. A large green metal machine, with round circular saws and a flat small metal console, sat in the middle of the trunk. Next to the edge of the machine was an item that made his blood run cold.

A syringe.

Why would a syringe be in the trunk of Zak's car?

"Some type of high-tech machine Omar is going to use to make frames for the artwork. He was whining about how it gives him the flexibility to use more than wood. It can cut metal, stone, and plastics. That bitch had a temper tantrum right in front of Dumay about me going to the airport to get it from the delivery service. So Adam made me do it," Zak said.

Julian leaned into the trunk to grab the syringe.

That's when it hit him.

That scent.

One he knew all too well.

The seductive, mixture of sandalwood and orange stung his nose, making his body weak.

Mena's perfume.

Julian felt his heartbeat, slow and methodical, slamming in his rib cage.

Stepping back, Julian looked over at Zak, who was leaning over the ground, assembling the easels neatly on top of each other, wrapping the legs with coarse string to hold them together.

Shadows spread across Zak's back from the darkness, but the cloak of night couldn't hide the massive tattoo etched across his skin.

Julian took another step forward.

The gothic lettering became sharper, clearer to Julian's eyes.

The tattoo was of a surname.

Juarez.

Chapter Sixty-Nine

"Where the fuck is she?" Julian demanded.

"Man, what you talking about?" Zak stepped over the easels he'd been stacking and turned to face Julian.

Two swift blows connected to the side of Zak's head.

Julian shook his throbbing right hand as he watched Zak stumble then crash down onto the pavement.

"I know who the fuck you are and what you did," Julian said, kicking Zak in the side before punching him twice more in the middle of the face.

Zak swung laconically toward Julian, failing to connect with any force as he slumped further down to the ground. Hacking loudly, Zak leaned forward. Blood dripped from his nose onto the dark pavement.

"Is that right?" Zak asked, pressing his palms onto the ground, bracing himself into a low crouch. Breathing heavily through his mouth, Zak looked up at Julian. With blood-stained teeth bared and hatred in his dark eyes, Zak struggled to his feet.

"Let's try this again," Julian said, impatience growing within him. He wanted to beat Zak within an inch of his life, but he knew the man was his only chance of finding Mena. Zak had grabbed her, thrown her into the back of his trunk, and took her somewhere. If Zak had hurt Mena, if he had killed her, there was no limit to the pain Julian would inflict on the bastard. But right now, he needed to stay calm and get as much information out of him as he could.

"What did you do with Mena?" Julian asked, adopting a monotone.

"I haven't seen her. What makes you think I did something to her?" Zak asked, standing slowly. He took one uneven step, then stopped and placed a hand on the side of the car to steady himself.

"Her perfume is all over the trunk of your car," Julian said.

Zak laughed lightly, "Sexy smelling stuff. I wanted to fuck her after I grabbed her, but there wasn't enough time for all that—"

Julian charged at Zak, reaching down to release his knife from the ankle holster before plunging the blade between Zak's left clavicle and rib cage. Pressing the knife deep into the gap, Julian stopped. Zak stumbled back, stunned by the attack, grappling for the hilt of the knife.

"I'd think twice before pulling that knife out," Julian said.

Zak's face turned ashen as a slow trickle of blood dripped from the wound along the side of the knife and plopped onto the ground below.

"I partially severed your subclavian artery," Julian explained, taking a step back from Zak. "Doctors debate how long it will take you to bleed out from that kind of wound to a major artery. Some say two minutes, others twenty. When I was on my SEAL team missions, I never had the chance to stick around and time it, so I can't tell you for sure. But what I do know is that the knife staying right in that position is probably saving your life."

Zak's hands dropped from the handle of the knife and rested against the car. Sliding down the side, his eyes were glued on the blade sticking out from his upper chest.

"Here's how this is going to work, Zak. Or should I call you Teo Juarez?" asked Julian.

A flash of recognition crowded Zak's face.

"You think I care that you found out my real name? So what? People change their names all the time," Zak said, his voice coming in short bursts through ragged breaths.

"Yeah, but people don't change their names and then leave their DNA all over the people they've been hired to kill, do they?" Julian responded. "The cops have your DNA from Ella Sapphire's fingernails, and your prints on the gun used to kill Irving Bond. They know you murdered them. There's enough evidence to send you to prison for a long time."

Zak scoffed, then leaned his head back. Julian could see him weakening as the color continued to drain from his tanned skin.

"Prison probably sounds like a good option to you right now, but that's only if you live long enough to make it there. If I snatch that knife out of your chest, you won't live long enough to see the inside of a jail cell," said Julian.

Zak's eyes widened as he looked at Julian.

"You ain't going to kill me in cold blood! You too good to do some shit like that," Zak said.

Julian squatted down in front of Zak, "When I was in the SEALs, I lost count of the number of confirmed kills I had after I hit one hundred. You think I would hesitate to take down another guilty criminal like you? Now tell me where Mena is!"

Sweat covered Zak's body, and his breathing grew more labored.

"Your little bitch is alive and being well taken care of," Zak said.

"Where is she?"

"Fuck you! I'm not telling you shit," Zak said.

Julian moved closer to Zak, squatting down to look him in the eyes. Zak shrunk back, trying to put distance between them, but he was too weak to move far. Julian placed his hand on the handle of the knife. Zak grabbed at Julian's wrist, but his grip was weak.

"C'mon man, don't do anything you'll regret ..." Zak struggled, his breathing shallower as blood coursed down his bare chest.

Julian watched the man, the look he'd seen countless times sneaking across Zak's face. The tell-tale signs of fear.

Tightening his grip on the handle of the knife, Julian twisted the blade.

Zak howled loudly from the movement, gasping for air.

Reaching into Zak's pocket, Julian lifted the cell phone out and walked away from the security guard. His thumb flying across the screen as he searched through the Contacts until he found the one he was looking for.

Boss Lady.

Pressing the green talk button, Julian strode toward the front parking lot as the ringing filled his ears. After the fifth ring, she answered.

"Where is Mena?" Julian barked into the phone.

"Mr. Montgomery! What a surprise to hear you calling from this phone. Should I surmise that you've dispatched of poor ... Teo Juarez? What a pity. He was such a loyal soldier to me over the years," Priscilla said, her tone taunting.

"I'm going to ask you one more time. What did you do to Mena?" Julian growled as he approached his motorcycle. Swinging a leg over the seat, he sat on the bike.

"Nothing. She's perfectly fine, and I'll be happy to arrange for her return to you ... alive ... but you're going to have to do something for me first ..."

Chapter Seventy

"What's the latest?" Julian asked, clenching the cell phone between his ear and shoulder as he reached over the limp body and buckled the seat belt. Easing the door closed, Julian walked around the back of the SUV. He grabbed more rope from the back compartment and headed toward the passenger side of the vehicle.

"Can you talk? Are you alone?"

"Yeah, I'm alone." Julian forced the words out, past the bitter tang in his mouth. Wiping sweat from his face, he looked down at the crumpled figure next to the back tire of the SUV.

"Don't have much time, but you deserve an update since you saved my ass earlier," Kendrick said.

"Did the bastards come clean about who hired them?" Julian squatted down and raised the lifeless arms, wrapping them with rope and securing the knot. He moved to the ankles and repeated the move, mechanically going through the motions without thinking of the ramifications of what he was doing.

"Not yet. Palmchat Island Investigative Bureau sent a team of agents, and they've had their best guys hold up in the interrogation room with them for hours, but they aren't talking. We got background on them—former PC-5 members who got disgruntled from the lack of cash coming their way and broke away from the gang. For the past few years, they've been mercenaries for hire and were connected to a string of murders, kidnappings, and thefts, but there was never enough evidence to convict them," Kendrick said.

Julian tapped the speaker button and rested the cell phone on the ground next to the body. Opening the back-passenger door, he lifted the man easily and placed him in the back seat.

"Anything on them that would implicate Dumay?" Julian asked. He shifted the man's legs to the side and reached over the body to buckle the seat belt around him.

"No, but PIIB agents have already been dispatched to their homes and hangout spots to gather evidence. We'll know something soon," Kendrick replied.

Julian glanced up at the full moon emerging from behind a storm cloud in the dark night sky. "How are you holding up?"

"Honestly, not so good. I just got back from Dumay's mansion in The Bluffs. PIIB said we had enough to hold her for questioning and to take her in custody, but when we got there ... the place was deserted," Kendrick said.

"It was?" Julian asked, startled by that piece of news.

"She was long gone. Looked like she hadn't been there in days. Furniture was covered. Pantry and refrigerator empty. We don't have any leads on where she could be. PIIB agents are canvassing the island for her. I thought I had her, but all I did was give her time to disappear."

"Don't worry," Julian said, easing the passenger door closed. "You're going to catch her. What do you need me to do?"

"What you've already done. I can't thank you enough for getting the Kuypers to a secure location. Stashing them at Quark's treehouse was a brilliant move," Kendrick said.

Julian felt his muscles tense.

"How'd you know that's where I stashed them?" Julian asked, walking around to the driver's door of the SUV. Opening the door slowly, he reached a finger along the buttons of the door and engaged the child safety locks for the back doors.

"I'm a cop. I have GPS tracking on my truck. Once I saw it parked in the middle of the Basil Mountains, I put it together. It was close to the same spot where we'd parked before we took off on foot to reach Quark's place," Kendrick said.

The tension eased from Julian's muscles as he closed the door of the SUV. He wasn't proud of what he was doing, but he'd had no choice. He had to follow the instructions exactly with no deviations. But if Kendrick could eventually track him through the GPS of the SUV, there was a chance, although slim, that his betrayal wouldn't have devastating effects.

Kendrick continued, "I had some of the agents from the Bureau head out there and guard the perimeter since I knew you'd have to show up for work at the Gallery to avoid any suspicion."

"And they say the Francois brothers are the best detectives on the Palmchat Islands. Desmond has nothing on you." Julian turned on the headlights of the SUV, illuminating the two sedated PIIB agents tied to a large mahogany tree. They'd wake up in about four hours from the tranquilizer he'd shot them with.

"Thanks for all your help, Julian. Seriously, I couldn't have done it without you," Kendrick said.

"Anytime. Try to get some rest before the sun comes up in a couple of hours," Julian said.

Kendrick laughed. "I'll sleep after I put Dumay behind bars ..."

Julian ended the call, then accessed the camera app on the phone. Turning toward the backseat, he looked at the slack faces of Yorick and Nora Kuypers, unconscious from the prescription strength sleeping pills he'd slipped into their tea. Snapping a picture of the tied-up couple, he attached the photo to a text and typed: *Delivery in thirty minutes. Mena better be alive.*

Chapter Seventy-One

A flash of lightning cracked against the sky, illuminating the bronze tile roof of the mansion as Julian neared the dock. The clouds grew darker, casting a large shadow over the island as large raindrops pelted his skin. Steering the jet ski onto the beach along the shore, Julian jumped off the machine. The sand sloped upward at a steep thirty-degree angle before merging with soft green grass that blanketed the ground in front of the massive three-story mansion. Running across the beach, Julian reached the stone driveway leading to an Arc de Triomphe style arch that served as the entrance to the property. Jogging through the structure, Julian slowed to a brisk walk as he rounded an oversized fountain spraying water in an intricate pattern. As he took the three steps up toward the loggia, Quentin Tufa emerged from the shadows of the veranda to the left.

"Right on time. Priscilla said you would be. I trust you came unarmed," Quentin said, lifting the hood of his raincoat over his head as a light rain began to fall.

The overcast sky brightened as morning dawned. Rain splattered against Julian's face as a heavily armed man walked around Quentin to frisk Julian. The man gave a tight nod, then disappeared back toward the beach.

"Where's Mena?" Julian asked.

"Where are the Kuypers?" Quentin asked.

"Ask Adam. Hasn't he been watching the live feed? " Julian asked.

"Of course, he has," Quentin said.

"Well, then you know that the Kuypers are tied up on the boat out there, like Dumay requested," Julian said.

"But why did you drop anchor so far away from the shore and take the jet ski into the island?" Quentin asked.

"Come now, Quentin. I know you didn't expect Mr. Montgomery to hand over that lovely couple before he got confirmation that we had held up our end of the bargain," Priscilla said, stepping through the double doors of the entrance to the mansion. Priscilla raised a large silver umbrella over her head and approached Julian.

"I need to see Mena," Julian said, turning away from Quentin toward Priscilla.

The woman gave him a warm smile, then linked an arm in his. "Of course, you do. Let's go inside. I'll take you to her myself."

Priscilla stopped and looked over her shoulder at Quentin, then said, "The boat has arrived to transport you off the island. On you way out, would you be a wonderful brother and phone the guards. Tell them to stand down as a good show of faith to Mr. Montgomery. No one should stand in the way of him leaving with Ms. Nix. Understood?"

Quentin nodded, then headed back to the veranda.

Priscilla led Julian into the opulent mansion, appointed with marble columns and carvings and luxurious wall art. The grand foyer was covered with a handmade rug, and a baby grand piano rested in the corner. To the left was a dining room with an oval table worthy of the Palace of Versailles and a massive crystal chandelier hanging overhead. To the right, what looked like a Picasso painting hung on a fabric covered wall.

As they walked through the foyer, the room gave way to a center gallery where a receptionist style console rested in the center. A woman dressed in a tailored business suit nodded at Priscilla as they passed by, turning right down another hallway.

"You're going to get a special treat on the way to see Mena. A first-hand tour of where the magic of my operations happens," Priscilla said, waving her hand through the air.

The hallway opened into a large ballroom, teeming with medical professionals.

"This is command central where workers clock in and check basic administrative information," Priscilla said, directing him to follow her through a short, curved hallway. They walked through what looked like an operating room, appointed with top of the line medical equipment before entering a narrow, curved stairway leading down to another level.

"What is this place?" Julian asked, following Dumay around a rectangular hallway surrounding an open garden filled with sago palms, grapeseed trees, and heliconia.

"This is the flagship facility for my operations. It took me a year to close on the purchase of the private island and build this mansion. It's been fully in service for about a month now. I was able to consolidate all of my assets from all over the world to this one location," Priscilla said, leading him around the rectangle and past several small bedrooms. "The indoor garden was designed to be an oasis of peace where my staff can go to relax from the stresses of their day, which is why I had it placed near their bedrooms on this floor. The sub-basement level is for my assets."

Descending another set of narrow stairs tucked in a corner, Julian was stunned by the complex sophistication of the home. The mansion looked more like a high-end hospital. Medical professionals walked past them as they entered a curved hallway lined with Greek-style busts.

"Such a pity that I will have to abandon this place now because of you and your friend, Detective Caillouet. The Palmchat Islands are no longer safe for me, but I've managed to successfully procure an alternative location for my operations, one more remote than this private island ..."

"This is where you hold the women you kidnap and force to carry the babies you sell," Julian said.

"Give the man a prize," Priscilla quipped, then pushed through the doors leading into another room filled with exercise equipment. Several people were working out in the room as a television broadcast the latest cricket match. Exiting the exercise room, Priscilla led him through a maze of two more rooms filled with recreational equipment—ping pong tables, arcade games, dart boards, and chess.

"And all these people ... they help you do this?" Julian was stunned.

"They are committed to the good work that we are doing for couples all over the world. Couples who have exhausted all options of having a child on their own. They decide to adopt but are increasingly disappointed in the adoption process and the unpredictability of the child they will receive. These couples would prefer to have certain guarantees, and I provide those guarantees for every child I create," Priscilla said, stopping near one of the hospital rooms.

Julian peered through the window. Two nurses flanked a pregnant woman restrained to a hospital bed. Her face was masked with a grimace as she gripped the railings of the bed, her legs propped high in stirrups. A doctor reached between her legs. One of the nurses dipped a towel in a bucket of ice and dabbed it along the woman's forehead as the other nurse stroked her arms gently, mouthing what must have been words of encouragement he couldn't hear from the hallway. The woman was giving birth to a child that very moment.

"That is a $500,000 child being born who will be delivered to a wonderful family. This child is the first in our genetic modifications to improve intelligence and athletic ability," Priscilla said.

"It's impossible to provide that kind of guarantee. I know you're using embryos stolen from unsuspecting couples who thought they were being sent to research facilities. Sure, you can test the embryos for their genetic make-up, but there's a limit to what you can guarantee about the unborn child," Julian said. The Kuypers hadn't been able to give any details about the alleged DNA modifications that Dumay was performing, and Julian wasn't convinced that she could do what she claimed.

Priscilla turned, her eyes dancing with excitement as she said, "We most certainly can provide those guarantees. There is a new technology being developed called NeoGen DNA Modification. No country allows geneticists to do this important research, but there is a contingent of wealthy benefactors that have been supporting them for the past decade."

Twisting through the maze of hallways and rooms filled with other women restrained in hospital beds, Julian had lost track of where they were in the massive mansion. Heading down another long hallway, he asked, "And you're one of these benefactors?"

"I have a more hands-on role in the project. I provide the embryos for the geneticists to perform their work. Once the embryos have been analyzed, any predisposition to more than five hundred medical conditions, including one hundred mental illnesses, are genetically modified, removed, and replaced with corrected DNA strands. That is how we provide parents with a guarantee that the child they purchase from me will be free of undesirable traits. I even ask the team to throw in the option of modifying eye color, hair color, and gender as a bonus—giving parents the ultimate designer baby ... for a price, of course," Priscilla said.

"That's why you're doing this? For money?" Julian asked, his gut churning from the direct confirmation of Dumay's morally corrupt criminal enterprise.

"Of course not. The money is a welcomed by-product of my efforts. Let's be real here. Each of these surrogates would have led lives that ranged from wretched due to their criminal proclivities to mediocre and forgettable due to their lack of ambition. What I have given them is a chance to contribute to humanity in a way that most on this planet could never have imagined. We are building a race of better humans, immune to the common diseases that plague our world and engineered to have every social advantage based on the known patterns of success, even if those superficial patterns are misguided. The children we create will have every advantage to guarantee success in life. Our means justify our ends," Priscilla said.

Julian trailed behind, glancing in another room two doors down from the woman giving birth. A face stared back at him, clouded by fear and suspicion. Her smooth honey-colored skin was dull, her dark brown eyes lifeless as she looked through him, uncertainty in her gaze. He stared, scrutinizing her features, recognizing her. He'd spent hours with Kendrick going through her cold case file trying to figure out how the missing woman could be connected to Ella Sapphire's murder and, later, why her hair had been found in the basement of the Genesis Gallery. The woman was Samantha Fox.

"How many women do you have down here?" Julian asked. His first priority was Mena, but he couldn't leave the rest of the women here. He had to find a way to set them all free.

"Only nineteen since I had to eliminate Ella Sapphire. But you know that already don't you. You delivered her baby. But I recently found out that you were connected to her in other ways, through another Navy SEAL named Broman Garrison. That is the reason you started working at my gallery. Too bad you couldn't save her," Priscilla said, her tone mocking.

Julian winced at her words, regret hammering through his body. He had failed Ella. But he wouldn't fail Mena, or the other women being held against their will. Some way he would free them all. Or die trying.

"Ella was trying to go to the cops, wasn't she? She was trying to be free of the prison you kept her in," Julian said, as they passed through an auditorium filled with dozens of theater style seats.

Priscilla sighed. "When Ella broke out and took Mena hostage, that was her third escape attempt. Three strikes and you're out. She'd discovered the other surrogates on her first two attempts. I have no doubt she was going to the police. But Zak is good at his job. He hunted the little bitch down and killed her, and you killed him. So, I'd say you got justice for Ella in the end, didn't you?"

Julian stared at the woman. Putting an end to Priscilla Dumay's designer baby factory was the only way to get justice for Ella, Mena, and the women forced to be surrogates.

"And Bond? You had to kill him too?" Julian asked.

"Bond double-crossed me! He was stealing art from my gallery and replacing it with forgeries and selling it on the black market as if the millions he earned for his services as a baby broker weren't enough. Bond stole the little boy on my direction, so we could complete delivery of the child to the Kuypers. But when you interrupted the exchange I'd arranged at the warehouse, he came up with a new plan. He saw the baby as leverage, a way to get the cops to give him immunity for his art theft crimes. He was going to save his own skin by giving me up. I couldn't let that happen. He had to die," Priscilla said.

"And Mena? What about her?" Julian asked, holding his breath as they reached the end of another narrow hall.

Priscilla stopped at the dark wooden door.

"See for yourself."

Chapter Seventy-Two

Mena's crumpled body lay hunched in the back corner of the room, her limbs visibly trembling as her head pressed against the cold tile floor. Her face was obscured by her tangled hair. Metal bars bisected the room, creating a cage that resembled a jail cell in what had once been a wine cellar. In the opposite corner from where Mena cowered was a small porcelain sink and a toilet. Two paper bowls filled with remnants of food were discarded near the front of the cage. Julian took tentative steps into the room, staring at Mena's body curled into the fetal position. She was breathing, but he wasn't sure if she was conscious.

"What the hell did you do to her?" Julian demanded, turning back to look at Priscilla.

"I taught her a lesson. The same one I'm about to teach you," Priscilla said, reaching for the heavy wooden door.

Julian lunged at the door, his fingers grasping for the edge as it slammed closed.

"Fuck!" Julian screamed, then pounded on the door. "Let me out of here. Now!"

"Well, that's something I don't plan to do." Priscilla's voice floated into the room from hidden speakers. Julian looked around the room trying to figure out where the sound was coming from and homed in on the flat white circles on the ceiling.

Priscilla continued, "I hate to renege on our deal, but it seems that you didn't hold up your end of the bargain, either. When you left Louis Campbell's yacht in the middle of the sea, something terrible happened, and it capsized, sinking to the bottom of the ocean floor with that lovely couple, the Kuypers on board. Since you reneged, then I could too."

"You think you've won, but you haven't. I'm going to get out of here, and when I do, I will track you down and make you pay for everything you've done to the surrogates and to Mena," Julian roared at the closed door.

"I applaud your confidence, however misguided it may be. Now because I do have a heart, I'm going to make your deaths as painless as possible. My team and I will be leaving the island in one hour. When we are safely away from the mansion, I will release carbon monoxide into the building giving you and Mena a chance to slip peacefully into death. I can't allow anything to remain that could incriminate me, including you two. That's why my security team is placing explosives inside and around this building as we speak. Trust me, dying from poisoning will be a lot less painful than burning alive. But if by some miracle you are able to survive the toxic gas, the horns blowing on our cruise ship will signal that we are a safe distance from the island. I will detonate the explosives, and in sixty seconds you'll be dead," Priscilla said.

The intercom crackled, and then silence filled the room. Julian banged against the door, kicking himself for not being more alert to Dumay's double-cross when she opened the door to the wine cellar. He'd been too worried about Mena and couldn't stop himself from getting closer to her.

Checking his watch, Julian only had an hour to get Mena out of the cage and free from the building. Reaching for the Swiss Army Skipper knife he'd smuggled into the mansion past the guard who frisked him, Julian began feeling around the bars for a lock.

"Julian ... is that really you?" Mena's voice was weak as she stared at him.

Julian squatted to the ground and reached his hands through the bars toward her. "Yes, it's me. I'm going to get you out of here. Everything's going to be okay."

Mena crawled toward him and placed her hands in his. "How did Priscilla capture you?"

"She didn't. I came here to save you," Julian said, giving her a small smile.

"How did you know how to find me?"

"Omar said you'd already left for Kenya, but I smelled your perfume in the trunk of Zak Webber's car, and I knew something bad had happened."

"And that was enough for you to try to find me?" Mena asked, frowning.

"More than enough. Zak wouldn't tell me where you were, so I talked to Dumay and ... we struck a deal."

A sob choked in Mena's throat as tears filled her eyes. "You never should have come looking for me. Oh God! You're going to die because of me."

"Hey, stop that. I'm exactly where I want to be," Julian said, clutching her arms in his hands. "I would do it again in a heartbeat. We're going to get out of here. I promise you that."

"It's too late. The cops may be able to catch her, but there's no way they'll be able to save us in time," Mena said, clutching his arms like a lifeline.

"That's okay. We're going to save ourselves." Julian looked down at his watch. Forty minutes left. "But I'm going to need your help. There's got to be a lock on these bars somewhere. If you can help me find it, I can use my knife to unlock it. Can you do that?"

Mena nodded, then stood on shaky legs. For the next half hour, they spent every minute pouring over each bar of the cage looking for a keyhole, crack, or other weakness that could be exploited. Nothing. Dumay had trapped Mena in a welded fortress with no way out.

Mena stopped Julian from examining the bars. "This is pointless. I was knocked out when they brought me in here. I don't know if the bars open or if they built this cage around me. We're almost out of time. Listen to me. There's a lock on that door."

Julian turned to look at the wooden door that Priscilla Dumay had slammed in his face, locking him inside the room with Mena.

"You can save yourself. Julian, listen to me. You have to save yourself. Please. We both can't die down here," Mena said, her words resonating confidently through short breaths. She reached a hand toward her chest as she slid down to the floor.

"What's wrong?" Julian asked.

"Chest feels tight, and it's getting ... kind of ... hard to breathe. Go ... Julian. Save yourself," Mena said. She rested her head against the bars as her hand fell to the floor.

Julian watched her fingers curl around the bottom of the steel.

Something caught his eye next to her fingers. A shadow he hadn't noticed at the bottom of any of the other bars. Dropping to the floor, he slid her hand away and plunged his knife into the shadowed keyhole, twisting the metal back and forth until he heard the unmistakable click. Grasping the bottom rung of the cage, Julian pulled out and up, lifting the outer door of the bars to the ceiling. Mena's body fell forward.

"You did it! I ... can't believe ... it," Mena said as she scrambled out of the cage.

"Don't try to talk," Julian said and glanced at his watch again. Fifty minutes had passed since Dumay locked them in the wine cellar. There wasn't much time left. Turning his attention to the wooden door, he plunged the knife into the deadbolt lock.

Chapter Seventy-Three

"Oh, my God! It worked!" Mena screamed, rushing toward Julian. She flung her arms around his neck.

Julian hugged her tightly, then released her from his grip. Twisting the knob, the door opened, and Mena staggered through. Getting out of the room was the first step. He still had to navigate them through the maze of hallways and bedrooms up two levels and out of the mansion before Dumay detonated the explosives rigged around the building.

Should he try to defuse the explosives instead? He was no bomb expert, but if he could intercept or scramble the frequency Dumay would use to detonate the flares, it could give them more time. Or waste the only time they had left ...

"The gas is penetrating this level," Julian said as a wave of nausea coursed through his body. A sledgehammer pounded within his skull, and he felt sluggish, as though he was moving through quicksand. He glanced at Mena. Her skin was flush as she struggled to get short, choppy breaths of air into her lungs. Her movement was becoming uncoordinated and unsteady. "We've been protected in this cellar with the one small vent, but it's more intense out here. We have to move fast, no stopping. We're almost out of time."

Mena nodded her head. "Do you remember how to get out of here and back up to the main floor?"

"I remember enough," Julian said, peering into Mena's beautiful brown eyes. Her gaze was intense and focused. He knew she trusted him, and he couldn't let her down. He wouldn't let someone he loved down ever again.

Grabbing his hand, she squeezed it tightly. "Let's get out of here."

Julian sprinted straight down the dark, narrow hallway, turning left at the dead end. He remembered a movie room behind one of the four closed doors. Grabbing the knob, he opened the door closest to him as Mena reached for the door on the right side. Damn it! A closet. The next door was locked.

"Julian," Mena called to him, pointing toward the room. "This way."

Following behind her, he leaped over the theater style seating of the large movie room and exited into an open area filled with lounge chairs and potted palms. Zigzagging through the furniture, he pressed past Mena, leading the way down another dimly lit hall which had been teeming with medical staff hours ago, tending to the surrogates held hostage in the luxuriously appointed rooms. As he rushed past three rooms, now empty, toward the door at the end of the hall, he prayed Dumay hadn't had the forethought to lock them in the sub-basement.

Pressing the metal bar in the middle of the steel door, it flung open. Pushing his muscles further, he increased the pace along the curved hallway until he burst through the second door and into the area Dumay had described as the recreational and exercise rooms for her staff.

The stairs leading up to the basement floor were hidden behind one of the rooms, but he couldn't remember which one. They were nearly identical. There was no time to check each one.

Mena's breathing was labored as she bent over. "Dead end? Did we take a wrong turn?"

Julian closed his eyes, ignoring the burning in his lungs and the abyss threatening to take him under. He only had seconds to make a decision, and the wrong one could cost him his life and Mena's.

"Straight ahead, the middle room," Julian said, taking off toward the oval-shaped enclosure. He entered the room, then turned. Mena wobbled on shaky legs.

"My head feels like it's splitting open. I'm so dizzy, I can't tell if ... I can't," Mena wavered, her body tilting to the right. Julian lunged for her before her body collapsed.

"Stay with me, Mena. Just lean on me and keep your face covered. I'm going to get us out of here," Julian promised. Half-carrying her, Julian slowed his pace and reached the back opening of the room. Ducking through the narrow doorway, they entered another curved hallway, now bathed in darkness. Julian pressed his hand along the stone wall, searching for the opening to the stairwell. Mena's body grew heavy next to his, as a coughing spell shook her body.

Slow, tentative steps forward, Julian kept moving until a gap emerged. The stairwell had to be within the dark room, but he couldn't see the steps. Mena was in no condition to walk up stairs that she couldn't see.

Reaching back for her, Julian lifted her.

"No, you can't carry me. There's no way you can get both of us up the stairs," Mena protested in his arms.

"The hell I can't. I've carried men twice your size for miles on my back. Carrying you out of a carbon monoxide filled building set to explode is going to be like a walk in the park," Julian said.

Mena gave him a faint smile, barely discernible in the dark hallway. "Well, when you put it like that ..."

Relieved that she acquiesced, Julian lifted her onto his back and ascended the stairs slowly, switching back twice as the stairs approached the basement level.

Kicking the door open, Julian rushed past an empty bedroom that had housed one of Dumay's medical staff and lowered Mena's body to the ground. Mena inhaled sharply, coughing between breaths. Her hands pressed against her temples as she hunched over at the waist. He'd give her a few more seconds, but then they needed to move. He had no clue how long Dumay had been gone, but ten minutes could pass faster than either of them expected.

As Mena stood up straight, she said through labored breaths, "I think I can make it."

A distant horn sounded three times, piercing the silence of the air.

I will detonate the explosives, and in sixty seconds you'll be dead.

Yanking Mena's hand, Julian raced toward the rectangular hallway bordering the indoor garden that spanned the bottom two floors. A quick left turn, then another and another. The stairs to the main level loomed ahead.

Julian turned toward Mena and scooped her in his arms, then raced up the curved staircase, taking the steps three at a time until they reached the main level. Muscles burning from the intense effort, his arms ached and grew numb as the mental countdown resonated in his head.

Forty seconds. Thirty-nine. Thirty-eight.

The main level was eerily silent, the only sound the pounding of Julian's feet as he maneuvered through the maze of operating rooms and into the common area.

Twenty-five. Twenty-four. Twenty-three.

He stumbled past the console table of the center gallery and entered the grand foyer adorned with the handmade rug and the now empty spot where the Picasso painting had hung. The double doors of the mansion stretched ahead. He had to make it in time.

Thirteen. Twelve. Eleven.

Bursting through the double doors, damp, humid air clawed at his skin as he raced through the covered entry loggia and into the open air. Rain smacked his face as he lowered Mena to the manicured lawn of the courtyard stretching in front of the mansion. Her steps fell in sync with his own as they raced around the oversized fountain toward the arched stone entry to the property. Ducking through the arch, the stone driveway to the beach stretched before them.

Three. Two. One.

Chapter Seventy-Four

Mena stopped, glancing back at the mansion. A ball of orange flame burst into the air, clawing at the sky. Turning back toward the beach, she took another step. Hot, wet air burned across her skin. The force of the explosion slammed against her back and rocked her vision with dancing stars as her body flung into the air. Waving her arms and legs frantically, she reached for Julian trying to hold on to him.

His body moved away from her, out of her reach. Twisting through the air, the world was devoid of sound. She moved in slow motion. Hot rain pummeled her body. Squeezing her eyes shut, she braced for the impact.

Crashing down onto a sago palm, her head snapped back sharply. Bouncing off the plant, she nosedived onto the soft grass of the lawn coming to a rest with her head pressed against the blades.

The roar of the blazing fire bellowed in her ears. Black smoke from the flames assaulted her nose, burning her throat and lungs. Pain like shockwaves racked through her body, the most welcome sign that she'd survived.

Just like Julian had promised.

Julian.

Where was he?

Mena lifted her head. A sharp ache sliced through her skull. Resting her head back against the wet, dewy grass, Mena took a deep breath. She had to gather her strength to find Julian. He'd saved her life. Now it was her turn to save his. He had to be alive. She was going to find him.

Pressing her palms against the slick blades of grass, Mena ignored the sharp throbs rattling inside her head and pushed up onto her knees. The air hissed with projectiles of rocks and debris from the mansion as rounds of explosions rocked the air. The searing air from the flames clawed at her skin. She knew she was far enough away from the danger. But was Julian?

Barefoot from shoes lost in the blast, Mena hurried past the line of sago palms and hibiscus bushes to the open field. Her eyes searched the canvas of flames dancing across the meticulous foliage. Heart pounding in her chest, she screamed, "Julian! Julian! Julian!"

Reaching the edge of the property where the grass graded into the sand of the beachfront, Mena quickly looked around. She rested her hands on her hips, trying not to hyperventilate. Her voice choked with unshed tears, she yelled, "Julian! Where are you? Julian!"

The whipping of helicopter blades overhead drowned out her cries. In the distance, military vessels with sirens surrounded a massive superyacht. Smaller convoys of coast guard boats headed toward the beach where she stood.

"Stay in place. We're coming to get you," a voice she recognized blared through a bullhorn. Detective Kendrick Caillouet. Somehow, he'd found Priscilla's private island. Sheets of rain grew heavier, plastering her hair to her skull. The water rushed down her face, blinding her. Blinking rapidly, she saw dozens of officers and agents in combat gear boarding the yacht. Priscilla was surrounded. She wouldn't get away with the heinous crimes she'd committed. All because of Julian. She had to find him.

The coast guard boat steered onto the beach. Kendrick jumped over the edge and rushed toward her.

"Mena, are you okay? You're bleeding," Kendrick said, concern in his eyes.

She wiped the side of her face, then looked down at her hands covered in rain and blood. Her injuries were the least of her worries now. "I can't find Julian. When the house exploded, the force threw us apart. I've been calling his name ..."

Kendrick placed his hands on her shoulders, gripping her tightly. "It's okay. We need to get you checked out."

Mena shook from his grasp. "No! I have to find Julian!"

Pushing away from the detective, Mena scrambled back toward the mansion, engulfed in flames. She stepped onto the paved driveway. Motionless near the curved arch, a body laid against the ground.

"Julian!" Mena screamed as she raced back toward the fire.

"Mena! No, don't go back there." Kendrick's words floated behind her.

She pushed her legs faster. As she came closer, she knew it was him, laying on his back, eyes closed. Instinctively, her pace slowed. Her mind and body refusing to acknowledge the image playing before her eyes. She didn't want confirmation, and if she didn't walk any closer, maybe she could convince herself that he was still ...

The rain had slowed to a sporadic drizzle. As the sun peeked from behind the dark storm clouds, a ray of light passed across Julian's handsome face. Mena's breath caught in her throat.

Glistening in the shaft of light was a wide pool of blood beneath his head, trickling across the stones of the driveway.

Chapter Seventy-Five

"You were very lucky," the doctor said, typing quickly with one hand on the tablet as he peered at the reading on the medical equipment next to the hospital bed.

"Doesn't feel like it." Julian chuckled. The pain subsided as the pain killers began to do their job. When he awoke hours ago in the intensive care unit of St. Killian Memorial Hospital, he'd been disoriented and in throbbing pain all over his body. Propelled through the air like a meteor, then crashing to the ground, he'd later learned that over seventy-five percent of his body had suffered bruises and contusions from the explosion on Priscilla Dumay's private island. He had a nasty gash on the back of his head and had been helicoptered to the Palmchat Islands' top trauma hospital to relieve pressure from an epidural hematoma, which had turned out to be much smaller than the paramedics had originally assessed.

Despite the seriousness of his injuries, his first thought was Mena, and if she had survived the explosion. Nothing had mattered more to him at that moment. Relief coursed through his veins when the emergency room attendant informed him that he was the only serious injury from the blast on the tiny private island. He'd gotten her out of there, and she was safe and alive.

"No hospital on the other Palmchat Islands has the expertise or equipment to treat your injuries. If the paramedics hadn't assessed your condition and insisted you be helicoptered over here immediately, your injuries could have been fatal."

"No real danger of that, I have a hard head," Julian responded.

"That's what your mom said," the doctor said, with a laugh.

Tears sprung to Julian's eyes. He hastily blinked them away as the warm comfort of knowing his mother was here with him flooded his body. "Where is she?"

He wasn't surprised that the PIIB had reached out to their counterparts in the FBI to ensure his mother was made aware of his dire condition. He hated that she had come all this way, but he knew he needed her.

"One of the orderlies took her and your cop friend to the cafeteria to get something to eat about ten minutes ago. They should be back soon," the nurse on duty said, as she waited for instructions from the doctor.

"The sutures from the gash on your head will be tender for about a week. Avoid messing around on that side of your head. The skull fracture is linear. It will heal over time and won't interfere with resuming regular activities. We need to observe you for a few more days and make sure that the hematoma has drained properly, and you don't have any complications," the doctor said. "Other than that, everything looks good here. Do you have any questions for me?"

Julian shook his head. The doctor gave the nurse further instructions then exited the room, closing the door behind him.

"You have one more visitor who's been waiting around to see you," the nurse added as she checked the level of his IV bag.

Julian perked up, his heart pounding in his chest. "Who is it?"

"A lady, really pretty. I didn't ask her name, but I took her some water a minute ago since she didn't go down to the cafeteria with the others," the nurse said.

A jolt coursed through Julian's body as he sat up straighter. "Can you tell her she can come inside?"

The nurse smiled brightly, then turned and left the room.

Julian tried to temper his excitement. Since his mom was here, the "pretty lady" could be Dawn. He knew his mother would likely reach out to her once she arrived. Despite Dawn's feelings for him, she'd grown close to both his and Broman's mothers. She would come to the hospital if only to support his mom.

Rubbing his fingers across his eyes, Julian leaned back on the bed as his excitement waned. Mena hadn't needed to come to St. Killian to get reports on his condition. Kendrick would have sent her regular updates on his status. Sure, he'd saved her life, but he was also the man she believed had moved on and had sex with Dawn.

"You gave me quite a scare earlier."

Julian's eyes flung open and rested on Mena's face. The beautiful velvety mahogany skin, round deep brown eyes with long lashes, the high cheekbones, and luscious lips. He took a deep breath, trying to calm the pounding of his pulse. He wanted to respond, but words escaped him as she came closer. Pulling a chair from the corner of the room next to his bed, she sat and leaned her elbows onto her knees. Her gaze was intense on his face, and he felt himself blush like a horny teenager.

"I must look like shit," Julian said after a pause.

"Quite the contrary," Mena said, trailing her hand down the side of his face. "The nurse said you'll make a full recovery, but you're going to be in the hospital for a while for observation."

"That's what they say," Julian said, rolling his eyes.

"How about you do what they advise this time?" Mena asked.

"What? You didn't like me crashing at your place after I got shot in the leg?" Julian laughed.

"Trust me, you don't need to get all banged up to have an excuse to spend time with me," Mena said.

"I don't?" Julian asked, a flutter coursing through his chest.

Now it was Mena's turn to blush.

Julian didn't want to make her feel uncomfortable. Changing the subject, he asked, "What the hell happened after the mansion blew up? I don't remember shit."

"The force of the explosion sent both of us flying through the air. I landed on the flower bushes and bounced down onto the ground. Had some bruises, a small cut, and stiffness but nothing major. You were pushed straight ahead and landed on the stone driveway. The paramedics said that's why your injuries were so much worse than mine," Mena said.

"I'm glad it happened that way—"

"Don't say that," Mena said, shaking her head.

"I mean it."

"You saved my life," Mena whispered.

"Only after you saved mine first."

"How? I don't understand."

"For the past three years, I was a shadow of a human being. Living but not really living, constantly punishing myself for Broman's condition and the deaths of my SEAL Team all those years ago. You came into my life, and I didn't want to be a shadow anymore. I wanted to be present with you, even if the circumstances that brought us together were grim. You saw the good in me, and you helped me to remember the good that I had in myself. That it was still there. So, you, beautiful woman, gave me back my life," Julian said.

"You're giving me too much credit. The real you wouldn't have stayed hidden for much longer ... maybe I sped up the process a bit." Mena smiled.

"I love you," Julian blurted out.

Mena's eyes grew wide as she stared back at him. He could have found a better way of telling her, but he couldn't hold it in any longer. He leaned toward Mena and grabbed her hands in his.

"I know you saw me with a woman on my boat, but it wasn't what it looked like," Julian said, the words rushing from his mouth. "It was Dawn. She was upset. She'd found out that the baby wasn't Ella's biological child and she tried to seduce me. But it didn't work. It didn't. I didn't have sex with her. Since I met you, no other woman has existed for me. Just you."

"You didn't ... move on? You weren't mad at me ..." Mena stopped, her words choked with emotion.

"I could never be mad at you," Julian said.

"Julian, I—"

"Hold on, let me get it all out. For the record, I have no problem with you taking the Fellowship. But you need to know that I would follow you anywhere. You want to go to Kenya, I'll go to Kenya. You want to go to Antarctica, I'll go to Antarctica. Hell, you want to go to Mars, I'll be in the spaceship right next to you," Julian said, a smile spreading across his face. "What I'm saying is that I don't care that we've only known each other for a short time. I know that I'm unconditionally and completely in love with you."

Mena bit her lip as tears filled her eyes. "You're in love with me?"

"More than I've ever loved anyone," Julian said. "I think we deserve a chance. I don't care if you don't love me back yet. We can take it slow, so you can figure out how you feel about me and if it can grow to something deeper or—"

Mena leaned over and kissed him. Julian ran his fingers through her hair, clutching her tightly toward him as he savored the sweet taste of her tongue.

Breaking the kiss, Mena pulled back and rested her hands on the sides of his face. "I'm in love with you, too."

Epilogue

Julian rested his head against Mena's bare stomach. The soft throbs of her heartbeat tickled his ear as he stroked a finger lazily along her thigh. The sun was bright in the cloudless sky, a break from the dismal rain of the past several days and the dark ordeal they'd endured. After two weeks in the hospital and another week of bedrest, Julian had been cleared for light physical activity, which gave him the perfect excuse to engage in the one activity he'd missed the most after he recovered from the brain injury. A blissful evening and early morning of slow, intense lovemaking had left him dazed and happily exhausted.

Rocking against the easterly wind, the boat cruised along at a steady pace, close to the shore of Amargo, the largest of the Aerie Islands.

Mena's hand ran through his hair, a sensual touch that awakened his desires, which had become insatiable for her. He never ceased to be captivated by her beauty. Her mocha skin glistened with sweat under the afternoon rays, giving her a sexy glow.

"I read the *Palmchat Gazette* online. The articles about THE ACCIDENTAL HERO are still the most popular," Mena said.

"Don't remind me," Julian said, groaning. The local newspaper had chronicled Julian's propensity for accidentally stumbling into dire situations and heroically saving those in trouble over the past several months. He'd been bombarded with calls from international newspapers for interviews, but he'd turned every single one down. He wanted his life to get back to normal now that Priscilla Dumay had been arrested.

"Some people dream of being a hero, and others can't help that that's who they are. You, my love, fall into the second category," Mena said.

"Well, I'm taking a break from saving lives to focus on having a life of my own," Julian said, as he trailed a line of kisses around her navel.

"Stop that. The doctor said light activity, and I need a nap. You wore me out," Mena said, sliding her hand down his back.

"Fine, take a nap," Julian said, reluctantly ceasing his kisses as he rested his head back on her abdomen. The breeze picked up as white popcorn clouds raced across the sky. Three weeks had passed since he'd rescued Mena from the clutches of Priscilla Dumay. When Priscilla had bargained Mena's life for the Kuypers', Julian knew he was taking a big risk that could fail. One wrong move and all three of them could have lost their lives. Leaving a trail of clues for Kendrick was the only option to give him the chance of having back-up as he went to rescue Mena and the other surrogates. His first move had been to trigger the silent alarm at the gallery before he left, which would alert police cruisers in the vicinity to check out the call from the gallery. As soon as they found Zak Webber bleeding in the parking lot, he'd be identified and rushed to the hospital. The knife plunged into his chest would be easily recognized by Kendrick as belonging to Julian, and he could start to put the pieces together.

Speeding along the mountain roads toward Quark's treehouse, Julian had gotten a call from Adam Russell with instructions: Bring the Kuypers to Louis Campbell's boat which would have the keys in the ignition. Store them in the master cabin, which had a security camera that could be accessed by Adam online. Once Adam performed the visual confirmation, Julian would need to sail the boat to the coordinates he received from Adam. After he arrived, Adam claimed they would perform an even exchange, and he and Mena would be able to leave unharmed.

Julian hadn't been fooled.

He'd been surprised by the PIIB operatives guarding the edge of the mountain, but quickly subdued them. Julian took the Kuypers back to Crescent Moon Marina and locked them in one of the spare cabins on the lower level of his boat. Using the camera on his laptop, he created a live feed which he supplanted with the feed that Adam believed was coming from Louis Campbell's boat.

Adam called like clockwork with the coordinates, which Julian programmed into the GPS of his boat, then pulled up the anchor before rushing across the deck to the Campbell boat. Maneuvering out of the slip, he programmed the longitude and latitude into the GPS and set sail to the private island as his own yacht drifted out of the slip. No doubt marina security would alert the police for the strange activity, giving Kendrick another chance to find the human cargo he'd left on board.

He hadn't known which, if any, of his breadcrumbs would work, but later learned Kendrick had found them all and put the pieces together. Shortly after Priscilla and her team of medical professionals, security guards and surrogate hostages had boarded a luxury super-yacht, the PIIB helicopters had descended on the area followed by police and coast guard boats surrounding the vessel. She and forty others involved in her crimes had been arrested. The nineteen surrogates were sent to St. Killian Memorial Hospital for evaluation, physical and psychological. Since their rescue, ten of the women had been released from the hospital, including the two from Kendrick's cold cases: Tamara Gardner and Samantha Fox.

Julian's mind drifted to the families without any knowledge that their embryos hadn't been destroyed as they'd directed. The stolen embryos were used to produce babies for sale to unsuspecting and desperate infertile couples. Child Protective Services was struggling to determine the right course of action for the surrogates who were currently pregnant with the babies of unknown parents, using the data Julian had stolen from the hard drive from Siamood Storage. PIIB had forensic specialists assisting in identifying the babies, although Kendrick had mentioned they weren't hopeful that the parents could be identified due to the genetic modifications to the DNA. The children would most likely be put up for adoption, like the baby Ella had given birth to. Dawn had been allowed to adopt the little boy, who she named Elliot, and she'd returned home to Jacksonville after Julian was released from the hospital.

The case against Priscilla and her team was growing stronger with each day, even as she refused to acknowledge her designer baby enterprise, the geneticists modifying the DNA, or the group of benefactors funding the work. Zak Webber had recovered from his stab wound and provided evidence on the kidnapping and murders, linking them directly to orders from Priscilla. Webber would get a reduced sentence for his cooperation. Adam Russell was working to secure a plea bargain in exchange for turning over more evidence against Dumay.

Mena sat up, a frown creasing her delicate forehead.

"What's wrong?" Julian asked.

"My fellowship," Mena started, then paused. "Priscilla was the main reason why the Board selected me. She was my biggest advocate. Now it feels wrong to accept the position."

"Don't say that." He looked her directly in the eyes, willing her to believe the truth in his words. "You earned that fellowship with your hard work and diligence, not because of Priscilla Dumay. What she did in no way detracts from the great opportunity you've been given."

"You don't think so?" Mena asked.

"Your qualifications speak for themselves. I'm no expert in orthographic art—"

"Ethnographic," Mena said, with a chuckle.

"Yeah," Julian said, pushing away his embarrassment. "What I'm trying to say is that the Board could never have been swayed by anything Dumay said if you weren't a top qualified candidate. Don't diminish your work and the reputation you've earned on your own."

Mena smiled, then leaned forward and kissed him softly on the lips. Parting his mouth, he allowed her tongue to enter, tantalizing and teasing him into a frenzy.

Moments later, breaking to catch their breath, Mena asked, "I'm going to ask the Board to delay my start again, to give myself more time to process ... everything."

"How much of a delay?" Julian asked, a thought teasing at the edge of his mind.

"Not sure yet," Mena said, with a smile. She tilted her head to look at him. "Why do you ask?"

"Think they'll give you eighty days?" Julian pressed.

"Eighty?" Mena giggled as Julian nuzzled the side of her neck with his nose. "Why eighty?"

"That's how long we'll need to sail across the Atlantic to Kenya," Julian replied, pulling back to stare into her soft chocolate brown eyes.

A smile spread across Mena's face as she wrapped her arms around his neck. "Eighty days sounds perfect."

Thank you for reading! I hope you loved the soul mates love story of Julian and Mena, how they worked to get justice for Ella, and how they brought down the demented designer baby organization of Priscilla Dumay.

If you enjoyed THE ACCIDENTAL HERO, then I know you'll love the next book in the series, THE RELENTLESS HERO.

Mena Nix has everything she ever wanted—a prestigious job and Julian Montgomery, the love of her life by her side. But secrets from her past lurk, conspiring to destroy the new life she's built for herself.

Julian Montgomery has a chance to rekindle his career as a special operative for a private security firm. He craves the action, but turns it down to protect his relationship with Mena.

While catching up with an old Navy buddy, Julian sees the museum that Mena works at under siege by a terrorist attack. Bodies are piling up and Mena's nowhere to be found.

Julian discovers that Mena has been kidnapped by one of the most ruthless criminals in Africa.

Can he outwit the diabolical mercenary and rescue the woman he loves before it's too late? Or will the secrets Mena has been harboring cost them their lives?

CLICK HERE TO READ THE RELENTLESS HERO TODAY!

https://bit.ly/therelentlesshero

Angel Vane has been entertaining readers with her brand of crime thrillers for women. Now you can get one of her novellas for FREE, you just need to go to the link and tell her where to send it:

GET MY FREE SHORT STORY NOW
https://BookHip.com/SFTKRK

Also by Angel Vane

HERO IN PARADISE SERIES

Ex-Navy Seal Julian Montgomery fights off threats to the new life he's trying to build with art conservator Mena Nix. A gripping romantic suspense series with diabolical enemies, unpredictable twists and steamy romance!

THE HIDDEN THREAT (Prequel Novella)

THE ACCIDENTAL HERO

THE RELENTLESS HERO

THE FALLEN HERO

THE UNEXPECTED HERO (Coming Soon)

STAND-ALONE NOVELS

Stand-alone romantic mystery novels all set in the fictional Palmchat Islands.

THE UNWORTHY WIFE

THE SILENT ENEMY

About the Author

Angel Vane has a dramatic personality, is prone to exaggeration and is in perpetual pursuit of her creative muse. She loves writing, reading, traveling, spa days and soap operas. Angel resides in Tomball, Texas.

For more information:
angelvaneauthor@gmail.com

About the Publisher

BonzaiMoon Books is a family-run, artisanal publishing company created in the summer of 2014. We publish works of fiction in various genres. Our passion and focus is working with authors who write the books you want to read, and giving those authors the opportunity to have more direct input in the publishing of their work.

For more information:
www.bonzaimoonbooks.com
info@bonzaimoonbooks.com

facebook.com/BonzaiMoonBooks
twitter.com/bonzaimoon